Le

Amish is a 1974-born, IIM (Kolkata)-educated, boring banker turned happy author. The success of his debut book, *The Immortals of Meluha* (Book 1 of the Shiva Trilogy), encouraged him to give up a fourteen-year-old career in financial services to focus on writing. He is passionate about history, mythology and philosophy, finding beauty and meaning in all world religions. Amish's books have sold more than 5 million copies and have been translated into over 19 languages.

www.authoramish.com
www.facebook.com/authoramish
www.instagram.com/authoramish
www.twitter.com/authoramish

'{Amish's} writings have generated immense curiosity about India's rich past and culture.'
— Narendra Modi
(Honourable Prime Minister of India)

'{Amish's} writing introduces the youth to ancient value systems while pricking and satisfying their curiosity ...'
— Sri Sri Ravi Shankar
(Spiritual Leader & Founder of the Art of Living Foundation)

'{Amish's book is} riveting, absorbing and informative.'
— Amitabh Bachchan
(Actor & Living Legend)

'Amish is India's first literary popstar.'
— Shekhar Kapur
(Award-Winning Film Director)

'Thoughtful and deep, Amish, more than any author, represents the New India.'
— Vir Sanghvi
(Senior Journalist & Columnist)

'{Amish is} one of the most original thinkers of his generation.'
— Arnab Goswami
(Senior Journalist & MD, Republic TV)

'Amish has a fine eye for detail and a compelling narrative style.'

'{Amish is} a deeply thoughtful mind with an unusual, original, and fascinating view of the past.'

'To understand the New India, you need to read Amish.'

'Through all of Amish's books flows a current of liberal progressive ideology: about gender, about caste, about discrimination of any kind … He is the only Indian bestselling writer with true philosophical depth—his books are all backed by tremendous research and deep thought.'

'Amish's influence goes beyond his books, his books go beyond literature, his literature is steeped in philosophy, which is anchored in bhakti, which powers his love for India.'

'Amish is a literary phenomenon.'

Legend of Suheldev

AMISH

&

THE IMMORTAL WRITERS' CENTRE

First published by Westland Publications Private Limited in 2020
1st Floor, A Block, East Wing, Plot No. 40, SP Infocity, Dr MGR Salai,
Perungudi, Kandanchavadi, Chennai 600096

Westland and the Westland logo are the trademarks of Westland
Publications Private Limited, or its affiliates.

ISBN: 9789387894037

10 9 8 7 6 5 4 3 2 1

Typeset by SÜRYA, New Delhi
Printed in India

Om Namah Shivāya
The universe bows to Lord Shiva.
I bow to Lord Shiva.

Nāsti me jātiḥ nāsti me dharmapanthāḥ
Nāsti vā bhāṣā nāsti me rājyam
Eko'yaṁ paricayaḥ ekaiva vyaktitā
bhāratamātuḥ sutā bhāratamātuḥ sutā
Jīvanam mama ātmā vā
Karmam mama śraddhā vā
Bhāratamātre khalu bhāratamātre khalu
Yadi mokṣaprāptiḥ yadi vā sampraśnam
Ekā pratyuktiḥ ko'si praśnasya
pṛcchet adhyakṣaḥ yadi vā parameśaḥ
Ekā pratyuktiḥ bhāratamātuḥ sutā
Eko'yaṁ paricayaḥ ekaiva vyaktitā
bhāratamātuḥ sutā bhāratamātuḥ sutā

Neither caste, nor religion,
Neither language, nor kingdom (state),
Only one identity I bear,
I am a child of Mother India.
My life, my soul,
My work, my faith,
Is all for Mother India.
Whether I attain Moksha,
or I stand on Judgement Day,
When asked who I am,
By the One Most High,
There will be only one answer:
I am a child of Mother India.
Only one identity I bear,
I am a child of Mother India.

To the late Himanshu Roy,
My brother-in-law.

There is no person that I have admired more. Ever.
You were the shade that protected me.
The light that guided me.
There is no fear of death now.
For you are on the other side, my brother.
I will keep breathing. I will keep walking.
For you would expect that of me, my brother.
But the feet will stop someday …
And that will be a good day.
For you will be on the other side.
Till we meet again …
Till we meet again, my brother.

Acknowledgements

Professionally, the last few years have been fabulous. Personally, they have been terrible beyond imagination. There was a time when I was so exhausted by the repeated blows of fate, that in one of my morning prayers, I looked up and screamed at Lord Shiva to stop testing me further. How this phase of my life will end, I don't know. Our ancients said that grief is the path to personal growth. I hope they were right ... But I know what has kept me going these last few years: my writing. It has been my refuge. It stops me from giving up. I'd like to thank all those who help me live, by helping me write.

My father-in-law the late Manoj Vyas, and my brother-in-law the late Himanshu Roy. Two men I have admired deeply. Their sense of honour, grace and dignity continues to inspire me.

Neel, my young son, my life, the purpose of my soul. The purest joy in the world is having him run into my arms shouting, 'Daaaaad!'

Bhavna, Anish, Meeta and Ashish, my siblings and my sister-in-law, for all that they do. They read the first draft, usually as each chapter is written. More importantly, they pick me up when I'm down. They are the souls I chose to be born with in this life. My soul chose well.

The rest of my family: Usha, Vinay, Shernaz, Preeti, Donetta, Smita, Anuj, Ruta, Mitansh, Daniel, Aiden, Keya, Anika and Ashna. For their consistent faith and love.

Gautam, the CEO of my publisher Westland, and Karthika, Shikha, Deepthi and Sanghamitra, my editors. If there are people outside of my family who are the closest to this project, it is this group. More than friends, they are like family now. Special thanks of course to Deepthi, who is in charge of the Writers' Centre. I look forward to doing many books in the Writers' Centre with her. The rest of the marvellous team at Westland: Arunima, Christina, Divya, Jaisankar, Krishnakumar, Madhu, Mustafa, Naveen, Neha, Nidhi, Raju, Sanyog, Sateesh, Satish, Shatrughan, Srivats, Sudha, Vipin and many others. They are the best team in the publishing business.

Aman, Vijay, Sharvika, Shubhangi, Padma, Seema and the rest of my colleagues at my office. They take care of my business work which gives me enough free time to write.

Hemal, Neha, Hitesh, Harsh, Punit, Beverly, Geetika, Prakash, Harshada and Team OktoBuzz. They have made most of the marketing material for the book, including the fantastic cover, and all the digital activities. I have worked with them for many years. Like fine wine, they get better with age.

Mayank, Deepika, Sneha, Naresh, Vishaal, Sarojini, Kirti and the Moe's Art team, who have driven media relations and marketing alliances for the book. Calm and wise in media relations, they are among the best media managers I have ever seen.

Ashish Mankad, a brilliant designer, and more importantly, a thinker, who helps guide and drive the art for my books.

Satya and his team who have shot the new author photos that have been used on the inside cover of this book. He made a rather ordinary subject look better.

Preeti, a publishing industry wizard, who works on the international deals for my books.

Caleb, Kshitij, Sandeep, Rohini, Dharav, Heena, Mohan and their respective teams, who support my work with their business, legal and marketing advice.

Mrunalini, a Sanskrit scholar, who works with me on research.

Aditya, a passionate reader of my books, who has now become a friend and a fact-checker.

Brij, Narayan, Archana, Navin, Sandeep and Ravichandran, my team at Nehru Centre, London, for their love and support.

Rajinder Ganju, from Sürya, who has typeset this book.

And last, but certainly not the least, you, the reader. Your consistent affection, understanding and encouragement is what I deeply cherish. Thank you so much. Lord Shiva bless all of you.

Foreword

I have always said that all my stories are the blessings of Lord Shiva. How they come to me, how they develop in my imagination, how I see them, everything, is His blessing. But He has blessed me beyond my capacity. I cannot write faster than a book every one-and-a-half to two years. And at that pace, I will die before I write down all the story ideas that He has already blessed me with. I cannot carry these stories to my cremation pyre.

Hence, the idea of a Writers' Centre. It was a suggestion from my team, and it made eminent sense to me. I work with a team of writers, to whom I relate the complete story, and the research material to be read. They then write the first draft, which I then work upon. So, the genesis of the story and the final writing is done by me, while a team drives the first draft. We have tried our best to ensure that the books from the Writers' Centre read like any other book of mine. But we wanted to honestly state, upfront, that these books are a result of a team effort, and not just my sole work. The writers in the Writers' Centre are paid, regardless of the fate of the book. And their names are on the cover, if they choose it. If they choose to remain anonymous, for whatever reason, then the co-credit is given to the Writers' Centre.

Now, what is this book about?

A giant tide of history for the last 2,000 years was defined by a flood of horrific violence. It wiped out all the ancient cultures of the world: Pagan Rome, mystical Egypt and Greece, Zoroastrian Persia, idol-worshipping Central America, and too many others. But one ancient civilisation stubbornly refused to die. One proud culture refused to break or be overwritten. It retreated at times, but is one of the rare few still left standing. And that civilisation is India.

When invaders came to our land, we needed heroes and heroines to lead us. Defend us. And we had many such—brave men and women who had the courage and determination to fight. But if you read our history in detail, you will find that the biggest challenge for these heroes and heroines was to somehow unite our fissiparous society to fight those foreigners. We did have a national consciousness, as the millennia old Vishnu Purana evidences, but the default tendency in us Indians is to fight each other. Infighting is our favourite pastime, which we stop only briefly when the enemy is at our doorstep. So this was the biggest challenge that confronted all our heroes and heroines—from Harihara and Bukka Raya, to Maharana Pratap, to Chhatrapati Shivaji, to Lachit Borphukan, to Rani Abbakka, to Maharaja Ranjit Singh, to Mahatma Gandhi, to Netaji Subhash Chandra Bose, to countless other great men and women. The challenge, always, was how to stop our constant infighting.

These leaders succeeded where others failed. They succeeded in uniting us.

Sadly, many of these heroes and heroines have been airbrushed out of our history books. And if there is one thing these great men and women demand from us, their descendants, is that we remember their tales. That we share their stories. That we celebrate them. And learn from them.

Today, more than ever, we need to hear these stories, the chronicles of these great people who united us and saved our land by making us confront the brutal foreign invaders, beat them back and survive.

This book is of one such hero, a fictional story inspired by real events. The story of the magnificent King Suheldev of the 11th century.

It is depressing that most people across modern India have not even heard of the name of this great son of India, let alone know his story.

But worse, and heartbreakingly, at present, we are a divided India. And therefore, there is dispute over which caste or community he belonged to. Many communities claim that he was one of them. British gazettes, written many centuries after the life of this remarkable warrior, can be used to support many competing claims. I don't know what the truth is. My truth is that he was Indian. A proud son of Mother India. So, I have not taken any stand on this. I do not say which caste he belonged to.

All I say in this book is that King Suheldev was a proud Indian, who fought to protect Mother India at a time when our land was threatened by the most vicious of foreign invaders. He united all—Hindus of all castes, Buddhists and Indian Muslims—under his leadership. They fought for their motherland. And won us a glorious victory. Heady, the thought, but there also is a learning from this great son of India: when we unite, as Indians, we are unbeatable.

My patriotism and love for Mother India compels me to narrate this story. But there also is another reason.

Regardless of community claims, one thing almost everyone agrees on is that King Suheldev was a *Shiva bhakt*—a devotee of

Lord Shiva. And as I said earlier, I believe that my storytelling skill is a blessing from the Mahadev too. One day I will leave this mortal body, and before I enter my next life, I may get an opportunity to stand before Lord Shiva. And then, the Lord may demand an answer from me. He had given me a talent: I could tell stories; then why did I not tell the story of one of His greatest devotees, King Suheldev? I will not hang my head in shame before my God. I must write. I will tell you the story of the time when, led by this great hero, India stood up, united, and defeated an army made of the fiercest and most brutal warrior-race that the world has ever seen, the Turkic hordes from Central Asia. We had not invited them. We had not picked a fight. They came. They plundered. We fought. We won. We saved our culture. When we Indians stand together, shoulder to shoulder, we are undefeatable.

If only we can be united.

If only …

I dream of the day when we will all say in one voice:

Jai Suheldev! Jai Maa Bhaarati!

Glory to King Suheldev. Glory to Mother India.

Chapter 1

Somnath, India, 1025 AD

The Indian warrior snarled, the veins on his forehead standing out starkly, his powerful biceps straining with effort, as his large, calloused hands squeezed the life out of his Turkic opponent. His foe hammered desperately on his broad chest, then clawed at his eyes. But the Turk's strength was almost spent and his feeble efforts made little impact on the grim warrior, who continued to ruthlessly strangulate the man he straddled.

The Turk's face turned red and his eyes bulged. Then his tongue protruded and he lay motionless. The Indian warrior continued to press down on his enemy's neck for a little while longer, then raised the head and banged it down hard on the rocky ground, cracking the skull. Just to be certain. Suddenly overcome with weariness, he let go of the dead man and staggered to his feet.

The warrior stood tall, with taut muscles that rippled across his lean frame, broad at the shoulders and chest, narrowing down to a slim waist and muscular legs. Innumerable scars criss-crossed his dark skin. Several new wounds had been added to his body today. He gingerly stretched his battered limbs, trying to ease the exhaustion and pain pervading his body.

A wounded Turk, a short distance away, saw his opportunity.

With massive effort, he got up, grabbed a sword and swung hard at the Indian warrior. Despite his tiredness, the warrior's innate agility and battle-honed reflexes saved him. He swayed back, the sword narrowly missing him. The momentum of the swing carried the sword safely past the warrior and left his attacker's right side exposed. The warrior punched him hard on the jaw, knocking him down. The sword slipped out of the Turk's hand.

The stunned Turk slowly tried to get up again. He managed to get into a kneeling position. The warrior scooped up the sword that had clattered to the ground, raised it high and thrust it down vertically into the back of the Turk's neck, right up to his heart. An instant kill.

The warrior rested on the sword. Exhausted. Bleeding. But he knew that there was no respite to be had. He was the crown prince of Shravasti, in the north of India. His soldiers and he had come rushing to Somnath, in the western coastal land of Gujarat, to join the Indians gathered there to protect the legendary Shaivite temple from the Turkic invader, Mahmud of Ghazni. They had just battled the advance guard and skirmishers of the Turks. They knew that the main Turkic army was yet to arrive. They had to rally. Once again.

The Indian warrior from Shravasti spoke to himself. *Come on, Malladev. Straighten up. Get moving. Regroup.*

But he continued to stand there. Leaning on the sword that was buried into the kneeling Turk. Breathing hard. Pumping oxygen into his lungs. Giving his fatigued body some more time.

'My prince ...'

Malladev turned towards the sound. He saw his loyal comrades all around him. All lying prone on the ground.

All dead. All except one. One look at the man's wounds and Malladev knew that it was only a matter of time before he would join the others. But he tried not to let it show on his face.

'Come on, Wasim,' Malladev said, his voice hoarse and tired. 'Are you going to let a few scratches like those slow you down?'

Wasim smiled weakly, then grimaced as his body was wracked by a bout of coughing, phlegm and blood coming to his lips. Malladev gently held him, massaging his back.

As his coughing subsided, Wasim spoke softly. 'We showed those Turkic bastards … didn't we?'

'We sure did,' Malladev said and smiled.

'But … there will be more …' said Wasim.

Malladev kept quiet. He knew Wasim was right.

'Great prince … You need to fall back … into the sanctum sanctorum. … It's the last line … of defence.' Wasim's words came out in an agonised whisper. Then his body spasmed, and he lay still.

Malladev embraced Wasim's body, then gently laid him down. 'May our Mother India bless you, my friend. May she always honour your sacrifice.'

Then Malladev rose slowly, whispering the words that always gave him strength. 'Om Namah Shivaya.'

The universe bows to Lord Shiva. I bow to Lord Shiva.

Then he limped slowly. Towards the main temple. Wasim was right. There was no time for rest. His job was not done. His life was not done. Not yet.

— EJ ӿЗԵЈĊᐃ —

Outside, the ocean waves lazily washed the land as they did every day, oblivious to the human tragedy taking place on the seashore. As the water swallowed more of the evening sun, the nearly cloudless sky glowed with vibrant shades of red, orange and purple. It was a surreal, beautiful sight, which may have been admired in a different time. But, at this point, the world seemed to be surrendering to vicious savagery. For at one of the holiest sites of probably the oldest surviving religion of the world, bodies of over-civilised people, and the temples of their Gods, were being laid to waste by foreign barbarians.

The Turkic forces were spreading rapidly through the huge temple complex, moving inexorably towards the main structure at the heart of the massive compound; the great shrine to Lord Shiva, in His form as the *Lord of the Moon God*, the *SomNath*. To the Indians, the Turks looked like the Chinese, with their round faces and slit-like eyes. But the actual Chinese knew the Turks as barbaric warrior nomads from Central Asia, and considered it wise to be afraid of them. For the Turks were people who were trained for one art alone: the art of killing.

Columns of smoke rose from various buildings of the temple complex. The corpses littered the ground. Statues of silver and gold lay strewn across the floors—broken, damaged, defiled. A group of Turkic soldiers laughed as they yanked at the golden horns on a massive statue of Lord Shiva's bull, Nandi. As the horns finally came loose, the men roared with glee and shouted obscenities.

As reverberations of the Turkic victory grew, so did the desperate pleas of the injured Indians barricaded in the sanctum sanctorum, the inner refuge of this, one of the greatest temples on the planet.

'Save us, great Mahadev …'

'Show your power …'

'Strike down those fanatics …'

'Why are you testing us like this?'

There did come a response—just one.

Thud! Thud! Thud!

A loud, menacing hammering at the doors of the sanctum sanctorum.

Malladev, who had remained silent till now, looked up at the barricaded door. His tears mingled with the blood that trickled down his face. The viscous mixture seeped into his mouth.

Bitter.

Like the destiny of his land. Of his faith. Of his people.

He looked up at the great *Shiva Linga*, the symbol of Lord Shiva, the *Mahadev*, the *God of Gods*.

His companions, just a dozen of them, edged closer together and exchanged anxious glances. This motley, ragtag bunch of bruised, battered men—many of them Brahmins who had never lifted a weapon till this day—were all that was left of an army of almost fifty thousand that had gathered to protect the fabled, stupendously wealthy Somnath temple.

A Turkic officer bellowed from the other side of the door. 'Open the door now or be tortured to death!'

Malladev drew in a deep breath. But he did not say anything. He held the Shiva Linga tight. Drawing strength from the magnificent idol.

On the other side of the door, even as the looting and the pillaging continued, one column of soldiers maintained discipline and marched resolutely towards the sanctum sanctorum. They were Sultan Mahmud's personal guards, elite warriors handpicked to accompany him everywhere in battle. Unlike the rest of the Ghazni army, which wore green tunics, the Sultan's guards had their own distinctive uniforms. In peacetime, they wore white. But when they went into battle, they were dressed all in black, the image of a roaring lion embroidered on their sleeves in white thread.

The marks of the long, exhausting battle were clearly visible on them, but they were in far better shape than the last defenders of the temple.

At a signal from their Turkic captain, ten men charged at the massive doors of the sanctum sanctorum with a battering ram. It crashed into the doors with a resounding bang, but barely made any headway. The doors stood resolute.

The Turks backed up. Took aim again. And charged. Heavy timber slammed into the doors with greater force this time. A minor creak escaped from the doors. The battering ram was readied again. Positioned just right. To collide with the central joint. The Turkic officer gave the order and the battering ram assaulted the door once again. Some of the doors' mighty hinges finally gave way. A crack of light filtered through, revealing the flickering shadows of the Indians who still clung on to the hope of defending their God, of defending their land's honour.

Malladev now touched his forehead to the idol's base, his eyes closed. Giving his final veneration to his God. He knew that he would not get another chance.

He whispered, 'We may die today, great Shiva … But we will return. We will return in the millions …' Malladev turned to his fellow defenders of the noble land of India, as his voice rose louder. 'We will return! We will rebuild! We will reclaim our Lord's honour! I swear on the name of the holiest of them all, Lord Shiva!'

The words infused the power of the Lord into the men huddled around him. Straightening their backs. Stiffening their resolve.

Malladev raised his hand high, pointing his sword at the door. 'Until death!'

'Until death!' bellowed the proud Indians alongside him.

And then, one of them shouted ancient words of immense power. Words that have electrified Indians for millennia. Words that reminded the Indians that they were Gods. That each one of them was a Mahadev.

'Har Har Mahadev!'

We are Gods!

Thud. Thud. Thud.

The battering ram was still at it with machine-like precision. The Turkic cries of maniacal pleasure at wreaking havoc were growing louder.

'Har Har Mahadev!'

We will die like Gods!

The huge doors of the sanctum sanctorum burst open with a loud crash.

'Har Har Mahadev!'

We will return like Gods!

The Turks charged into the hallowed sanctum sanctorum of one of the holiest temples in the world, screeching like beasts.

'Har Har Mahadev!' roared Malladev, as he and his fellow Indians charged at the Turkic defilers.

The rage and defiance of the defenders stopped the advancing Turks in their tracks. The barbarians did not expect such resistance. Many Turks were killed in the initial rush. But they outnumbered the defending Indians by many multiples. They just kept coming. And coming. And coming.

Each Indian took down at least five Turks before he fell. But fall they all did.

Fall they all did.

Till the only one left standing was Malladev. Exhausted beyond measure. Injured beyond human capacity to bear. Bleeding desperately. Screaming all the time. He kept fighting. Kept fighting.

Alone.

Against too many to count.

He did not throw his sword down in surrender. He did not waver. He did not plead for mercy. He kept fighting.

Malladev thrust his sword into the belly of an attacker. As his victim fell to the ground, the sword slipped out of Malladev's blood-soaked hand. He reached quickly to his side for his last knife. Swung it across to slash through a Turk's throat. Some enemies pushed him hard against the wall. The knife slipped out of his hands.

There were ten people around him now. All stabbing him at the same time. Slicing blades into him. Again. And again. And again. Brutally. Without respite.

And yet, without any weapons, Malladev kept fighting. He kept fighting. Slashing his nails across the eyes of one opponent, punching another in the throat. Screaming in fury all the time.

A loud commanding voice was heard. 'Step back!'

The Turks immediately obeyed. Their heads bowed in respect. A massive man, with an ugly, battle-scarred face, came forward.

Malladev was against the wall. Panting desperately. Bathed in blood. Drowning in agonising pain. Staring with defiance at the gigantic man standing in front of him.

The sultan. Yamin-ud-Dawla Abul-Qasim Mahmud ibn Sebuktegin. More commonly known as Mahmud of Ghazni.

Mahmud held his right hand out. His mighty war sword, dripping with blood, came into view.

Malladev kept staring into the eyes of Mahmud with pure, raw, defiance. He whispered the words he wanted to die with, 'Om Namah Shivāya.'

The universe bows to Lord Shiva. I bow to Lord Shiva.

'Go to hell,' growled Mahmud, in a fearsome, gravelly voice. And he swung his sword. Beheading Malladev with one mighty blow.

— ᴇᴊᴊ ᴋᴣᴒᴄᴧ —

'Damn, that *kafir* had a lot of blood in his pathetic body,' complained Mahmud, as he dabbed at his face to get rid of Malladev's blood that had splattered on him.

'Hail the sultan!' cheered the guards.

Malladev's killer acknowledged their cheers with a nod, then turned towards the gilded Shiva Linga at the heart of the sanctum sanctorum.

Even to the cynical eyes of Mahmud of Ghazni, it was a magnificent sight. He gazed at it for a long time. A hush fell upon the room, broken only by the crackling of fire outside as more and more of the temple complex was put to flames.

Then a fifteen-year-old boy, surrounded by bodyguards, walked in, carefully picking his way across the floor, made slippery by large patches of sticky blood congealing on it.

The boy, named Salar Maqsud, was Mahmud's nephew. He was stocky and of medium height, but he already had broad shoulders and muscled arms that indicated long hours of work with the sword and shield. He was fair-skinned, with high cheekbones. His roundish face would have been unremarkable but for his large eyes, which were unusual for a Turk. His eyes had a hazel colour that went from appearing light-green to dark-brown, depending on the light. Most people who met the boy found themselves almost hypnotically drawn to the eyes; unless he was in a fury, when even grown men found themselves quailing at the thought of locking gazes with him.

'This is a great moment, My Lord,' said Salar Maqsud, bowing to his uncle. 'My heartiest congratulations to you.'

Mahmud's face broke into a wide smile. He was never particularly expressive in public, but there was genuine affection in his eyes as he ruffled his nephew's hair. 'Maqsud, my boy!' He gestured at the Shiva Linga. The idol was jet black, shining brightly with the precious stones embedded in it. Most strikingly, it hung suspended in mid-air. 'What do you think of that?'

'What evil sorcery is this?' whispered Maqsud. 'May Allah protect us.'

Mahmud laughed out loud. 'There is no sorcery here. Only some clever trick by the sly idol-worshippers. Does anyone have any idea what the secret is?'

'Perhaps there is an invisible support, My Lord?' ventured one of the soldiers.

Mahmud ran his sword under the Shiva Linga. Nothing there.

Khwaja Hassan, the prime minister of Ghazni, who was in charge of revenues and accounts, stepped up. 'We should remove the canopy above, My Lord.'

Hassan, being an educated Persian, had acquired a lot of knowledge about the region. He knew that the canopy above the *linga* was made of lodestone, which acted as a natural magnet on the *linga*, which also had a mix of lodestone and some metal in it.

Mahmud nodded. As the first stone was removed from the canopy, the idol swerved to one side. When the next stone was removed, the idol perceptibly shifted downwards. Bit by bit, the canopy was dismantled till the idol finally came to rest on the ground.

'You see, my boy?' said Mahmud to Maqsud. 'No magic here. Just a devious trick.' He looked once again at the *linga*. 'So this is what all these imbeciles died trying to protect,' scoffed Mahmud. 'They will not forget this day in a hurry. But let's make it even more memorable.' He turned to one of his men. 'Fetch me a hammer.'

The man immediately procured a hammer, dropped to his knees and respectfully offered the implement to the sultan.

As Mahmud hefted the hammer, Hassan's voice interrupted him. 'A thousand pardons, My Lord, but a delegation of businessmen has assembled outside. They are respectfully submitting that if you spare the idol, they will offer any tribute you deem fit, to be paid into the royal treasury every year.'

Mahmud smiled mockingly. 'Hassan, my dear prime minister, always ready with your calculations! How much do you think I should ask for to leave this idol alone?'

The prime minister spoke in a soft tone. 'These men will pay any amount you demand, My Lord. Destroyed, this statue is worthless. If kept secure, it could be a lucrative source of revenue for years to come. Think of all the things you could do with the money. The armies you could raise, the magnificent buildings you could construct, the blessings you could shower on the people of your kingdom.'

Mahmud stroked his beard thoughtfully. 'Hmm, tempting,' he conceded. 'Especially if I were an effete Persian focused only on money and luxury.' His gaze hardened. 'But I am not Persian. I am a faithful Turk. On the day of judgement, the Creator will search for me. What will he say that day? "Where is that Mahmud who sold the greatest of the idols to the unbelievers for gold?'"

Hassan quietly slunk back. Head bowed. Outwardly penitent. The thoughts though, buried deep inside his own mind, were different. *Locust-eaters … These Arabs and Turks …*

Mahmud turned to his nephew Salar Maqsud. 'Look carefully, my boy. One day, this holy mission will be yours. You must strike down your enemy without mercy, whoever they might be. Destroy everything they hold dear.'

Maqsud nodded, his eyes shining with the light of hero worship. 'Long live the sultan!'

Mahmud rested his left foot on the base of the idol. He stretched back for maximum swing and grunted loudly as he smashed the hammer down with all his strength.

And broke the soul of India.

Chapter 2

Ballala, the massive wrestler, roared as he lunged forward, arms outstretched. But his yell faded away as his wiry opponent neatly sidestepped him, leaving Ballala's meaty hands clutching at thin air. With a frustrated scowl, he turned to face the young man who had just made him look foolish.

The wrestler's face was red with exhaustion and anger, his body smeared with mud from the arena. His barrel chest heaved up and down as he tried to suck some air into his lungs.

His opponent, by contrast, hardly looked like he was wrestling. He was tall and wiry. His hair, which hung till his shoulders when he left it open, was neatly tied in a bun. Like his opponent, he wore a *langot*, a loincloth, which showed off most of his extremely fit body.

His shoulders were unexpectedly broad for his slim frame, and his body narrowed down dramatically to a hand-span waist and washboard abs. Taut muscles rippled across his chest and arms. His legs were lean and sinewy. He moved like a big cat—languid and graceful, but with an underlying energy that suggested he could erupt into sudden, explosive action in the blink of an eye.

Though the youth was barely eighteen, his torso was already marked with several scars. His palms were callused, and the middle finger of the left hand was crooked from an old break.

Just below the ribs on his right side, there was an indentation. It was an old wound that had healed but left its mark.

The young man grinned mockingly. Only a thin film of sweat on his forehead revealed that he was exerting himself in any way. But for all his apparent effortlessness, he constantly moved on his feet, alertly watching his opponent and taking care to stay out of grappling distance.

Around the arena, a raucous crowd cheered or jeered, depending on whom they were backing.

'Move, Ballala, you fool! I've bet my horse on you!' yelled one man.

'You shouldn't have bet a horse on a donkey, you idiot!' called out another man.

'I hope a million fleas from a dog permanently infest your armpits!' growled back the first man.

'Try putting those fleas in Ballala's *langot*. That might speed him up a bit!' came the cheerful retort.

The crowd hooted in delight.

Ballala's face coloured as he heard the taunts. He growled at his opponent, 'You've been dancing around all morning. Stand in one place and fight like a man.'

'Catch me, if you can, old man,' smiled his young tormentor.

The furious wrestler put his head down and charged like an enraged bull. The young man let him come, then sidestepped rapidly at the last moment, dropped to the floor and stuck out his right foot, tripping the wrestler and sending him sprawling to the ground with a crash that resounded through the noisy arena. As he lay there stunned, his opponent pounced on him, turned him around and pinned his back and shoulders to the ground.

Most of the crowd cheered, but there were also some loud groans. 'Go to hell, Ballala, you stupid butt-face,' yelled a corpulent man, wiping the sweat off his face with a cloth draped around his shoulders. He whirled around, irritated, as a thin man tapped him on the shoulder.

'I'll take my money now,' said the thin man, grinning triumphantly from ear to ear.

'Here, take it. I hope some prostitute steals it from you! I hope you buy bad wine that gives you a pounding headache! I hope you get rotten food that wrecks your stomach!' shouted the fat man. He threw a bag of coins at the man. 'Take this as well,' he said, removing the sweat-drenched cloth from his shoulders and hurling it in disgust, exposing a pair of sagging, pendulous male breasts.

'Don't worry, I'll put the money to good use,' came the cheerful reply. 'When I've spent it all, I'll come back for another bet. And you better keep the cloth. You'll give our women a complex.'

Meanwhile, the young tormentor of Ballala had risen gracefully to his feet. He joined his palms in a namaste and held them above his head, acknowledging all sections of the crowd. Then he went up and touched the feet of a slim, grey-haired man who had been watching the fight intently from one side of the arena.

'Greetings, *Gurudev*,' said the young man to his *teacher*.

The older man patted his back fondly. 'You did well, Prince Suheldev. But you teased Ballala for too long. You should have finished it earlier.'

Suheldev smiled the loopy grin that made so many women go weak at the knees. 'A boy can also have some fun, Gurudev!'

As both the guru and the student laughed, some aides came forward, bearing wet towels and the prince's clothes. Suheldev used some of the perfumed towels to wipe the mud off his face and body. Then, in practised, sweeping movements, he wrapped a *dhoti* around his hips, ignoring the admiring glances from many young women who still hung around, staring dreamily at their prince. Suheldev's guru handed him a miniature Shiva Linga pendant. He reverentially touched it to both his eyes, kissed it and slipped it around his neck, whispering the holy words as he did.

'*Om Namah Shivāya.*'

The universe bows to Lord Shiva. I bow to Lord Shiva.

Suddenly, a harried-looking, dark-skinned, white-haired man pushed his way through to Suheldev.

'My prince,' he said politely, but hurriedly.

'Iqbal,' said Suheldev. 'What happened?'

Suheldev could tell that something was wrong. Iqbal, his father's loyal aide, should have been in his afternoon *namaaz* at this time. Only a disaster would have caused him to miss his prayers.

Iqbal looked devastated. 'Your presence is urgently requested at the palace, Prince.'

'Let's go,' Suheldev said immediately.

———— EJJ ⅏ʒↄⅩↄ ————

'You should have stopped Malladev *dada*! I had told you!'

Suheldev glared accusingly at his parents, King Mangaldhwaj and Queen Vijayalakshmi. Anger and grief bursting through every pore of his body.

When Malladev, Suheldev's elder brother, and the crown prince of the kingdom of Shravasti, was leaving the palace to go defend Somnath temple, the younger prince had made several attempts to stop him. Pleading desperately. Malladev had tried to reassure Suheldev that victory was certain and that he would not die fighting. He had said that kings from across North India were mobilising to stop Mahmud of Ghazni. Suheldev had argued that nobody would come and that Indians were too divided to mobilise together, even against a barbarian like Mahmud. But Malladev had not listened. Then Suheldev had tried to emotionally blackmail his parents to stop their eldest son from leaving. Instead, they had proudly blessed him as he had ridden off, with a contingent of the kingdom's finest soldiers, to Somnath.

'Malladev is a hero,' said Vijayalakshmi calmly. Even through the grief clouding her face, she remained a strikingly attractive woman. Her hair had a reddish hue from the henna that she used to conceal the increasing number of strands that were greying. Her waist, visible below the royal purple blouse she was wearing, was thickening slightly. But apart from that, there were no other signs that she was well into her forties. Her eyes were tinged with sadness but showed no hint of a tear; her voice remained steady.

'*Dada's* death is on your hands!' bawled Suheldev, tears flowing freely from his eyes now. 'You could have stopped him! But you didn't!'

'Don't insult Malladev by crying for him, Suheldev. Be proud of him. Be proud of the way he died. This country will remember his sacrifice.'

'You think this country will remember the sacrifice of people like us? Of our subaltern caste?'

'Those who are true patriots will remember. I don't care about the rest. I am proud to have given up one son for a noble cause. I would happily sacrifice more if needed.'

King Mangaldhwaj had listened silently to this exchange.

A slightly shorter, much older version of Suheldev, he had a dark, weather-beaten face that was clearly the result of many hours spent in the open, under a blazing sun. An old scar ran across his left cheek, starting just under his eye and going right across till his jaw. A handlebar moustache accentuated his already imposing appearance. With age, his shoulders had stooped slightly, and his waist threatened to expand into a paunch unless constantly watched. But he still largely retained the sturdy physique of the fierce warrior that he had been in his prime. His eyes could blaze with passion and anger, just as Suheldev's were at that moment. But he was looking at his son with tenderness and concern.

Mangaldhwaj walked up to Suheldev and put his arm around him. 'Son, you are a prince. Act like one. You will not cry. Celebrate Malladev's bravery. Learn from it.'

'I don't believe this!' cried Suheldev. 'Celebrate? Celebrate *dada's* death?'

Without saying another word, the prince stormed out of the room.

— EJJ ⅄�ð⌒ᒑᐃ —

Suheldev sat quietly next to the small lake. It was more of a pond than a lake. And yet, it was special for him. It was where Malladev had taught him how to swim. It was where they would come regularly. To talk. To wrestle. To throw stones. To argue. To gossip.

To do nothing.

To be brothers.

'It's in the wrist, Suhel,' whispered Malladev.

The ten-year-old Suheldev kept marvelling at the ripples on the water.

Having seen a flat pebble bounce on it six times as his sixteen-year-old brother, Malladev, had flung it on the water's surface. Suheldev stared at his much taller elder brother, the hero. Then looked down at the pebble in his hand nervously.

He adjusted his grip, pressing his forefinger on one side. 'Like this, dada?'

'Yes,' said Malladev. 'And stop noticing the girls staring at you.'

There was a gaggle of ten-year-old girls at a distance, ogling at Suheldev. Even at this young age, Suheldev had a dashing, mischievous air about him. It made him appear exciting to many girls. Suheldev grinned at his brother and looked back towards the water. Focusing.

The pebble crashed into the water and sunk with a plop. Not even one bounce.

Suheldev wiped a tear from his eye. He still couldn't get it right. Couldn't even throw a pebble right. Despite all of Malladev's attempts to teach him.

He hadn't learnt to be as good as Malladev at anything. Not in warriorhood. Not in knowledge. Or caring for the kingdom's citizens. Or respecting his parents.

Suheldev looked up at the sky.

Why him? He was the better one.

I was always a useless prankster.

Why him?

It should have been me … It should have been me who was dead.

A sudden noise interrupted his flow of thoughts.

Suheldev turned around. 'Gurudev,' he said, getting up, trying to hide his unhappiness at being disturbed.

'Sit, sit,' said Kashinath, sitting beside his student. He sighed. 'Oh, it feels good to sit. Old age is a curse …'

Suheldev said nothing.

'I will miss Malladev too,' said Kashinath softly. He looked directly at Suheldev. 'You will be the crown prince now.'

'I can never take *dada's* place. He was ...' Suheldev's voice choked up.

Kashinath gently patted his shoulder.

'He was amazing ...'

Kashinath spoke gently. 'That he was ... But now he's not here. And we have to make our peace with that, right?'

Suheldev went back to silence.

'Everybody who is born will die one day, son. It's what we do in between that matters.'

Suheldev remained silent.

'I know you're not in the mood to discuss anything, but would you care to indulge this old man in a conversation just for a bit?'

Suheldev sighed and looked away.

'Malladev always answered my questions. No matter when I asked them.'

Suheldev turned back to look at Kashinath.

Kashinath smiled gently. 'Thank you, my prince. Now, my question ... How does our clan celebrate *MahaShivaRatri*?'

Suheldev stared blankly at his teacher. Not understanding the point of the question. For the answer was obvious. It was an answer every child in the clan knew.

'Please, indulge me,' his teacher said with a smile. 'For Malladev's sake.'

'Our men show their devotion to Lord Shiva by carrying a massive Shiva Linga on their shoulders during *MahaShivaRatri*,' replied Suheldev, referring to an ancient custom followed on the *great night of Lord Shiva*.

'Exactly,' nodded his teacher. 'We worship Lord Shiva in our own way, right?'

Suheldev nodded. *Yes.*

'Now my next question. Which Vishnu do we consider the most venerable?'

Suheldev held his breath in irritation, wondering why Kashinath was asking questions to which he already knew the answers. 'The sixth Vishnu, Lord Parshu Ram,' Suheldev said eventually. 'Our ancestors served as a warrior group and helped him fight evil-doers. We were His sword arm.'

Kashinath smiled approvingly, ignoring the note of irritation in Suheldev's voice. 'And whom did Lord Parshu Ram worship?'

'The Mahadev, of course,' responded Suheldev.

'Thank you. Now, tell me, our people are not considered full Kshatriyas. So how come we have a kingdom of our own?' asked Kashinath.

'Because my grandfather united our people and turned them into a fighting force that carved out a kingdom.'

'Yes. And what is it that unites us?' asked Kashinath softly. 'What makes us one people?'

'Devotion to Lord Shiva,' said Suheldev, finally understanding what his guru had been leading up to.

Kashinath smiled slightly. 'All our people are one family because Lord Shiva is our God. Malladev was your brother, but so is every boy in every household in this kingdom. Malladev understood that. He knew, deep in his soul, that we cannot say that defending our Lord's temple is not our problem.'

Suheldev remained mute.

'Do you know what has happened to the shattered pieces of the Somnath*ji* Shiva Linga?'

Suheldev shook his head. *No.*

'Mahmud is taking them back to Ghazni, my prince. He has announced that he intends to use these shattered pieces of the Shiva Linga to pave the steps of a new mosque that he will be building. Every day, hundreds of feet will step on and desecrate the remains of the *Mahadev's idol*.'

Suheldev did not say anything, but his jaw tightened and he clenched his right fist.

His teacher sat with him silently for a while, then patted his shoulder and left.

Suheldev kept staring into the distance. Deep into the still waters of the lake. A tiny air bubble pushed up to the surface and broke through. Releasing the air it imprisoned, from the depths of the waters, into the glory of the open winds.

Words that Malladev had said before leaving came flooding back to him.

'The Turks did not stop at Afghanistan and Balochistan. That was our land too, once. They did not stop at the holy Indus river. That was our river too, once. Even if they conquer the entire land of Mother India, they will not stop. They will not stop the humiliation. They will not stop the war. They will not stop the killing. The more we appease, the more they will demand. The more we surrender, the more they will attack. They will never, ever stop. The only way they will stop, is if some Indian dares to stand up and say: Enough is enough.'

A few soft tears started flowing down Suheldev's cheeks. He held on tightly to the Shiva Linga pendant hanging around his neck.

He could almost hear his brother's kind and encouraging voice.

'You have it in you, Suhel. I know you can do it. Fight for me. Fight for Lord Shiva. Fight for the great land that cradles us. Fight for Mother India.'

Chapter 3

Ajitpal, the emperor of Kannauj, grimaced as he scratched at an insect bite on his arm. Once, in the not-so-distant past, his capital had been the shining jewel of a mighty empire. Under the great Mihira Bhoj, Ajitpal's ancestor, Kannauj had held sway from the foothills of the Himalayas in the north to the Narmada river in the south, from the Sutlej river in the northwest up to Bengal in the east.

But now, the kingdom had been reduced to a shadow of its former glory, though Ajitpal still clung to the title of emperor, which had been claimed by his ancestors by right. But privately, many already referred to him by his much-reduced stature: king. The whispers had become louder a few years ago, when he had tried to resist the Ghazni army and suffered a humiliating defeat that had left him with no option but to accept Mahmud as his overlord.

Ajitpal glared at his minister. 'This lowborn upstart dares to demand a meeting with me as if we are equals. And I actually let you talk me into it.'

His minister, Vrishabh, bit back a sigh that threatened to erupt. Vrishabh was a slender old man with an unnaturally youthful face that belied his mostly grey hair. The hair on his crown was longer, and tied in a knot, signifying his Brahmin background. His neatly trimmed beard too was largely white, with only occasional strands of black. He had a dignified air and his brown eyes usually sparkled with wit and humour. At the moment, though, he was struggling to conceal his irritation. It had taken weeks of negotiations to set up the clandestine meeting in a remote forest clearing.

The rendezvous point was located close to the border of Kannauj with the neighbouring kingdom of Haridway, also known as Haridrohi, or enemy of Hari, due to the belief that it had once been ruled by Hiranyakashipu, father of the legendary hero and devotee of Lord Vishnu, Prahalad. Hiranyakashipu was so incensed by his son's devotion to the path of the Vishnu, that he repeatedly tried to get him killed. Instead, Hiranyakashipu was himself slain by Lord Narsimha, who was recognised as the fourth Vishnu.

Ajitpal had used the pretext of a hunting trip to reach the location, keeping his meeting with Mangaldhwaj a carefully concealed secret. But that hadn't stopped him from grumbling endlessly about it. Vrishabh tried, once again, to calm him down. 'Your Highness, the message was clear. King Mangaldhwaj—'

'Don't refer to him by his trumped-up title,' snapped Ajitpal.

'Forgive me, great emperor. Mangaldhwaj requested a meeting and said it could be of mutual interest. One does not usually send such a request unless it is of some significance. What harm can there be in at least hearing out what he has to say?'

'Fine, I'll listen, though it turns my stomach to be breathing the same air as him.' A shiver ran through Ajitpal, almost like his soul was disgusted with what he had allowed himself to be talked into. He again slapped at his wrist. 'Uff, these bugs. They're eating me up alive. Why the hell did I agree to come to this miserable place?'

Vrishabh kept quiet, but couldn't help looking around. Soft rugs covered every inch of the considerable ground covered by the massive tent, which was made of velvet and embroidered with golden thread. Ajitpal was comfortably seated on a throne, placed on a platform.

Once, the king had been a well-built, handsome youth. But his fine physique had long since vanished, and the person who sat in the tent was a jowly man verging on corpulence. His sallow skin and bloodshot eyes added to the general air of decadence that hung about Ajitpal.

An attendant fanned Ajitpal energetically, while others scurried to serve him food and wine and indulge his every whim. Two armed guards stood at the base of the platform, and there were another two at the entrance of the tent. Outside, a group of twenty soldiers formed a circle around the entire tent to make sure no intruder could sneak in from any point.

If it hadn't been for the occasional chirping of a bird or sound made by a wild animal that trickled in through the tent, it would have been impossible to tell they were in a forest.

Ajitpal understood Vrishabh's silent reproach, and it made him even more irritated. 'Well, don't just stand around looking glum. When is your "honoured" guest expected?'

'He should be here any time now, great emperor,' replied Vrishabh.

'Well, go and find out. And get someone to take these seats away. They won't be needed.'

'Your Highness …' Vrishabh began in an appalled tone, but fell silent as Ajitpal glared at him.

Ajitpal's thoughts could almost be heard in the angry silence. *He is not my equal. Mangaldhwaj will sit on the ground, exactly where he belongs.*

Vrishabh, despite his deep misgivings, signalled to the king's attendants to remove the seats, and exited from the lavishly furnished tent with a bow towards his emperor. There had been so many other royal orders that his emperor had forced him to carry out, which had disgusted him even more.

Ajitpal did not even bother to acknowledge Vrishabh's bow. He signalled to an attendant, who hastily placed a platter filled with delicacies in front of him. Ajitpal sniffed appreciatively, then began shoving the food into his mouth.

— ᴇᴊ ᴀᴈᴧᴄᴧ —

Though Suheldev had agreed to accompany Mangaldhwaj, he remained sceptical about his *father's* idea. 'Nothing will come of this, *baba*.'

Suheldev and Mangaldhwaj had been riding for a few days, accompanied by a small bodyguard corps.

Mangaldhwaj adjusted the reins of his horse to keep his ride in line with Suheldev's. 'I am sure Ghazni's armies will turn towards our part of India soon. We cannot possibly take him on alone. We will need allies. Yes, it's true Ajitpal lost to Ghazni, but he still has one of the strongest armies in this region. He may just be willing to form an alliance with us. We Indians have divided ourselves on so many counts. Perhaps it will take a common threat from outside to unite us.'

'*Baba*, do you honestly believe he'll be able to look beyond our caste and his?' asked Suheldev.

Mangaldhwaj shrugged. 'I don't know. But history can be our ally. Think of India's greatest emperors. Chandragupta Maurya and Bindusara, Samudragupta and Vikramaditya. None of them was born Kshatriya. It wasn't so long ago that a man was defined by his *karma* rather than his birth.'

'*Baba*,' said Suheldev, rolling his eyes, 'that was very, very long ago …'

'Maybe. But we need to remind ourselves of those days. Invaders did not dare attack us then. We were unconquerable.'

'Yes, because in those days we actually fought foreigners together. Today, we are more interested in fighting each other.'

'Then let us try to revive those days. Who knows, Ajitpal may surprise us.'

Suheldev snorted and shook his head, laughing slightly. Mangaldhwaj glared at his son, and then turned, looking ahead. Looking far ahead.

— EJJ ℋℨ⌐JℂΔ —

Ajitpal desultorily nibbled at the delicacies spread out in front of him. The second *prahar* of the day was drawing to a close. In short, it was close to noon, and lunchtime was not very far away, but Ajitpal's stomach was already almost bursting with the food and wine he had been steadily consuming out of sheer restlessness and boredom. He burped, and felt the acidic taste in his mouth. It worsened his already sour mood.

I am from the line of the great Mihira Bhoj! These bloody countrymen of mine need to show me the respect I deserve!

Still brooding, he picked up a goblet and gulped down the wine in it. Some of the liquid dribbled down his chin. Irritated, he wiped it with the back of his hand.

'Great emperor, your honoured guests are here,' said Vrishabh as he entered the tent, ushering in Mangaldhwaj and Suheldev with utmost respect.

'Welcome,' said Ajitpal. He didn't get up to receive his guests. Instead, he gestured towards the ground. 'Please be seated.'

Suheldev's eyes flashed with anger but Mangaldhwaj put a restraining hand on his shoulder and silenced him with a glance.

'Thank you, but we would prefer to stand, Your Highness,' Mangaldhwaj said courteously, as he noticed Vrishabh looking at him apologetically.

'Suit yourself,' shrugged Ajitpal. 'You wanted to meet me. Well, here we are. Speak.'

Mangaldhwaj composed himself briefly, then began. 'Great emperor, I am sure you will agree that Mahmud of Ghazni is the single greatest threat to the peace and integrity of our land. You have already suffered at his hands. It will not be long before he targets the rest of us. What he has done to the Somnath*ji* temple has filled all of India with rage—'

'That was some time ago,' interrupted Ajitpal. 'The *vasant ritu* has already passed since then and the *grishma ritu* too is drawing to an end. It will be forgotten soon. In any case, we can rebuild the temple later ...'

Ajitpal was referring to the passage of two of the six Indian seasons, that of *spring* and *summer*. He seemed to think that it was a long period of time.

Mangaldhwaj was shocked. An insult to their God being forgotten so quickly? But he still wanted to try his best for an alliance. He wanted the support of the powerful Kannauj army. 'Your Highness, it is a foolish man who stands by silently while his neighbour's house burns, for the fire will surely spread to his home as well. Mahmud will not stop at Somnath. He will keep coming deeper and deeper into India. None of us will be safe.'

'You needn't worry for my safety,' said Ajitpal, smirking. 'My army can take care of anything.'

'Your Highness, we would like to propose an alliance with

you. Once you declare your intent, other kingdoms will also take heart and rally around to the cause. Say the word, and we will all stand shoulder to shoulder with you. Then we can defeat any Turk!'

Ajitpal laughed incredulously. 'Are you serious? A few generations ago, your ancestors were raising animals and cultivating land for us higher castes. And today, you dream of standing shoulder to shoulder with me, a pure Kshatriya? I am a descendant of Mihira Bhoj! I am a descendant of our great God Lord Lakshman Himself!'

Mangaldhwaj retained his unfailingly polite tone. 'Yes, My Lord. Mihira Bhoj was a great emperor, one who all Indians respect till today. But please remember that he treated all Indians as his own. And it is also true that you and your clan are descendants of Lord Lakshman. But do not forget that Lord Lakshman's elder brother, Lord Ram, treated all, including subaltern-caste people, with respect.'

'Well, I am not Lord Ram!' growled Ajitpal. 'Behave according to your status and I will show mercy. Don't forget who you were in the past.'

'What does the past have to do with this?' burst out Suheldev. 'We live in the present and my father is here to deal with you as one king to another.'

Ajitpal raised his hand angrily. 'Mangaldhwaj, I realise that your people do not have the benefit of a proper education, but you need to teach your little rascal that one does not become a king just by winning a few skirmishes and grabbing a little land. You need to be born a Kshatriya to be considered true royalty.'

'There have been great kings and emperors in the past who were not born Kshatriyas—' began Mangaldhwaj.

'That was in the past,' snapped Ajitpal, interrupting him.

'And as this insolent pup of yours just pointed out, we live in the present, and you have to deal with me. I humoured you by agreeing to this ridiculous rendezvous, but don't cross your limits. Know this once and for all: I will never disgrace my illustrious family by joining hands with a low-born fool with delusions of grandeur.'

Suheldev pushed aside Mangaldhwaj's restraining hand and shouted, 'Yes, you earn great honour by bowing your head before a foreigner, but you would disgrace yourself by joining hands with a fellow Indian, you arrogant idiot!'

'Silence!' thundered Ajitpal, sweeping away all the dishes on the table in front of him. 'You impertinent wretch, I should have your tongue pulled out for your impudence.'

'Your Highness, they are your guests,' pleaded Vrishabh. 'Please, I beg you.'

Ajitpal turned towards his minister. 'This is all your fault! You talked me into this! I will deal with you later!' Then he addressed Mangaldhwaj and Suheldev. '*You* may have forgotten *dharma*, but *I* have not. I will forgive your arrogance for this first and last time. Leave my domain and never come back. If I ever see your faces again, I will have you executed on the spot.'

Suheldev began to respond, but Mangaldhwaj seized him by the hand and hustled him away.

—— EЛ Ӿꞝꞁ꒱ ——

A party of about a hundred and fifty men made their way back home with Mangaldhwaj and Suheldev. While they were all soldiers in the Shravasti army, none of them was wearing a uniform. They did not want to be easily identifiable. Some carried bows and quivers; the rest had lances, axes and maces.

All of them had swords and daggers tied to their hips, with shields strapped on to their backs.

The bulk of the party was in the centre, with Mangaldhwaj and Suheldev riding in their midst, while another group of twenty brought up the rear. Two scouts rode ahead, followed by an advance guard of twenty men.

'May Lord Mahadev curse this idiot Ajitpal!' fumed Suheldev. 'Nothing good can happen in India till we have jackasses like him ruling our land.'

Mangaldhwaj shook his head sadly. 'With Indians like these, we don't need Turks to defeat us. We are pretty good at defeating ourselves. Divided, we will continue to fall.'

Just then, one of the scouts came galloping back, signalling to the men to halt. The riders stopped and parted ranks so that the scout could reach the king.

'What's the matter?' asked Mangaldhwaj.

'There are some soldiers at the lake, My Lord,' replied the scout. 'About fifty men. They're wearing the colours of Ghazni.'

The lake the scout was referring to was like an informal waystation, where all caravans on the route stopped to water their horses and get some rest. It was a few kilometres away, through a wooded path.

Mangaldhwaj looked beyond the scout. 'Where's the senior scout?'

'He's keeping an eye on them, great king. He sent me back to inform you.'

Mangaldhwaj nodded approvingly, happy to see standard protocols being followed. 'Let's go take a look,' he said. He signalled to Suheldev and two other soldiers. 'You come with us. Everybody else, drop back. Keep an eye on us, but stay concealed.'

The small party rode up towards the lake. The senior scout was hiding behind a tree, his horse tied to another tree further back. One of the soldiers made a bird sound in a low tone as they approached so that the scout wouldn't be startled.

The scout turned around, saw the riders, and saluted quietly. Mangaldhwaj and Suheldev dismounted, handed over the reins of their horses to the youngest soldier, and walked up to the scout.

'What is it, Abdul?' asked Mangaldhwaj softly.

Abdul shook his head to indicate that he had no idea, and pointed towards the lake. A large tent had been set up next to it. About fifty men in the distinctive green tunics of the Ghazni army were sitting around a fire, while a couple of men kept guard, though they weren't particularly alert.

'Let's go find out what they are up to,' said Mangaldhwaj. He looked back. The rest of the soldiers were some distance away, but visible. He turned to the younger scout. 'Go to them with my instructions. They are to stay close by and keep themselves hidden. I don't think there should be any trouble, but if they see any sign of it, they should rush to our aid.'

As the men took cover, Mangaldhwaj, Suheldev, Abdul and another soldier rode up to the camp, making sure that their horses walked at a leisurely pace. It was twilight, and a gentle breeze was blowing.

The forest line was about two hundred metres away from the lake, but the approach to it was a grassy plain with no obstructions.

Perfect for grazing horses—or for mounting a cavalry charge, thought Suheldev.

'Stop right there,' one of the sentries called out as the riders approached the camp. 'Who are you?'

Mangaldhwaj raised his hands. 'We are horse traders, on our way to Bahraich. May we approach?'

As the sentry hesitated, a burly, obviously Turkic-looking man dressed in a fine silk robe stepped out of the tent. He was completely bald, but made up for it with a thick beard that reached his chest. He had a roundish face with thin slit-like eyes, like most Turks. His robe was stretched tight across a massive paunch. 'What's going on?'

The Turk exuded an air of entitlement that immediately set Suheldev's teeth on edge.

The sentry gestured. 'These are horse traders, My Lord. They asked for permission to approach.'

'Horse traders, eh?' asked the man. 'Where are your horses?'

Mangaldhwaj bowed. 'By the grace of the Gods, we were able to sell all of them in Kannauj. We are on our way home to pick up some fresh stock. With your permission, we would like to stop by the lake for a while.'

'Are you blind, you fool?' asked the Turk arrogantly. 'Can't you see this place is taken? Move on!'

'But surely there is enough room and water for all of us,' said Mangaldhwaj politely.

'You insolent bastard, do you know whom you are talking to?' thundered the man. 'I am an envoy of the great sultan, Mahmud of Ghazni himself. Get out of here while you still have your skin on your back, you worthless pieces of pig shit.'

Mangaldhwaj bowed hurriedly. 'I am so sorry, My Lord. I had no idea that I was talking to such a grand person. We will leave right away. But before that, may I ask if—'

The envoy yelled loudly, 'I am not buying anything from you, bloody Indian rat! Get out! You're lucky I'm leaving you alive. Otherwise you'd be squealing like the pigs our men gutted at the Somnath temple.'

Suheldev drew in his breath sharply. He spurred his horse hard and rode straight at the envoy. Even as the startled Turk screeched in terror, Suheldev flung himself off the horse and landed on top of him. Both of them went down in a tangled heap.

The other guards rushed towards the two men, but Mangaldhwaj and the soldiers accompanying him pulled out the swords that they had been concealing in their bedrolls and attacked them. Seconds later, thundering hooves echoed loudly as the rest of the Shravasti party came galloping to their assistance.

Suheldev repeatedly punched and kicked the envoy, who initially tried to hit back but finally covered his face with his hands and curled up in a foetal position. After a while, strong hands pulled the seething Suheldev away, off the defenceless man. The envoy was hauled to his knees roughly.

'Search the tents,' Mangaldhwaj told one of his soldiers. Then he walked up to the Turk. 'You said you were an envoy of Mahmud. What message were you conveying from the sultan? And to whom?'

The envoy spat at him. A gob fell on Mangaldhwaj's right shoe.

'Let me ask him,' said Suheldev.

He backhanded the man on his right cheek. The envoy sagged back, then coughed and spat out blood and two teeth.

'Shall I ask again?' asked Suheldev. 'I can keep doing this all day.'

'You dog, the sultan will have your head for this,' growled the envoy.

Suheldev smiled, but it was a mere tightening of the lips, with no humour. 'Wrong answer,' he said, punching the envoy on his nose. There was a cracking sound as the Turk's nose fractured. His nose swelled up immediately and blood began to pour out of it. He struggled to breathe and opened his mouth to suck in some air, wheezing as he did so.

'We found something,' yelled Abdul, who had been searching the envoy's tent. He brought out several scrolls. 'Sealed letters addressed to various rulers in this region. There's one for you as well, great king of Shravasti.'

Abdul handed over a scroll to Mangaldhwaj. The envoy's eyes widened when he heard the title.

'Mangaldhwaj!' the Turk rasped, staring at the king. 'Your women and children will be sold as slaves. You and all your men will be killed, just like that coward son of yours. How he shrieked before the sultan took his head off. We all laughed our guts out.'

A red haze settled over Suheldev's eyes. He pulled out his sword. 'Shriek for me, you son of a bitch,' he screamed, slashing at the Turk's stomach.

The envoy howled in agony as he clutched at his stomach and collapsed, writhing. Blood spurted from his ruptured abdomen, and his slippery intestines fell out to the ground.

'Looks like he's really laughed his guts out this time,' said Suheldev curtly, wiping his sword clean. He saw his father staring at him. 'What? Didn't you hear what he said about *dada*?'

'Breathe,' said Mangaldhwaj, calmly. 'Anger has its place too. But information on the enemy is far more important than immediate vengeance.'

Suheldev remained silent. Defiant.

'Anyway, what's done is done,' said Mangaldhwaj. 'Let's see what the letters say.'

Mangaldhwaj read a scroll, then looked up thoughtfully. He

turned towards Abdul. The other scrolls were also opened and handed over to the king of Shravasti.

Mangaldhwaj quickly read the other letters too, then gestured to Suheldev to walk a short distance away.

Mangaldhwaj spoke calmly. 'The letters basically say that every king should swear allegiance to Ghazni, send him half of his revenue collection every year, and give him troops whenever he asks, or be prepared to be invaded. From the seals that I've seen on some of the scrolls, it seems that quite a few of the kings have accepted the terms—including Ajitpal.'

'That hypocrite was lecturing us about honour,' said Suheldev bitterly. His eyes widened as a thought occurred to him. 'Ajitpal may have met this fellow just before meeting us. Maybe he didn't want his people to know about his shameful surrender.'

'True, but do you realise what you have done in your anger, son? You attacked Ghazni's envoy in front of his bodyguards, and we had no choice but to help you, otherwise you would have been killed. This will bring the full wrath of Ghazni down on our heads if Mahmud finds out. And we are not yet ready to fight him head-on.'

'What do we do?'

'We will have to keep this little encounter a secret for as long as we can.' Mangaldhwaj turned back towards the camp and signalled to the captain of the Shravasti guards to approach him. Many of the Ghazni soldiers were dead. The survivors had been taken prisoner. Mangaldhwaj's order to the captain was clear. 'There can be no witnesses to what happened here.'

The captain immediately drew his sword and walked towards the Ghazni prisoners. His guards understood and pulled out their blades as well. The Ghazni prisoners wailed in terror as they realised what was to happen. They had heard of the Indian concepts of honour and treating prisoners-of-war with mercy. They appealed for clemency, promising to turn against Sultan Mahmud. Crying desperately. The cries were cut short as they were quickly clubbed to their knees and executed.

'What are our casualties?' asked Mangaldhwaj, as soon as the executions were done.

'A few wounded. Nothing serious,' he was told.

'Patch them up and let's get out of here,' said Mangaldhwaj. 'But first, we need to get rid of the bodies. Take them into the forest and bury them deep, so that the wild animals can't get at them. Pack some salt on the bodies as you bury them. That will keep the smell of the decomposing bodies from becoming too obvious. Take the salt from their stores. They must have some. Cover the ground that you dig up with leaves and branches, so that no one will be able to tell that the soil has been disturbed. Take everything that is useful and destroy the rest. Leave no trace of what happened.'

— ᴇᴊᴊ ᴎᴅᴧᴊᴄᴧ —

Mangaldhwaj yawned and stretched by the fire. As the sun rose, he bowed to it and mumbled a quick prayer. He briefly considered doing a few rounds of *Surya Namaskar* but decided against it. He was still tired from the previous day, and there were many hours of hard riding ahead.

It had been late into the night by the time the men had finished removing all traces of the clash with the Ghazni envoy and his party. They had ridden out immediately after that, wanting to put as much distance as possible between themselves and the spot. Due to the darkness, they had maintained a slow pace, but Mangaldhwaj had kept the exhausted men and animals going as long as he dared before allowing them to camp for the night. They had barely managed a couple of hours of sleep before it was time to rise again.

'Pranam, *baba*,' said Suheldev, coming up to his father and touching his feet.

Mangaldhwaj gestured to Suheldev to sit beside him. 'You don't look like you've slept much.'

Suheldev shook his head. 'There were too many thoughts running through my head.'

'And what were you thinking?'

'Ajitpal knows we were in the vicinity. Once word gets out that the Ghazni envoy has mysteriously disappeared, he will not take long to put two and two together ... Or at least get suspicious ... But there is another thing. Did you hear the men talking last night? They were excited. They realise now that the army of Ghazni is not invincible. Their soldiers can be killed, if we take them by surprise.'

'So, what's on your mind?' asked Mangaldhwaj. He had been thinking along the same lines, but he wanted to hear what his son had to say.

Suheldev took a deep breath, almost as if speaking it out loud would confirm his final decision. '*Baba*, I will not return home with you. We will put the word out that I was responsible for the envoy's death while you had already moved on ahead. I will go into hiding with whichever of these men are willing to come with me. I will live like a bandit and roam through the region, striking at Ghazni's men whenever I get the chance. I am sure that many more will join me. You can say that I am acting against your wishes and you are not involved in any way. We will stay in touch secretly.'

'It will be a hard life for you, my son.'

'Hardship does not scare me … I took a vow to avenge *dada*, and I will do so, whatever it takes.'

'You are taking on the might of Ghazni with just a handful of men. It will be like an ant fighting an elephant.'

'I know, but even an ant can make an elephant miserable,' Suheldev said and smiled. 'It just has to know when and where to bite.'

Mangaldhwaj looked long and hard at his son. When he finally spoke, his voice was choked with emotion. 'Becoming a leader is not about being able to fight or argue or make speeches. It's actually about realising what must be done for the greater good. And doing it, regardless of the personal costs …'

Suheldev held his breath, not used to open compliments from his father. Those compliments were usually reserved for the good son, Malladev.

Mangaldhwaj pulled his younger son into a bear hug. 'Malladev would have been proud of you, my boy … I am proud of you …'

The two men embraced for a long time. Then Suheldev gently disengaged himself from his father.

Mangaldhwaj touched Suheldev's face and whispered, 'Go with Lord Shiva, my son. Fight for Mother India.'

'Har Har Mahadev …'

'Har Har Mahadev …'

Suheldev touched his father's feet once more, and then walked away.

He did not look back.

Chapter 4

'That deer is already dead, Suheldev. You don't have to stab it to death again. Here, let me skin it.'

Suheldev scowled at Abdul. The hawk-nosed, curly-haired scout was one of the fifty men who had followed him into his self-imposed exile a few weeks ago. Since then, the band had largely stayed in a forested area that overlapped the border of the kingdoms of Kannauj and Haridway.

Owing to the dense vegetation, the border was extremely porous. On a couple of occasions, Suheldev and his men had conducted minor raids in Kannauj, then slipped back into Haridway, where the soldiers of Kannauj could not follow them. During this time, they had also befriended the inhabitants of a village that marked almost the last human settlement in Kannauj before one entered the border area.

The residents of the village were poor but hospitable, and generously offered the band whatever assistance they could provide.

'I know you're just trying to take over my chore, Abdul,' said Suheldev. 'But I've told you before, I don't want preferential treatment. We're all equals here. I'll do the same tasks as everybody else.'

Abdul smiled slightly and shook his head. 'You're just like your elder brother.'

Suheldev's gaze softened. Abdul's father, who had served as Mangaldhwaj's bodyguard, had died protecting the king. A grateful Mangaldhwaj had given Abdul's mother employment in the palace and ensured that her son received a proper education along with his own elder son.

Abdul and Malladev were the same age and Abdul had quickly become Malladev's closest companion. When Abdul had indicated that he wanted to join the army, no one had been more delighted than Malladev.

Abdul had accompanied Malladev on several expeditions. Strong of both body and character, he had quickly proven himself a tough, resourceful soldier. On a recent campaign though, he had suffered a serious injury. He was still recovering from it when Malladev had volunteered to ride to the defence of the Somnath temple. Abdul had begged Malladev to let him accompany him, even in his injured state. But Malladev had refused, saying there would be other battles to fight in the future. Abdul's injury had barely healed when news of Malladev's death had reached Shravasti. He believed that if he had been there in Somnath, then Malladev would have still been alive.

Suheldev gently touched Abdul's shoulder. 'There is no greater compliment for me than being compared to *dada*. But you know as well as I do that I am not as great as he was. Not even close.'

Abdul looked at Suheldev, an expression of pure misery on his face. 'I should have been with him at Somnath*ji*.'

Suheldev sighed. 'Then you would have been dead too.'

'It would have been better than living while my friends and comrades lie dead.'

'Abdul, your injury was not your fault. In any case, we

cannot roll back time. Instead of mourning your friends, focus on avenging them.'

Abdul nodded, rubbing his face, almost like he was pushing the misery off it. 'You're right … Why don't you finish skinning that deer? Maybe we can take some of that meat to our friends in the village and trade it in for some nice home-cooked food?'

Suheldev nodded. 'I'll give you about a quarter of it. Take one of the men and go.'

—— EJJ ℋ3ᴧᴄ̌Δ ——

'Please, sir, have mercy on us,' said the old villager, tears rolling down his cheeks as he clutched the foot of the man seated on a horse. 'If you take away all our grain, what will we eat? We'll starve to death.'

The Turkic officer, Salik Khan, drew back his foot from the stirrup and viciously booted the man in his face, sending him sprawling to the ground, blood streaming from his nose.

'Shut your mouth, you fool,' Salik growled. 'Your king's orders are clear. A proper tribute has to be paid to our great sultan of Ghazni. And everyone must pay their fair share.'

Many Turks from Mahmud's army had volunteered to stay in the Indian kingdoms that had surrendered their sovereignty to the sultan of Ghazni. Technically they were officers of the local Indian kingdoms. But in effect, they acted as Mahmud's representatives in these realms, commanded soldiers, and ensured that Ghaznavid instructions were followed. And, of course, these Turks also ensured that they looted for themselves personally. The plunder of India, the richest land in the world, was an opportunity for most Turks to make enough of a fortune for generations to come.

The old man rose unsteadily to his feet. 'And will the king go hungry like the rest of us?'

'You impudent imbecile,' roared Salik, drawing his sword. 'I'll have your head for this.'

A young man rushed forward, bowing low to Salik. 'Please My Lord, spare him! Spare him! I beg you … He's half mad anyway …' The young man pulled the old peasant back. 'Come on, *baba*, let's go. As long as we live, we can always find more food.'

The officer nodded in approval. 'You're a smart fellow. What's your name?'

'Kishna, My Lord,' said the young man, his eyes downcast.

'Hmm … Well, Kishna, keep this old fool out of my sight. And tell him to mind his tongue, or I'll rip it out of his mouth.'

Kishna hurried away, half helping, half dragging his father alongside. As Salik watched them go, a senior soldier who served as his sergeant rode up to him. 'Even after we take away all their grain, we still won't meet our target, My Lord.'

'Dammit! Just my luck to have this miserable area assigned to me.' As he looked around, his eyes fell on the village temple. 'I'm sure that must contain some valuables.'

The sergeant looked shocked. He was an Indian, after all. 'You mean to loot a temple, My Lord?'

Salik looked at his sergeant nonchalantly, but there was menace in his voice. 'Do you have some doubts?'

'My Lord … I … But would the king approve?'

'The king doesn't have to know of everything that goes on in every remote part of the kingdom. In any case, the great Sultan Mahmud of Ghazni has set the tradition in India of looting temples. And he is now the king's overlord, so the king should have no reason to complain. We are only following tradition!'

Salik laughed as he said the last line.

The sergeant looked nervous but bowed. Surrendering, as usual, to the Turk.

Darkness does not win because it is strong. It wins because the lamps stop fighting.

— EJJ ⅓⅃⅃∆ —

The old man was almost hysterical, his voice quivering as he cried out for help. 'The bastards are going to loot the temple. Will no one stop them? Will you just watch?! Cowards!'

'*Baba*, stop! You will get yourself killed. In the name of the Mahadev, let's just get out of here.' Kishna was weeping too, but he was resolutely pushing his father on the main road that led out of the village.

'What's going on here?' asked Abdul, surprised to see practically the entire village population running away. Some of them were bloodied or had swollen faces, but most simply looked terrified, even though they were physically unharmed.

Kishna looked up in alarm, then heaved a sigh of relief as he recognised Abdul. 'It's the king's men ...' he said, instinctively looking back towards the village, clearly terrified. 'They are led by a Turkic maniac. They've looted all our belongings. And now they're even ransacking the temple.'

'Let's go to the prince and get help,' said Abdul's companion instantly.

Kishna's father suddenly stepped up. 'It will be too late by then. Who knows if they'll just stop at looting the temple. What if the Turk destroys it? What if they do here what they did at Somnath*ji*?'

Abdul had been in the process of turning his horse around. He froze as soon as he heard the old man's words.

'Come on, Abdul,' said his companion urgently.

Abdul shook his head. 'You go and get help. I'm going to the temple.'

His companion reached out and put his hand on Abdul's arm, speaking tenderly, 'Listen to me, Abdul … This is a bad idea …'

Abdul gently removed the restraining hand. 'No, it's not a bad idea … It is Allah giving me a small opportunity to make a stand. Now go.'

Abdul spurred his horse towards the temple while his companion raced off. Within a few minutes, Abdul had reached the vicinity of the temple. He saw some men in the distance, bringing out the temple chests in which the offerings were kept.

Hidden behind the dense forest line, Abdul silently dismounted and tied his horse. A safe distance away. He pulled his bow forward and crept slowly towards the temple.

He was now close enough to hear the soldiers. But yet, hidden well by the darkness and the trees.

'Get the idols and jewellery as well,' commanded Salik.

Abdul quietly pulled an arrow, nocked it to his bow, aimed quickly and shot.

A good archer doesn't need to spend too much time aiming. The arrow whizzed forward, sharp and true, striking a soldier in his chest. The soldier went hurtling back with the force of the blow, the missile buried deep in his heart, as the jewellery he was carrying spilled all over the ground.

There were angry shouts of confusion from the soldiers.

'Take cover!' shouted Salik.

Abdul quickly ran to a different position. Far from where he had been just a few moments ago. He quickly drew another arrow, nocked it and let fly. It found its mark. Another of Salik's soldiers went down.

Salik was screaming now. 'There are many enemies! Upon me! Stay close! Shields steady!'

Salik was a ruthless man, but an excellent soldier. He had trained his troops well. They quickly formed a tight defensive line. The temple behind them. The forest line in front. Staying low. Protected by their shields.

Abdul kept running to different areas behind the forest line. Trying to fire arrows from various directions. Some got through. Felling soldiers. But most were deflected by the defensive shields.

Salik started suspecting something was wrong. There was too long a time gap between different arrows. If there were a lot of enemies, then the arrows would be fired a lot quicker.

Maybe there are fewer enemies than I thought.

Salik ordered his soldiers to remain steady. And quickly slipped out from the back, using the darkness for cover.

Within a few minutes, he was behind the forest line. Sword drawn. Trying to track the enemy soldiers. He walked carefully in a long arc, trying to get behind the enemy position.

The hunted wanted to turn the tables and become the hunter.

Stealthily, Salik crept forward, following the sound of the last arrow released. And the faint beats of footsteps.

Salik was impressed by the technique and the carefulness of the movements. *Whoever the enemies are, they are well-trained.*

He heard a soft sound. It was unmistakable. The sound of a bow being stretched. Just ahead. Salik inched forward. Slowly. Stealthily.

His eyes had adjusted well to the darkness now. He could make out the rough shape of a human being.

By the twisted balls of a diseased horse! Just one man! Just one man pinning my entire platoon!

Salik moved quickly, just as the sound of another arrow being released was heard. Abdul had shot one more missile at Salik's soldiers, who were in front of the temple. He didn't notice Salik himself creeping up behind him.

By the time he realised, it was too late. Salik hammered Abdul's head from the back with the hilt of his sword. And Abdul collapsed. Unconscious.

— EJ⌐ ꝋꝋ⌐ —

The whip whistled through the air, lashing into Abdul's back. Yanking skin. Drawing blood. He bit down hard on his lip to avoid crying out but could not prevent a muffled groan from emerging. His knees sagged, and he would have fallen if his hands had not been tied by a rope that hung from the branch of a tree.

Abdul had been brought back to the temporary camp commandeered by Salik. The granary of the village was being used as the troop's barracks. And the village headman's house next door was being used by Salik as his personal quarters. The village was empty, except for Salik and the king's soldiers. All the villagers had escaped a few hours ago. Abdul was being tortured in the open square in front of the temporary barracks.

'Tsk, tsk,' said Salik mockingly. Carrying a goblet of wine, the Turkic officer walked around Abdul and looked at his back. It was a bloodied mess, with several gaping wounds where the whip had torn the skin.

'Oh dear, that looks awful,' said Salik with fake concern. He took a swig of the wine, grinning mockingly as he examined Abdul's back closely. Then, suddenly, he spat out the wine directly onto Abdul's lacerated back.

Taken by surprise, Abdul jerked forward in pain, the alcohol scorching his wounded back. 'Ya Allah!' he cried out.

Salik froze for a moment. Stunned. He quickly came around Abdul, grabbed his hair and yanked his head up so that he could look his captive in the eye. 'You are a Muslim?!'

Abdul didn't answer. Glaring at Salik, fury dripping from every pore of his body.

'Trying to protect a temple?! What sort of Muslim are you?!'

Abdul stared back with undisguised contempt. 'A better one … than you …'

'How dare you oppose me?!' thundered Salik. 'You are a Muslim!'

'I am … an Indian first …'

Salik slapped Abdul hard. 'You fight for infidel Hindus rather than a Muslim like me?!'

'I fight … alongside my Indian brothers … against a Turkic monster …'

Salik hit Abdul hard, cracking his nose. And he kept hitting. Again. And again. Repeatedly. Till he was exhausted.

And then he hit Abdul some more. Stopping only when Abdul sagged on the rope. Unconscious.

Salik turned to his soldiers. 'Let the bastard hang here all night. I'll decide tomorrow how exactly he should be killed.'

— EJJ ℋ℥ᴎᔑ —

The guard stretched and yawned, then looked wistfully at his comrades, who had already abandoned their posts and were curled up on the ground, snoring away contentedly. As the youngest person in the squad, he had been delegated the task of staying up all night and keeping an eye on the prisoner.

Abdul was still hanging there. Motionless.

Is he dead?

The soldier shook his head and shrugged his shoulders, answering his own question in his mind. *Why should I care?*

He looked at the temporary barracks a short distance away, where most of his fellow soldiers were.

I could be sleeping right now.

This is such a waste of time. Who's going to have the nerve to attack an army camp? Those miserable villagers who couldn't even protect their own homes?

Taking a quick look around to make sure no one was watching, he sat down on the ground. Using the tree to prop up his back, he stretched out his legs, sighing with pleasure. In minutes, he dozed off. He did not notice the figure that stealthily crept up on him, knife drawn. Nor did he sense the hand that came up close. His consciousness was dragged out of his sleep only when his mouth was clamped shut. But his consciousness was too slow. He was still groggy as the knife sliced through his throat. Deep. He never really woke up completely.

— EⅡ ⅩⅢⅡⅭⅢ —

Salik sniffed in his sleep. The smell of something burning reaching his subconscious brain even before he woke up with a start. He called to his attendants, snatched up his sword and ran out.

As he emerged from his commandeered house, he froze in shock. The doors to the temporary barracks in which his men had been sleeping had been locked, and the building set ablaze. Since the building was originally a granary, there were no windows. He could now hear the desperate screaming from inside, as his soldiers were being slowly roasted alive. Some of them were banging on the locked doors, trying to break them down. But Salik noted with a sinking heart that some attackers were standing in front of the doors with bows drawn, ready to cut down his men if they managed to get out.

There were probably a hundred Indians in the square. He saw the dead bodies of his own soldiers that he had posted as night guards.

Where did these bastards come from?

Salik didn't realise that most of the Indians in the square, holding weapons, were the villagers he had just evicted. They had come back. They had been roused to fight. Roused by a leader he had never heard of.

Salik looked around. There were just four men with him. He looked back at the temporary barracks. The desperate screams of his soldiers rattling the night. He whispered urgently to the four with him, 'It's hopeless. We can't help them. Let's get out of here. Two ahead of me. Two behind. Move!'

The men scurried to the left. Heading quickly for the trees. Just a few hundred metres away. Once they reached behind the forest line, they could disappear easily. Or so Salik planned.

Unfortunately for him, the massive flames were radiating light in all directions. Drowning out the shadows of the night in many parts of the clearing.

And even more unfortunately, Salik was up against a ruthless foe. One who understood guerrilla warfare well.

He and his soldiers ran straight into forty men waiting for them.

Before Salik even knew what was happening, two of his lead soldiers were cut down. He swerved his sword around in all directions, keeping the enemies away. He heard desperate screams behind him. He didn't need to turn to know that his soldiers behind him had also been massacred.

He was alone. He kept swinging his sword. Keeping the enemy soldiers away. Screaming loudly. 'I will not go down easily! I will kill at least ten of you before I go! Come on!'

But they didn't come close. They kept a distance. Feigning charges and pulling back at the last minute. Salik kept swinging. Thinking he was keeping them away. Thinking that the Indians were behaving like the typical cowards that he had always believed they were.

Reality dawned on him only after some time.

They were playing with him. Toying with him. Like a merciless hunter did with a cornered animal.

Suddenly, someone from behind slashed brutally with a long sword. At the back of his right thigh. Salik howled in agony as the blade severed the hamstring cleanly, crippling his leg. Blood burst forth in a flood. He fell face down in the dust.

He could hear the laughter of those around him.

Taunting.

Screaming obscenities.

Salik turned on his back, still lying on the ground. Swinging his sword around. In every direction. But his enemies kept a distance. Again.

Salik screamed in fury. 'Kill me, you infidel bastards!'

He kept swinging his sword. Hitting only the air. Rage and frustration building in him. A stone was thrown at him with stunning accuracy. Hitting him exactly on his right wrist. The sword flew out of his hand. An Indian immediately rushed forward, picked up Salik's sword, and walked back slowly. Laughing all the time.

'Kill me!' screamed Salik. 'You filthy cowards! Kill me!'

'All in good time ...'

Salik could make out from the tone of the voice that this was the leader of the Indians. The Turk turned his head to see a tall, lean man emerge from the shadows. The light of the flames made the vision clearer. The Indian leader's skin was dark. Long hair tied in a bun. Scraggy beard. Scars on his body. Many still fresh. Proud adornments of battle. He had the gait of a panther. Charismatic. Attractive. Scary.

Salik felt fear grip his heart. Something inside told him that it would not be a quick death. That he would suffer a lot of pain. That he would be kept alive till the last possible moment. He tried to incite his enemy. 'I have destroyed your temple idols. If you have the guts, kill me! Avenge your powerless pathetic pagan Gods!'

Salik heard a soft laugh. And his heart sank further. This was not an ordinary enemy. He was not foolish like most of the Indians that Salik had met till now. For Indians were very easy to incite if you insulted their Gods and superstitions. They seemed to prefer hot-tempered vengeance, rather than cold, calculated retribution.

But this one was different. This Indian leader was different.

'Oh, I will kill you. But not with anger. I will do it slowly. I will do it leisurely. I will ensure that your soul will remember. And it will not dare to come back to India.'

Salik could only imagine what awaited him. What awaited his soul. He lost control of his bladder. The only time it had ever happened to him in battle.

To his mortification, it was noticed by the Indian leader. He heard that soft, menacing laugh again.

'We haven't even begun ... And look at you ...'

Salik saw the leader turn to his followers. He heard the leader speak loudly and clearly.

'What did I tell you? These Turks are cowards. Like all bullies, they are cowards. We have to make them regret the thought of even looking at India. We have to make them urinate in their clothes if they even think of attacking India.'

Salik heard the Indians around him laugh. He had never heard Indians use this tone with a Turk before. He turned back to the leader. Terrified to the marrow of his bones.

'Make sure your soul remembers my name. So that it cowers in fear whenever it hears it.'

Salik slunk back, trying to drag his body away. The Indian leader kicked him hard on the chest, knocking the wind out of him.

'Remember my name. Remember Suheldev of Shravasti.'

— EJJ ꜳꜱꞀČᴧ —

Abdul opened his eyes. Every part of his body ached. Like each cell had been thrown into a hurricane, whiplashed for an aeon, and then stitched back together into a devastated body.

He heard the voice he recognised well. 'You'll recover soon.'

Abdul tried to rise. 'Suhel ...'

Suheldev gently pushed Abdul back onto the bed. 'Stay on your back.'

'How long ... have I ...'

'Almost an entire day.'

Suheldev and his men were still in the village. And they intended to remain there till Abdul recovered. The villagers were busy cleaning up the remnants of the battle. Repairing their homes. Restoring the village temple. Removing all traces of the bodies of the king's men. They would pretend that Salik and his soldiers had left the village with their booty. And that they had no idea where Salik went after that.

'Is the ... temple ... safe?' asked Abdul, still weak from the severe beating he had received from Salik and his men the previous night. But his mind was alert. The local medicine man was good.

Suheldev ignored the question. He spoke firmly. 'Don't do this again.'

'Suheldev ...'

'I know what you were trying to do. You don't need to prove anything. Don't do this again.'

'But that Turk was ... The temple idols ...'

'We will make new idols.'

Abdul remained silent.

Suheldev continued. 'Our faith is our strength. But the Turks have turned our faith into our weakness. They know that we will go to any extent to protect our idols, even sacrifice our lives. And they use that as a pressure tactic. To break our resolve. To defeat us easily.'

'But ...'

'Listen to me. It's my faith. I know ... The Divine is everywhere. In the stars and the skies, in the trees, in the rivers, in the wind, in all of us. Our faith is what actually puts God Himself into an idol. If we all die, then our faith dies. If our faith dies, then who will worship the idols? Remember, new idols can always be made and *pran pratishtha* done on them. But if our faith dies, then it is all over. And our faith exists only in our beating hearts. So, if there is a choice between saving an idol or us, I will always choose us.'

Abdul looked away. A soft tear rolling down his cheek. 'You ... don't understand.'

It was Suheldev's turn to remain silent. He let Abdul speak.

Abdul's tears picked up pace. 'I feel ... guilty ... I had to do something ... I had to fight ...'

'You have nothing to feel guilty about. You have nothing to do with the Turks or the crimes they commit.'

Abdul turned back towards Suheldev.

Suheldev's voice quivered slightly, his strong emotions bursting through. 'You are not one of them. You are one of us.'

Abdul's tears flowed quicker.

Suheldev held Abdul's hand firmly. 'You are one of us. I trust you. Completely. I want you to fight by my side. But the aim of fighting a battle is to win, not to become a martyr.'

Abdul remained quiet.

'Remember what I told you earlier. What I learnt from *baba*. What I learnt that day of the attack on the Ghazni envoy. No angry vengeance. We will have cold, ruthless retribution.'

Abdul looked at Suheldev with respect. Till now, he had shown the prince respect only for his birth. But now, he respected him for the man that he was becoming. The leader that he was becoming.

Abdul whispered, 'Yes, My Lord.'

Suheldev smiled and touched Abdul's shoulder. 'Continue to call me Suheldev.'

Abdul shook his head. 'No, My Lord.'

Chapter 5

Peshawar, 1027 AD

The archer held the bow steady with his left hand. With the right, he slowly pulled back the string, till it almost touched his lips. He held his right elbow high, parallel to the ground, so that it virtually formed a straight line with the arrow. This ensured that his powerful back and shoulder muscles would take the strain rather than the much weaker elbow. Then he pulled the string back one more notch and released the arrow.

His target was a young man dressed in the robes of a Buddhist monk. His chest was shielded by a battered piece of armour made of bamboo, which had clearly seen better days. He gripped a staff lightly in his right hand. His body was small, but lean and ripped with muscles. Without a single ounce of spare fat anywhere.

The monk stood still as a statue as the arrow sped towards him. Then, at almost the last possible moment, his hands moved in a blur. The staff clashed with the arrow, deflecting it harmlessly to one side where it crashed into a rock wall.

Applause rang out from above. Many novice monks, most of them little more than children, had been watching this scene from a safe height, sitting atop the tall rocks that fenced the circular sand pit. The two stunt boys looked up and grinned.

But it wasn't for long. Their smiles vanished as a stern voice was heard.

'Ashvaghosh! Sanghamani! You should have been back in the monastery an hour ago. Ashvaghosh, the abbot wants to see you.'

The two young men suddenly looked like little children who'd been caught playing a prank. They hurriedly stored their equipment in a small enclosure, clambered out of the training pit and sprinted up a steep hill. Crude steps had been cut into the side of the hill, and there were almost a hundred of them. It was a tough climb, but apart from a slight shortening of breath, neither seemed unduly fatigued by the time they reached the top and saw the wooden gates of the main monastery complex.

The two scurried into the complex, which had been their home and school for most of their young lives. Ashvaghosh often thought he could probably walk around the entire area blindfolded and identify every room by touch. He had no memory of ever having lived anywhere else.

The monastery was laid out like a rectangle within a rectangle. The students' dormitories were in the outer rectangle, as were the stores, granary and rooms for visiting pilgrims. Four passageways led to the inner rectangle, which housed the teachers' cells, the classrooms, the dining hall and library.

The complex was spacious and neatly laid out, but the architecture was simple and unfussy. The buildings were made of bricks, had a squat shape and were mostly of an earth-coloured hue—the complex was designed for utility rather than beauty. The only exceptions were in the courtyard of the inner rectangle, which housed a prayer hall and a majestic stupa with a distinctive white dome. The entire complex was located about fifty kilometres from the bustling town of Peshawar, or Purushpura, as it had once been called.

'Where's the abbot?' Ashvaghosh asked a young monk.

'In the prayer hall,' he was told.

Ashvaghosh muttered his thanks and rushed to the prayer hall. Ashvaghosh knocked as softly as possible on the wooden doors, half hoping that the abbot would be deep in prayer and would not hear the sound.

'Come in,' called out the abbot cheerfully.

Ashvaghosh sighed ruefully and entered the hall. Three storeys high, it was the tallest building in the complex. It was dominated by a huge statue of a seated Buddha, itself almost two storeys high, placed at the far end. The walls were completely covered with elaborate, colourful murals depicting various scenes from the life of the Buddha. No matter how many times he entered the room, the majesty of the statue and the beauty of the murals left Ashvaghosh awestruck.

The abbot, a renowned philosopher and teacher named Chandrakirti, was seated on a rug in front of the statue. He gestured at Ashvaghosh to wait, then resumed his prayers. After some time, he folded his hands and bowed deeply to the statue. Then he turned around towards Ashvaghosh, who was standing respectfully near the entrance.

'Come here, boy,' he said, patting the space next to him. 'Sit with me.'

It was hard to tell Chandrakirti's age. He had a shaved head, a ruddy, round face and a sturdy physique. There were hardly any wrinkles on his face, though the presence of deep laugh lines suggested that he was not devoid of a sense of humour. But he was not smiling as he looked at Ashvaghosh.

The young monk walked across to the abbot, bowed and sat down cross-legged opposite him. 'You wished to see me, Master?'

'Yes, Ashvaghosh,' said Chandrakirti. 'Your teachers are worried about you. You've always been one of our better students. But I hear that, increasingly, your mind seems to be out in the martial arts training pit, even when you're attending classes.'

'I'm sorry, Master. It's just that ...'

'It's just what?'

'It's just that I like it ... And don't you always say that we should follow our *swadharma*? Isn't it my *personal dharma* to learn martial skills? For the good of the monastery?'

'These skills are purely for self-defence, Ashvaghosh. You have been told that repeatedly.'

'I know, Master, but ...'

'But what?'

'Please don't be upset by this question, Master.'

'I never get upset.'

Ashvaghosh gathered some courage. To say something to the abbot that he never had. 'Isn't protecting our motherland also part of self-defence? We practise these skills but never use them, even as our land is ripped apart by cruel foreign invaders.'

Chandrakirti sighed and shook his head. 'You spend too much time thinking about the outside world. That's not good for a monk.'

'But Master, isn't it selfish to cut ourselves off from the world and try to lead a good life when there is evil all around us?'

'And how should one combat this evil that you speak of? With violence? With killing?'

Ashvaghosh paused. He knew the abbot would not like his answer, but he went ahead anyway. 'If need be.'

'Violence is no solution to anything, Ashvaghosh. It only

creates a chain reaction that ends up destroying everybody. The desire for revenge is a fire that consumes both the target and the seeker. You cannot conquer hate with more hate, or anger with more anger. The only way to conquer your enemy is through love and forgiveness. If he hits you on one cheek, offer him the other.'

'Pardon me, Master, but I feel people often mistake love of peace for weakness. They look upon those who talk of love with contempt and keep pushing them. If I turn the other cheek and somebody hits me again, then what am I supposed to do?'

Chandrakirti remained silent. Impassive.

'I am sorry, Master,' said Ashvaghosh, folding his hands together into a penitent namaste. 'I have spoken too much.'

Chandrakirti reached over and patted Ashvaghosh gently on his shoulder. 'My child, you were left here as an orphan, when you were a little boy who could barely walk. Many other young children join us every year. Most of them are able to adjust to the life here. But I fear that the way of the Buddha may not be for you. Perhaps you belong in the world outside.'

'Don't say that, Master. This monastery is the only home I've ever known. Please don't be angry with me.'

A gong rang out loud. The day of the monks was ordered, to a large extent, by the gong and the time buckets it made. The abbot smiled gently. 'I must return to my duties.' As he rose, he gently patted Ashvaghosh on his head. 'I am not angry with you, my son. But I want to leave you with one thought. Do you really want to fight against evil? Or are you just seeking an apparently credible excuse to plunge into violence? It is easy to take that path, but very difficult to return from it.'

Chandrakirti walked out, leaving Ashvaghosh deep in thought.

As the abbot strolled down the corridor, an ancient memory came rushing back to him. He stopped walking as he closed his eyes momentarily. The voice rang crystal clear in his ears. Even today. After all these years.

It was the voice of a distraught woman. *Please, please, Guruji, take him in your monastery! I beg you! He won't have a chance outside!*

Chandrakirti turned back to see Ashvaghosh, in the distance, still sitting in front of the magnificent statue of Gautam Buddha.

Please don't tell anyone who he really is … Not even him …

Chandrakirti sighed. He had honoured the promise to this day. But the secret weighed heavy on his gentle soul.

— EJ ᏈᎦᏨᏦᎠ —

The palanquin bearers stopped abruptly, then unceremoniously dumped their burden on the ground.

The noble woman inside called out, in a thick Turkic accent, 'What's going on?'

The bearers ignored her and took to their heels. Inside the palanquin, Hamida anxiously clutched her two small children, a six-year-old boy and a three-year-old girl, to her bosom. Despite having two children—and having lost a third during a difficult pregnancy—she retained a slim figure. Her gorgeous green eyes, milk-white complexion and long black hair gave her a lustrous beauty that made it almost impossible for onlookers to take their eyes off her.

'I'll find out what's happening, Ammi,' said her son, wriggling furiously in an effort to free himself. 'Let me go.'

Hamida only held on to him tighter, her anxiety increasing as she heard raised voices, cries of agony and the clash of swords. After a few moments, there was silence. Then, the veils of the palanquin were parted.

A very courteous voice was heard. 'Please come outside, My Lady.'

Hamida stiffened with fear, but the thought of her children made her gather up her courage. 'How dare you interrupt my journey? Do you know who I am? My husband will have your head for this.'

'If you could please step out. We promise that no harm will come to you or your children.'

Hamida knew she had no choice. She stepped out of the palanquin, forcing her children to remain inside. Her heart picked up pace quickly. In panic.

All the soldiers escorting her had surrendered their weapons and were standing bunched together, herded meekly like sheep. As she glared at them contemptuously, they averted their gaze, unable to look her in the eye.

Hamida turned towards the man who had addressed her. He was a tall, lean man, who was looking at her with a twinkle in his eyes.

'What is the meaning of this?' she demanded.

Before the man could answer, Hamida's son burst out of the palanquin, brandishing his toy sword. 'Who wants to fight me? Come on, I'll take on all of you.'

'Whoa … Easy there, tiger,' said the man, nimbly sidestepping the boy's thrusts. 'You might just hurt me.'

'I will kill you if you hurt my mother.'

'It's a good thing I don't intend to hurt your mother then.'

The boy became silent. And suddenly noticed the man's magnificent horse. The child's martial ardour was forgotten in an instant.

'Do you want to ride the horse?' asked the tall man, smiling broadly.

'Can I?' asked the boy, his eyes gleaming. 'Really?'

Not looking at his mother, who would have definitely forbidden it, the child eagerly held out his arms. The stranger chuckled, picked him up and placed him on top of the horse. Then he handed the reins to his lieutenant. 'Abdul, take him for a slow trot. Keep him within his mother's eyesight.'

'Why have you stopped us?' demanded Hamida. 'What do you want?'

The man smiled lazily and Hamida couldn't help noticing that he had a certain rakish charm. 'Well, My Lady, to be honest, I am more interested in the money that these men were taking to be deposited in the treasury of Kannauj. But I must say, the tales of your beauty are no exaggeration. In fact, they don't do you justice.'

'You know who I am?' asked Hamida. 'Then you must also know my husband? And what will happen to you if—'

The man smiled again, interrupting Hamida. 'Yes, I know that your husband is Qasar Khan and that he is serving as Mahmud Ghazni's ambassador to the king of Kannauj. I am aware that you are on your way to join him. I am also aware that a lot of the money your soldiers are carrying is, eventually, to be sent onward to Ghazni ... We can't allow that. I have been waiting patiently at this spot for the last few days for your convoy.'

Hamida stared at him, intrigued. *The information about the money was supposed to be a secret. How does he know?*

'I have many well-informed friends,' said the man, almost as if he could read her thoughts. 'But as I have already told your son, you need not fear for yourself or your children. You will be handed over safely to your husband soon enough.'

Hamida looked down, suddenly weak-kneed with relief. 'I thank you,' she said, her voice threatening to crack. Then a thought struck her. 'Wait … are you … Suheldev?'

The man smiled and bowed. 'Guilty as charged! So, you too have heard of me?'

'Yes, the tales about you are no exaggeration,' said Hamida, smiling. 'In fact, they don't do you justice either.'

Suheldev threw back his head and roared with laughter. 'Touché, My Lady. And what exactly are the tales about me that you've heard?'

Hamida hesitated for a moment. 'That you are a former prince … And a bandit. And that all Turks need to stay away from you.'

Suheldev smiled and bowed his head. 'Only the Turks who hurt us … Others, such as yourself, who have done us no harm, have nothing to fear.'

Hamida smiled. Clearly, she was smitten.

Suheldev looked towards one of his men. 'Escort Lady Hamida and her children, with all respect, to the borders of Kannauj.' Turning to Hamida, Suheldev continued. 'Do convey my greetings to your husband and to King Ajitpal.'

Hamida smiled. 'I'll tell them that the bandit prince sends his regards.'

— ᴇᴊᴊ ꜱᴊᴏᴊᴄᴀ —

'Do you have to do this?' she asked.

She had spoken to him countless times already. Begged. Pleaded. Argued. But her son wasn't one to allow his resolve to waver, especially once his mind was made up.

But she was a mother. She still had to try. One last time.

'Mother, we've spoken about this,' the young man replied firmly.

The woman sighed. 'The journey will be long and dangerous. May Allah guide and protect you.'

She hugged her son close, then turned away abruptly, tears streaming down her face.

A few hours later, late at night, the youth quietly left his home. He had prepared thoroughly for this. He knew the mind of the sultan. Only a few could be trusted with the knowledge of what he was setting out to do. The stakes were high. Secrecy was key to the success of his mission. He had donned the rough garb of a mendicant, riding his favourite horse and leading another pack horse by the reins.

The guards had been told to expect him. They nodded quietly and allowed him to pass. As he neared the last of them, a hand reached out and held his horse's reins. It belonged to a thickset soldier with a tear-shaped birthmark on his right cheek. The man's face was prematurely wrinkled due to his long hours in the sun. He had close-cropped black hair interspersed with patches of grey.

The soldier spoke in a low voice, 'My Lord, I have personally made the arrangements, but you know how tricky things can be. Do be careful.'

The rider acknowledged this with a nearly imperceptible nod. 'Yes, Ozgur.'

Ozgur let go of the reins. But not before adding, 'Your mission is sacred but difficult, My Lord. I will pray for your success. For Allah. And for the holy land.'

'For Allah. And for the holy land.' Saying this, the young man spurred his horse onwards, melting into the darkness, slipping noiselessly out of Ghazni.

Chapter 6

Chandrakirti hurriedly shoved a semi-conscious Ashvaghosh into the prayer hall. 'Bar the doors,' he directed. A few monks already gathered there ran to do so.

Ashvaghosh sat slumped on the floor, bleeding heavily from a cut above his right eyebrow.

'Ashvaghosh,' said Chandrakirti.

The young lad looked up.

'How many fingers?' asked Chandrakirti, holding up one.

Ashvaghosh wiped away the blood that was obscuring his vision. 'One,' he replied.

The abbot moved his finger first to the right, then to the middle and then to the left. Ashvaghosh's eyes followed the movement.

'Good,' said Chandrakirti. 'There's no major damage to that thick skull of yours.'

He looked around and did a quick mental count of the monks gathered there. There were ten, apart from him and Ashvaghosh.

'The others?' Chandrakirti asked.

'They didn't make it, Master,' replied Dhammajyoti, the only one in the room apart from the abbot who knew the truth about Ashvaghosh's parents.

Chandrakirti closed his eyes as a spasm of grief rocked him. The sounds of battle were now near as a handful of monks, armed only with staffs, made their last stand against the Ghazni soldiers outside.

The local rulers, the king of Mesank, Balavrata, and the king of Pushkalavati, Daeshim, had capitulated and converted to Islam. As had many of their subjects. But the Turks were still not satisfied. The next target was the monasteries. The Turks were most brutal on the Buddhists—that was the religion that the Turks themselves had recently converted from. And the version of Buddhism that they had practised, before they converted to Islam, did believe in idol-worshipping. The Turkic word for idol, *'but'*, was derived from 'Buddha'.

But, according to the Turks now, worshipping idols was a grievous crime which was punishable by death. Of course, many idol-worshippers, who had never massacred or attacked those who rejected idol-worship, could never understand what it was about idol-worshipping that got the Turks into such a frenzy.

Smoke began to rise as each of the buildings inside the monastery was set ablaze. Monks who had been hiding inside them came stumbling out, blinded by the smoke and frantically coughing in an effort to clear their lungs. They were brutally cut down.

The Turks built a huge bonfire in the main open square of the monastery. Sacred texts that had been lovingly written and carefully preserved over millennia were pulled from various rooms and from the library, and tossed into the flames.

The invaders had not reached the prayer hall as yet. Not as yet.

'They will be here soon,' said one monk fearfully. 'May the Buddha have mercy on us.'

'The Buddha will save us, my child,' replied Chandrakirti. He walked up to the giant statue of the Buddha and fell at its feet. As the monks watched, he pushed down hard on the statue's right toe.

The monks gasped as the back of the statue swivelled open, revealing a hollow space large enough for two men to stand in. There was a trapdoor on the floor. Chandrakirti yanked it open and pointed to steps leading down. 'The monks who built this monastery were careful planners ... That tunnel will take you many miles from here. Dhammajyoti, you are in charge. Get them to safety. Quickly now. There is no time to waste.'

The monks scrambled down the steps till there were only Ashvaghosh, his friend Sanghamani, and the abbot left.

'Hurry up,' said Chandrakirti, his voice calm, despite the devastation of everything that the monk held dear.

'You first, Master,' said Ashvaghosh.

'Someone has to stay behind to shut the secret door,' said the abbot. 'I will try to buy you time. Go now.'

Ashvaghosh shook his head stubbornly. 'Not without you.'

Chandrakirti groaned softly, then shrugged in resignation. 'Fine,' he said. Then his eyes widened as he looked just past Ashvaghosh's right shoulder. 'Oh no!'

'What ...?' Ashvaghosh began to turn his head.

A moment later, the abbot's fist crashed into his jaw, knocking him out cold. He crumpled and would have fallen to the floor if Chandrakirti had not grabbed him.

'Here, take him,' said Chandrakirti, handing the unconscious Ashvaghosh to Sanghamani. 'Ask Dhammajyoti to tell him how he came to the monastery. Go now, my children. May the Buddha bless you.'

'Goodbye, Master,' said Sanghamani, his voice breaking, in accord with his heart. He slung Ashvaghosh over his shoulder and climbed down the steps.

The abbot walked back and pulled the toe of the statue

upwards, back to its original position. The passage was concealed once again.

Chandrakirti sat down before the Buddha's statue. 'I have dedicated my life to peace and I will die violently. I wonder what *karma* of my previous life has caused this, Great Lord.' He closed his eyes and took a deep breath. 'Give me the courage to die well, Great Buddha. Without hatred. Without anger.'

There was loud banging on the door. He could hear the Turks ramming against the massive wooden doors, trying desperately to break them. Then a loud Turkic voice reached Chandrakirti's ears.

'Burn the place down! We will smoke out the *kafir* dogs left inside!'

Chandrakirti bowed to the statue and rose to his feet as hungry flames began licking at the building. He walked in a tranquil manner towards the entrance and opened the doors. As he stepped over the threshold, his long *angvastram* caught fire.

Chandrakirti walked a little further, sat down on the ground in a lotus position and started to chant. His burning angvastram had fallen just a little behind him.

'*Buddham Sharanam Gachchami.*'
I go to the feet of the great Buddha.

The sweeping wind fanned the flames of the monk's saffron *angvastram* further. Till it rose high and caught his *dhoti*. The fire lapped up and singed the monk's legs. But he remained stationary. Calm.

'Buddham Sharanam … Gachchami.'

The cruel wind did not die down. It kept fanning the flames with fresh bouts of oxygen. The flames burnt brighter still. The sickening smell of burning flesh began to fill the air.

Chandrakirti's chanting grew louder. But his face remained calm. His eyes shut. His being detached from the pain tormenting his body. His soul focused on Lord Gautam Buddha, the great proponent of non-violence, peace and compassion.

'Buddham … Sharanam … Gachchami.'

The thin outer layer of his skin began to fry and slowly peel away in some places. Even as the blaze intensified, the abbot's face remained calm.

'Buddham … Sharanam …'

His trembling voice showed the obvious struggle of his body. His tranquil face showed the magnificent serenity of his soul.

' … Gachchami …'

The soldiers stared at him, initially horrified, and then with increasing fascination. Some of them fell to their knees, tears streaming down their faces as they witnessed Chandrakirti's supreme courage, dignity and obvious spiritual power, in the midst of a horrific death. They remembered the religion they had followed till just a few years ago. They remembered this chant only too well. For these Turks had also, once, chanted the same words of peace and love. Words they had been told to forget. Words that they had been told were those of 'evil idol-worshippers'.

The spell was broken by a loud command. 'Archers, cut him down.'

'Buddham …'

Seconds later, a volley of arrows ripped into the abbot's body, sending him toppling backwards.

… Sharanam … Gachchami …

The monk's body died.

But his immortal soul did not carry any of the burden of the pain and torture the body had been subjected to. The soul went in peace. It went with compassion. It went with love.

It went to the lotus feet of Lord Buddha.

Chapter 7

Two Years Later, 1029 AD

The last hypnotic notes of the qawwali slowly faded away. The crowd sat in silence, transported to another world. They were seated in the courtyard of the building that housed a Sufi saint, Sheikh Nuruddin, and his followers. The building stood in one of the many lanes that criss-crossed the city of Panchala, sometimes called by its relatively modern name, Bareilly.

The building where the Sufis lived also served as a community centre, free kitchen and rudimentary hospital for residents of the area. It was a modest, mud-plastered dwelling. The walls were bare, and there was little by way of furniture. The Sufis who resided there simply spread sheets on the ground and slept on them.

Located close to an overwhelmingly Hindu neighbourhood, the Sufi centre had initially been regarded with suspicion by the residents, but they had soon been won over by the kindness of Nuruddin and his disciples. The Sufis had little wealth, but they were happy to share whatever they possessed, and this generosity—and their espousal of a philosophy based on love and tolerance—had quickly gained them many friends.

The singer cleared his throat and began another song. He had barely gotten through the first line when a group of ten men barged in.

'Stop this blasphemous nonsense at once,' said their leader, a gangly, turbaned man with a beak-like nose and intense anger reflecting on his face. One of his companions had a sword; the others carried crude spears and axes.

The singer stopped and looked at Nuruddin. The cherubic Sufi master rose to his feet, gently patting down his long, curly locks that had become dishevelled as he had ecstatically moved his head in sync with the music. 'Welcome, Maulvi sahib. What can I do for you?'

The maulvi, Zayan, stared at him with undisguised contempt and hatred. 'I have told you before, Nuruddin, stop this rubbish. It offends Allah and all true believers.'

'I am delighted to meet someone who can actually speak for Allah,' replied Nuruddin sarcastically. 'But please do tell me, what is so offensive?'

'You sing songs here in honour of Draupadi, that … that …'

Nuruddin interrupted Zayan, his tone polite. 'Careful what you say about Lady Draupadi, Zayan. She was a princess of our land. Of Bareilly. She is honoured here.'

Draupadi, who had lived some millennia ago, was the wife of the famous Pandavas, the heroes of the Indian historical epic *Mahabharat*, and had been a princess from this very land. From Panchala. All the people from Bareilly, regardless of their religion, respected this great princess of antiquity as a Goddess.

'Draupadi was not one of us!' shouted Zayan. 'She was … she was … Forget her! How dare you mingle freely with these infidel barbarians?'

'What barbarians?' asked Nuruddin. 'All I see are my fellow Indians. Whatever their religion, they are all equally dear to me.'

'You better decide where your loyalties lie,' snarled Zayan, his voice dropping menacingly low. 'Are you a Muslim or a so-called Indian?'

'What a stupid question.'

Zayan seethed in fury. 'Stupid? How dare you call me stupid?'

'I didn't call you stupid. I called your question stupid. Because you are asking a heart if it belongs to the body.'

'What?'

'My heart carries the message of Allah. But every cell in my body carries the soil of Mother India. My body emerged from this land. And after my death, it will merge with this holy land once again.'

'Holy land?' Zayan ridiculed, raising his voice. 'You have the audacity to call this home of unbelievers a holy land?'

'Maulvi sahib, you may not be aware of this, but Islam had friends in this land well before it was adopted by the Turks,' replied Nuruddin. 'The clan of Datt Brahmins fought alongside the Prophet's grandson, Imam Hussain, at Karbala, and many were martyred along with him there. Their descendants still live on in India and are called Hussaini Brahmins. The Hindu king of Sind, Raja Dahir, gave asylum to some members of Imam Hussain's family. When Raja Dahir died fighting Mohammed bin Qasim, Imam Hussain's family too was massacred. So, tell me, who do you think is a true friend of Islam? Those who sheltered the Prophet's family like the Indian Hindu king Dahir, or those who slaughtered them like the Arab marauder Mohammed bin Qasim?'

The maulvi looked nonplussed for a moment, then changed tack. 'What about all this singing? You know music is prohibited in Islam.'

'Is it?' asked Nuruddin. 'But the Holy Quran clearly says in verse 55 of the Surah Al-Isra that Allah gave the psalms to David. Why would Allah, in his wisdom, allow David and his followers to sing and play music, if music was prohibited?

Many scholars have cited the Hadith to say that the Prophet only disapproved of music that promoted evil behaviour and licentiousness, he had no problem with music itself.'

'Why do you make no efforts to lead the infidels away from their false gods?' demanded Zayan, not wanting to lose face in front of his followers.

Nuruddin shook his head. 'You have read the Holy Quran. How can you forget the verse that says, "To you be your religion, to me be mine"? Haven't you read that?'

One of the young men who had accompanied Zayan was growing tired of this verbal duel. 'Are the two of you going to talk the whole night?' he sneered as he turned to the Sufi, pulling his sword half out of its scabbard as a threat. 'Listen Nuruddin, we have had enough of your blasphemy. We are not here to argue over scriptures with you. We know the true meanings of our Lord's words. This is your last warning. Pack up and get out of here or we will slaughter you and your disciples.'

Nuruddin was clear. 'We are not leaving, young man. We are not fighting with you either.'

The young zealot, clearly agitated, had had enough. He drew back his left fist and unleashed a punch at the Sufi. A split second before the punch could ram into Nuruddin's face, it was blocked by an open palm. The sound of the impact resounded across the courtyard. The zealot scowled as he looked at the broad-shouldered, barrel-chested, young man who had blocked his fist. He seemed to be a disciple of Nuruddin, but was very different from the other docile devotees. He had wavy hair, high cheekbones, and clearly Turkic features. His hazel-coloured eyes were blazing with fury.

'If you touch the saint, I'll kill you,' warned the young Turk in an eerily casual tone.

'Aslan, stand down,' said Nuruddin sharply to the young Turk.

Aslan ignored his master and continued to keep his eyes fixed on the zealot. The man grunted and shifted his gaze. Stepping back slightly. Seemingly surrendering. But a second later, he drew his sword rapidly and slashed at Aslan.

Aslan, however, had been expecting the sneak attack. He swayed back, allowing the blade to whistle by his chest harmlessly. As the attacker's swing completed its arc, Aslan stepped in and grabbed his wrist, twisting it. The sword clattered to the floor. The man was now off balance and leaning forward. With his free hand, Aslan punched him hard at a spot just under the ear. The man crumpled to the ground.

Aslan picked up the sword. He held it easily, like it was simply an extension of his arm.

Instructions that had been drilled into him years ago came flooding back to his mind.

Check your breath. Is it coming fast? That is your body reacting to stress. It will make you useless in a fight. Suck in a deep breath. Hold it. Then let it out. Slowly. Again. And again. Till your breathing is relaxed and steady. Good. Now, position your feet apart; shoulder-width; not more, not less. You fight right-handed, so put your right foot forward. It extends your reach. But make sure that the weight is evenly balanced. Stay on the balls of the feet, so that you can move easily in either direction. Keep your knees bent slightly. The idea is to be like a coiled spring. Excellent. Now, move your sword a little. Twirl it a couple of times if you like. Get the feel of it. Now, take guard. Hold the sword out. The wrist should be relaxed and in line with the forearm. Adjust your arm till you feel the weight of the sword being taken by the back, shoulder and biceps. These are big muscles. Using them will allow you to fight longer without tiring.

Aslan went through the entire routine in a matter of

seconds, his body instinctively following old patterns that he had repeated thousands of times till they had become embedded in his muscle memory. His eyes moved quickly from left to right and back, scanning the men for potential threats.

The attackers paused. They were a mob rounded up by Zayan and had been expecting to rough up a few harmless, submissive devotees. Confronted by a warrior who obviously knew what he was doing, they hesitated.

'Come on,' said one of them finally, a young man with a slight hunch. 'He's alone. We can take him.'

'Maybe … but I'll take quite a few of you with me,' warned Aslan. 'Who wants to die first?'

'Aslan, stop this at once,' said Nuruddin. 'I will not have any bloodshed for me.'

For just a second, Aslan's eyes darted towards where Nuruddin stood. The hunched man decided to take advantage of his distraction. He lunged forward, drawing his axe back for a kill blow.

Peripheral vision saved Aslan. By the time he fully registered what was happening, his subconscious brain had already reacted. His hand moved in a blur, almost of its own volition. The sword slashed across the attacker's throat, severing the carotid artery.

The young man dropped the axe and fell to his knees. He clutched at his throat, as if trying to seal the gash. Blood spurted out from between his fingers and formed a puddle on the ground. With a barely audible sigh, he toppled over, landing face down on the now bloodied ground.

Zayan howled with rage. The young man now lying dead was his nephew. 'You gutless cowards, surround the bastard! Kill him!'

'There's been enough killing for one day,' an authoritative voice cut across the courtyard. A tall man arose from the crowd. He had a shawl wrapped around him, which he shrugged off to reveal a sword. Twenty more men stood up along with him. All of them were similarly armed.

The man walked up to Zayan. 'That boy's death is your fault. If you want to live, then take his body and leave quietly. Otherwise I'll put you on the ground next to him.' He gestured to the other men who had accompanied Zayan. 'The same goes for all of you.'

Zayan's men hurriedly picked up their fallen comrade. Scared witless now. Eager to flee. A mob is usually made up of cowards. They have no grit. Courage enters their souls quickly, when they think they are in control. But it departs their souls equally quickly. A few telling blows are enough. They scurried away in haste.

Zayan was the only one from the mob still left standing. He directed a poisonous glare at Aslan and Nuruddin. 'This isn't over,' he hissed.

Aslan glared back at Zayan. The bloodlust clear in his eyes. 'If you come back here, Zayan, then the next time it will be your body that will be carried out.'

Zayan quickly scurried away.

The tall stranger walked up to Aslan. Smiling slightly. 'You are a brave man.'

'Thank you,' said Aslan. 'You have bought my soul by saving my life. What is the name of the man who owns my soul now?'

'My name is Suheldev,' replied the tall stranger.

Aslan smiled slightly. *At last … finally, we meet.* But he kept his thoughts to himself. 'The bandit prince …'

'So, you've heard of me?'

'Who hasn't?' replied Aslan. 'You're a legend.'

It was true. In the years that had elapsed since Suheldev had walked out of his father's camp, he had become famous throughout North India. Along with his small band of warriors, he raided kingdoms that had acceded to Ghazni, slipping in and out of them seemingly at will. Killing the Turks stationed there. Doing what the subjects of those kingdoms wanted their cowardly rulers to do.

He would suddenly spring up at some place far away from his last known location, stage a surprise strike and then vanish, inflicting heavy casualties and hardly suffering any losses himself. Even if his men fell in battle, none of them was ever left behind.

With every successful attack, the aura around Suheldev had grown stronger, till some people had actually begun to credit him with supernatural powers. But he never attacked civilians, and he paid them handsomely for information or for any supplies he took from them. Therefore, he was loved by the general populace as much as he was hated and feared by their rulers.

Suheldev couldn't help smiling at the obvious awe in Aslan's eyes. He gestured at the sword Aslan was still holding. 'Looks like you know how to use that.'

'I was trained as a soldier,' said Aslan. 'But I have given up that life. Now, I stay here and serve the great Sufi saint, Nuruddin.'

Nuruddin had been stunned into silence when Aslan killed Zayan's nephew. Now he spoke, his voice hoarse. 'Aslan, you cannot stay here anymore. There is no place here for murderers.'

'But Nuruddin sahib, I was just trying to protect you,' protested Aslan.

'I didn't ask for your protection,' said Nuruddin. The Sufi's voice was calm but the pain and anguish in his eyes were obvious. 'I had told you that I didn't want any bloodshed. I would rather have died myself than live with the guilt of that poor boy's death on my head. Please leave right now.'

Aslan's face fell as Nuruddin turned and strode away. He looked down at the floor, seemingly devastated. He dropped the sword, then wiped his eyes with the back of his hand and shook his head slightly. When he looked up, he saw Suheldev staring at him, his eyes full of sympathy.

'Well, my friend,' said Suheldev softly, 'you may be done with violence, but it seems violence is not done with you. The maulvi will definitely want you to be tried for murder. You have two choices: you can take your chances at a trial, or you can run for your life. If I were you, I'd take the second option.'

Aslan spread his arms helplessly. 'Where will I go? What will I do?'

Suheldev looked at him silently for a long time, as if weighing a decision. 'You can ride with me, if you like. You have skills I can use, and it would be a shame if someone like you ends up hanging from a tree because of some fanatical idiots. What do you say?'

Abdul, standing behind Suheldev, was clearly unhappy with this decision. He didn't trust Turks.

Aslan didn't take long to make up his mind. 'Lead the way, great prince.'

Suheldev pointed at Aslan's fallen blade. 'You'll need that.'

Aslan bent down and picked up the sword. It was his weapon now. If one could see from the ground level, one would have noticed a slight smile on Aslan's face. As if he had gotten exactly what he needed.

Chapter 8

'My Lord, this trader, Halil, is accused of continuing with the heathen practices of his Yazidi ancestors in secret, though he claims to have converted to Islam,' said Hassan, the prime minister of Ghazni. 'A raid at his home has turned up an idol of their false God.'

Mahmud frowned at the fair, green-eyed man standing in chains. The Yazidis had long been persecuted because of their belief that God placed the world under the care of seven angels, of whom the chief was Melek Taus, the Peacock Angel. According to Yazidi belief, Melek Taus rebelled against God and was thrown into hell. He stayed there for forty thousand years till his tears quenched the fires of the underworld. God then forgave him and restored him to his position. But the Abrahamic faiths saw a resemblance between the story of Melek Taus and that of Satan, who was also cast into hell by God.

As a result, the Yazidis were termed devil worshippers and subjected to ruthless massacres and pogroms. The fact that they were idol-worshippers made them an even greater target of violence and persecution.

'These are serious charges,' said Mahmud. 'Are they true, Halil?'

Mahmud knew Halil as a very successful trader who paid large taxes. As such, the crown had no complaints about him. Until now.

'No, great sultan,' said Halil, bowing low. 'These are lies, spread by rivals jealous of my wealth. It is true that my father followed the Yazidi way, but I have seen the light and I am a true believer now.'

'Hmm, and what about the idol?' asked Mahmud.

'It must have been planted in my home by my enemies.'

Mahmud turned to the prime minister. 'Is there any other evidence against him?'

'No, My Lord,' replied Hassan.

Before Mahmud could say anything, he was interrupted by his nephew. 'My Lord, with your permission, may I question this man?'

All eyes in the packed court turned towards Salar Maqsud. He smiled confidently as he looked at the sultan.

'Go ahead,' said Mahmud.

Maqsud inclined his head gratefully, then turned towards the prime minister.

'Where is the idol that was seized?' he asked. 'I would like to see it. And get me a hammer and chisel as well.'

An attendant rushed out and returned after a while, carrying all the items. The idol, a beautiful gold statue, depicted a figure that was largely human. However, it had the wings and webbed feet of a peacock. On its head, it wore a crown of peacock feathers, coloured blue, turquoise and green, not vastly different from the peacock feather crown that the Hindu God Lord Krishna wore. There was a black snake emblazoned on the abdomen of the idol of Melek Taus, very similar to the legendary snake of Kundalini, the representation of the latent feminine energy according to the Hindus. Two bright green emeralds served as the eyes of Melek Taus.

'Thank you,' Maqsud told the attendant, with exaggerated politeness. Then he turned towards Halil, the trader. 'So, you feel nothing for this piece?'

'Only hatred and disgust,' insisted the man.

There was a piercing look in Salar Maqsud's hazel eyes that made Halil squirm and look away.

After a long pause, Maqsud spoke up once again. 'Please take this hammer and break the idol's right wing.'

'What?' Halil looked horrified.

'You heard me,' said Maqsud, his voice steady and calm. 'Do it, or I will have your right arm chopped off.'

Halil hesitated, then picked up the hammer wordlessly and swung it hard at the idol. The right wing of Melek Taus shattered.

'Wonderful,' said Maqsud, clapping softly. 'I applaud your commitment to the true path. Now chisel out both the eyes.'

Halil's face turned ashen.

'Something is coming out, my friend,' said Maqsud. He spoke softly, but his voice dripped with menace. 'It's either the idol's eyes or yours.'

Halil's hands trembled, but he managed to chisel out one eye of the idol, and then the other. As he completed the task, tears began to stream down his face.

'Look at the foolishness of the kafirs,' laughed Maqsud. 'Their so-called Lord of the World does not even have the power to protect himself, and they actually believe that he can save them.' Then he turned to the trader. 'But why are you so upset? Does this statue mean so much to you?'

Halil shook with emotion but managed to control himself. 'May I go?' he finally asked, his voice hoarse.

'I have just one last task for you,' smiled Maqsud. 'Throw this piece of junk on the ground and spit on it.'

With a cry of pure rage, Halil slashed at Maqsud with the chisel. Maqsud leapt back and instinctively threw up his left hand. The chisel slashed through the palm, without doing any serious damage, but drew some blood.

Before Halil could attack again, a tall, slender figure came charging up from behind and shoved him hard, knocking him off balance. As Halil staggered, Maqsud seized his right wrist, which was still holding the chisel, and twisted it brutally.

Halil yelped with pain and went down on his knees. The chisel clattered as it fell to the floor. 'Stop, please stop!' he pleaded desperately.

Instead, Maqsud gave his wrist one more twist. A loud crack

resounded through the court, and many present there winced as Halil's wrist snapped like a twig.

The court guards quickly seized the man, now moaning with agony and fear, and dragged him away. The tall man who had come to Maqsud's aid grabbed his hand and examined it anxiously.

'I'm fine, Kerim,' said Maqsud gently, his voice loving and tender. 'It's just a scratch.'

'You should see a physician,' said Kerim, with a voice filled with concern even as he discreetly caressed the back of Maqsud's injured hand.

Sultan Mahmud interrupted their conversation. 'Maqsud, my young lion,' he exclaimed, his voice booming through the court. 'You are a treasure. How can I reward you?'

'The honour of serving you is all the reward that I need, My Lord,' said Maqsud.

Mahmud smiled warmly in response. He clapped his hands. 'Court dismissed.' Then he beckoned Maqsud. 'Come to my private quarters for dinner. I want to talk about something with you.' He looked around and noticed Maqsud's father, who was married to the sultan's sister. 'Actually, bring your family. I haven't seen my sister in a while and it will be good to spend some time with all of you. But first, listen to this pretty boy of yours and get your hand attended to.'

It was late in the evening when Maqsud and his family entered the sultan's lavishly furnished personal chambers. Their feet sank into the soft Persian carpets that blanketed the floor. The walls were covered with elaborately embroidered tapestries depicting battles and hunting scenes. The divan on which the sultan reclined was covered with a cloth made from the finest silk imported from India.

Mahmud was talking softly to a shifty-looking individual who was said to be his spymaster. On spotting his guests, he hastily ended the conversation and dismissed the officer. Mahmud may have invited the entire family, including his own sister, but he ignored everyone besides his favourite nephew. 'Come in. Make yourself comfortable.' He pointed at Maqsud's bandaged hand. 'All well?'

Maqsud bowed. 'Yes, My Lord. The doctor didn't want to take any chances.'

Mahmud nodded. 'Just as well. That lovely slave boy of yours would have kept on nagging you if you hadn't shown yourself to a doctor. He's quite a beauty, that fellow. Sometimes I'm almost tempted to demand you hand him over to me.'

Maqsud kept quiet but Mahmud noticed the expression that flitted across his face.

'Don't worry,' Mahmud said, laughing loudly. 'I remember what it's like to be young and in love.'

A wistful expression settled on the face of the sultan of Ghazni. Maqsud knew immediately that Mahmud was thinking of Ayaz, his own slave and great love. One whom the sultan adored so much that he had been crowned the king of Lahore.

With an effort, Mahmud snapped out of his mood. 'Enough love talk.' He turned towards Maqsud's mother. 'I hope your husband is taking good care of you.'

'Very much so, thank you for asking,' she said. 'Brother, you seemed somewhat irritated by what your previous visitor was saying. Is everything all right?'

Mahmud's brow wrinkled. 'Apparently there is some Indian prince who is becoming quite a nuisance. I might have to do something about him soon. He goes by the name of Suheldev.'

'Aslan! Wake up!'

Aslan awoke with a start. Instinctively, he reached for his sword. He blinked, momentarily disoriented.

'Whoa, take it easy.' Suheldev backed up reflexively. 'You don't need that. You are with friends.'

Aslan looked at him, puzzled, then realised that he had half-drawn his sword out of its scabbard. His hair was soaking with sweat and his pulse was racing. He took a deep breath and sheathed his sword. With an effort, he sat upright, leaning against the tree. He wiped his forehead with the back of his hand.

Gradually, his breathing returned to normal as his brain realigned with reality. *I am part of Suheldev's band now. We spent the night in this forest.*

Suheldev was peering at him curiously. 'Are you alright?'

Aslan nodded. 'I'm alright. It was just a dream.'

'You're awake now. Time to go.'

Chapter 9

India, 1030 AD

The sun set over a field littered with the dead and dying. Oblivious to them, thousands of men grimly fought on. Just then, bugles rang out, signalling an end to the day's carnage. The end of the battle-day. And a simultaneous call to put down weapons.

Govardhan paused when he heard the bugles. He had just disarmed his opponent and brought him down to his knees after a long, brutal duel. *There's time for one more killing blow*, he decided and raised his mace to bring it down on the man's head.

'Stop, Govardhan,' yelled Mahipal Tomar, from a distance. 'The battle-day is over. Don't dishonour yourself. Don't dishonour your king.'

Mahipal, the king of Delhi, was distantly related to Govardhan, though when Govardhan's mother had once tried to explain the exact long-winding familial connection between the two, his head had started swimming halfway through. The best he had been able to figure was that his father and Mahipal were distant cousins, more than five times removed.

Govardhan sighed. The king was a good man, but sometimes he could be too honourable for his own good.

A case in point was his decision to engage the enemy in a battlefield barely twenty kilometres to the west of Delhi, even though his advisers had pointed out to them that it would be better to stay within his well-fortified capital.

Mahipal had scoffed at the suggestion. 'What? Skulk behind my city walls while the invader walks all over my land? Looting the villages under my protection? And I suppose I should wear bangles while I am at it? The lion does not hide from the jackal. He tears him to pieces for having the audacity to enter his territory.'

Privately, Govardhan had agreed with the sensible advisers rather than the chivalrous king. But as an officer in the king's army, he had no choice but to obey orders. It hadn't helped that Mahipal had actually wanted to engage the Turks much further on, well beyond Delhi, but the sheer speed at which the Turk army had moved had almost caught him off guard and forced him into battle on a ground not of his choosing.

It was not for nothing that the Turks were counted among the best armies in history. Ruthless, fast-moving, hard-charging. Able to intimidate enemies with just their sheer barbarism and cruelty.

But the Rajput army had stood strong and held the Turks in check. Govardhan too had spent an exhausting day battling the enemy troops, culminating in a brutal duel with the soldier of Ghazni who was now at his mercy.

The man had been a formidable opponent and it was foolish to leave him alive so that he could come back refreshed the next day. But Kshatriya honour decreed that weapons could not be used after the end of the battle-day.

Then an idea occurred to him.

The dazed Turk was flat on the ground, his palms open on the side. Govardhan lowered his mace and reached for the man, pretending to be helping him up. As he did so, he casually placed his foot on the man's right hand. Then he stepped forward, twisting his foot brutally, making sure that for a few seconds his entire weight was resting on his foe's fingers and wrist.

Over the years, Govardhan had often been told that he was appropriately named. Because he resembled a mountain: massive, craggy and imposing. He towered over most men, and was almost as broad as he was tall, with huge shoulders, a barrel chest, a thick waist and bulging biceps, thighs and calves. The combined weight proved too much for his opponent, who shrieked in agony as the bones of his fingers and wrist were crushed to pieces. But his cries were drowned out by the noise of thousands of soldiers disengaging from battle.

'That should keep you out of trouble,' said Govardhan, smiling broadly. Then he casually bent down and patted the Turk on his head. He turned and started walking back. It was a long way towards the Tomar camp.

He smiled as he walked, gesturing in a friendly manner to the other Delhi soldiers walking with him. It had been a good day for the Tomar army. They had fought the troops of Ghazni to a standstill.

Govardhan's face clouded slightly as he recalled how his horse had died, run through by the spear of the man he had just incapacitated. Then he shrugged. It could have been worse. He was still alive, and not badly wounded, which was more than could be said for many of the men who had begun the battle in the morning.

As he entered his personal tent, a manservant ran to help him strip off his armour, then handed him a bucket of cold water. Govardhan poured it over his body, not even bothering to remove his clothes. He gasped with mingled relief and pleasure as the water coursed over his aching muscles. The manservant handed him a dry cloth, which he used to vigorously towel his leonine mane. Then he smoothed his handlebar moustache, twirling it to perfection quickly.

A messenger was announced. Govardhan allowed him to enter.

The messenger bowed low as he said, 'King Mahipal is asking for you, Commander.'

'Tell His Highness that I'll be right there.'

Govardhan hastily changed into clean clothes and walked over to the king's tent. He expected that they would discuss the new tactics of the Turkic commander, Kerim, who was apparently the lover of the Turkic commander-in-chief in India, Salar Maqsud.

The tactics were astonishingly good. It wasn't like the raiding style of Mahmud. It was a destroy-the-enemy-capacity-for-war style. More suited for conquest and rule, rather than just raid and plunder. He had also heard that these superior tactics of Kerim had been witnessed in the battles he had won while marching up to Delhi. And they weren't uniformly standard strategies. They varied with each region, with each battle that was fought. Suitable to the land and the particular enemies being fought against. It was almost like Kerim and his lord, Salar Maqsud, understood deeply the culture, nuances and expected tactics of different communities within India. It was the vastly superior troop strength of the Tomar army that had saved the day for them; a day that had ended in a stalemate. But the Tomar army needed to do something radically different the following day if it wanted to win the battle. That is what Govardhan expected the discussions to centre around.

However, Govardhan was dismayed as soon as he pulled

aside the curtain of the royal tent. Festivities had begun, with several of the king's favourites clustered around him, babbling excitedly. The wine was already flowing and delicious dishes were being served on huge platters.

They think war is a party, thought Govardhan sourly.

Unlike most of the men present in the tent, he had not enjoyed a privileged childhood. His father had been killed in battle when he was still a toddler, and his ancestral estate had been taken over by his uncle. Govardhan and his mother had suffered the daily humiliation that is the lot of impoverished nobility, forced to live off the grudging charity of more prosperous relatives.

Govardhan had joined the army as soon as it was possible for him to do so. He had spent the next decade fighting his way up the ranks, till he had been given charge of a thousand men, and a small estate of his own. His uncle had died shortly after that, but Govardhan was still unable to get over the bitterness of his deprived childhood. Besides, the years of hardship he had endured had left him with a distinctly cynical attitude towards life. Unlike King Mahipal and his nobles, who firmly believed in the Kshatriya code of honour, chivalry and courtliness.

'Come, come, Govardhan,' said Mahipal. 'You fought well today.' A bearded, strongly built man of medium height, Mahipal was beaming with delight. 'Tomorrow, with the blessings of the great Goddess Bhavani, we will send Mahmud's puppy back to Ghazni with his tail between his legs.'

'He lost many men today, Your Highness,' said Govardhan politely. 'More than ours, I'm sure.'

'We will end it tomorrow. One frontal charge will take care of the Turks.'

'My Lord, his cavalry is still dangerous. And I suspect that he may have reserve troops that—'

Mahipal waved his hand contemptuously, interrupting Govardhan. 'Whatever he tries, we will be ready. Come, let us discuss tactics for tomorrow.'

The king of Delhi moved towards a table on which various ivory figurines, representing cavalry, infantry, archers and other military units, were arranged. His courtiers and commanders followed. They all had cups of wine in their hands.

Several hours passed before Govardhan finally walked back to his tent, his head buzzing. There had been a long discussion, accompanied by several more drinks, before the session had finally ended.

'Get a good night's sleep, my lions,' Mahipal had said cheerfully as the men trooped out. Despite the large amounts of wine he had consumed, the king's legs were steady and so was his voice. Not for the first time, Govardhan had marvelled at Mahipal Tomar's capacity to absorb alcohol without being affected in any way.

Govardhan entered his tent and collapsed on his bed. Not changing his clothes. Not rinsing his mouth. He just shut his eyes and felt his mind go blank.

Darkness.

And then there was light.

He was in a field.

He looked around.

What am I doing here?

Something didn't feel right. The light was falling oddly. Almost like the sun was flickering.

What the hell?

He was moved forward suddenly. Through the field. Racing

through the tall grass that surrounded him. Moving much faster than was humanly possible. Moving at the speed of sound.

And then he suddenly came to a halt.

A clear field.

Several bodies were lined up in a row. The bodies of his men. Being cremated.

In the background, he heard wailing. The smoke stung his eyes. The heat of the blaze drew sweat from his body.

Then he saw one cremation pyre that was unlit. There was a body on it. Wounded. It was the Turk he had fought at close of battle-day. The one whose hand he had crushed. Blood flowed freely from the Turk's battered hand. Suddenly, the Turk opened his eyes. His mouth moved, like he was speaking. But no sound came out.

What the hell is going on?

Then, the Turk's pyre too caught fire. The heat singeing Govardhan even more. He was pulled closer. The smoke was suffocating.

And then he heard the Turk's voice. Clear. Eerie. *You are next,* kafir.

Govardhan awoke with a start, his heart pounding. As he looked around, he suddenly realised that there really was smoke around him, and it was starting to fill his tent. He leapt out of bed, grabbed his mace and ran out of the tent.

The scene that confronted him was straight out of hell. The sky was still dark, but there was light everywhere. Light from the many tents that were ablaze. Horses were stampeding in terror, trampling over men who tried to stop them. Battle cries and screams rang out as some men attacked others, and mowed them down. A man bumped into him, screaming at the top of his lungs. As the man regained his balance, Govardhan saw that his face was a bloody mess. Blood was pouring out of his right eye and the eyeball was almost completely out of the socket, barely hanging by a thin nerve and some sinew.

Peripherally, Govardhan sensed a rider looming up on his right. He turned just in time to block the sword that slashed down at him. Sparks flared as the weapon clashed with his mace. The Turkic rider pulled his horse to a halt. He raised his sword again, ready for a kill-strike. But Govardhan swung his mace before that. Powered by Govardhan's giant height and beastly muscles, the mace thudded into the horse-mounted Turk, drawing a howl of agony from him as his ribs fractured. A few seconds later, one of Govardhan's men speared the Turk through the throat. He tumbled to the ground. Govardhan grabbed the horse's reins before it could flee and swung himself onto the saddle.

'What the hell is going on?' Govardhan demanded from the man with the spear.

'The Turkic scum attacked while we were sleeping, My Lord,' shouted the soldier over the deafening noise of battle. 'They must have killed our sentries.'

Govardhan looked around. A dreadful foreboding in his heart. *Shit. This is a disaster. I must get the king out of here.*

'I'm going to the king's tent,' yelled Govardhan. 'Gather as many of our men as you can and come there. Now!'

Govardhan spurred the horse and galloped towards Mahipal's tent. Twice, Turkic infantrymen sprang at him. Without pausing, he batted them away with his mace and kept riding.

As he neared Mahipal's tent, he saw the king emerge in full armour. His favourite horse was already standing by the entrance. There were approximately fifty riders guarding the tent. Govardhan brought his horse to a halt and leaped off.

'Thank goodness you're safe, My Lord,' said Govardhan. 'We need to leave! Fast!'

Mahipal glared at him. 'Run away from the battlefield? Are you mad? I am a Tomar!'

Govardhan looked at him incredulously. 'My Lord, the enemy attacked at night. He broke the rules, not you. There is no shame in saving your life under such circumstances. There will be other battles. But you must live. Delhi will fall if you die!'

Mahipal did not budge. 'What kind of Kshatriya are you, Govardhan? I will go home as a hero, alive or dead. Now, follow me, or get out of the way!' He mounted his horse, then pointed his sword at a flag in the distance. 'Men, their coward commander, Kerim, is hiding there. I say we charge straight at him and finish this fight once and for all. Who is with me?'

The others raised their swords and bellowed stridently.

Mahipal roared, 'Jai Bhavani!'

Glory to Goddess Bhavani.

'Jai Bhavani!'

The king of Delhi galloped off towards the Turks. His brave men followed him in a frenzied charge.

It's suicide, thought Govardhan despairingly. Briefly, he considered mounting his horse and escaping. But for all his pragmatism, the code of Kshatriya duty was too deeply ingrained in him.

One last charge it is then, he thought grimly, putting his foot in the stirrup and swinging himself up. As he did so, he suddenly saw a Turkic archer take aim at him. At that very instant, an Indian soldier stabbed the archer from behind, through his heart. The archer involuntarily released the arrow, which narrowly missed Govardhan. But as it whizzed past the horse's head, the startled animal reared up, throwing off its unprepared rider. Govardhan landed painfully on his back and saw lights flash before his eyes as his head thudded against the ground.

And the world went black.

— EⅡ ౪ɔⅎĊΔ —

'Commander, commander, are you alright?'

Govardhan heard the voice. But it sounded like it was distant. Faint. From far, far away.

He had this strange sensation that he was stuck at the bottom of a well.

How did I get here?

He tried to swim upwards but his limbs felt sluggish. They didn't obey his commands.

'Commander, can you hear me?'

Somebody is really looking for me … I wish they'd just let me sleep …

Then he felt his shoulder being shaken roughly. In that instant, he snapped back into full consciousness and found himself seated upright, held up by one soldier as another peered anxiously at him.

'I'm … fine …' he said in a voice that came out as a croak.

He nodded at the soldier, then winced as a shooting pain went through the back of his head.

'Careful, Commander … that was a bad tumble,' said the soldier. It was the same man who had killed the Turkic rider whose horse Govardhan had taken.

Then he suddenly recalled that a battle was going on. 'Where … is …'

'I've got some thirty of our men together,' the soldier said, pointing at a group of riders. 'We came here, as ordered by you. The king and his men have charged towards the Turks. What do we do, My Lord?'

'We join them ... of course,' said Govardhan, heaving himself to his feet. Still a little unsteady. 'Help me get another horse.'

As he said the words, Govardhan heard howls of triumph from the distance. A few moments later, anguished wails rang out too.

Govardhan looked in the direction that Mahipal had charged towards, and felt a sharp pain stab through his chest. Tears sprang to his eyes. 'Oh no ... Lord Ram, have mercy ...'

The great king Mahipal Tomar's severed head was being brandished on a spear as the soldiers of Ghazni whooped and hollered. The Delhi king's face was frozen in an agonised rictus. His eyes were wide open, righteous anger still burning in them. Blood dripped from his neck onto the spear.

Seeing the grisly sight, some of the Indian soldiers threw down their weapons and raised their hands in surrender. They were ruthlessly cut down by the Ghazni troops.

Loud shouts began emanating from the Turkic side. 'No prisoners! No prisoners! Kill all the *kafirs*!'

The Turks did not follow the warrior code of honour in anything. All they sought was victory.

Govardhan stared at the scene as if hypnotised, his brain struggling to process what his eyes were relaying. He felt a hand on his shoulder and snapped out of his trance.

'Commander ...' said the man uncertainly.

Govardhan looked at him, then at all his other men. Each of them was staring at him, waiting for his next words.

The choice was clear. *Death or dishonour.*

One of the soldiers spoke up. 'What do we do, My Lord?'

No. Actually, the choice was different. *Die today, or live to fight another day. Die today, or seek vengeance later.*

'Disengage,' Govardhan said finally, and saw relief flood into the eyes of his soldiers.

And they rode away. Away from the decapitated head of their righteous king, who had lost with honour. Away from the treacherous Turks, who had won with deceit.

But most of the riders who followed Govardhan had the same thought. *It doesn't matter how the Turks won. They won. That's all that matters.*

Chapter 10

The innkeeper had been waiting for him. Tired after several hours of fast riding, the young man locked himself in his room and slept through the rest of the day. At night, he arose refreshed, and resumed his journey. He followed a similar pattern for the next few days.

Although he had initially been alert, the monotony of the solitary journey, coupled with the steady rhythm of his horse, lulled the youth into a state of somnolence. He yawned a couple of times, then slowly felt his eyelids begin to close as his chin dropped towards his chest …

'Halt, who goes there?'

The young man snapped out of his slumber, irritated at his carelessness. Still, it was too late to do anything about it now.

'I come in peace, brother,' the young man said in a calm tone.

'Ride forward slowly and keep your hands where I can see them.'

The young rider obeyed. As he came closer to the source of the voice, he saw two campfires. About eighty men were clustered around them. Two men stepped away from the group and approached the rider. One of them had a round face, slit-like eyes and high cheekbones, and was very obviously a Turk. The other was a dark-skinned giant and constantly looked around. Careful. Alert.

I wonder who you might be, thought the young rider of the dark-skinned man. You look Indian. *But he kept his thoughts to himself.*

The Turkic-looking man peered hard at the unexpected visitor. The darkness of the night made it difficult to see the young rider clearly, but it was obvious that he was powerfully built, with broad shoulders, muscular arms and a sturdy chest.

'Who are you?' the Turkic-looking man asked the young rider, his accent confirming his origins.

The young rider spread his hands wide. 'I am a seeker of God, brother. I am looking for a master to guide me on my spiritual journey. I have heard that some great Sufi saints live in India. Perhaps that is where my search will take me.'

'India, huh?' asked the Turk. 'That's an interesting coincidence. Some of the brothers around the fire are from there. They have recently converted to the true faith and are on their way to Ghazni to see the famous mosques that have been built by the great sultan.'

'Well, then, they are in for a treat,' replied the young rider. 'Those buildings are truly beautiful.'

'Would you like to join us for dinner? You can stay the night and leave in the morning.'

The young rider did not hesitate. The risks were too high. 'Thank you for your kind offer. But I would prefer to ride on.'

The Turk stared at the young rider for a long time. Finally, he nodded. 'Well, we shall not keep you.' Then, as the young rider began to trot away, he called out. 'What did you say your name was?'

The young rider had already decided on a false name to work with during his mission in India. He had been advised well. 'Aslan ... My name is Aslan.'

'Yes, I know your name is Aslan.'

Aslan woke up to find Suheldev standing over him, sporting a smug grin.

'Dreaming again, eh?'

Aslan nodded wordlessly, rose and began to brush at his clothes with his hands. Self-conscious. Had he revealed anything? Then, pretending nonchalance, he rolled up the thin blanket on which he had been lying. His saddlebag had served as a pillow.

Suheldev appraised him for a long time. 'Are you sure you want to go out on this mission again?'

Aslan had gotten into the practice of leaving Suheldev's band for long periods of time. He had told Suheldev that he was spying on the Turks, who had returned to northern India on a conquering mission. Any intelligence on their new tactics was very valuable to Suheldev. And Aslan usually came back with useful information. So, the prince had no objection to Aslan leaving. But, of course, any mission like this carried risks.

'We've discussed this before,' said Aslan. 'I'm a Turk. I know the language and the customs. It makes sense for me to spy on them for you. Don't worry, I'll be fine. I'll head out now and meet up with you in some time.'

'Alright. But be careful, my friend.'

Aslan smiled. 'Careful is my middle name.'

'It's a silent word then?'

Aslan burst out laughing. He embraced a smiling Suheldev. 'You take care of yourself too, prince.'

Chapter 11

She walked up to him, bent low, offering him a generous view of her cleavage, and whispered, 'I need to speak to you alone.'

'Thanks, but no thanks,' said Govardhan, reddening instantly.

For all that his appearance suggested, Govardhan was singularly awkward around women. And this woman, while clearly past the first flush of her youth, was still quite attractive. There was a certain harshness to her face though, and her make-up was a little too garish for his liking.

'You fool, I can save the lives of your men and you!' she hissed softly. 'Come to my tent!' Then she ruffled his hair and spoke in a loud, teasing voice, ensuring that everyone around would hear, 'Come along now, big boy … Don't be shy …'

The woman rose and walked languorously towards her tent, swaying her hips, shooting Govardhan a seductive look as she went. Govardhan stood up and followed, his ears burning, as the others yelled encouragement and cracked crass jokes.

Just a few more hours, he reminded himself. *Tomorrow morning, we'll be in Sirat.*

Sirat was the capital of Manohargarh, a small kingdom neighbouring Meerut. After the crushing defeat of the Tomar army, Govardhan and his men had decided to head there, hoping to offer their services to its ruler Jaichand, who was Mahipal

Tomar's son-in-law. When they had reached the Manohargarh border, Govardhan had declared as much to the guards.

The captain of the guards had nodded sympathetically. 'I'm sure the king will be delighted to see you,' he had said, sending Govardhan on his way.

They were just a few hours' ride away from the city of Sirat. They had decided to rest the night and ride on the next morning. A group of wandering minstrels and dancers had appeared from nowhere and quickly set up camp close to where Govardhan's soldiers had settled down for the night.

On their invitation, Govardhan and his men had joined the minstrels for dinner.

And he now stood in one dancer's tent.

'Come and sit here,' she said, patting the space next to her on the bed.

'I'm fine here, thanks,' he said stiffly.

The woman sighed. 'You idiot. I'm not going to molest you. Do what I'm saying.'

Govardhan warily obeyed. He found himself concentrating on the pale shades of the tent cloth. He didn't even turn towards her. His cheeks a deep beetroot red.

'That's much better,' said the woman loudly. Then she leaned in close and spoke in a much lower tone. 'Don't go to Jaichand. He is an ally of Ghazni. He will probably hand you over to the Turks.'

'But he's King Mahipal's son-in-law,' protested a surprised Govardhan.

'Speak softly!' hissed the woman, her voice a harsh whisper.

Govardhan immediately lowered his voice. 'Sorry … But he *is* King Mahipal's son-in-law.'

'Yes, and did you see him fighting with you in the battle

where King Mahipal died? He chose to stay neutral and sided with the eventual winner. The gossip is that his wife is so furious with him that she's not even sharing his bed.'

'How do you know all this?'

The woman laughed. 'Oh, you'll be surprised how much powerful men blabber in front of "dumb women" … Especially when they're all blissed out.'

'And why are you telling me this?'

'Because some of us still love our country. We work in secret to help a true patriot. A true leader. The only one who is willing to fight and is also capable of winning.'

Govardhan immediately knew who the woman was speaking of. *Suheldev of Shravasti.*

Govardhan leaned forward. 'Do you know him? Can you put me in touch with him?'

The woman leaned backwards, rummaging through a pouch that hung by the side of her bed. She extracted a miniature Shiva Linga from there and handed it to Govardhan. 'There is a village about twenty miles down the road, away from Sirat. Go to the headman's home. Preferably at night. Don't take more than one or two men with you. The whole bunch of you riding into a village is bound to set tongues wagging. Show him this Shiva Linga. Say that Urvashi gave it to you. And ask him to introduce you to the true devotee of the Mahadev.'

Govardhan took the Shiva Linga respectfully, with both hands, and reverentially touched it to his forehead.

'Thank you,' he said. Then an embarrassed expression appeared on his face. 'I wish I could reward you in some way, but I have nothing of value.'

'If you join the person I told you about and kill at least twenty Turks, consider your debt to me settled.'

Govardhan had many more questions in his mind. What had the Turks done to Urvashi? Was there anything he could do to help her? Who was she really? But it was obvious from her expression that the conversation was over.

Govardhan rose. He stood in awkward silence for a while. And then left the tent.

— EJJ ⅍ↄↄ⅃⅌ —

'Rise and shine,' said the guide, shaking Govardhan.

The commander winced and shielded his eyes as the rays of the rising sun forged their way through the dense cover of the trees.

Around him, birds chirped noisily as the forest woke up to another morning.

So much for staying alert, thought Govardhan, disgusted at himself.

He had followed Urvashi's instructions, even though some of his men had feared it was a trap. He had had his doubts too, but his instincts had told him this leap of faith was not going to be in vain.

So, three different villages, a village headman, a money-lender, and another farmer later, he had met the man who walked with a minor limp in his right leg. He had emerged from the forest that was a short distance north of the spot Govardhan and his men had been told to camp at. A few kilometres to the south lay almost two hundred acres of sugarcane fields, while a nearby stream ran along the length of the forest line.

'What's your name?' Govardhan had asked the man.

'You don't need to know that yet,' the man had replied. 'But I'll tell you if the meeting goes well.'

From thereon, this mystery man had guided them into the forest, zigzagging his way ever so often that, after a point, even the scouts with Govardhan couldn't keep track of where they were going. The branches of many trees, especially the banyans, reached out like overhanging arms, plunging most of the path into shadow and putting the already tense men further on edge. Shrubs and bushes clawed at Govardhan and his comrades, who warily picked their way through, keeping a sharp lookout for wild animals and poisonous thorns. At many places, the path was thick with overgrown grass and weeds, forcing the men to hack their way through.

Suddenly, the guide had stopped in a clearing where there were a few boulders, and the stream ran deeper into the forest. The guide declared that this was the area where they all would wait. And the wait had lasted a long time. The entire night, in fact.

'How long was I out?' Govardhan asked the guide.

The man shrugged. 'A few hours. Looks like you haven't slept peacefully in a long time.'

'Our friend didn't turn up?' asked Govardhan. He picked up his waterskin bag and drank a little of the life-giving nectar from it. Some of it trickled down into the thick beard that had grown over the past month.

'Maybe your snores scared him away,' quipped the guide. 'Come on, let's get back to your camp.'

Govardhan's men looked at him expectantly as he entered the camp. He shook his head tiredly. 'We'll try again tonight,' he said and walked to the stream.

He splashed some water on his face and was just about to drink from the stream when he heard a horse neighing.

Govardhan looked up sharply and found himself staring

at several horsemen across the stream. Under their chainmail armour, they were clad in long bright yellow tunics and white dhotis, with red cummerbunds—the colours of the Manohargarh army. Since they had come through the sugarcane fields, they had not been visible until they suddenly emerged next to the stream.

For a moment, both sides froze as they spotted each other. Then, Govardhan scrambled to his feet and turned as one of the riders unslung a bow from his shoulder and drew an arrow.

'Run!' yelled Govardhan to his men. 'Run!'

He sprinted to his horse as the Manohargarh soldier released his arrow, which dug into the ground just a few feet away from the fleeing Govardhan.

'The forest,' yelled the guide frantically. 'Get into the forest.'

Govardhan leaped onto his horse, pulled the guide onto the saddle behind him and spurred the animal. Behind him, he heard more arrows being shot. One of Govardhan's men screamed as an arrow pierced his back. A horse went down to a lucky arrow that smashed into the beast's neck, piercing below the brachiocephalicus muscle to slice through the jugular vein. The rider managed to roll clear and was quickly grabbed by another of Govardhan's men galloping up from behind.

The enemy cavalry thundered across the stream. And rode hard into the forest, chasing Govardhan and his men.

Suddenly, a bow twanged and one of the pursuers toppled off his horse, clutching at an arrow in his throat. Govardhan whirled around, stunned.

A loud voice was heard. 'Shoot at will!'

More arrows were shot from high up in the trees as the hunters suddenly became the hunted. Even as Govardhan looked on, bewildered, men seemed to erupt out of the ground and began attacking the Manohargarh soldiers.

They're camouflaged in the leaves, realised Govardhan. *They were here all along!*

The guide suddenly dismounted from Govardhan's horse and raced towards the battle, drawing his sword as he ran.

'Come on, men, let's help our friends,' shouted Govardhan, charging into the fray as well. As he did so, he noticed a tall man yelling instructions. A Manohargarh cavalryman had spotted the man too and galloped towards him. As his horse neared the man, the rider slashed at him with his sword. His target blocked the attack with his own sword, but the impact knocked him off balance and forced him down on one knee.

The rider drew back his sword, preparing for a backhand cut. Before he could complete his stroke, Govardhan hurled his mace at him. It connected squarely with his forehead. Though a helmet protected the soldier's head, the ferocity of the blow left him stunned. Even as he reeled in his saddle, Govardhan rode up, grabbed him by the throat and pushed him off his horse. The tall stranger finished him off with a single blow to the neck.

Govardhan dismounted, picked up his mace and looked around to see if more help was needed. It wasn't. Most of the enemy soldiers were already down and the others had fled. He turned and saw the tall man approaching him.

'Thanks for your help,' said the man.

'I should be the one thanking you,' replied Govardhan. 'Prince Suheldev, is it?'

Suheldev smiled. 'Absolutely right, great king.'

Govardhan blinked. 'You must be confusing me with someone else.'

Suheldev arched an eyebrow. 'Am I? What's your name, then?'

'Govardhan,' replied the big man.

Suheldev smiled. 'Like the mountain? It's a good name for you.'

Govardhan rolled his eyes. 'You must be the five thousandth person to tell me that.'

'Then you have had the good fortune of meeting five thousand brilliant, witty people!'

Govardhan laughed good-naturedly.

Suheldev turned to his men. 'Offer the surviving Manohargarh soldiers amnesty if they join us. Our quarrel is only with their king, not with them.'

Suheldev's soldiers saluted and rushed to carry out his orders.

Suheldev turned to Govardhan. 'I guess you have not heard the bad news. That's why you were surprised when I called you "king".'

'What bad news?'

Suheldev took a deep breath and patted Govardhan on his shoulder. 'After killing King Mahipal Tomar, the Turks carried out a massacre in Delhi. All the males who remained there were killed, and the women and girl-children sold into slavery. Temples were looted, houses burned and artisans' workplaces destroyed.'

'But why?' asked Govardhan, horrified. 'I can understand killing soldiers, but why do this to innocents?'

'The Turks call it total war,' said Suheldev. 'Not only do they kill their enemy soldiers, they also annihilate entire cities. All males, even children, are killed. All women are sold into slavery or given to their soldiers to abuse. They believe it ensures that their enemies will never rise against them again since the ability to carry out war itself is destroyed. Soldiers don't fight just by themselves, right? They need the support of others, such as farmers who give them food and ironsmiths who give them weapons. If you destroy them all, then how will an enemy ever rise again?'

'That is barbaric.'

'Yes, well ... the Turks like that reputation for themselves. Anyway, as part of the slaughter, every male who was in any way linked to the Tomar clan was killed. King Mahipal's sons, brothers, nephews, cousins—even the babies weren't spared. There are now only two male relatives of King Mahipal left alive who could possibly claim the throne of Delhi. There's Jaichand, but his claim is an indirect one, through his wife. And then there's a relative who's linked to him through blood. You.'

'But ... but, I'm only a distant relative of the king.'

'You're now his last surviving heir. The Turks know it and so does Jaichand. They want you dead, great king. Assassination orders have been issued.'

'How do you know all this?' asked Govardhan.

Suheldev did not answer Govardhan's question. He smiled as the man who had led Govardhan into the forest the previous night walked up to them. 'I trust Abdul took good care of you?'

Govardhan began to nod, then froze as he registered the guide's name. Suheldev and Abdul burst out laughing at his expression.

'Relax, big man,' chortled Abdul. 'If I had wanted to harm you, I could easily have slit your throat last night.'

Govardhan kept quiet.

'Do you have any questions?' asked Abdul. 'Go ahead, ask. I know you want to.'

'Well ... umm ... why are you fighting against, you know, your fellow Muslims?'

'Because I am an Indian and the Turkic Muslims are enemies of India,' said Abdul simply. 'You just killed some soldiers of Manohargarh. Did I ask you why you fought against your fellow Hindus? You fought for the good of Mother India, right?'

Govardhan smiled, accepting the logic. Abdul grinned, patted Govardhan on his shoulder, and walked away. Govardhan continued to stare at his retreating back.

Suheldev stepped up to Govardhan. 'I don't care where my Indian soldier comes from. As long as he is willing to fight the Turks, he is one of us. Do you agree, great king?'

'Please stop calling me that,' Govardhan said, wincing. 'As long as the killers of my king Mahipal Tomar are alive, I can't even imagine anyone else as the king of Delhi. And in any case, I have no wish to be a king. I am a soldier and all I want is to follow a good leader.'

Suheldev remained silent.

'I want to follow somebody who is not just willing to fight the Turks, but also knows how to defeat them,' continued Govardhan. 'Somebody who understands how the Turks think and is willing to do whatever it takes to beat them. King Mahipal was a great man, but he was too gentlemanly for this enemy, and it cost him his life. Jaichand is too cowardly to fight the Turks and so are many of the other kings here. In fact, I think there is only one man in all of North India who can defeat the Turks, and I believe I am looking at him right now.'

Suheldev's expression turned serious and he looked Govardhan squarely in the eyes. 'You are a Kshatriya royal. Will you be able to take orders from me?'

'Just a few moments ago, you said that you wouldn't care about a man's background. You would only look at whether he was willing to fight for our motherland.'

Suheldev smiled slightly.

'I am sick and tired of being on the losing side,' said Govardhan. 'I want those bastard Turks defeated.'

A broad grin spread across Suheldev's face. He held Govardhan by the shoulders. 'Welcome to my band, brave Govardhan. Jai Maa Bhaarati!'

Glory to Mother India.

'Jai Maa Bhaarati!'

— ᴇ᛬ᴜ ᚼᔆᚱᴊᴄᴧ —

Govardhan and Suheldev's men were clearing out all signs of their presence in the forest. The fallen soldiers of Manohargarh were being given proper funerals. Those who had survived had already pledged their loyalty to Suheldev. It was a matter of a few hours before the band would ride out.

Abdul came up to Suheldev and whispered, 'Aslan has returned.'

'Did you have someone follow him?'

Abdul nodded. 'Salim kept an eye on him without revealing himself. He kept track of him most of the time. But there were times when he just disappeared. Aslan is very careful and takes a lot of precautions. When Salim got a tab on him again, Aslan was rushing back to us. My man had to use a shortcut to get back before him.'

A moment later, Aslan jogged up to the duo.

Suheldev turned to him. 'What is it?'

'I think the Turks are about to raid a defenceless village a few hours' ride from here,' said Aslan. 'I overheard some soldiers discussing the orders to attack a small settlement, though they didn't know why exactly.'

'Any chance that you were noticed?' asked Suheldev. 'It could be a trap.'

'I kept myself concealed in some bushes close to their camp,' replied Aslan. 'But I could hear the sentries talking to each other.'

Suheldev and Abdul didn't look at each other. But Abdul took a quick breath. And Suheldev let out a long, deep breath. Aslan had come to realise that this was some form of coded communication between these two. He kept his face expressionless.

That's right. My story matches whatever that fellow Salim told you. Did you really think that after training with some of the finest warriors in the world, I wouldn't notice that I was being shadowed?

The only thing Aslan said aloud was, 'We should hurry if we want to help those poor people. We may already be too late.'

How long will they suspect me? When will they realise what my true mission is?

Chapter 12

The vultures rose reluctantly into the air, screeching as they expressed their displeasure at having their feast interrupted. The smell of charred flesh and burnt huts combined to produce a sickening odour. Body parts were strewn all over the ground. There were so many corpses that, in some cases, it was difficult to identify which limb belonged to which body.

'Allah be merciful,' whispered Aslan, tying a cloth around his nose and mouth.

Suheldev and his men had ridden as fast as they could to get from their meeting place with Govardhan to the settlement, but they had arrived too late. The burning huts were clustered together in a rectangular layout. One rough track that apparently served as the thoroughfare passed through the middle. Most of the bodies were lined up along this track.

As they rode grimly through the scene of the massacre, one of them, a young lad who had joined Suheldev's group only recently, suddenly leaned forward and threw up violently. Even after he had emptied his stomach, he continued to retch dryly for a while.

Aslan rode up to the boy and gently patted him. The recruit looked away, embarrassed.

'I'm sorry,' he mumbled.

'Don't be,' said Aslan. 'You're still human ... which is more than can be said for the monsters who did this.'

'I think that one's still alive,' said Govardhan, pointing to an old man—or what was left of him—lying face down on the ground at some distance from the main scene of the carnage. His right arm and left leg were both chopped off. There was a trail of blood along the ground where he had dragged himself for a while before collapsing.

'Go check him out,' said Suheldev, as he looked around for threats.

Aslan and Govardhan galloped towards the old man, followed by a couple of others. They dismounted and walked up to the desperately injured man. Aslan knelt and gently turned him over.

The fair-skinned old man's hair was completely white, and his face was wrinkled and haggard. The horrific suffering he had endured was writ large on his entire being.

'Water ...' he croaked, his eyes squeezed shut against the sunlight. 'Give me ... some water ... for Lord Ram's sake.'

Aslan put his waterskin bag to the man's lips. He slurped down some water greedily and nodded gratefully.

'Thank ... you ...' the old man whispered, opening his eyes for the first time. Suddenly, an expression of pure terror appeared on his face. 'No ... no ... mercy ... mercy ...' he yelled, the sudden burst of sound startling the men around him.

Govardhan bent forward, speaking gently to the old man, 'Don't be afraid, my friend ...'

Govardhan didn't notice that, for a fleeting moment, an expression of deep worry had crossed Aslan's face.

Do these people recognise my face?

Govardhan continued speaking gently to the old man, while offering more water from his own waterskin bag. 'This man's name is Aslan. He may be Turkic, but he is one of us.'

Aslan, though, was not paying attention. *Great Allah, please protect my identity. Protect it till I have completed my mission for you.*

The old man closed his eyes and seemed to drift back into unconsciousness. His breathing was slow and ragged.

Aslan bent over towards Govardhan and whispered very softly, 'I don't think this old man can survive. He has lost too much blood … He is in too much pain … Should we … Should we do the merciful thing?'

Govardhan was about to answer, when, from the corner of his eye, he saw something move. He lunged to cover Aslan and himself, pulling up his shield as he did so.

A split second later, an arrow slammed into the shield.

Aslan immediately pulled his own shield forward as well. 'Cover yourself, Govardhan!'

'We're under attack,' yelled Govardhan, as he crouched behind his shield. 'Everybody down! Shields up!'

The men instantly took cover. A few more arrows flew in their direction, but bounced off the shields. Suheldev, who had leaped off his horse the moment he heard Govardhan's warning cry, noticed that all the arrows were coming from behind a particular hut near the outskirts of the village. He quickly ducked behind one of the huts that was next to the main track.

If I go around the huts, I'll come out behind the archer.

He raced through the fields, taking care not to make too much noise.

Around here should be okay.

Cautiously, he peered out from behind the tall darbha grass. Sure enough, about fifty feet ahead of him, he saw an archer kneeling behind a hut. The archer had a small but very well-designed recurved bow and a few arrows in a hip quiver. Every once in a while, he would get off a shot, then duck behind the hut, pull out the next arrow, and nock it on the bow-string, waiting for another opportunity.

A blue cloth covered the archer's head and face. His torso bore a piece of battered leather armour. From his slight build, he didn't seem to be more than a teenaged youth, at best.

Suheldev felt anger coursing through him. *A chit of a lad, and he's got my entire band cowering.*

He drew his dagger and moved rapidly towards the archer. Stealthily. Making as little noise as possible. When Suheldev was but a few feet away, some sixth sense warned the archer. He whirled around just as Suheldev lunged at him, knocking the bow aside. The arrow shot harmlessly into the air.

An instant later, Suheldev grabbed the archer by the throat and shoved him to the ground. Snarling, he crouched over him and drew back his right arm to strike with the dagger …

And then froze.

As the archer hit the ground, the cloth covering his face fell away to reveal … a young woman with chiselled features. A sharp nose rested over a full, generous mouth. But it was the eyes that were the most arresting part of her face. They were huge, dark, deep-set and lotus-shaped. And they were blazing at him with pure rage.

Wow …

Suheldev felt something twist within his chest as he gaped at her, his mouth open. An instant later, the gentle ache was replaced by a wave of agony that shot through his body as she kneed him in the testicles.

Suheldev grunted with pain. The dagger slipped from his hand as he jack-knifed forward, his hands instinctively moving to cup his injured parts.

Quick as a flash, the woman shoved him aside. As he tumbled to the ground, she snatched up his dagger and knelt astride him, reversing their positions.

The woman uttered a feral cry and stabbed at Suheldev's chest. Despite the throbbing pain he was suffering, he managed to grab her wrist in the nick of time. She clawed at his eyes with her other hand. Suheldev caught that hand as well and the two grappled furiously. The woman was much smaller than Suheldev, but surprisingly strong.

Suddenly, an arm swung around the young woman's neck and pulled her backwards. She gasped and dropped the dagger. Freeing her hands from Suheldev's grip with a jerk, she clawed at the arm, desperately trying to relieve the pressure on her neck.

'It's okay … release her,' croaked Suheldev, still in considerable pain.

Abdul, who had sneaked up behind the woman, and was now holding her in a death grip, ignored Suheldev. The woman continued kicking, trying to swing back and hit Abdul with her elbows. Breathing desperately, in large gasps, through her mouth. Struggling against the pressure on her neck.

'Abdul, release her!' Suheldev's voice was much firmer.

Abdul finally did as ordered. The woman coughed repeatedly as air finally flowed freely into her tortured lungs. She massaged her neck, shooting a baleful glare at Abdul.

Turning to the woman, Suheldev continued, 'Who are you and what are you doing here?'

The woman growled, 'Kill me and be done with it!'

'We don't want to kill you.'

'You've killed these poor villagers already. Let me join them with honour …'

Suheldev sighed. 'You've got things mixed up … We didn't kill these villagers. We're here to help.'

'Then why was Sukhia *kaka* screaming?'

'I don't know. Why don't we go ask him?' Suheldev gingerly rose to his feet. Then he yelled out loud so that his men could hear him, 'All clear, we're coming out. Don't shoot.'

The woman retrieved her bow and marched ahead where Aslan and Govardhan were warily crouching by the mutilated man.

'That's quite a woman,' muttered Abdul to Suheldev. 'It's a good thing for you that I turned up when I did.'

Suheldev looked at Abdul and frowned. 'I had things under control.'

'Really?' asked Abdul, laughing softly. 'That's what you call control now?'

The woman, meanwhile, had reached Aslan, followed closely by Suheldev and Abdul. She froze when she saw Aslan's face.

'A Turk!' she spat, unslinging her bow.

'Wait,' said Suheldev, urgently. 'Don't shoot! He's one of us.'

The woman stared at Suheldev for some time, then at Aslan. Finally, she seemed to come to a decision and lowered her bow. She turned back towards the wounded man.

Aslan looked up at her and shook his head sadly. 'He's gone, I'm afraid. I think his heart stopped. After those terrible injuries, it was only a matter of time anyway.'

The young woman covered her face with her hands and sank down to the ground, her shoulders shaking.

Suheldev came up behind her. 'I'm sorry for your loss,' he said gently.

The woman did not respond. Her face still covered by her

hands. Her shoulders shaking gently. No shrill crying. No loud sounds. Overcome with grief. And yet strong. Resilient. Gritty.

Suheldev gently touched the woman's shoulder. She shrugged his hand off.

Wiping her eyes, she looked at the old man lying on the ground. *I'm sorry. I'm sorry, Sukhia* kaka.

—— EJl ೫うJĊ△ ——

It had been a few hours since Suheldev and his band had come to the ravaged village. They had organised funeral rituals for the deceased.

The young woman stood stoic, staring at the cremation pyre that was consuming what remained of the old man. Suheldev couldn't help but admire the strength of this woman. He had discovered that her name was Toshani. She was from one of the forest tribes south of the Yamuna river, and had been part of the army of Kannauj. She had deserted the troops when her king had surrendered to Mahmud of Ghazni. She made her living as a hunter now, and had come to sell her kill at this village of leather-workers. The villagers had bought her animal, but, in addition, Sukhia had also treated a serious injury that Toshani had suffered during the hunt, one that was life-threatening. As any good warrior should, she was grateful to those who had saved her life. She had gone out hunting, to bring in a kill that she could offer free to the village, as a gesture of gratitude. And it was that thought of kindness that had saved her from the devastation the Turks had wreaked on the unfortunate village. For she wasn't there when the barbarians from Central Asia had attacked.

'These people are leather-workers?' asked Suheldev. He had noticed some of the implements around the village.

The woman's voice was bitter. '*Were*. People can't do without them when carcasses have to be cleared and leather goods have to be made. But they don't want these people around ... So they have to live by themselves ... Easy targets for invaders ... And ... despite all their suffering, they were the kindest, most generous people I have ever met ... I should have been here with them.'

'Then you would have been dead too.'

'Exactly,' said Toshani, turning her attention back to the cremation pyres.

Suheldev looked around. One thought kept troubling him. *Why in Lord Shiva's name are the Turks interested in this leather-workers' village?*

Aslan had studied the tracks of the Turkic horses. They were still fresh. They couldn't have gone very far. It was also clear from the tracks that it was a relatively small Turkic platoon.

Suheldev had already decided what he was going to do. He looked at Toshani. 'There must be retribution for this massacre. The Turks have to pay. With blood. Agree?'

Toshani turned to Suheldev. Eyes blazing. She didn't speak a word. But her answer was obvious.

'Then ride with us. Give me your blood, and I will give you your vengeance.'

Toshani remained silent. Her grip on her bow tightened and she gave an almost imperceptible nod.

Chapter 13

The Indian screamed as the arrow pierced his right shoulder. Gradually, his high-pitched cries subsided. 'Let me go ... please ...' he pleaded, tears streaming down his face.

The Turkic archer, standing at a distance, cursed loudly, while the other Turk soldiers guffawed. There were about thirty soldiers in all. Four of them were supposed to be on guard duty, but their attention was focused on the drama unfolding within the temporary camp.

The soldiers had already pitched their tents in an open field. Tracts of tall darbha grass—considered sacred by both Hindus and Buddhists, and renowned for its medicinal properties—grew wild all around the camp. In some patches, it had reached a height of over seven feet.

The tents were in two parallel lines, with the commander's tent in the middle of where the lines ended, forming a sort of 'U' shape. In the space between the two facing sides, the soldiers had set up the evening entertainment, at the expense of their four captives. Three were bound and lay huddled in a corner, while one was being tortured.

'This cursed wind is making a mess of things,' said the archer. He had missed the spot marked with coal on the Indian's left shoulder. 'The light is also quite faint now. The sun has almost set.'

'Or maybe you're just a lousy shot,' jeered a fellow Turk.

'Let's see if you can do better,' challenged another.

The Turkic archer stepped forward once again to a line drawn on the ground, about a hundred metres away from where the helpless Indian, who had been stripped naked, was tied to a pole. It was a warm evening, but the captive was shivering uncontrollably.

'I am changing the odds for the bet,' announced a Turk. 'One to ten that the arrow will hit the marked spot.'

A heated argument broke out among the soldiers. Some were arguing that the odds could not be changed now. Some were saying that they could, since the Indian captive kept shifting around, despite being tied up, making the job of the archer difficult.

'Stop this!' interjected a thickset man with salt and pepper hair and a tear-shaped birthmark on his right cheek. 'Our orders are to bring them in alive.'

'It's alright, Ozgur,' said the officer-in-charge curtly. 'The order only said alive, not how alive. Half-dead will do just as well.' He turned towards the archer. 'Carry on.'

The archer bowed theatrically. 'Thank you, sir.' Then he turned towards the target and spoke loudly, so that his voice would carry clearly. 'Don't worry. I'll not miss the left shoulder this time.'

As he heard the archer's words, the intended target began to plead even more frantically, sobbing in desperation. A trickle of urine ran down his leg.

The Turks roared with laughter but the archer frowned. 'This bastard's whining isn't letting me concentrate,' he complained. Then he smiled cruelly as an idea occurred to him. He pulled out a knife and advanced towards the Indian captive. 'Stick out your tongue,' he ordered.

The captive shut his mouth and shook his head desperately, his eyes wide and pleading.

'Fine,' said the Turk. 'I'll just have to get it out myself.'

He drew back his fist and prepared to punch the man in the stomach. Then, a look of shock appeared on his face. He peered down at his chest and saw an arrow protruding there. He opened his mouth to speak, then coughed, as blood rose in his throat.

The Turk turned towards his comrades, took one step, then fell to his knees. The men had been laughing and chattering, unaware of what had happened. All conversation stopped abruptly as they gaped at the fatally wounded archer.

Danger had come in. Stealthily. Quietly.

The silence was broken by loud war cries.

'Har Har Mahadev!'

Suheldev and his band suddenly erupted out of the tall grass surrounding the camp. Having spotted the Turks from a distance, they had crouched low and come up right to the periphery of the camp, creeping noiselessly through the darbha grass.

Toshani, who had shot the arrow that killed the Turkic archer, let loose a few more arrows that found their mark, then picked up a scythe and joined the attack.

Govardhan charged into the battle, his eyes alight with bloodlust. The Turkic soldiers took one look at the fearsome giant and scrambled away from him. All except one young lad, who had barely started to get a beard. The boy lunged at Govardhan with a sword. Govardhan batted the sword aside with his mace, then rammed into the boy with his shoulder, knocking him to the ground. But the boy sprang to his feet again. He slashed wildly, first from left to right, then right to left.

Brave. But stupid and inexperienced.

As the lad continued to swing his blade, Govardhan stayed beyond his reach. Thinking that the big man was retreating before him, the youth became even more reckless. He swung wildly at Govardhan's head, leaving himself completely unprotected to a counter-attack. A second later, he howled in agony as Govardhan's mace thudded into his rib-cage. There was a loud cracking sound, and the boy was knocked off his feet. He clutched at his injured side and winced as he tried to draw a breath.

That should keep him out of action for a while.

Then Govardhan saw, with growing incredulity, that the lad had dug his sword into the ground to support himself, and was trying to get back on his feet.

Govardhan sighed. He admired courage when he saw it. Even in an enemy. But this was not the time for fine sentiments. He smashed his mace down on the boy's shoulder, shattering his collarbone—and his resolve.

The boy began pleading, fighting back his tears. 'Mercy! Mercy!'

Govardhan had drawn back his mace for the killing blow. He hesitated as he looked into the eyes of the boy, who suddenly seemed like a lost child desperate to get back to his parents. Govardhan brought his mace down, and held out his hand, gesturing that he had accepted the enemy's surrender. Just then, Abdul stepped up and stabbed the young Turk through the heart. As he died, the Turk stared at Govardhan, as if accusing him of breaking a promise.

'What the hell?' protested Govardhan. 'The poor bastard had surrendered.'

'We don't have any place to keep prisoners.'

'But he was in no condition to fight,' said Govardhan. 'He was no longer a threat.'

'Not now,' said Abdul. 'But he would have recovered. And then he would have fought us again. This is war, not a game. Your code of honour won't work here.'

Govardhan opened his mouth to argue further, then decided against it. He remembered that he himself had felt his former king Mahipal's attitude towards the Turks too honourable.

I guess the great king affected me more than I thought.

Abdul smiled. 'You're learning.'

Govardhan grunted and looked around. Taken by surprise, most of the Turkic soldiers had died in the first few minutes of the fight. But some were still battling on, though the odds were heavily against them.

A Turkic soldier had pushed one of Suheldev's men to the ground and was choking him with his left hand. He raised his right hand, which held a dagger, to finish off his opponent. Then he howled in agony as Toshani suddenly appeared behind him and viciously swung her scythe at a point just below his elbow, cutting through skin, tissue, muscle and nerves, right through to the bone. The dagger dropped from the man's numbed fingers. But Toshani wasn't done with him. She swung her scythe again, this time burying the blade into the back of the man's head. He toppled to the ground, the scythe embedded in his skull.

Toshani bent down to retrieve the scythe, which was very fortuitous for her, because another Turkic soldier behind her had swung his sword right then, at the exact spot where her neck had been an instant ago. Instead of decapitating her, the blade swung harmlessly above. The swishing sound of the blade cutting through air startled Toshani and alerted her to the danger. Before she could react, Govardhan bellowed a warning and charged to help her. The Turk turned around to face the new threat just as Govardhan swung his mace. It connected with the Turk's right eye, turning it into a bloody, pulpy mess.

The Turk screamed in agony and dropped his weapon, both his hands instinctively going towards his crushed eye. Toshani, who had retrieved her scythe by then, deftly slit the carotid artery in his throat, ending his misery.

Meanwhile, Aslan and Suheldev battled a couple of soldiers near the fire that had been lit to cook dinner. One of the soldiers had his back to the flame. As he retreated before Aslan's onslaught, the edge of his tunic caught fire. He screamed loudly as he felt the blaze begin to singe him, and frantically tried to beat it out.

Aslan put him out of his agony with a clean blow to the neck. The body fell to the ground, still burning. Aslan saw a pitcher of water lying nearby. He snatched it and doused the corpse with it, extinguishing the flames. Suheldev, who had finished off his opponent as well, walked up to him, intrigued.

'He's already dead, genius,' said Suheldev. 'Why are you putting out the fire?'

'The cremation of a believer is strictly forbidden in Islam,' said Aslan. 'The human body is a gift from Allah. In life or in death, it must be treated with the greatest respect.'

'So … as a devout Muslim, you would fear death by fire?' asked Suheldev, thoughtfully, his head cocked to one side.

'It's a horrible way for anybody to die, Muslim or non-Muslim,' said Aslan, curtly. 'Shit, one of them is getting away.'

He dashed into the long grass in pursuit. Out of sight of the others in Suheldev's band.

The Turkic soldier ran as rapidly as he could, but Aslan was able to keep pace with him easily enough. He let him get a fair distance away from the camp, then dived and tackled him from behind. The two crashed to the ground. The cornered Turk lunged up with a snarl on his face, his sword drawn back to strike, then stopped abruptly when he saw it was Aslan.

'My Lord!' he said in disbelief. 'What are you doing with—'

'Keep your voice low, Ozgur,' hissed Aslan, cupping his hand over the Turk's mouth.

Ozgur nodded, showing that he understood. Aslan removed his hand.

'You've become even older and uglier than I remembered you,' said Aslan, the warmth in his voice belying the words.

Ozgur laughed good-naturedly. 'The last time I saw you was in Ghazni, My Lord. Are you still on your mission to—'

'Yes,' interrupted Aslan. 'Now listen to me …'

Aslan leaned in close to Ozgur and the two had a hurried conversation in whispers, making sure that they were well-concealed in the tall grass.

When the exchange ended, Aslan patted the man on the shoulder. 'Good, you should leave now. I will meet you again when I need you. But, for now, you have to stay with Kerim. Understood?'

'Yes, My Lord.'

'And before you go, punch me in the face.'

Ozgur looked horrified. 'I can't do that, My Lord!'

'It's an order,' said Aslan. 'Do it, or I'll ask you to stab me next.'

'But, My Lord …'

'It's an order, Ozgur! And make sure it's a good, hard punch.'

Ozgur swallowed hard, then unleashed a savage blow on Aslan's right cheek. The skin got cut and blood began flowing immediately.

Ozgur looked contrite and began to apologise but Aslan reassured him with a gesture and made a shooing motion with his hand, signalling that he should leave. It was only after Ozgur had scurried away that Aslan allowed himself to wince and touch the spot where he had been hit.

'Shit, he really takes orders seriously,' he muttered to himself.

— EꝒ ꝄꝌꝌꝒꝂ —

'Hope you got him after that,' said Suheldev, pointing at Aslan's injured cheek, which had swollen up and turned bright red.

'I almost did, but the bastard managed to get away.' Aslan pointed towards the recently rescued Indian captives. 'What's their story? Have you figured out why that settlement was wiped out?'

'They don't seem to know much. They just say that the Turks came with what appeared like clear orders. Destroy all the leather-making equipment and kill most of the workers. Capture the best of them and bring them to the main Turkic commander. And they were asked repeatedly about other leather-worker villages in the area. It's bizarre.'

Aslan didn't say anything. He looked keenly at Suheldev. He could almost see the prince's mind whirring. *Will he work it out?*

'Unless …' Suheldev began, and then paused.

'Unless what?' asked Aslan.

'The Turks believe in total war, right? Destroy the enemy's capacity to battle.'

'Yes … And …?'

'After the ransacking of Delhi, they have not started any new battle campaign. They have remained camped in Delhi. The reasoning is very simple. It's peak summer now. It's too hot for them, because they are used to the Central Asian cold. And they will not want to fight in the monsoon either. It's impossible for anyone to wage large battles during the Indian rains. So, they are waiting for winter. The Turks will begin their next battle campaign then.'

Aslan pretended that he didn't understand the argument that was being built up. 'What does that have to do with leather?'

'I'm coming to it. All Indian armies have metal armour only for the officers and richer soldiers. The common soldiers use thick leather armour. Without leather-workers, the common soldiers will have no armour. They will become easy prey to Turkic weapons.'

Aslan was getting impressed. 'Go on …'

'Also, the metal shields of the officers have to be covered with leather during winter; otherwise they will be too cold to use. So even metal shields will become useless without leather-workers. Indians have never truly realised the massive importance of our leather-workers in warfare. They were always available. But if the leather-workers are all gone, our capacity to make war is radically reduced. And since all leather-worker villages are isolated, it will not even be noticed for a long time that they are being systematically destroyed.'

Aslan smiled faintly. He was finally sure. He had found his man. He had found the Indian leader who could truly pose a threat to the Turks. Charismatic leader, Prince Suheldev was. No doubt. Able to get people of all castes and religions to fight under his command. Sure. Brilliant warrior and tactician. Certainly. But most importantly, he understood the mind of his enemy.

This is the man the Turks should be wary of. This is the man that I must …

Aslan's thoughts were interrupted by Toshani.

'Excuse me, Prince, I wanted to …'

'Suheldev.'

'Sorry?'

'Suheldev, not Prince.'

Toshani smiled. 'Suheldev, I wanted to thank you. These days, our Indian kings and princes don't even care for their own citizens, let alone others. These villagers are not your people. And yet, you helped. You have saved some of them. And even more, by letting me join the rescuers, you have helped me settle a debt to them.'

'There is no need for thanks. What I did was my duty. It was my *dharma*.'

'Then it is my *dharma* to fight by your side from now on. I will—'

Their conversation was suddenly interrupted by Abdul, who came rushing up to them. 'We need to leave, My Lord!'

'What happened?' asked Suheldev.

Abdul pointed at the horizon. In the distance, several beams of light were clearly visible. They were approaching the camp, and moving rapidly. 'The Turks have more men nearby! At least a battalion, by the looks of it!'

Suheldev cursed. Then he yelled to his men at the top of his voice, 'Ride out!'

Chapter 14

Suheldev knew that the situation was tough. He did not have all his men. They had managed to prevail over one small Turkic raiding party because of the element of surprise. But this was different.

We cannot outrun them. Sooner or later, our horses will get exhausted. Once they catch up with us, it will all be over. We are hopelessly outnumbered.

The wind rushed through Suheldev's hair as he urged on his galloping horse, keeping his head and body in a low crouch. The rest of the group raced along with him.

Behind them, the beams of light were not getting any closer, but they were not fading away either. The Turkic cavalry was maintaining the gap.

Suheldev's life, and the lives of all those who followed him, were hanging by a slender thread.

His eyes swivelled towards Abdul, who was leading the group. One of Abdul's special skills was that once he travelled across a path, he never forgot it. As Suheldev's most trusted scout, he had often conducted recces of various terrains and knew them like the back of his hand. Suheldev was counting on that knowledge to help make their escape.

Suddenly, Abdul stopped. Like many others in the band, he was carrying a torch. Now, he raised it and waved it around, signalling to the others.

'This way … Follow this way,' yelled Abdul. 'Double file. Stay close!'

The others reined in their horses and followed side by side. The Turks began to close the distance between them.

Suheldev gritted his teeth, fighting down the panic that threatened to overwhelm him. The words of his teacher came flooding back.

Panic is useless. It serves no purpose. Calm down. Breathe.

Suheldev breathed deeply. Slowly.

Forcing the pace of his heart down.

Focusing.

He looked to the side. Even in the faint moonlight, he could make out that there was a long field of sugarcane, stretching a considerable distance downriver.

Breathe.

Focus.

Suddenly, an idea hit him.

This can work.

'How far to the river?' asked Suheldev.

'Barely two hundred metres from here,' said Abdul. 'Listen, you can hear it flowing.'

Suheldev cocked his ears and then smiled. 'Yes … good. Now, take everybody to the river and get them across. Take Toshani as well. Leave ten fighters with me.'

Toshani spoke up immediately. 'I'll stay. I can be one of the ten.'

Suheldev glared at her. 'There's no time to argue.'

'Then don't argue,' she retorted. 'I'm probably the best archer here. You know it.'

Suheldev opened his mouth to dispute this, then decided against it. 'Fine.'

He quickly rattled off the names of the people he wanted left behind, including Aslan and Govardhan.

'Keep torches with you,' he told them. Then he nodded to Abdul. 'Go now. Lord Shiva willing, we'll meet again at our usual hideout.'

Abdul clasped Suheldev's hand briefly but fiercely. 'Allah be with you, My Lord,' he said. Then he raced off.

Suheldev turned towards the warriors left with him. 'Set fire to the sugarcane.'

Aslan and Govardhan exchanged puzzled looks but followed the order. As did the others. Suheldev himself took a torch and held it to a tall stalk. The flame caught, then began flickering, as if about to go out.

'Come on, come on,' muttered Suheldev.

As if heeding him, the fire suddenly leapt up, enveloping the whole stalk. A generous gust of wind blew suddenly, fanning the fire further. It soared from stalk to stalk, racing across the field. Suheldev grunted with satisfaction.

'Thank you, great Mahadev,' he whispered, wiping the sweat from his forehead.

Soon, the whole field of tall sugarcane was ablaze. A towering wall of fire. Suheldev and the others fell back about fifty metres. But even from that distance, they could feel the heat.

'Why have we set fire to only that part?' asked Govardhan. 'The Turks can still outflank us.'

Suheldev just smiled. 'Watch ...' Then he turned to the others. 'Bows ready. Take down anybody who tries to come through the fire.'

All of them dismounted from their horses and waited. Arrows nocked on bowstrings. Feet spread wide. Breathing steady and calm. Ready for battle.

A few minutes later, they heard the first wave of the Turkic company roaring up towards them.

Suddenly, oaths, screams and curses rang out all along the Turkic line, accompanied by loud splashes and the panicky neighing of horses.

Aslan, Govardhan and Toshani whipped around to stare at their leader inquiringly.

'The grassy field suddenly gives way to quicksand at the other side,' Suheldev explained calmly. 'There's only one safe passage through this area—the field that we've just set ablaze. If they want to catch us, they're going to have to ride through this field of fire.'

'And the faithful dread being burned, dead or alive,' said Aslan. He said it so softly that it was almost a whisper, but Suheldev heard him.

Suheldev turned to Aslan. His face was hard as stone. 'That's right. The moment you told me that, I knew it would come in handy someday. They use our beliefs and our faith in idols against us. We'll use their beliefs against them.'

Just then, a Turkic rider came charging through the blaze, his clothes on fire. Toshani expertly shot an arrow at his horse's saddle strap. Severing it cleanly, while causing only a surface wound on the beast. The saddle came loose rapidly, and the Turk was hurled from the animal. After rolling on the ground a few times, he came to a rest near Govardhan. The big man leaned down, lightly touched his mace to the Turk's head a couple of times as if aligning his aim, then drew back the weapon and swung with all his might. The Turk's skull shattered on impact. He was put out of his misery. Instantly.

Another horse emerged through the fire. Toshani shot another arrow, hitting the rider in his right eye. He screamed and fell from his mount, back into the fire. The greedy flames immediately raced up his body as he ran mindlessly, screaming, before collapsing to the ground.

A few more Turks fought their way through the flames and were promptly mowed down. There was a pause. Suheldev heard raised voices in Turkic, and more horses neighing. He turned towards Aslan, who seemed unhappy. Suheldev assumed that it was because he was seeing his fellow faithful being burned alive. But the Shravasti prince didn't bother. He had to save his own people. And all tactics were justified in war.

Unknown to Aslan, Suheldev had learnt a little bit of the Turkic language. Knowing the enemy was important. The prince could make out that the soldiers were screaming, refusing to ride through the fire. The Turks were normally not afraid of death. They were brave warriors. But they were afraid of *this kind* of death.

Though Suheldev could broadly understand what was going on, he felt like testing Aslan. 'What are they saying, Aslan?'

Aslan answered promptly. 'The Turkic commander is ordering his men to douse the fire.'

He has spoken the truth.

Suheldev mounted his horse and edged up on the saddle, trying to look across from the height. 'It'll take time. They don't have easy access to the river. And it's a nice big blaze.' He looked back. 'The rest of our band must have gotten across by now. I think it's time for us to also make a dash for it.'

His band quickly mounted their respective horses.

'Let's go!'

They raced to the river in a frenzied gallop. As they approached the water, the shape of a narrow wooden bridge loomed in front of them. Apart from taking a boat—and there were none available at the moment—it was the only way to get across the river.

In the dim moonlight, the river was barely visible below the bridge. The water seemed to be moving sluggishly, but Suheldev knew from past experience that the appearance was deceptive. The river current was strong and could easily wash away a man, or even a horse.

Suheldev pointed at the bridge. 'Move quickly! The moment we're across, destroy the bridge!'

He looked back, and could make out that the blaze at the fields was slowly burning out. The Turks would be able to make their way through soon.

The prince knew that they had little time. 'Move! Move! Move!'

They raced across. Aslan was among the first to reach the other side. He quickly began hacking at the poles of the bridge. 'Help me,' he yelled to Govardhan. 'We'll time it so that the bridge collapses within seconds of the last person getting across.'

The last person happened to be Suheldev, who had waited to make sure everybody else had gotten across. He urged his horse onto the bridge while his comrades yelled at him to get a move on.

While riding hard, Suheldev pointed at the torch held by one of his men. Ordering Govardhan to set fire to the bridge—the fire would destroy the bridge much quicker. He raced forward, his horse's hooves drumming rapidly on the wooden crossing.

'Hyah!' he screamed, kicking his horse faster, as he saw Govardhan grab a flaming torch and rush towards the bridge poles.

'Put it to flames!' shouted Suheldev loudly.

All of his soldiers were across. Suheldev was almost over to the other side.

Then, suddenly, he stiffened.

A lone Turkic archer had come racing through the now dying fire and shot a poisoned arrow. It was shot wildly, without any real hope of hitting anybody.

But by sheer bad luck, the arrow had found Suheldev. Slamming into his back with brutal force.

The prince swayed in the saddle. Holding the reins and continuing to ride would cause the arrow to tear through more of his flesh. But, admirably, he held on. He had to. He still hadn't crossed the bridge. Time seemed to slow down as he found himself listing towards his right. His vision blurring. A common effect of a wound caused by a poisoned arrow.

But he held on. The arrow ripped through more of his flesh.

He knew he was nearing the end of his strength. But he held on. He had to cross the bridge.

He heard the sounds of the hooves of his horse change. It wasn't the loud clip-clopping of horse shoes banging on wood anymore. It was the muffled shoosh of horse feet on riverbank ground. He didn't need to turn back to check. He knew he was over to the other side. He had crossed the bridge.

Burn the bridge!

His order did not escape his mouth. It was a mere few seconds since he had been shot, but it felt like aeons to Suheldev.

I've crossed the bridge! Burn it!

Time slowed down even more. Then he was falling through the air. He fell and fell, for what seemed like forever. He hit the ground with a thud, banging his head against the hard banks of the river.

And the world went black.

Chapter 15

Toshani stared, stunned, as she saw Suheldev crash to the ground.

She bellowed, 'Suheldev!'

She turned to the Turkic archer, on the other side of the river, riding towards the now burning bridge. She drew her bow forward, screaming as she ran ahead, pulling an arrow and nocking it in one smooth movement.

It's not easy shooting a moving target, at a far distance. One is not shooting the arrow where the target is, but where the target will be a few seconds later. And Toshani's task was made infinitely more difficult by the presence of a strong wind, which could make the arrow movement unpredictable. Even worse, the light was terrible, for there was the dim moonlight, disturbed by the erratic emanations of a raging fire.

But Toshani was no ordinary archer.

Almost instantaneously, her mind calculated the distance, trajectory, the wind direction, the speed of the horse of the Turkic archer thundering towards the burning bridge.

And she shot the arrow.

The missile flew rapidly across the river and slammed into the Turk, right into his chest, puncturing his right lung. The Turk started listing to his right, the horse continuing to gallop.

Govardhan and Aslan stood stunned by the exquisite

archery on display. They had never seen such accuracy over this distance.

'Get Suheldev!' shouted Toshani.

Govardhan started running towards Suheldev's prone body, as he saw more Turks emerge on the other side of the river.

But Toshani was not done. The Turkic archer who had shot Suheldev was still on his horse. Incapacitated. But still alive. She immediately drew another arrow, nocked it and fired. It thumped into the Turk's left shoulder.

Another one. It ripped into the Turk's abdomen.

The Turk fell off his horse.

But Toshani didn't stop. She drew another arrow and fired. It flew in a smooth arc and struck the Turk's chest once again, this time piercing his heart.

But Toshani was still not done.

She shot another arrow. Which impaled the Turk's throat.

But she was still not done.

She drew another arrow, nocked it to her bow and was about to fire, when Aslan grabbed her arm.

'I think he's dead, Toshani.'

Toshani turned towards Aslan, the fury of the Mother Goddess in her eyes. Aslan stepped back. Afraid.

He spoke in a softer tone. 'I think he's dead …'

Toshani turned back. She saw the gargantuan Govardhan heft Suheldev onto his shoulder as though he was a child. The burly warrior was now racing towards the safety of the tree line. Where they would not be visible to the Turkic archers on the other side of the river.

Toshani, Aslan and some of the other archers in Suheldev's band remained on the riverbank. Watching the Turks assemble on the other side. Ready to shoot if any of them were stupid enough to attempt crossing the bridge, which was now being swallowed by massive flames. The boards would collapse at any time. The Turks knew that.

A few moments later, Suheldev's men roared in triumph as the bridge crumbled into the river with a huge splash.

The Turkic commander ordered one of his soldiers to take his horse into the river and make it swim across. This soldier was the sacrificial lamb. For the other Turks remained stationary. Waiting to see if it was safe to swim across the waterway.

To Toshani's grudging admiration, the Turkic soldier did not argue. He did not care about the risk to his life. He immediately began goading his horse into the river. The horse stepped into the waters gingerly. It grew in confidence as the current did not seem that strong. It went deeper and deeper into the river. It must have been a third of the way through, when one could sense the panic in the beast's movements. The Turk turned around. To look at his commander. One last time. The horse neighed in terror as the current swept it away, its rider still on its back.

'That should hold them for a while,' said Aslan. Then he looked back. Govardhan and many of the others had disappeared into a thick grove of trees about fifty metres away.

'Let's go!'

— EᒍᒍᎥ HᲘᎴᑎᏨᎴ —

'He needs a proper physician,' said Toshani.

Suheldev's band was safe, for now, in the grove. It would take a very long detour for the Turks to cross the river. At least a full night's ride. Therefore, they had laid Suheldev down and Aslan was about to attempt to pull the arrow out.

'Do you see a proper physician here?' asked Aslan. 'Look, I've seen plenty of battlefield wounds and I have a basic idea of healing from my time with the Sufis. Right now, I'd say I'm his best bet.'

Toshani scowled, unconvinced. 'Listen to me, Turk. If anything happens to him ...'

Aslan shut his eyes and took a deep breath. When he spoke, his voice was calm and measured, but distinctly cold. 'Toshani, I may be a Turk, but I am not a monster. And I am not an angel either. I cannot guarantee anybody's life. But believe me, I will do my very best not to harm Suheldev. He is my friend and leader too.'

Govardhan intervened. 'Is there a physician whom we can trust? Anyone nearby?'

One of Suheldev's men shook his head. 'There is one. But his village is at least a day's ride from here.'

'That settles it then,' said Govardhan. 'There's no way he can bounce around for a day with that shaft stuck into his back.' Govardhan turned to Aslan. 'Go ahead. Do what you need to.'

Aslan nodded and rushed to his horse. There was some equipment in his saddle bag.

Govardhan, meanwhile, turned towards the soldiers and directed them towards perimeter defences. Just in case some Turks managed to cross the river.

Aslan returned soon. A rucksack on his back. Govardhan and Toshani bent down, close to Suheldev, who had been made to lie down on his stomach. The arrow was protruding from Suheldev's back at an angle.

Aslan squatted next to Suheldev. He gently touched the arrow and peered at the spot where it was lodged.

'Should we pull out the arrow now?' asked Govardhan.

Aslan shook his head. 'Let me first check that it's not stuck in a bone. If it is, and a piece of the arrowhead remains behind, it will kill him slowly and painfully.'

Aslan gripped the shaft and gently twisted it. Only a little. Suheldev moaned in agony. Toshani winced at the sound, but Aslan grunted in satisfaction.

'The shaft is moving freely,' said Aslan. 'That's good.'

He doused a clean piece of cloth with the disinfectant that he usually kept in his saddle bag, and then rolled it into a compress. He handed it to Govardhan. Then he pulled out a pair of pincers and gave them to Toshani.

'I need you to enlarge the wound slightly and keep it open. The arrow needs to come out as smoothly as possible.' Toshani paled slightly, but nodded grimly and dug the pincers into the wound. Suheldev groaned and stirred.

'Just a little while longer,' said Toshani in a soothing tone, stroking his head gently. 'It will be over soon.'

Suheldev relaxed at the sound of Toshani's voice. Aslan pulled out a pair of forceps. Very gently, he lowered them into the wound, feeling his way gingerly down the shaft till he came to the arrowhead. He used the forceps to enclose the arrowhead and get a good grip on it. Once satisfied that the arrowhead would not slip, he pulled it out.

The arrow came loose with a sucking sound. Blood began to flow immediately. Aslan grabbed the improvised compress and pressed it hard against the wound, staunching the blood flow.

'No bone damage and no excessive bleeding. He's a very lucky man.' Aslan cleaned the wound with the disinfected cloth. He then reached into his rucksack and pulled out a small pouch. From it he retrieved a suturing needle and fibres made from the guduchi plant. 'I have learnt some of your ayurvedic techniques as well. Guduchi fibres are the best for stitches. They have antiseptic properties too.'

Govardhan held Suheldev's shoulders down to ensure that the prince didn't move, as Aslan started sewing the wound shut.

'Can you make the stitches smaller?' asked Toshani. 'The scar will end up being quite big.'

Aslan smiled, continuing to focus his attention on Suheldev's wound and what he was doing. 'I am not an expert surgeon, Toshani. Better for Suheldev to have a bigger scar than an open wound.'

Toshani didn't argue. The logic was irrefutable.

With the stitching done, Aslan checked the wound meticulously. He seemed satisfied. He reached into his rucksack and pulled out a flask. 'Okay, I just need to clean the wound once again now.'

Govardhan sniffed the air. 'That's wine. You don't even drink. Why the hell are you carrying it?'

'For occasions like this,' said Aslan. 'It's a very strong wine. It's not for drinking. It's a great disinfectant. Now hold him down. This will sting a lot.'

He quickly washed the wound with the wine. Suheldev moaned involuntarily, but Govardhan pushed down on his shoulders firmly, ensuring that he didn't move around and re-open the wound.

'Good, good, that should keep any nasty infection away,' said Aslan. Then he turned to Toshani. 'Let's use the other piece of long cloth in my rucksack to bandage him up nicely.'

Toshani nodded. When they were done, she turned to Aslan. 'Is he going to be all right?'

Aslan shrugged. 'I've done the best I could with whatever I had. Suheldev is young and strong. Insha'Allah, he will recover completely.'

'Thank you,' she said. She hesitated for a moment, then spoke again, haltingly. 'I'm sorry I was rude to you.'

'It's alright … We were both worried about him. And you were right, we do need to get him to a proper physician.'

With the tension having eased, Govardhan couldn't resist cracking a joke. 'Too bad I didn't know about your little wine stash. It wouldn't have lasted very long!'

Aslan laughed softly. 'That's precisely why I kept it a secret!'

— ᴇᴊ ᴴᴰᴧᴄᴧ —

Suheldev woke up slowly. His eyelids heavy. Struggling against the enforced ennui of the painkilling herbs and the even stronger anti-poison medicines given to him. His entire body felt sore.

The light diffused slowly, through his slightly opened eyes, into his consciousness. As his eyes adjusted to the light, he looked to his side. There was someone there. Seated on a chair. Sleeping. Daylight shining behind; almost like a halo around the person's head. Giving the figure a divine appeal.

What …?

His eyes adjusted a little more as he blinked rapidly. And he saw relatively clearly. He was lying on a cot in a hut. There was nobody else there. Apart from the young woman sleeping on the chair. A cold compress in her hand. It was obvious that she had been caring for him. And had probably fallen asleep. Out of tiredness, perhaps.

Toshani …

He smiled. Or at least he wanted to. He was not sure if it actually showed on his face.

Sleep took over once again.

— EJ ℋℷ∩ℐᏟ△ —

Suheldev's eyes opened. The light was soft. Just a lamp in a niche in the wall.

It's night. How long have I been asleep?

He coughed and shifted his position slightly. He heard the sound of someone getting up from the far corner of the room. As the person came close, Suheldev recognised her. It was Toshani.

The effect of the painkillers was receding. But, despite his severe pain, Suheldev's heart actually picked a romantic beat.

It was difficult to miss the mood.

The soft diffused light of the lone lamp. The moonlight filtering in from the open door. The distant sound of the village guard singing a song. A song of the divine love between Lord Krishna and Lady Radha.

It was for the first time that Suheldev was getting a good look at Toshani with her hair open and her face scrubbed clean. He had found her attractive even when he had first seen her, though she had been covered with sweat and dirt. But it wasn't till now that he realised that she had a stunningly beautiful face.

Breathing became difficult.

He smiled. Or at least tried to.

A look of concern appeared on Toshani's face. 'Why are you grimacing? Is the pain too much? Should I ask for more painkillers?'

No. I'm not grimacing. I'm trying to smile.

But no words came out.

'Suhel?'

Mmm … Suhel … Not Suheldev … I like it …

Sleep took over once again.

—— ᗴᒍᒍ Ꮗᕎᐣᒍᒼᐃ ——

Suheldev blinked rapidly as he woke up. The light was strong. The sun was definitely up. He stirred slightly.

Toshani was in front of him in no time.

He smiled.

Toshani smiled in turn. 'Feeling better now?'

Yeah! The expression came out right …

'Water …' he whispered. His voice was little more than a croak.

Toshani turned to another soldier sitting at the back. He got up, poured some water from an earthen pitcher lying nearby into a small earthen cup, and helped Suheldev drink it.

'Take gentle sips, not big gulps,' Toshani advised.

Some water trickled down both corners of his mouth and onto his chest. She wiped it clean. Gently.

It struck him as a little odd to find the fiery Toshani being so gentle and caring towards him. Even nurturing …

Suheldev turned to his soldier. 'Find … Govardhan …'

The soldier saluted and left the hut.

Suddenly, memories of the battle with the Turks came flooding back. 'Any losses … on our side?'

'No,' replied Toshani. 'Everyone survived. No serious injuries.'

Good.

Then, Toshani smiled naughtily. 'No serious injuries on anyone except you. Perhaps you ride too slowly.'

Suheldev laughed softly. *Ah, there's the woman I recognise.*

Govardhan walked into the shed. 'Praise be to Lord Ram that you are alright.'

Suheldev whispered softly, 'Jai Shri Ram …'

Glory to Lord Ram.

Govardhan and Toshani repeated, 'Jai Shri Ram.'

'But,' continued Govardhan, 'you can also thank the village doctor who has treated you, and this young lady who has taken excellent care of you. She has stayed by your bedside all through while the rest of us have taken turns to rest.'

Suheldev's eyes turned towards Toshani. There was a shy smile on her face. Matched by the embarrassed smile on his. Awkward silence. No words spoken.

Unfortunately, Govardhan was not one to notice the delicate nuances of the situation. He carried on speaking, as if there was nothing to be noticed. 'You have been out for a couple of days. Aslan fixed you up initially. He saved you, truly. For we discovered later that the arrow was poisoned and could have caused tremendous damage if it had remained inside. Then we brought you to this village doctor, who has provided us this derelict shed to hide in. He came up with some foul-smelling concoction that he has been applying to your wound every few hours. Clearly, it has worked!'

'Where is … Abdul?' asked Suheldev. 'He'll be … worried.'

'I'm right here, My Lord,' said Abdul, standing at the door of the hut. 'I'm not worried anymore.'

'My friend …' whispered Suheldev.

Abdul stepped into the hut. 'Govardhan sent a messenger to me and I got here as fast as I could. You need to rest for a few days before you're fit to travel. We'll set out after that. Aslan should be back by then as well.'

Suheldev frowned. 'Where has … he …'

'He's gone on yet another one of his spying missions,' said Abdul. 'He took off as soon as he was sure we'd be safe here. Said he'll be back soon.'

Suheldev looked at Abdul. But didn't say anything. At least not out loud.

Aslan gave us correct information on the village raid. He saved my life at the river battle. It's about time that I start trusting him completely. He may be a Turk. But he is one of us.

But Suheldev also knew that Abdul would have probably sent a man to tail Aslan. And set up a strict perimeter guard around their own temporary camp. He knew that there was no point in arguing with Abdul, to try to convince him about Aslan's trustworthiness.

He let it be.

Chapter 16

Deep in the forests, far from any habitation in the Gangetic plains, a small Turkic platoon had assembled. Fine, unbeatable, ferocious soldiers guarded the lone, military tent. Their lord and commander, Salar Maqsud, had just ridden in. As always, in a hurry. He had rushed into the tent to meet his lover. And the soldiers waited. Alert.

Maqsud lay comfortably in the bed that occupied most of the small military tent, his head on Kerim's lap. Kerim ran his hand down Maqsud's broad shoulders slowly, smiling. Maqsud smiled back, running his hand along Kerim's face.

'I could lose myself forever in your eyes,' whispered Kerim.

'You are the light of my life, my darling.'

Kerim bent down and kissed Maqsud gently. Languid. Slow. Full of love. As they disengaged, Kerim breathed deeply.

'Enough of this, Maqsud,' said Kerim. 'Let's go home now. Let's go back to Ghazni.'

Maqsud shook his head. 'I can't. You know I can't. It's the orders of the sultan himself.'

'Why is this so important?'

'Because it is.'

'No, it's not. All that matters is you and me. You have done enough for the sultan already. Tell him that this cannot be done. It's impossible. And then …'

'I can't do that.'

'Maqsud …'

'I can't, Kerim. We Turks will be remembered by history only if we conquer and rule one of two countries. Either India or China. They are the most populated and wealthy nations on earth. We will be blessed with heaven and virgins in our afterlife only if we lord over these prosperous lands of idolaters and pagans, destroy their unholy cultures, and bring them to the true faith. Once either India or China falls to the sword of Islam, the entire world will capitulate and become Dar-ul-Islam. That is the task that Allah has given us.'

'Maqsud, you think Allah has ordered you to kill millions of people? Seriously? Allah would never do that. Love is the only—'

Maqsud held up his hand and covered Kerim's mouth. Gently. 'I have told you before, my darling. Don't say these things out loud. They are blasphemy. If any of these words reach the sultan's ears, then we are …'

Kerim took another deep breath and looked away. He loved Maqsud deeply. And for his love, he was willing to suppress his Sufi ideology, his beliefs. 'But if the sultan wants to conquer and rule, why does he need you to travel around India? Incognito? This is dangerous. I have been using the tactics you have told me. And we have been winning battles. But I told you before, we have too few men in our army. We can defeat the Indian armies, but we don't have enough soldiers to suppress the Indian citizens. More Turks need to be sent from Ghazni. With a larger army, we can conquer and rule. The sultan needs to be told that.'

Maqsud shook his head. 'No, Kerim. We Turks are fierce warriors. The best in the world. But our army, including all the soldiers in Ghazni, is not large enough to *rule* all of India. There are just too many Indians. We are only strong enough to charge in, plunder and then retreat to safety in our own kingdom of Ghazni. If we want to rule, we have to break the Indian resistance permanently.'

'Break their resistance permanently? There are probably a few hundred million of these Indians. How can you ever …'

'Forget the lands of South India. Most of them are militant, aggressive Hindus. But much of northern India, especially the elite, has become effete and non-violent. They celebrate vegetarianism and women's rights. They are weak. We can conquer North India first, consolidate our rule, and then go south.'

'But even North India has too many people. This is such a large land, and—'

Maqsud interrupted Kerim. 'You don't understand. I have been spending years here, blending in, studying them … With only one aim: to understand their strange culture. What I have learnt is that there isn't one North India. There are actually three.'

'Three?'

'Yes. There is the North India of the upper caste Hindus. We have picked their kingdoms off one by one in our raids. Their silly notions of battle-honour have ensured that they can't defeat us. And their caste-pride has ensured that the common people don't fight for them.'

'And the second?'

'The second is the North India of the Buddhists. In India, most of the Buddhists are from the trader castes. And their greatest numbers are concentrated in Punjab, Afghanistan and Bengal. They are the easiest to defeat. They believe in non-violence, love and compassion. And they actually think that since we Turks were Buddhists till a few years ago, we won't be brutal with them.' Saying this, Maqsud sniggered.

Kerim didn't find it funny. For his parents, from whom he had been taken away when he was a child, were Buddhists.

Maqsud immediately realised what he had done, and moved quickly on. 'The third group is the North India of the subaltern caste Hindus: people like the peasants, the farmers, the artisans, etc. That is where there will be true resistance to our rule. That is what I have learnt.'

'But if they are the subaltern castes, then they will not be organised. There will be no leadership to decapitate to break their resistance.'

'Actually, they are more organised than we think. Some of the subaltern castes have founded their own kingdoms. And there are a few among them who can lead the resistance. I have been tracking one particular leader. I have been researching him.'

'Can't you just …'

'Assassinate him?' asked Maqsud. 'I have thought of that. There were some opportunities too. But if we kill him by subterfuge, we will end up making him a martyr, an inspiration, which will make the resistance stronger. Another leader could rise. We can't have that. We have to kill him at the right time, at the right place. We have to defeat this leader in an open battle. Fair and square. Where we can make an example of him. Publicly. We have to lure him to an open war. And then we have to massacre every single one of his followers. So that we can put the fear of the One God in anyone who wants to be like that Indian subaltern-caste leader. Maybe we will parade his mutilated body around all of North India. Maybe torture him in public. That is what will break the resistance. Then we will rule till Judgement Day.'

Kerim kept quiet. If his love for Maqsud wasn't so deep, he would have been horrified by now. He couldn't understand how someone could be so loving and caring one moment, and such a monster the next. *I should listen to Ozgur. For Maqsud's own good. Maybe then we can …*

'You didn't ask me his name, my love …' said Maqsud, playing with Kerim's hair.

'I'm sorry,' said Kerim gently. 'I got distracted. Who is this man who will suffer your wrath?'

'Suheldev of Shravasti.'

Kerim waved his hand dismissively. 'Forget Suheldev for now. You will be leaving in a few hours. Give me something to remember you by.'

And Kerim bent down to kiss Maqsud.

— EJJ ⱨϧⱭЇ⳨△ —

The doctor left after changing the bandages. Suheldev hated the procedure, mainly because it hurt like hell. It made him feel so vulnerable. His body seemed to be utterly delicate all of a sudden. So delicate that even contact with air felt like someone was clawing him viciously. The medicinal balm was a little soothing. But it was not enough.

Toshani now re-entered the room after having discarded the older bandages. She was the second reason Suheldev hated the procedure. He felt embarrassed to be so exposed and helpless in front of her. He would speak of anything, except his injury. 'Umm … the … the perimeter … about the …'

'The perimeter guards are alert and strong,' said Toshani. 'Abdul is managing that. Forget about them. How is your pain?'

'I'm okay … I'm okay … I think I can … ride out of here tomorrow.'

Toshani smiled. 'Sure, you can.' She brought a cup forward. 'But for now, drink this.'

'What is it?'

'It's something the doctor has made. It will give you good sleep. And help heal the wound quicker.'

Suheldev obediently drank the infusion. He wiped his mouth slowly with the back of his hand and whispered, 'Yes, I can … ride …'

'Of course, you can.'

'The perimeter … guards …'

'Don't worry. Sleep.'

'Yes … Abdul … will take care …'

Suheldev's eyes closed slowly as sleep took over.

Chapter 17

Ozgur looked around nervously. He could have sworn that he had seen his lord's horse. He had been tracking it for the last two days. Trying hard to catch up. His lord moved fast!

Ozgur had left as soon as the news had come in. Kerim had ordered him to leave immediately.

Trees and dense tall grass had blocked out the light to a significant extent. It was still afternoon, but it felt like late evening. Rays of light broke through gaps in the foliage, giving a surreal feel to this secluded spot.

The beauty of the setting, though, was completely lost on Ozgur, who kept darting glances from side to side.

Where is he?

Suddenly, he felt a finger prod his back hard.

A calm, playful voice was heard. 'I could have killed you about ten times in the last five minutes.'

Ozgur sagged with relief and turned around when he heard the voice. 'My Lord Salar Ma—'

Ozgur's words were cut off as his mouth was held tight. His lord hissed in warning.

'How many times have I told you, Ozgur? Do not use my real name when I am not with the Turks. Even the trees have ears.'

A penitent Ozgur touched Salar's beard. 'I am so sorry, My Lord. Please forgive me.'

'In India, my name is Aslan. That is the name you will use. Always.'

'Yes, Lord Aslan.' The bruise from Ozgur's blow was still visible on Aslan's face and the Turkic soldier winced when he saw it. 'Forgive me. I may have been over-enthusiastic in obeying your orders.'

Aslan waved aside his apology. 'Don't worry about it. Why are you tracking me? What news is so important?'

'Lord Kerim sent me. With an urgent message, Lord Aslan.'

'What is it?' asked Aslan.

'My Lord …' Ozgur seemed to be hesitating.

'Out with it, Ozgur! Tell me quickly. I have to get back to Suheldev's camp.'

'My Lord … Lord Kerim just received word that …'

Aslan was getting impatient. 'In the name of Allah, Ozgur. Don't take forever! What is the news?'

Ozgur took a deep breath. 'A communication from Ghazni says that the sultan is no more.'

'What?!' exclaimed Aslan. 'The sultan is dead? Are you sure?'

'Lord Kerim has confirmed it personally. It is true.'

'But he was always in excellent health. What happened?'

'Nobody knows. It is true what you say: Sultan Mahmud rarely suffered from even a cold. He used to recover from battle injuries very quickly too. But he died suddenly. In Ghazni itself. We're not sure what happened. No details are available, though there are plenty of rumours—right from a traitor's hand to some mystery illness. I have heard some of the men say the *kafirs* may have used dark magic to avenge the sultan's attacks on Indian temples.'

Aslan slumped to the ground, stunned by the enormity

of what he had just heard. It was as if the axis of the world had suddenly tilted. Sultan Mahmud had been a larger-than-life personality. A colossus who evoked hero worship in his followers and intense fear and hatred among his enemies. It was impossible to suddenly imagine a world without him.

Ozgur came gently to the main point that Kerim had asked him to communicate to Aslan. 'My Lord, you have to come back to Ghazni now. Lord Kerim has said that—'

Aslan interrupted Ozgur. 'What will I do there now? With the sultan gone—'

It was Ozgur's turn to interrupt Aslan. 'My Lord, there is talk of a civil war between the sultan's sons. The Turkic armies in India are being called back to Ghazni. We have been ordered to fight on the side of the rightful heir.'

Aslan shook his head. 'The sultan dead. Civil war in Ghazni. Wow, the world has become a different place overnight.'

'Are you coming back to Ghazni, My Lord?'

Aslan remained silent.

'I have to inform Lord Kerim of your decision, My Lord,' said Ozgur.

'I will come,' said Aslan. 'But not immediately.'

'My Lord? But why? You have an important role to play in Ghazni. You must—'

'My true future is not in Ghazni. It is in India.'

Ozgur remained silent.

'I will finish my work with Suheldev and then come to Ghazni. You can tell Kerim that.'

'Yes, My Lord,' said Ozgur, as he saluted smartly.

'Farewell, my friend. Allah be with you.'

'And with you, My Lord.'

After Ozgur left, Aslan stayed slumped on the ground for

some time. Finally, with a sigh, he rose and jogged to where he had left his horse. The animal nuzzled him affectionately. He patted it absentmindedly, swung onto the saddle and spurred the horse into motion. It was a ride of many days to Suheldev's hideout.

—— ⵉⵊⵍ ⵅⵝⵍⵛⵄ ——

Suheldev was annoyed by his slow recovery. The pain was getting bearable, but he still had his moments of weakness. He was able to get up from his bed now. He could stand for some time. And walk too, but very slowly.

For a naturally active person like Suheldev, staying confined for long hours in bed was the worst form of torture. Initially, he had no choice as his body was simply too weak. But as his recovery had progressed and he had regained some strength, it had become more and more oppressive to simply lie around. The stultifying heat didn't help either.

His ears perked up as he heard what seemed like some drops of rain hitting the roof. Some more drops followed. Then suddenly, the heavens opened up.

'Rain!' exulted Suheldev, with childlike delight.

He slowly dragged his legs out of bed. The physician sitting beside him got up to offer help, but Suheldev waved him away. Using his hand, he pushed himself up onto his feet.

The physician looked at him questioningly.

'I'll be back soon,' said Suheldev. 'Let me just have a glimpse of the rain.'

The physician nodded reluctantly. 'Okay. But don't get wet. The last thing we need is for your wound to get infected.'

Suheldev made a face, but nodded his assent. He had been

moved a few days back from the hut to a house of a wealthy merchant in the next village. So that he could be better taken care of. With its large, airy, well-lit rooms, arched doorways and walls decorated with beautiful frescoes, the house was a distinct improvement from Suheldev's previous quarters.

The house was built in a rectangular shape, with an open courtyard in the middle. The traditional Indian style of architecture. Suited well to the Indian climate as it aided air circulation and natural light. The floor of the courtyard was paved with clay bricks, and a champa tree occupied pride of place in the centre. The courtyard also served as a meeting place where the residents of the house would gather for companionable moments.

Suheldev walked out of his room into the covered gallery that overlooked the central courtyard. He stared up at the sky. At the rain pelting down. Careful to stay away from the edge of the awning, protected by the roof from the rain above. He breathed in deeply. Savouring the fragrance of freshly wet earth. One of the most nourishing aromas known to man.

Suheldev's mind reacted the way most Indian minds did to the first rain.

Happiness. Joy. Spiritual ecstasy. Romance. Love at the return of life.

He couldn't help but smile, silently thanking his God, the great Mahadev, for keeping him alive to enjoy one more monsoon.

He closed his eyes. Letting the music of the rain intoxicate his mind. His soul.

An ancient tune, one that he had heard when he was young, came back to memory. It was a song that celebrated the love of rain. And the rain of love that the season caused.

He began humming the tune. Softly.

And then, as if guided by Kamdev, the God of Love Himself, Suheldev's eyes opened and he turned for a reason he did not understand.

And he froze.

Some distance away, at the diametrically opposite end of the courtyard, stood Toshani.

She hadn't bothered to stand under the awning. She had come out into the open courtyard. Standing in the pouring rain. Eyes shut. Face turned up towards the sky. Drenched to the bone. Her clothes plastered against her.

Suheldev had stopped humming. But the tune continued to play in his mind. Louder than ever.

Lord Kamdev, have mercy …

Suheldev had only seen Toshani dressed like a warrior. Until now. He suddenly became aware that her body was every bit as attractive as her face. Her arms and shoulders were well-defined and muscular, but they were lithe rather than bulky. Given her slender frame, her breasts were surprisingly large, something he had not noticed earlier due to the leather armour she always wore. Coupled with a narrow waist and sturdy hips, they gave her an unexpected, but very alluring, curviness. The raindrops seemed to lovingly caress her as they slid down her taut, firm, young body.

Suheldev stared at her. His mouth open. Breathing agonisingly slow. For what seemed like forever. She must have sensed his gaze, because she opened her eyes and turned to him. Their eyes locked, and she stared right back at him.

Look away. Look away.

But Suheldev's eyes were not in his control anymore. He couldn't bring himself to turn away.

Toshani did not look away either. She just stood there. In the rain. Staring at Suheldev. Letting him stare at her.

No words were spoken. No words were needed.

A smile. Slight. Faint.

She smiled at me. She ...

'My Lord!'

Suheldev felt a surge of anger at the disturbance. He turned towards the main door. It was Abdul. He turned back towards Toshani. She was gone.

Goddammit!!

'My Lord,' said Abdul, walking swiftly towards Suheldev. 'Aslan has returned.'

$$-\text{EJ } \text{כׄ}ɔ\text{ʃ}\text{Ċ}Δ-$$

'By the great Lord Shiva,' whispered Suheldev, shocked.

Suheldev was in his room now, lying on the bed, as the doctor had ordered. Sitting by the bed, in comfortable chairs, were Govardhan, Toshani, Abdul and Aslan. Toshani had changed her clothes. Neither Suheldev nor she acknowledged, even with their eyes, what had just happened in the rain.

All had been forgotten. All attention diverted. Everyone was gobsmacked by the news of the death of the one they thought of as the devil himself: Sultan Yamin-ud-Dawla Abul-Qasim Mahmud ibn Sebuktegin of Ghazni.

'How did he die?' asked Govardhan.

'Nobody seems to know,' said Aslan. 'My sources are junior soldiers, not officers. So they do not know all the details.'

'I lost the chance to kill that pathetic bastard myself,' growled Govardhan. 'I lost my chance to avenge Somnath*ji*.'

Aslan did not say anything. He stared at Govardhan. His

face expressionless. It was impossible to read what he was thinking.

'Did he suffer?' asked Abdul.

Aslan nodded. 'I heard he suffered a lot.'

Abdul ran his open palms across his face, in gratitude to his God. 'Allah may take time, but He always gives justice. He always punishes those monsters who deserve it.'

Again, Aslan remained silent.

Toshani looked at Suheldev, almost instinctively knowing what he would be thinking. She turned to Aslan and asked softly, 'What are the Turkic armies doing now?'

'They are all going back to Ghazni,' said Aslan. 'Apparently, civil war has broken out between his successors.'

'So, is India free of the Turkic menace?' asked Toshani.

Before Aslan could respond, Suheldev cut in. 'Only for now ...'

Aslan raised his eyebrows, once again impressed by Suheldev's astuteness. Truly, he would make a formidable enemy to the Turks.

'Yes,' said Aslan, 'the prince is right. It may take a few years, but the Turks will certainly return.'

Abdul glared at Aslan. 'Is that a warning or a threat?'

'Abdul ...' said Suheldev, counselling patience through his tone, rather than his words.

'It is not a threat, Abdul,' said Aslan. 'Just a statement of fact. You can choose to disbelieve it if you want to. It may surprise you, but I too have an interest in Prince Suheldev's career.' Aslan wasn't lying. 'In any case, I will not be around to irritate you much longer.'

'Where are you going, my friend?' asked Govardhan.

Aslan smiled at him. 'I am not needed for now. At least, not until the Turkic civil war is over. I thought I would return to my Sufi path. Try to find a master. Try to relearn some peace.'

Suheldev burst out laughing. 'You are a natural-born warrior, Aslan. I don't think you are made for the Sufi path.'

'The Sufi path unmakes and then remakes you, my friend.'

Suheldev patted Aslan's hand. 'Then may Lord Shiva guide your path. I will not hold you.'

Aslan bowed his head and held Suheldev's hand tightly. 'Thank you, my prince.'

'Do you have you any idea who will win the civil war, Aslan?' asked Toshani. 'Which son of Mahmud will be the enemy we will have to face in due course?'

Again, Suheldev cut in. 'From what I have heard, Mahmud's sons are not that important. The one who matters most is his favourite general. Whichever side he supports will probably win the war.'

Aslan said nothing. *How much does Suheldev know? What are his sources of information about the Turks? Does he know any other Turk besides me?*

'Which general is this?' asked Govardhan.

'The Turkic commander-in-chief in India, General Salar Maqsud.' Saying this, Suheldev looked towards Aslan. 'Am I right, my friend?'

The name cut much closer to Aslan's heart than Suheldev realised. Admirably, Aslan kept the shock and surprise off his face.

Chapter 18

The scout raised his right arm, his fist clenched tight. The signal to stop. Abdul and Govardhan, who were directly behind him, immediately halted, gesturing to the others behind them to follow suit.

It had been a few weeks since Aslan had left in search of his Sufi path. Suheldev had recovered almost completely from his injuries. He could ride out now. And he had decided that they had spent enough time in one place. While the bulk of the Turkic armies were moving back out to Ghazni, many Turks still infested the countryside. Staying in one place for too long, even now, was still a risky proposition for Suheldev's band. Therefore, the prince had ordered that they ride out to another village that was a secure base for them. One that was a few days' ride away. His entire brigade was with him.

Suheldev goaded his horse and ambled up to Abdul and Govardhan. He gestured, raising his right palm upwards, the thumb and forefinger lying flat while the other three fingers curved upwards. *What is it?*

Govardhan put a finger to his lips, then jerked his thumb at the scout. *We need to be quiet. He's seen something.*

The group was travelling through a rough track in the forest. The path opened up into a clearing. The scout was at the very edge of the path, peering through the dense vegetation towards the clearing.

Suheldev rode up to the scout, taking care not to make any noise. After a moment's hesitation, Abdul and Govardhan followed. As Suheldev approached, the scout nodded at him, then pointed towards the clearing.

Two young monks in ragged clothing were sitting there. On the ground. They looked tired. Haggard. Hungry. Defeated by fate and the elements.

They were surrounded by four men, all of whom held swords. The four ruffians wore shabby, mismatched clothing. And had long unkempt hair and thick beards. The feral smell that emanated from them made clear that they hadn't bathed in weeks. Their facial features very obviously showed that they were of Turkic origin. Perhaps they were deserters from the Ghazni army.

One of the monks held a thick wooden staff. The other was unarmed, though an old bow that seemed to be on the verge of falling apart lay on the ground by his side.

'I have already told you … we have nothing of any value,' said the monk with the staff. 'You should leave.'

'We'll give the orders here,' said one of the four Turks. 'Take off your clothes.'

'You're making a big mistake,' warned the monk.

The bandit guffawed. 'Let's see. There are four of us fighting men versus two of you weepy little non-violent wimps. We have weapons, you have toys. And we're the ones making a mistake?'

'Yes,' said the monk calmly. 'You're heavily outweighed. And I have told you before, we are not hiding any gold under our clothes.'

'That young fool is going to get himself and his friend killed,' hissed Govardhan. 'Should we step in?'

'In a moment,' whispered Suheldev. He was intrigued by the quiet confidence of the young Buddhist monk.

'Last warning ... Do what you've been told ...' said the leader of the bandit Turks, raising his sword threateningly, ' ... or I'll send you both to meet the pagan lotus feet you people love so much.'

The monk moved so fast that Suheldev and his companions barely registered a blur of motion. He jabbed his staff hard into the leader's stomach. The air was knocked out of the man in an explosive whoosh. As he folded over from the impact, the monk brought the staff up, straight into the man's descending jaw. There was a clicking sound that reverberated throughout the clearing and the man collapsed, out cold even before he hit the ground.

The other bandits froze momentarily, then let out a roar of anger as they charged at the monk. He struck again with the staff, this time making a low, sweeping motion. One of the Turks suddenly found his legs swept out from under him. He cried out in surprise as he fell heavily on the back of his head. And lay there on the ground. Unconscious.

The third man raised his sword and brought it down straight at the monk's head, trying to split his skull. The monk swiftly brought his staff up horizontally and blocked the blow. The force of the Turk's swing wedged the sword into the staff. Even as he grunted in frustration and tried to pull his sword loose, the monk simply let go of the staff. The Turk was caught off balance and lurched forward. The monk quickly swung his hand up in a Kalaripayattu chop. The blow to the neck knocked the Turk senseless.

The fourth Turk had been trying to get behind the monk. The monk, through all the fighting till now, was not blind to his peripheral vision. He swivelled around at a demonic pace. The Turk swung hard at the monk's neck, attempting to behead him. Only, his target was no longer there. The bandit gaped as he realised that the monk had bent backwards till his back was almost parallel to the ground. The sword had passed harmlessly over him.

'By the great Lord Mahadev …' whispered Suheldev, awed by the sheer brilliance of the fighting talent on display.

Before the Turkic bandit could control the swing and try another strike, the monk straightened up and struck with an open palm into his opponent's solar plexus. With the full momentum of the monk's rebounding back behind it, the blow had the effect of a coiled spring being let loose. The bandit fell backwards and landed with a hard thud. He lay on the ground, gasping for breath like a stranded fish.

The second bandit, who had been knocked off his feet and had momentarily blacked out, had regained his senses. He reached for his sword, which was lying on the ground next to him. Then he froze as an arrow swooped into the ground barely an inch from the sword.

'The next one will be through your wrist,' warned the second monk, who already had another arrow mounted on the bow.

'Don't shoot,' croaked the man, hastily withdrawing his hand.

'Wise choice,' said the second monk. Then he raised his voice. 'And those of you behind the trees … Come out … Slowly … Keep your hands where I can see them.'

Suheldev and his friends looked at each other, startled. Then Suheldev threw back his head and laughed. Still chuckling, he urged his horse into the clearing.

'Bravo!' said Suheldev to the monk who had single-handedly demolished four men without even breaking a sweat. 'Bravo!'

A few of Suheldev's men immediately dismounted and began tying up the Turkic bandits.

'And who might you be?' growled the monk with the staff.

'Me? I'm just someone who appreciates good warriors. But who are you? Where are you going? Where are you coming from?'

'We've come a long way, from a village near Purushpura,' said the archer monk. His companion scowled at him, irritated that he had divulged this information to strangers.

'Are you monks from the famous Buddhist monastery there?' asked Abdul.

Both monks immediately turned to stare at him. They didn't say anything. But the answer was obvious in their expressions.

Abdul continued in a gentle voice. 'We had heard news of its destruction some time back. We had also heard that … I mean … that the abbot …'

'Yes …' whispered the monk with the bow, the pain in his voice crystal clear. 'The abbot died. He died trying to save us … He was … We heard that he was still alive when they put him to flames …'

'Bastards,' growled Abdul. 'Attacking defenceless men in this manner. This is against the rules of Allah.'

The Buddhist monk's expression changed immediately. 'You are a Muslim?'

Suheldev answered for Abdul. 'He is an Indian first. Just like you.'

The monks remained silent.

Abdul's tone remained polite. Concerned. 'Are you the only survivors?'

The monk with the bow spoke up. 'Eleven of us made it out of the monastery. One died on the way here. The other eight are old men who joined various monasteries along the route. But the two of us didn't. Because it is not water but blood that flows in our veins. The old monks tried to tell us that revenge is a fire that consumes the person who nurtures it. They advised us to cultivate forgiveness. But I am no saint. I want vengeance. I burn for vengeance. I will destroy the monsters who killed our great abbot.'

'But are you actually willing to kill?' asked Suheldev. 'I was told that you monks believe that any violence is a sin. Won't killing someone come in the way of your *moksha*, your *salvation*?'

The monk's eyes were burning with anger. '*Moksha* can wait. Evil must be stopped first.'

'And it will be stopped. I swear by the name of Lord Shiva and Lord Buddha. Join me. Join my tribe of warriors. And I promise you that we will avenge the dishonour done to Lord Buddha. We will avenge the crimes done upon your monastery. We will avenge your abbot.'

The monk with the staff stared at Suheldev, genuine curiosity in his voice as he spoke. 'Who are you?'

'I am Suheldev of Shravasti.'

Both the monks immediately held their breath. Who hadn't heard of Suheldev? The tormentor of the Turks. They dropped their weapons and went down on their knees.

One of the monks spoke up. Loudly and clearly. So that even the Divine could bear witness. 'We pledge our loyalty to you, great prince. We swear on the name of the great Buddha.'

Suheldev dismounted from his horse, walked up to the monks and pulled them up. 'And I, Suheldev of Shravasti, pledge my loyalty to you. We will fight like brothers. We will defeat the foreign horde that defiles our land.'

The monks folded their hands together in respect.

'What do I call you both?' asked Suheldev.

The monk who had fought with the staff spoke up. 'My name is Ashvaghosh and this is my friend Sanghamani.'

'Which part of India are you from originally?'

'I am from Bengal,' said Sanghamani, 'and Ashvaghosh is from Burma.'

'Well, Ashvaghosh and Sanghamani, we have extra horses. You can ride with us. But first …' Suheldev stopped speaking and pointed at the four Turks kneeling in the distance, hands and legs tied, guarded by his men.

One of Suheldev's men walked up and offered two swords to the monks. Ashvaghosh and Sanghamani seemed to hesitate.

Speaking of killing is much easier than doing the actual killing itself.

Suheldev spoke firmly, but without any harshness. 'We fight enemies and death every day. Our band survives because we will kill to protect each other. I need to know that the two of you will not hesitate to do what must be done, when lives are at stake.'

Sanghamani took the sword that was being offered to him, but he didn't unsheathe it from its scabbard. Ashvaghosh hesitated to even hold the sword.

Suheldev spoke up once again. 'Don't see it as killing four Turks. In fact, see it as you saving countless Indians who would be killed by these murderers in the future. It is true when they say *ahimsa parmo dharma*. That non-violence is the greatest dharma. But they also say *dharma hinsa thathaiv cha*.'

Violence that protects dharma is justified.

'Protecting your countrymen is *dharma*. Fighting for your motherland is *dharma*.'

Ashvaghosh and Sanghamani unsheathed the swords.

They did what needed to be done.

Chapter 19

'Oh, come on! You're going to have to do a lot better than that if you're on my team.'

Toshani was glaring at Suheldev and Govardhan, who studiously looked down. Having spent the last few years in almost constant battle, Suheldev's men were getting restless now that the Turkic forces had largely withdrawn. So, the prince had decided to organise some martial games in order to occupy their minds, boost their morale and strengthen their camaraderie.

The very first event was an archery contest, in which the two teams were led by Sanghamani and Toshani, respectively. Toshani had shot superbly, drawing gasps of appreciation from the assembled spectators. But both Suheldev and Govardhan had turned in sub-par performances, leading to their team being routed. The very competitive Toshani was not amused, and was giving both men a piece of her mind, dismissing their feeble protests that it was just a game.

'Both of you are supposed to be trained warriors. Weren't you ever taught how to use the bow?'

Suheldev cleared his throat sheepishly. 'It isn't really my favourite weapon. I prefer to do my killing up-close.'

'Me too,' chimed in Govardhan.

Toshani clicked her tongue in disgust. 'I could kill both of you a dozen times before you ever got close enough to lay a finger on me. Come on now, let's head off for some practice. The games will have to carry on without the two of you for a while.'

Suheldev and Govardhan exchanged glances, but they already knew Toshani well enough to realise that it was pointless trying to argue with her once she had made up her mind. They quietly followed her to a field nearby that served as an improvised archery range.

Abdul noticed them go and nodded at some of the men. Five of them immediately began tailing the trio at a discreet distance. Even in seemingly peaceful times, Abdul insisted on security protocols being rigidly adhered to.

'If the Turks could only see me now, they wouldn't fear me at all,' whispered Suheldev to Govardhan. 'Bullied by a chit of a girl.'

The big warrior winked back at his friend.

'I heard that,' snapped Toshani.

The two men hastily subsided into silence.

'Right, show me how you shoot,' said Toshani once they reached the range. 'You first,' she told Suheldev, pointing at the target, a scarecrow about a hundred and fifty metres away.

Suheldev nodded and carefully shot an arrow that grazed the scarecrow's thigh before dropping into the field beyond.

'Not bad, eh?' he beamed, turning towards Toshani. His expression faltered as he saw her glaring at him, stone-faced. 'Come on! It's a hundred and fifty metres away! I got the target, didn't I?'

'You do everything wrong,' said Toshani. 'It's a wonder you manage to get anywhere close to the target. You grip the bow too tightly. You don't pull the bowstring back far enough. Your angle of release is wrong. You spend too much time aiming, which causes your shoulders to tense up. You're not properly balanced on your feet. And your hand jerks when you release the arrow!'

'Did I do anything right?'

'Shut up!'

Suheldev fell silent.

'Again.'

Suheldev raised the bow once more. This time, Toshani stood behind Suheldev and held his arm as she demonstrated the correct form. Suheldev suddenly became acutely aware of her proximity. The feel of one of her hands on his wrist and the other on his shoulder, the slight pressure of her breasts on his back, her legs barely, tantalisingly touching his, her intoxicating fragrance …

'Did you hear a word of what I said?' asked Toshani angrily.

'Sorry … Sorry …'

'Great prince!' One of Suheldev's men came racing up.

Suheldev took a deep breath, trying to compose himself. Toshani stepped back.

'Yes?' asked Suheldev, his voice a little rougher than usual.

'Great prince, Gurudev is here to see you.'

A smile spread across Suheldev's face. 'Gurudev!' he said joyfully. Then he looked at Toshani. 'Uhh … we'll certainly practice again.'

— EⅡ ⅩⅤⅮ —

Abdul spotted him. A lone being, staring into the horizon as the orange sky announced the imminent setting of the sun. His tonsured head was bent low, chin resting on his right knee.

One arm wrapped around, just below his knee; the other lying next to his ready staff.

He's been doing this a lot of late, sighed Abdul. *Better find out what's on his mind before he makes it a habit to sit this exposed everywhere we go.*

Calmly, noiselessly, Abdul walked up to him and sat beside him. He said nothing. That was Abdul's gift: he instinctively knew what the other person needed to feel at ease. He waited.

The sky darkened further. It now looked pinkish. The Sun God was ending his work for the day in this land of India, and carrying His great energy further west.

Ashvaghosh broke the silence. 'Don't you ever struggle with your identity, Abdul? Don't you ever feel like you're stuck in this horrible place between two parts of you; you want to belong to both and yet you do not belong to either?'

Abdul looked at him. *By Allah, I forget sometimes that Ashvaghosh is, after all, only a boy.* He was careful not to let any sympathy show on his face.

'Yes … and no,' he said slowly, turning his gaze back to the far horizon that Ashvaghosh was staring into.

Abdul didn't explain further. He didn't ask the obvious question either. Questions at an inappropriate time usually put people on the defensive, getting their guards up.

'I always wonder how you do it …' said Ashvaghosh. '… Navigate that space between your brotherhood and your motherland … your religion and patriotism … Don't you ever feel frustrated … frustrated that you even need to choose, or put one before the other?'

Ashvaghosh now turned to face Abdul.

Abdul met his questioning gaze now. *Poor boy … He's really a tortured soul … His heart still can't justify the need for killing … Perhaps if he knew …*

But Abdul brushed that thought aside.

'Yes, it is frustrating. It is frustrating that some of my countrymen, a few of my friends included, have begun to think that Muslims are an intrinsically violent lot who are blinded and crazed by the teachings of their religion. It is frustrating that my loyalty to this land is questioned every now and then. Yes, it is very frustrating.'

Ashvaghosh nodded. This, he expected. 'Is that why you fight with such vehemence against your brothers, for the freedom of this country?'

'The Turks are not my brothers,' Abdul said tersely. 'Even if they are Muslims, they are not my brothers. The brotherhood is about being a family. Do you think the Turks actually behave like family? Tell me, who murders his family simply because his demands are not met? He's not a Muslim, he's just a power-hungry man wanting to have absolute control. Religion is the garb under which he does it. It makes for a good marketing pitch to get a following among those Muslims who are naïve enough to get carried away. For they don't think that these self-proclaimed "true followers" of the faith will lie to their brothers. Having said that, there are some "pragmatic people" too—non-Muslims included—who recognise that it is only about power. Many of them convert and side with the Turks, not because of "faith", but simply to be on the winning side. They hope that they can, maybe, even earn enough of the Turks' trust to have some power of their own. But that's the cruel joke. A power-hungry man is shrewd. He plays these "pragmatic people" to ensure he remains the sole decision-maker. He will always lay down the definitions, the rules; he'll change them on a whim and he'll expect full, unquestioning compliance. His followers will always be pawns. They will always be slaves, at his mercy, because that is the idea he relishes.'

'But how can he enslave his own brothers? How can they remain his pawns forever? Especially once ... I'm not saying it will happen ... but once, say, everyone decides to convert and become a Muslim? There will be nobody to oppress, no idol-worshippers to kill, right?' Ashvaghosh was curious.

'You're not listening carefully enough. The power-hungry Turk considers no one equal enough to be a brother. They're all slaves—"brother" is just a label that makes it a more palatable idea. As for whether an all-Muslim country will satiate his hunger? Of course not! This power-hungry man will not stop even when everybody converts. He will prey upon whichever section of Muslims he wants to, and he will get the social narrative to change around it to harass them. Do you think the Turks' all-Muslim homeland is peaceful? No! Now that all are Muslims in their homeland, they will raise the chant of "Who is a *true* Muslim?". Those they want to oppress will be accused of not being "true Muslims", which of course, they will present as the will of Allah. This game never stops.'

'But ... but one could argue that you are a pawn here in India too ... That you are not being asked to kill for a faith. Instead, you are being asked to kill for a nation.'

Abdul kept the smile off his face. *And the coin finally drops.*

'Answer me this, who controls the heavens?'

Ashvaghosh frowned. 'What does that have to do ...'

'Humour me for a little while ... Who controls the heavens?'

'God. Or the Universal Law. Basically, the Divine.'

Abdul smiled. 'Complicated answer. But I'll accept it. Now tell me this. Who controls the Earth that we live on. Who is the most supreme power here?'

'I … I don't know.'

'Think of it this way. When any man is in trouble, is in pain, is close to death, who does he cry out for?'

'His mother …'

Abdul touched Ashvaghosh's shoulder. 'Your mother is there for you, even when she isn't physically present. Just crying out for her gives you strength. Gives you what you need to survive. The supreme power on this planet is the mother.'

Ashvaghosh remained silent.

'Lord Ram said that mother and motherland are greater than heaven. Prophet Mohammed said that heaven is at the feet of your mother. Who can love you as much as your mother can?'

Silence.

Abdul's voice shook with emotion. 'And some foreigner comes and tries to … to your own mother … If you don't fight for her then, if you don't fight for your own mother, then what kind of man are you?'

'But my religion preaches non-violence. It is wrong to …'

'Ashvaghosh, remember this—India will remain secure only if there are enough men who choose India over everything else. And I mean everything else. If I have to choose between my religion and India, I will choose India. Every. Single. Time. As long as there are enough Hindus, Jains, Buddhists, Muslims and Christians who think like that, our country will be safe.'

'But an eye for an eye makes the whole world blind. That's what my abbot taught me.'

'Ashvaghosh, if you are the only one who believes this philosophy then you will be the only one left blinded. And they aren't blinding you. They are blinding your mother. Non-violence has a place in a civilised society. Yes. But not when you are facing barbarians who kill for pleasure. Don't make a fetish out of non-violence. Remember, when you have to fight, then you have to fight.'

Ashvaghosh remained quiet. He looked down at the ground. In thought.

Abdul's voice was kind, gentle, as he spoke. 'Defending your mother, even if you have to do it with violence, will not get counted as bad *karma*.'

Ashvaghosh turned to Abdul. His eyes were moist. 'Perhaps you know what it's like to have a mother. I don't.'

Now was the right time.

'Your friend Sanghamani told me your life story. Apparently, it was narrated to him by one of the old masters who left the monastery with you. Ask your friend about how you came to live at the monastery. You are alive because your mother sacrificed her life to save yours. Because she did everything she could to protect you when you were a helpless little baby.' Abdul picked up some of the earth on the ground and dropped it into Ashvaghosh's hand. Then he pointed up at the sky. 'And now, she is up there, looking down at her grown-up son, demanding that you be a man and defend the mother of us all.'

Ashvaghosh started crying.

Abdul held Ashvaghosh's hand tight. 'Jai Maa Bhaarati!'

Glory to Mother India. Victory to Mother India.

'Jai Maa Bhaarati!'

Chapter 20

Suheldev dismounted his horse and walked briskly towards his basic military tent. A guard immediately drew the curtain aside as he saluted smartly.

'Great prince, he's waiting inside for you.'

Suheldev patted the guard on his shoulder and smiled as he walked into the tent. A tall, grey-haired person stood quietly at the other end of the tent. The advancing years had caused his shoulders to droop somewhat, but he had remained slim and dignified.

'Gurudev!' said Suheldev joyfully. He rushed over to Kashinath and bent to touch his feet with respect.

Kashinath pulled Suheldev up and engulfed him in a huge bear hug. 'My prince ...'

Suheldev smiled, holding his guru tight.

'My prince, your brother Malladev would be so proud of you. So proud of what you have become. You know, back home in Shravasti, children play with toy swords and pretend to be you, fighting the soldiers of Ghazni and their wretched allies.'

'I didn't do it all by myself, Gurudev. I have a band of heroic warriors who are as dedicated to our land as I am. And I have the quiet support of thousands of common people who provide us with all we need. We could never have survived for so long without their help. The kings of Manohargarh,

Kannauj and other kingdoms may have allied with Ghazni, but their people have assisted us. They are true patriots. I even have some friends in the courts of these kingdoms that are officially our enemies!'

Kashinath laughed softly. 'I would love to get to know these friends of yours someday … What cannot be denied though is that you have lit a fire across the land. And with Lord Shiva and Maa Bhaarati's blessings, this fire will consume the Turks.'

'Om Namah Shivaya,' whispered Suheldev, holding the miniature Shiva Linga pendant tied around his neck. 'Jai Maa Bhaarati.'

Kashinath's eyes teared up as he looked at the man before him. This little prince had been an imp of a child. Happy-go-lucky by nature and with a complete disregard for rules, this young boy was hardly who Kashinath had imagined would be the one chosen to take on the responsibility of defeating the Turks. But who could say what is planned in the minds of Time and Lord Shiva? He patted the young prince's shoulder and whispered, 'Om Namah Shivaya. Jai Maa Bhaarati.'

Suheldev stepped back, folded his hands together into a namaste and said, 'I am so sorry to be direct, Gurudev, but I don't think that you came all this way here just to compliment me and my men. I can make out that there is some important news. What is it?'

Kashinath sighed. It was clear that he was controlling his emotions. Like any good minister should. 'It is time for you to come home, Prince …'

'What happened?'

'It's your father …'

Suheldev immediately held Kashinath's arms, his face creased with worry. 'What happened?'

'It's cancer. It has struck suddenly. It has grown too quickly ...'

Suheldev was too stunned to react. He had met his father in secret just a few months ago. He had seemed completely fit and healthy.

Kashinath's voice was gentle. 'You need to return to Shravasti immediately. The throne cannot be left ...'

Wisely, Kashinath did not let the rest of the words escape his mouth. He knew that, in the last month, when it became obvious to Mangaldhwaj that his days were coming to an end, urgent messages had been sent to several kingdoms in the area. Many carried by Kashinath himself. Mangaldhwaj had reached out to those kingdoms who were willing to form a confederacy under Shravasti's leadership. And who better to lead that united army than the one man who had heroically stood up to the might of Ghazni all these years? Suheldev.

But Kashinath didn't say any of this to Suheldev. Now was not the right time. Let the son grieve for his father first. Later, the prince would be told of the duties he had to fulfil for the king.

— EⅢ Ӿらⴖ⫯Ⴢ —

It had been a few days since Suheldev had received word of his father's illness. He had set out with his followers early the next day itself. En route to Shravasti, Suheldev and his band had camped a short distance from a lake.

The temporary campsite had been well-selected. While they were close enough to a town to replenish supplies, they weren't so close that they would receive unwelcome visitors. When they were in territories outside of their direct control, anonymity and discretion were their allies. The site had a water-source close by. There was open land between the forest line and the camp, to prevent any surprise attacks. But for added precaution, sentries had been posted at key locations. There was open ground on the other side of the camp to make a rapid retreat, if necessary. Since this was a temporary camp, things had not been completely unpacked. Weapons, money and important documents remained tied within bags fixed on horses and bulls, so that they did not lose key resources in a quick escape. Those horses and bulls were, of course, guarded round the clock by sentries.

Suheldev was wary and cautious when necessary. And this caution had ensured that he had lost very few men in the last few years when he had been battling and harassing the Turks.

'It is a beautiful place,' said Govardhan.

He and Suheldev were sitting by themselves, eating their dinner. They had walked a little away from the camp. Closer to the lake. Enjoying the beauty of the surroundings as the sun set slowly over the horizon. Their weapons were unsheathed and placed next to them. Ready to use in case of an attack.

A true warrior never gets so lost in beauty that he forgets his combat training. A true warrior is always ready for battle.

Suheldev remained silent.

Govardhan touched Suheldev's shoulder sympathetically. 'Are you alright, my friend? Do you want to …'

Suheldev shook his head. 'Talking about this will not help me. It will only make me sadder. Let's talk about something else.'

Govardhan nodded. *No point talking about things that we can't do anything about. Best to sweep it under the carpet and focus on something else. He can think about his father when he meets him.*

Govardhan changed the subject. 'Do you know that this beautiful place was liked a lot by the Sufis as well?'

Suheldev smiled. 'Yes ... Sad that the Sufis have moved away. The Turks didn't just torture the Hindus. They tortured the Sufis too.'

A voice was heard from behind them. 'Yes, they called them impure Muslims.'

Suheldev and Govardhan turned around rapidly. Govardhan, almost instinctively, reached for his sword.

'Relax, Govardhan,' smiled Kashinath genially. 'I am a friend.'

Suheldev touched Kashinath's feet in respect as he said wryly, 'A friend whose footsteps are almost impossible to hear.'

Kashinath laughed softly as he sat down next to Suheldev. He refused the offer of food from Govardhan. 'I have eaten already.'

Govardhan resumed eating. Between gulps he asked, 'So, why do the Turks hate the Sufis so much?'

'That is a good question,' said Kashinath. 'One of the problems with our modern Indian rulers is that they have lost the curiosity that possessed our ancestors. Only when you are curious will you try to understand other ways of life. Especially of those who are your enemies. For, if you don't understand your enemies, how can you defeat them? Even more importantly, unless you are curious about and understand your own society as well, how will you know how to mitigate your own weaknesses and increase your own strengths?'

Suheldev nodded. 'Know yourself. And know your opponents.'

Kashinath patted Suheldev's shoulder and smiled. 'So you do remember some of my teachings.'

'I remember *all* your teachings, Gurudev,' said Suheldev softly, before putting some more food into his mouth.

'But you still haven't answered my question, Gurudev,' said Govardhan. 'Why do the Turks hate the Sufis so much?'

'Every community, every way of life, has some strengths and has some weaknesses. This is true of the Islam of the Turks and the Hinduism of us Indians.'

'That still doesn't answer my—'

'Patience, patience, my warrior friend,' smiled Kashinath, patting Govardhan's hand. 'Let me finish my point. The strength of the Islam of the Turks is that it is socially inclusive, but its weakness is that it is theologically intolerant. On the other hand, the Hinduism of us Indians is theologically inclusive and liberal, while socially we are intolerant.'

'Woah …' said Govardhan, pulling back, his eyes wide open, taking a deep breath. 'Too many big words. You lost me.'

Kashinath leaned back and guffawed loudly.

'Gurudev, I am an uncomplicated warrior,' said Govardhan, laughing along. 'Make your words simple, please!'

'Alright, alright. When I say theological, I mean how we approach different belief systems in God. When I say social, I mean our attitude to different groups, classes and communities who practice our own religion. So, when I say the Turks are socially inclusive, I mean that, at least theoretically, all Turks who practice Islam are believed to be equal before their God. Because of that, there is tremendous unity and strength of purpose within their community. They will fight as one against their enemies.'

'And their weakness?'

'Their weakness is that they are theologically intolerant. They believe that their God is the *only* true God and that all other Gods are false. They believe that their religion is the *only* true religion. And there is a hierarchy in the way Turkic Muslims treat other religions. Followers of Christianity and Judaism can be allowed to live, but they must do so as subordinate people called *dhimmis*. But all other religions, especially those of idol-worshippers, are considered completely sinful. That's why, not just Hindu temples in India, but also Zoroastrian fire temples in Persia, Buddhist viharas in their own Turkic homeland or in China, are all to be destroyed ...'

'So that is their weakness,' said Suheldev.

'Exactly. If you go around the world picking fights with everyone who disagrees with you, it's only a matter of time before everyone will ally together to fight you. That's the problem with their theological intolerance. They make enemies out of everybody. This is precisely the issue that the Sufis will solve.'

'How so?' asked Govardhan.

'I'll come to that in a minute,' said Kashinath. 'But before that, we must understand the strengths and weaknesses of today's Hinduism as well. Theologically, Hinduism is very liberal. Because we are polytheistic and believe in idol-worshipping, we don't have a problem with anyone believing in a different God. We see God in everything, so it's a very easy step for us to see the presence of God in Jesus Christ of the Christians as well. Or to worship Allah of the Muslims too. And by doing so, we don't lose our Hindu religion either. Have you ever heard of a Hindu king attacking and breaking anyone else's temple or place of worship?'

Govardhan shook his head. 'No. Never.'

'Exactly. It is very, very rare. Almost unheard of. Why is that? Because we Hindus believe that there is Divine in everything. So, breaking someone else's place of worship is a sin. In fact, there are times when a Hindu king defeats another Hindu kingdom, and then goes to the defeated king's main temple and steals the royal idol there. Then that royal idol is brought, with respect, to the victor king's personal temple and consecrated there. Why does a winning king do that? Because he believes that, by doing so, he will gain the blessings of the defeated king's God as well. In fact, in Hinduism, we have no problem with having Goddesses too, something that cannot be allowed in the Islam of the Turks.'

'And our weakness is our caste system,' said Govardhan, stating the obvious.

'Yes,' said Kashinath. 'The Turks may have oppressed others. But we have oppressed our own. We have divided our own people using this birth-based caste system. That is our sin. And as a result of this caste system, we are almost constantly fighting each other. Internally divided, we are easy prey for foreign invaders. There was a time when India was considered an unconquerable land. And that was a time when we did not practice the evil caste system that exists today. That is not a coincidence. Because we hadn't divided ourselves into different communities and castes based on birth, it was almost impossible for any foreigner to conquer us. Have you heard of Alexander?'

'No,' said Govardhan. 'Who is he?'

'Among the Europeans and the Persians, he is considered the greatest conqueror in history. For us Indians, though, he is a nobody. Because he was fought to a standstill by some minor kings in western Punjab, just inside India's borders. He hadn't even battled the Nandas, our main Indian empire at the time, and yet had to retreat in ignominy. It was almost impossible to defeat us in the past. But now that we have divided ourselves along different castes, foreigners just pick us off one by one. We have become so easy to conquer.'

Suheldev took a deep breath and stared at the lake, processing what Kashinath had said. 'We have to solve our social problem. And the Muslims have to solve their theological problem.'

Kashinath frowned. 'Not all Muslims. Indian Muslims do not have the problem that the Turks have. They are theologically liberal. Does Abdul hate idols? Does Iqbal kill cows just to spite Hindus?'

Suheldev shook his head. *No.*

'Indian Muslims, are, in many ways, like the Indian Hindus. They have no problem respecting the religions and Gods of others. And Indian Muslims too are divided along caste lines. What I was speaking about is a problem for the Islam of the Turks. And that of the Arabs as well. And this theological intolerance is what the Sufis will solve.'

'How so?' asked Govardhan.

'With a very simple change. The Sufis are saying that their religion, Islam, is the true religion *for them*. And that my religion, Hinduism, is the true religion *for me*. They aren't changing their belief in the truth of their faith. They are just opening the space for people of other faiths to have their own truths as well. Apparently, it is said amongst them that there is no compulsion in religion. As of now, there are very few Muslims in India. And the way of the Turks will never work at increasing the number of Muslims here. Because attacking our country's way of life only makes the Hindus more angry and rebellious; and we are by nature a very rebellious people. But mark my words, if Islam ever becomes a big religion in India, it will be because of the Sufis. Their openness and liberalism will bring down the defences of the Hindus. The Turks are wrong if they think they can keep destroying our temples, insulting our faith, and we will surrender. We will never surrender that way. In fact, they may just unite us in our hatred for them. But many Indians may surrender to the love of the Sufis.'

'The Sufis are doing good work for their religion, a religion based on faith and compliance,' said Suheldev. 'But I do not want Hinduism to die. It is one of the few ancient cultures that still survives till today. Most other major idol-worshipping cultures, like Rome, Greece and Egypt, have been wiped out. Even Zoroastrianism is almost dead in its ancient homeland of Persia. Some people call all our ancient cultures pagan. It's supposed to be an insult. If Hinduism dies, the world loses the last major connection with the ancient way, religions based on wisdom and the spirit of questioning. We cannot allow that. And therefore, we have to solve our social problem. We have to destroy the caste system that divides us, and causes such oppression and pain.'

'Precisely,' said Kashinath. 'We need reformers who will annihilate the caste system based on birth. And take us back to our original ancient way.'

Govardhan reached across and held Suheldev's hand. 'This man will be our reformer. Centuries from now, they will recall his name. And they will use Suheldev's example to teach all of us Hindus that if we want our faith to survive, if we want to honour our great ancestors, if we are truly patriotic, then we must destroy the birth-based caste system.'

Chapter 21

Queen Vijayalakshmi stared at her son for a long time, too overcome to speak. Holding his shoulders. Using him for support. Giving him support.

The queen and the prince were alone in her chambers. Normally, the return of their prince, a hero of the Resistance, should have led to wild celebrations in Shravasti. But everyone knew how ill their king Mangaldhwaj was. Everyone knew how rapidly the disease had grown. There was a pall of gloom that had descended over the city. Suheldev had ridden in quietly, at the head of his band. While his people were housed in different rooms in the palace, he had come immediately to his mother's private chambers.

A solitary tear escaped Vijayalakshmi's battle-hardened, strong eyes. Like the tiniest of openings in the veneer of the mighty Goddess Shakti, showing that she, too, was vulnerable. She embraced Suheldev tightly. 'My son ...'

'*Maa* ...'

They held each other in silence. Grieving in stillness for the man they both loved. Her husband. His father.

Suheldev pulled back. In some tiny corner of his heart, he still held hope.

Hope. The greatest source of human strength. And the greatest source of human grief.

'How … Is there … The doctors …'

Vijayalakshmi gazed at her son. She didn't say anything. At least, not with her mouth. But her eyes said it all.

Suheldev started crying.

— EJI ЖЗ∩Ċ∆ —

Many courtiers, relatives and others waited outside the palace chambers that had been converted into the king's hospice. Like a weakened pride waiting for the death of an aged, once-magnificent lion.

They parted as Suheldev appeared. Led by his mother. Giving them way to the chambers. All of them tried to catch Suheldev's attention as he walked forward. Trying to show sympathy and concern. Many genuine. Some not. Suheldev was going to be the king soon. Some wanted to build bridges. But the prince ignored all of them.

The curtain was pulled aside. Suheldev took a deep breath and steeled himself.

Vijayalakshmi, dignified and strong, held her son's hand. 'He has changed since you saw him last …'

Suheldev nodded and followed his mother into his father's chamber. He stepped through the doorway, to find many physicians and his guru Kashinath gathered around the bed. They moved aside and Suheldev saw his father.

He stopped. Rooted to his spot in stunned disbelief.

The figure lying on the bed was a pale shadow of the hulking warrior that Suheldev remembered. One he had seen just a few months ago. Mangaldhwaj had become so skeletal that the skin seemed to be stretched tight against his bones. The outline of his skull seemed faintly visible. He tried to smile when he saw Suheldev, but it turned into a grimace as a cough shook his emaciated frame.

The prince rushed to Mangaldhwaj's bed and went down on his knees beside it.

'*Baba*,' whispered Suheldev.

Mangaldhwaj raised a claw-like hand and feebly patted his son's head. Even that little effort seemed to exhaust him and his hand fell back to the bed.

Suheldev gently picked up his father's hand, trying not to wince at how thin it had become. Very carefully, he brought it to his lips and kissed it tenderly.

With an effort, Mangaldhwaj spoke. It was barely a whisper. 'Good you came … I can die in peace …'

'Don't talk of dying, *baba*,' said Suheldev, his voice soft and grief-stricken. 'You're going to be fine.'

Mangaldhwaj smiled faintly. 'You never were a good liar … At least, not to me …'

Suheldev remained silent. Holding his father's hand. Drawing strength from a withered limb attached to a mighty soul.

'Still … at least I outlived that monster Mahmud …' Mangaldhwaj started to laugh, but it turned into a rasping cough.

'Rest now, *baba*. We'll talk tomorrow.'

Mangaldhwaj shook his head. He had a lot to say. And he didn't know how much time he had. 'They will return … Trust me … The Turks … will return.'

Suheldev nodded. Agreeing with Mangaldhwaj. He could see what a tremendous effort it was for his father to speak. He did not want to prolong the conversation further and weaken his father even more.

Mangaldhwaj looked at Kashinath, who rushed to the bedside immediately. The king turned towards his son again.

'I have made plans to …' said Mangaldhwaj. ' … Gurudev knows everything … Speak to him …'

Suheldev looked briefly at Kashinath and then turned back to his father. 'Yes, *baba*. I will speak with Gurudev.'

Mangaldhwaj took a deep breath. Like it was his final effort. He held his son's hand with surprising strength, his eyes suddenly blazing, his face fierce. 'My son … keep fighting … Never surrender … Fight them wherever you find them … Fight them to the end … Even if you are the last man standing … keep fighting … keep fighting … Never surrender … Those foreign bastards … will not rule our motherland … They will not … defile—'

Mangaldhwaj's words were cut short by a sharp burst of coughing. Thick, viscous sputum oozed out of the edge of his mouth. A physician rushed forward to try to wipe it away. But Mangaldhwaj turned his face. And stared at Suheldev again. Into his son's eyes. Into his son's soul.

'You will keep fighting … Promise me …'

'I promise you, *baba*. I promise you …'

Mangaldhwaj took another deep breath. 'Jai Maa Bhaarati.'

And he shut his eyes. Within seconds, he was asleep. Only the slight rise and fall of his chest indicated that he was still alive.

— EJ ᵾᴣᴧᴄᴧ —

The royal physicians stayed close to Mangaldhwaj. Tracking his pulse regularly. Testing the consistency of his breathing. Administering medicines methodically when required. Nobody knew how long it would be. Patients had, sometimes, survived in this state for months as well.

Suheldev and Vijayalakshmi sat at a distance. Looking at the king lying on the bed.

Sometimes they sat in silence. Sometimes they spoke to each other, reminiscing about things they had done with Mangaldhwaj. Finding comfort in the memories of the past is wise, when the future is too despairing to think about.

'He would have loved to see you get married,' Vijayalakshmi said with a sigh.

Suheldev looked at his mother. But did not say anything.

'No, it's not just about you having a son and producing an heir to the throne,' continued the queen.

'I know,' said Suheldev. 'I have been speaking to Gurudev. I know the alliances that *baba* has struck with various kingdoms. To form a confederacy, with Shravasti at the head. And I guess I will need to get married to princesses in some of these kingdoms to cement the alliances.'

'No, it's not that either. That was important for Mangaldhwaj too, but it wasn't the only thing. He genuinely wanted you to find someone who would complete your life. Who would make you happy.'

Suheldev smiled slightly and looked at his father. He said softly, 'Who wouldn't want what you and *baba* have, *maa*? It's not that I haven't thought of it. But, love can be a distraction. Especially in times like this, when our country and culture are at stake, I guess leaders don't have the luxury of a personal life.'

Vijayalakshmi held her son's hand. 'Wrong. In fact, it is especially at times like this that a leader needs love in his life. It is one of the things that will keep you connected. That will keep you human.'

Suheldev remained silent.

'The biggest fear in fighting a monster is not that one will lose to him. The biggest fear, in fact, is that in fighting the monster, we ourselves will become like the monster. We will certainly defeat the Turks. I believe that. But, in defeating the Turks, if we become like them, if we lose our innate liberalism and open-mindedness, then what is the point of winning?'

'But their ruthlessness can only be fought with our ruthlessness. How can we not change when we fight them? It's almost as impossible as saying that we can cut off their heads without some specks of their blood falling on us.'

'Some specks of their blood will fall on us. Yes. But it can be cleaned. Love is that cleanser. If you keep your heart filled with love, then you will not change. And if the leader doesn't change, hopefully, the people won't either.'

Suheldev chose silence once again.

'I have been watching her. She is a good woman. Marry her.'

Suheldev turned to his mother in surprise. He didn't know how to react.

'I am your mother. I can see your heart. And your father would have said the same thing that I am telling you. You have our blessings. Marry Toshani.'

Suheldev smiled as some tears slipped out of his eyes. He put his arms around his mother and rested his head on her shoulder.

Chapter 22

The doorman's voice was loud and clear. 'Great king of Shravasti, a visitor is requesting a private meeting.'

Suheldev twitched, feeling a pang of discomfort. Even guilt. Like he didn't deserve the title.

It had been a few weeks since Mangaldhwaj's death. The old king's debilitated body simply could not fight the cancer anymore. An ordinary son is allowed the privilege of grieving for a long time over the loss of a beloved father. But an unfortunate prince is not even given the time to be with himself.

Many ceremonies had been conducted over the last few weeks. The cremation of Mangaldhwaj, with the honours due to a ruler. The quiet puja, in recognition of Suheldev as king, for the throne could not be allowed to remain empty. The recognition of diplomats from across the kingdoms that had pledged loyalty to Shravasti. The confederacy was forming. Mangaldhwaj's dream was taking shape.

But now, the time had come to organise a ceremonial coronation. Suheldev had decided that it would not be an ostentatious affair. But he did send out invitations to all the kings and queens in the region, including those who were not a part of the Shravasti-led confederacy. Ajitpal of Kannauj had, unsurprisingly, declined. But had sent his minister, Vrishabh, to represent him.

With the coronation ceremony concluded, Suheldev had retired to his chambers with his inner circle. However, within minutes, there were visitors lining up to meet him.

Kashinath, Abdul, Govardhan and Toshani were the only ones in the room with Suheldev. The king's guru looked at the hourglass.

'You don't have much time,' said Kashinath. 'There are already some other people waiting to meet you, and right after that, it will be time for the special dinner you are hosting, My Lord.'

Suheldev wrinkled his nose. 'How many times do I tell you, Gurudev, even if I am the king, I am not your lord. Please don't call me that.'

Kashinath put his hands together into a namaste. 'I will not insult the throne of Shravasti by not referring to its occupant with respect. Now, let's not waste time on an unnecessary argument. Why don't you meet your visitor, and then we can proceed to your other engagements?'

Suheldev sighed. 'Alright. Why don't all of you go get ready? I'll meet you in a bit.' He turned to the doorman. 'Who is the visitor?'

'Lord Vrishabh, the prime minister of Kannauj, Your Highness.'

Suheldev froze. His fists clenched tight. The ruler of Kannauj had always thought of Suheldev as a subaltern-caste upstart. And he had also sided with Ghazni in a few battles.

'My Lord,' said Kashinath softly. 'At least the prime minister has come. They have not insulted us by missing the coronation completely.'

Suheldev remained silent. Clearly unhappy.

'Suheldev,' said Toshani, 'regardless of how others behave, we must treat a guest with honour. That is *dharma*.'

Suheldev nodded. 'All of you leave. I will handle him.'

Abdul felt the need to intervene. 'Listen to me, great king—'

He was cut short by Suheldev. 'All of you, please leave. I will handle this.'

Kashinath looked at the rest, signalling clearly that they must obey. Then he bowed and left the chambers. The others followed, Toshani leaving last.

Soon, the prime minister of Kannauj was led into the room.

Vrishabh's gait was slow and confident. His demeanour, stiff and unfriendly. He pulled his hands together into a namaste. 'Jai Shri Krishna.'

Glory to Lord Krishna.

'Jai Shri Krishna,' repeated Suheldev.

'Greetings, great king. Please accept my condolences on the death of your respected father. My master, Emperor Ajitpal, regrets that he could not personally attend the ceremony.'

'I'm sure he does,' said Suheldev dryly.

The king of Shravasti looked at the doormen and signalled for them to leave. They hesitated. To leave the king completely alone with the prime minister of an enemy kingdom was unorthodox. But they knew better than to question Suheldev. They quickly left the chambers.

Suheldev rose from his chair and stepped up to Vrishabh, towering over the diminutive Brahmin prime minister of the Kshatriya king of Kannauj.

Vrishabh, however, didn't step back. He looked up at Suheldev, a confident smile on his face, and whispered, 'How have you been doing, my friend?'

Suheldev smiled warmly and embraced Vrishabh. 'Very well, Vrishabh*ji*.'

Vrishabh looked at the closed door. And then back at

Suheldev. 'By the blessings of Lord Krishna, our secret alliance remains a secret.'

'It must … I never did get to thank you properly for all the help you sent me in my years in the forests.'

Vrishabh stepped back, continuing to hold Suheldev's arms. 'That was the very least I could have done. You were risking your life. Risking it all for our motherland.'

'Believe me, your help probably saved my life quite a few times.'

'I'm glad to hear that … And thank you for giving me the chance to serve my motherland. Serve it through you … I only wish I could have openly joined you.'

'You're a much bigger help to me and our motherland while serving in the court of Kannauj,' said Suheldev. 'Now, tell me, what is happening with King Ajitpal?'

'He's not happy about your becoming king, but he will not attack you alone. Not without the army of Ghazni to support him. He cannot take on your confederacy of twenty-one kings and chieftains all by himself.'

'Hmm.'

'The confederacy was a wise idea.'

'My father was always wise.'

'That he was … However, there is something you need to know.'

'What?' asked Suheldev, intrigued.

'You have a traitor in your ranks.'

— EJ H3JCA —

The gathering of twenty-one kings and chieftains rose to their feet as Suheldev entered the large hall. Suheldev had especially arranged to meet these twenty-one separately because they had agreed to Mangaldhwaj's suggestion to form an alliance, a confederacy, against the Turks.

Their small kingdoms and principalities had been carved out as the great imperial powers of North India had declined, giving way to many smaller states.

Suheldev greeted everyone with a namaste, then gestured that they should take their seats. He sat down on the simple throne at one end of the hall, with his aides standing around him.

'Thank you, great kings, for honouring me with your presence,' said Suheldev. 'My father had a vision. A vision that has come to fruition now. A vision that only when we are united, will we able to fight off foreign invaders like the barbarian Turks. I look around me and I see men whom I have admired all my life. Great sons of India, with the wisdom, strength and patriotism to do what must be done to protect our motherland. Jai Maa Bhaarati!'

The fervent cry was echoed throughout the hall. 'Jai Maa Bhaarati!'

'You agreed to be part of a confederacy led by my father. He was a great man and no one can ever truly replace him. But I will try my best to carry on his life's work and dream. And I intend to stick to the terms that had been agreed with my father. This confederacy will have only one aim: common defence against foreign invaders. We will not interfere in each other's internal affairs. The autonomy of each kingdom will always be respected.'

'Hear! Hear!'

'We will create a common army to fight the foreigners. Your internal police will remain independent.'

One of the kings asked Suheldev, 'When do you see the Turks returning?'

'They are fighting a civil war now. The snakes have given us time to prepare. But they will return. There is too much money in India. And they are poor compared to us. Whoever wins the civil war in Ghazni will need money to pay off his allies to buy loyalty. They will be back. We must not become complacent. We must use this time to prepare for war. Agreed?'

King Shankar, the ruler of Chatri and the oldest person in the room, stood up. Despite his advanced age, his voice was still firm and he commanded the respect of every person present at the conference. 'King Suheldev has spoken wisely. It is only a matter of time before the Turks return. If anyone can stop them, it is him. In the last few years, while the rest of us were living lives of luxury in our palaces, he was fighting the Turks and their lickspittles.' He turned towards Suheldev and bowed. 'Your father was not just a great visionary and a brave warrior, he was also a loyal friend to all oppressed people. He was the first to extend diplomatic recognition to our kingdom, at a time when everybody else shunned us. I had the privilege of considering him a brother. I would be honoured to call you my comrade-in-arms. I agree with your proposal. Let's create our own joint army. Long live King Suheldev!'

The others joined him one by one, till the whole hall resounded with their cheers. Suheldev stood up, folded his hands into a namaste, and, with humility, bowed his head. Then he raised his hand, gesturing for quiet.

'Thank you for your trust and support, great kings. I swear in the names of Lord Mahadev and Lord Ram, that I will never give you reason to regret it. I have some plans that I will announce in court tomorrow, but I wanted all of you to hear about them first.' He gestured first to Abdul and Govardhan. 'Based on my experience of fighting the Turks, I believe that, apart from the regular army, we should also create two corps of light cavalry, who will serve as scouts and guides and carry out surprise attacks. Abdul and Govardhan will raise and lead these corps, which will include many of the people who were in my band.' As Abdul and Govardhan bowed, Suheldev told them, 'Make sure that each of your men gets at least some training from the two Buddhist monks. Those skills will come in handy.' Next, Suheldev turned to Toshani. 'I have always believed that we need to encourage more women to join our armies. Our ancient militaries had many women warriors. They too have the same beating, patriotic heart that the menfolk have. Why should they not have the opportunity to defend our motherland? So, I plan to set up a volunteer regiment of women warriors. Toshani, you will command this regiment. We will call it the Maa Kali regiment!'

Toshani's face shone with delight. She bowed towards Suheldev and all the kings present.

'Moving on, it saddens me to tell you that there was a traitor in the court of Shravasti.' Suheldev clapped his hands. 'Bring him in.'

The assembly gasped as some guards roughly shoved a man into the room. A man they all recognised. His hands were tied and his face was battered and bruised. He looked around the room with frightened eyes.

Suheldev pointed at the prisoner. 'This wretch has huge land holdings and commanded three thousand soldiers. But he was not satisfied with that. He has been conspiring against all of us with King Ajitpal of Kannauj, under the instructions of the scoundrel from Ghazni, Salar Maqsud. I would never have suspected him, but a source whom I trust completely told me about him. When confronted, he confessed.'

'Mercy, My Lord! I served your father faithfully … Forgive my mistake … Mercy!'

Suheldev looked at him grimly. 'I can give my life for a friend. And I have no hesitation in taking the life of an enemy. You condemned yourself the day you decided to conspire against me with an enemy of our kingdom.' He gestured to the guards. 'Get him out of here.'

The man fell to the ground and began weeping loudly. The guards seized him by his arms and dragged him away, as he continued to plead for mercy. Every eye in the room followed him as he was hauled out.

Suheldev waited till the prisoner had been taken away, then resumed speaking. 'There will be no mercy for traitors, but out of respect for his service to my father, I will grant him a quick death. The traitor's property will be confiscated, and he will be stripped of his military rank.'

He looked around the room, making sure that the message he wanted to convey had registered. From the grim looks on everybody's faces, it was clear that it had.

'There is one last thing, great kings,' said Suheldev. 'I have read many of our ancient texts, our ancient stories. There is a tradition that was honoured by all our Gods. A tradition that we have forgotten. It is believed that when Lord Ram was preparing his army and his brothers for the final battle to establish his kingdom Meluha, he had done this. It is believed that Lady Sita, when she went to war, had done this. It is believed that when Lord Shiva, Lady Sati, and their sons, Lord Ganesh and Lord Karthik, would go to fight battles, they too would do this. It is believed that Lady Sati's sister, Lady Kali, joined them too. It is believed that everyone from Lord Parshu Ram to Lord Rudra, from Lady Mohini to Lord Krishna, would do this. It was a good tradition. A tradition that we have forgotten. A tradition that we don't honour anymore.'

The kings looked at each other. Surprised.

'There are traditions from the past that divide us. And there are traditions from the past that unite us. What we honour from our past will decide our future. The choice is ours.'

Every one of the kings present had the same question. *What tradition is King Suheldev speaking of?*

'As a country, we have chosen to divide ourselves. And by dividing ourselves, we have chosen defeat over victory. Let us choose unity. Let us choose victory ... Let us choose the traditions that support unity.'

The entire assembly remained silent.

'There was a time in ancient India when marriages were common across different communities. That supported unity. There was a time in India when we celebrated each other's festivals. That supported unity. There was a time when temples were open to all communities. That supported unity. There was a time when the same well gave water to everyone in the village. That supported unity. There was a time when we all ate together. That supported unity.'

Suheldev clapped his hands, and a truly gargantuan platter, carried by ten people, was brought in. Various royal retainers followed, carrying dishes of food.

'In the traditions of our great Gods like Lord Ram and Lord Shiva, let us all eat together, from one plate, to show that we are all, truly, united. We have all pledged our loyalty to our mother, to this great nation of India. By eating the food grown on her soil, her blessing, from one plate, we honour Maa Bhaarati.'

Silence descended upon the room. The kings exchanged glances. Raised from birth to believe in segregation in all personal matters like food and marriage, the notion of breaking caste rules to share a common plate was unnerving for several of them.

Suheldev felt the need to give another push. 'Our motherland is calling out to us. Will her children keep dividing themselves? Or will they unite?'

As the silence lengthened uncomfortably, Suheldev's face began to redden. In frustration. In anger.

Then Govardhan stepped forward.

Govardhan was born a Kshatriya, and that too in a royal family. Therefore, he was, technically, the highest-caste-member in the chamber, according to the so-called rules of caste hierarchy.

Govardhan looked at Suheldev, then spoke up in a loud, ringing voice. For the words were meant for the entire assembly. 'We have fought together, killed together and bled together. The brotherhood forged in battle is stronger than any rules written in any book. I am a proud Kshatriya. And I am proud to call you my king, prouder to call you my guide and proudest to call you my brother.' Then the Tomar commander turned to the other kings. 'I am no expert on our scriptures. I know very little of what is written in them. But I do know this: if we don't stop stupidly dividing ourselves, we will lose everything to those foreign barbarians. And our culture, our land, our temples, our *dharma*, will all be destroyed.'

Govardhan sat down next to the massive plate. He looked up at all those gathered around him. 'I don't know about you all, but I am starving.'

Saying this, he tore a piece of roti, dunked it in a bowl of dal, and put it in his mouth. Suheldev, his eyes moist, sat down and started eating too. Slowly, all the kings shuffled up to the massive platter, one by one, and took a bite of the food.

Suheldev gestured for Abdul and Toshani to join them too. And they did.

They were supposed to take just a symbolic bite from the *thali*. But everyone ate their entire meal together. From that one large plate.

Children of Mother India. United.

A bond forged in blood was consecrated with what Indians are most passionate about: food.

— EJJ ⅓⌒⌒⌒⌒ —

'I've thought it over deeply, Suhel …' said Toshani. She seemed to be hesitating. Her eyes were moist. 'But I think … No …'

'What do you mean, no?' asked Suheldev, immediately agitated.

It had been a few weeks since the gathering of the twenty-one kings at the Shravasti royal hall. Having consolidated his rule and commenced the building of a massive army, Suheldev had wanted to do what his mother had given him permission for. What his heart wanted to do. So he had asked Toshani for her hand in marriage. But, to his surprise, Toshani had refused to answer immediately, and instead asked for time to think it over. Her answer, after a week, had left Suheldev hurt and confused.

'Suhel …' said Toshani. 'You know I care deeply for you …'

'And this is the way to show it, right?' asked Suheldev, his anger showing on his face. He was still mourning his father. His heart was raw and filled with grief. And the natural reaction of a grief-stricken heart to more pain, is anger.

'Listen to me, Suhel …' said Toshani calmly, finally able to get a hold over her emotions. 'I am not going anywhere … But this is not the right time. Remember what your father asked of you. Remember what he demanded. Never ever stop fighting. Not until the Turkic threat to Mother India is completely finished.'

'What does this have to do with my marriage?! I will not get distracted. You will not allow me to get distracted.'

'You don't need me for that, Suhel. I know you will never get distracted. I know you will never stop fighting for the motherland. Not until you have even one breath left in your body.'

'Then why … Why hurt me like this?'

'Because you will not be fighting alone.'

'What?! Who cares what other people think? What does that have to do with—'

'Listen to me, Suhel … You need an army willing to die for you. And I have always agreed with you that India does not lack in brave men and women. We have the bravest people in the world. Our problem has always been that we'd much rather fight each other than a common enemy. We are too divided for our own good.'

'What in Lord Shiva's name does that have to do with my marriage?'

'We Indians overthink everything, Suhel …'

'Yes, we do! You are doing it right now!'

Toshani smiled sadly. 'No, I am not. But many of your noble followers will. They will keep thinking of what will happen to them after the war with the Turks is over. Will you become too powerful? Will you become the new emperor of North India? Will they lose their independence?'

'That's ridiculous! We aren't even sure that we will defeat the Turks.'

'They have faith in your generalship, Suhel ... And that is the problem. For they assume that you will lead them to victory. They are not thinking about tomorrow. They are thinking about the day after tomorrow.'

Suheldev took a deep breath. 'What does this have to do with my marriage?'

'Think about the greatest empire-builder in recent Indian history.'

'Guru Chanakya?'

Chanakya, the main advisor to Emperor Chandragupta, was considered by most to be the builder of the great Mauryan empire, which encompassed almost all of the Indian subcontinent, and beyond.

'Why did people follow him? Not just because he was brilliant. Not just because he was a fantastic organiser. Not just because he was ruthless.'

Suheldev finally understood what Toshani was saying. 'Because it was also obvious that he had no personal stake in the empire-building project ...'

'Exactly. Nobody would even dream that Guru Chanakya had any selfish interest in building the empire. If your followers start thinking that you have some selfish interest in this war, will they go all the way for you? They should never think that you are fighting for your dynasty, or your children, or your own personal kingdom. They MUST believe that you have no selfish interest in this war. There is a reason that most of the greatest leaders in Indian history have been single; almost like sanyasis. Because then their followers believe that this leader is committed only to the people. Nobody wants a Dhritarashtra for a leader. Everyone wants a Lord Ram. If we Indians trust the intentions of our leader, we will go to any extent for him or her.'

'But ...'

Toshani knew that Suheldev would bring up what his mother had said. She smiled. 'Suhel, I have known you for a long time. You are so steeped in dharma that you will never ever become monstrous like the Turks.'

Suheldev shook his head. And sighed.

'You know what I'm saying is right,' said Toshani. 'It's unfair. Of course, it is. To both you and me. But we must bear this unfairness. For Mother India ...'

Suheldev remained silent. Unhappy.

'I'm not going anywhere. I have the Maa Kali regiment to raise. I am here. Let's win the war. Let's see off the Turks. And then we'll see ...'

Suheldev shook his head and looked down at the ground. Unhappy and resigned.

Chapter 23

Ghazni, 1033 AD

The gigantic soldier tightened his grip, squeezing down hard on Maqsud's throat with his right hand. His left hand had firmly clamped down the hand in which Maqsud held his sword. Maqsud gasped for breath and tried desperately to loosen his adversary's grip, but the giant was too strong, even for the bulky Maqsud.

Maqsud kicked and punched the man, but it had no effect. His strength was beginning to fade and darkness began descending before his eyes.

Suddenly, the giant grunted and his chokehold eased slightly. Then his face contorted into an expression of agony as he released Maqsud and clutched at his back, into which a long dagger had been thrust. He swivelled his neck, groaning in tremendous pain, and saw his attacker.

Kerim.

Raw fury shone on Kerim's angelic face as he twisted the dagger further in, ramming it through brutally till it pierced the man's heart.

As the giant dropped dead to the ground, Maqsud coughed and drew deep, rasping breaths. He winced as he gently rubbed his bruised neck. His hazel eyes had become bloodshot and moist. His usually wavy hair was slicked down with sweat. Maqsud continued massaging his neck, soothing it, trying to draw in deep breaths into his oxygen-starved body.

It had been more than two years since Suheldev had formed his confederacy and started raising a standing army. Not that Maqsud had been tracking events in India. The civil war in Ghazni had dragged on for a long time. A very long time.

As Salar Maqsud felt his strength returning slowly, he looked at Kerim. The love of his life.

Kerim stood protectively in front of Maqsud, his back towards him, his sword drawn against any threats.

But there were no major threats left. Maqsud looked at the prone body of Asur, the giant Assyrian soldier that Kerim had just killed. Maqsud spat on the corpse.

The bastard nearly got me.

He rose slowly, waving away the offer of support from Kerim. Then he looked at the badly wounded figure who lay a few metres ahead. Mohammad, the younger son of Mahmud of Ghazni, was prone on the ground, bleeding from multiple wounds. As he had collapsed, Maqsud and his men had rushed to capture him, even as Mohammad's elite guards had made a last, furious attempt to protect him. Asur, whom Kerim had just killed, had been Mohammad's personal bodyguard, his constant companion and protector since he was a child. With his death, Mohammad was truly alone for the first time in his life.

Maqsud ran his fingers through his damp hair. He took his time doing it, deliberately drawing out the tension for the man lying in front of him.

As Maqsud's shadow fell on him, Mohammad made an effort to get to his feet. He managed to push himself up on all fours, but his exhausted body was unable to rise any further.

Maqsud patted his back gently, almost tenderly. 'The war is over, cousin,' he whispered softly. Then he kneed Mohammad viciously in the ribs.

Mohammad howled in pain and toppled back to the ground, where he lay, utterly spent. 'In the name of Allah, kill me … Get it over with …'

Maqsud shook his head. 'Your brother will decide what to do with you. But I'm sure it won't be anything as merciful as a quick death.' He turned to some of his men who had gathered around them. 'Tie him up. Keep him isolated and well-guarded.'

'Maqsud, whatever my brother Shahid has offered you, I will double it!' yelled Mohammad, finding a burst of energy in his desperation. 'Just let me go!'

Maqsud walked up to Mohammad, bent down, and caressed his face. His cousin shuddered and tried to back away.

'Do you know why you are such a pathetic leader, cousin?' asked Maqsud. His tone was cold and cruel, almost like he was disgusted that he had to speak to this miserable man. 'It is because you simply do not understand men and their motivations. If you truly understood me, you would know that my loyalty is not for sale. You have nothing of your great father in you.'

Maqsud gestured to his men. They hauled Mohammad to his feet and dragged him away.

Then Maqsud turned to Kerim. His eyes warm and affectionate. A broad smile on his face. He spoke in a gentle, loving tone; it was almost like he was a different man. 'So, how many times have you saved my life by now?'

Kerim smiled and embraced Maqsud. 'It's not right for me to keep track of how many times I save my own heart.'

Maqsud smiled and caressed Kerim's face.

— EЛ ӿ϶ᏃᏟᐃ —

Maqsud drew the curtain aside and entered the tent, to find Kerim waiting for him.

It had been only a day since they had captured Mohammad, effectively bringing an end to the long-drawn-out civil war among the Turks. They were on their way back to Ghazni with the prisoner. It would be up to Shahid, the elder brother of Mohammad and the true heir to the Ghazni throne, to decide how justice would be served.

Maqsud had ordered his troops to camp for the night. They would recommence their journey to Ghazni the next morning.

'How are you?' asked Kerim to Maqsud, smiling, as he signalled to one of Maqsud's servants, who immediately brought a bucket of warm water.

Maqsud dunked his head in the bucket and stayed in that position for a while. He finally emerged with his hair and beard soaking wet. Playfully, he shook his head, sending drops of water flying onto Kerim. The slave gave his lover an indulgent smile, but remained silent.

Maqsud dismissed the manservant. They were alone now.

'How long have you been a slave to the Sultanate?' asked Maqsud.

Kerim shrugged his shoulders. 'To be honest, I have lost count.'

Maqsud walked over to Kerim and affectionately stroked his face. 'I can ask Lord Shahid for anything, since I have delivered the Sultanate to him. I will ask for your freedom.'

Kerim smiled, stepped closer and kissed Maqsud gently. 'But even if the Sultanate frees me, I will always remain *your* slave.'

Maqsud smiled and kissed Kerim back. They held each other for a long time. Drawing strength and love from each other.

'And I know the other thing that I have to ask from the Sultan,' said Maqsud as he laughed and patted Kerim's backside.

Kerim pulled back. His good humour suddenly vanished. He seemed distressed.

Maqsud's shoulders sagged. He had known this day would come when the civil war ended. He knew that he had to do it. But he didn't want to see Kerim upset. 'Kerim, my love, listen to me. India is—'

'Maqsud, sometimes I think that you don't even care about what I want,' interrupted Kerim.

'It's not like that, my love. But you know that I have to—'

'No, you don't have to. Your oath to Sultan Mahmud means nothing anymore. The sultan has been dead for some years now.'

'Kerim …'

'You have done enough for Ghazni. You have done enough for the Sultanate. Now let's forget all this and get away from here. Just you and me. Forget India. Forget the conquest of that land.'

'I can't do that …'

'Why not? I've told you before. The oath means nothing now.'

'It's not about my oath to Sultan Mahmud.'

'Then why can't you forget about India?'

'Because I can't!'

'Why? You have to answer me!'

'Because I want it! I want to rule that land! I want to rule those people!'

Kerim held his breath. He closed his eyes and shook his head. The wealth of India, the richest land in the world, had seduced his love.

Kerim held Maqsud's hand as he said tenderly, 'Listen to me my darling, wealth means nothing. Wasn't it our own great Imam who advised that we should treat wealth like it is the dirt below our feet. For when dirt comes above your head, it becomes your grave.'

Maqsud's eyes became hard as stone. 'I am going there, Kerim. I am going to conquer India. And you will sit by my side when I rule it. Is that clear?'

Kerim remained silent. An expression of misery and sadness on his face. The sadness of one who cannot save the one he loves.

'Is that clear?'

Kerim nodded. *Yes.*

— ᎬᎫ �జᏏᏁᏣᐃ —

'Welcome, great Khwaja Hassan,' said Maqsud, bowing his head slightly to the prime minister of Ghazni. 'Please make yourself comfortable.'

Maqsud knew that he had to show respect to the Persian prime minister of Ghazni. Effete and always focused on money, someone like Khwaja Hassan was an obvious figure of ridicule for the warlike Maqsud. But Hassan was a survivor. He was the prime minister to Sultan Mahmud for many years. And had now inveigled himself into the inner circle of the new sultan, Shahid.

Hassan smiled and sat down. This was Maqsud's private palace. He lived away from his parents and other family members.

Hassan glanced at Kerim, who was standing a little farther away. 'How are you doing, fair Kerim?'

Kerim bowed low in respect towards the prime minister, bringing his right open palm up to his forehead, in the traditional Persian form of greeting. 'I am well, great prime minister.'

Hassan appreciated the respect shown by Kerim to his native Persian culture. Something that the ruling warrior classes, neither the Turks nor the Arabs, ever showed. The prime minister turned back to Maqsud. 'The sultan is pleased with you, great Salar Maqsud. I come bearing many rich gifts from him. He has also instructed me to inform you that his offer still stands. You can choose the governorship of any province you desire. Ask for anything you want. You will be denied nothing.'

Maqsud smiled. 'I only ask for two things. The noble sultan knows what they are.'

Hassan beamed. With a flourish, he handed over a sealed letter to Maqsud. 'The proclamation of freedom for your ... uhh ... friend.'

Maqsud grabbed the scroll and glanced at Kerim before tearing the seal apart. He rolled the scroll open and read it twice, looking more and more happy with every word he read.

He looked at Kerim again and smiled. A warm and loving smile. Then he turned back to Hassan. 'Is there anything else?'

Hassan smiled even more broadly as he said, 'Yes, there is something else.'

The prime minister reached into his pouch and took out another scroll. This time with even more flourish.

Salar Maqsud grabbed the scroll like a child lunging for his favourite sweets. He quickly broke the seal and started reading, impatiently racing through the flowery language and pompous phrases till he came to the all-important part.

'In appreciation of your courageous service and unwavering loyalty to the empire of Ghazni, His Majesty the Sultan, in his boundless graciousness and generosity, is pleased to appoint you commander-in-chief of the Imperial Army. You are directed to assume charge of your new post with immediate effect, and begin preparations forthwith for an invasion of India. To this end, you are authorised to gather all the men and resources of the Army, leaving behind only the brigades required to safeguard the realm, and proceed to India in order to bring it under the light of the true faith, and the benevolent and just rule of His Majesty, Sultan Amir-i Shahid.'

The letter had been signed by the sultan, and affixed with the seal of the Sebuktegin Ghaznavid empire.

Maqsud's expression was triumphant. This would be an invasion on a far larger scale than anything even Mahmud had mounted. The late sultan had simply conducted raids and returned once his goals had been achieved. But Maqsud aimed to conquer and rule India. He turned to Kerim once again, his excitement and anticipation clearly visible on his face. Kerim, on the other hand, did a very good job of hiding his true thoughts.

'Congratulations, great general!' said Kerim loudly. 'India will soon be at Ghazni's feet.'

Maqsud smiled. He turned back to Hassan, raised the scroll and said, 'Please convey my complete and utter gratefulness to the great sultan for this noble gesture. I will conquer India soon and add it to his Sultanate.'

'The sultan expects nothing less,' said Hassan. He seemed

to hesitate a bit before he continued speaking. 'May I ask you something?'

'Of course, Prime Minister.'

'You could easily live a life of luxury as one of the most powerful men in Ghazni. Why are you so hell-bent on embarking on another tough campaign?'

Maqsud carefully rolled up the letter, then looked up at Hassan. 'I had made a promise to my uncle, the late Sultan Mahmud. I had vowed that I would conquer all of India and turn that domain of infidels into a land of believers. I made that vow after he told me that he believed I was the only man capable of fulfilling his vision.'

'Yes. A vision that the great Sultan Shahid shares as well.'

Of course, Hassan didn't know that Maqsud intended to not just conquer and convert, but to rule India as well; at least North India. And with the fabled riches and vast resources of that territory in his control, he would be one of the most powerful men in the world. Certainly more powerful than Sultan Shahid. Perhaps rivalling the Song emperor of China. Or, if fate was kind, even stronger than the most powerful man in the world: the mighty Chola emperor Rajendra, who ruled all of southern and eastern India, along with most of South-East Asia.

Hassan bowed and left. As soon as he did so, Maqsud turned to Kerim. 'Summon the officers for a meeting right away. We have lots of preparations to make. We're going back to India. And you will be leading a regiment, Commander.'

Chapter 24

Emperor Rajendra Chola frowned as he finished reading the scroll, then stared at the person who had brought it to him. Kashinath kept his face impassive, trying hard to ensure that his nervousness was not visible.

But Kashinath's nerves were understandable. It was not every day that one met the most powerful man in the world. And if they had to fight the Turkic hordes in the north, they needed the emperor's help. The negotiation was particularly difficult. For Kashinath was asking for help against Salar Maqsud, who had already entered north-western India. And was blazing a trail of destruction. And while asking for help, Kashinath was offering nothing tangible in return to Rajendra Chola. No money. No land. No offerings of submission.

Swarthy, tall and well-built, with a handlebar moustache, Emperor Rajendra Chola was one of the greatest conquerors India had ever seen. His conquests included the Andaman and Nicobar Islands, Sri Lanka and the Maldives. He had successfully raided Malaysia and Indonesia and brought them under his control. The kingdoms of Thailand and Cambodia paid him tribute and were therefore, nominally, a part of his empire. Earlier, having established his supremacy in South India, he had marched right up to the Ganga river, defeating the Pala rulers of Bengal and Bihar along the way.

To commemorate that historic expedition, and in what was clearly a very emotional moment for the mighty monarch, he had taken on the title Gangaikondaan, the *one who brought the waters of the holy Ganga*. He had even had a new capital city built, named Gangaikonda Cholapuram.

It was hard to be in the presence of such a man and not be awed.

Rajendra stared at Kashinath, letting the silence play out uncomfortably.

Kashinath continued to stand, his hands folded respectfully in a namaste. Silent. Waiting for the great man's decision.

The stakes were very high.

Rajendra finally broke the silence. He spoke softly, but his deep baritone could be heard clearly. 'Let me get this straight. A king is actually inviting me to send my army into his kingdom?'

'Great *Arya*,' said Kashinath to Rajendra Chola with utmost respect, for the king was among the *most noble* in India, 'my master, King Suheldev, is only seeking your help against the Turks.'

'What's to stop me from taking over his kingdom myself?' asked Rajendra.

'King Suheldev acknowledges you to be an emperor with great vision. The Turks are a menace not just to any one kingdom, but to all of India. The more Indian kingdoms they defeat, the more resources they get and the more powerful they become. Wouldn't it be better to help stop their invasion early on?'

Rajendra pursed his lips and went back to staring at Kashinath thoughtfully.

'Great emperor,' continued Kashinath, 'isn't it more desirable for you to have your fellow Indians at your borders, rather than the savage Turks?'

Rajendra smiled. 'So, you think I cannot defend my land from those barbarians from Central Asia?'

'Of course you can defend your land, My Lord,' said Kashinath humbly. 'That's another reason for you to help us.'

Rajendra Chola frowned, clearly not understanding Kashinath's point.

Kashinath clarified. 'North India may not be a part of your *empire*, My Lord. But it is a part of your *land*. Bound by the Himalayas to the north, washed by the Western and Eastern Seas at the arms, and by the Indian Ocean at its feet, Mother India is the land of all of us. We cannot allow foreign thugs to defile our mother.'

Rajendra Chola remained silent. But the sentiment on his face was obvious.

Kashinath knew that Rajendra was a staunch devotee of Lord Shiva. 'Remember what these barbarians did to the great temple of Lord Shiva at Somnath, My Lord. King Suheldev is also a devotee of Lord Shiva. In fact, King Suheldev's elder brother died defending the Somnath*ji* temple.'

Rajendra suddenly held his breath. Kashinath noticed that the mighty Chola had clenched his fists.

'What was his elder brother's name?' asked Rajendra softly.

'Prince Malladev, My Lord.'

Rajendra Chola remained silent. Apparently impassive.

In his mind, the great Chola whispered a soft prayer to Lord Shiva. Pleading with the Mahadev, the God of Gods, to bless the brave Malladev's soul.

Finally, he nodded. 'You will get your answer tomorrow, noble Kashinath.'

Kashinath bowed low in respect to the emperor, and said loudly, 'Jai Maa Bhaarati.'

Glory to Mother India. Victory to Mother India.

Rajendra Chola looked surprised at the unorthodox farewell greeting from Kashinath. Unorthodox words for what was, essentially, a diplomatic visit. No words of praise from the diplomat for his king. No words of praise for the Gods.

Praise. Only for the motherland. Only for India.

The words were in a form of Prakrit, the common language of the part of India where Suheldev lived. But the emperor knew what the words meant.

Rajendra Chola smiled, and replied, '*Bharatha Thaai Vaazhga.*'

Those words were in Rajendra Chola's native tongue, Tamil.

But Kashinath knew what they meant. He had learnt a little bit of Tamil along the journey to Cholapuram. He smiled and bowed his head again. He knew the answer he would get the next day.

Bharatha Thaai Vaazhga. Long live our Mother India.

— ᎬᏗ ᎻᏛᏞᏟᎠ —

A little while later, four men sat closeted in a sparsely decorated but elegant room. The private chamber of Rajendra Chola. Along with the great emperor were his eldest son, the crown prince Rajadhiraja; his commander-in-chief, Senapati Kirtivarman; and the leader of his Intelligence Services and Special Forces, Narasimhan.

Rajendra began without any preamble. 'Why should we get involved? We have already done what needed to be done. That scum of the earth, Mahmud, has been killed. The Somnathar Mahadev's honour has been avenged. We have no stake in this battle between the North Indians and Salar Maqsud. And why should we fight for those in the north who have made an obsession out of non-violence? Those who follow Lord Buddha look down on us Hindus as violent and conservative. Even the Hindus up north have been influenced by Buddhism.'

'You may be right, *appa*,' Rajadhiraja said politely to his *father*. 'It may be that the non-violent liberals up north are incapable of defending themselves. It may be that the non-violent liberals are sanctimonious and supercilious towards us. But, they are still *our* non-violent liberals. If some foreign barbarian attacks them, we have to come to their defence. And perhaps, finally, those non-violent liberals will realise the importance of us aggressive Shaivite Hindus to the culture of India!'

Rajendra Chola laughed. 'We don't need their approval, son.'

Narasimhan bowed and said, 'With all due respect, great lord, as it is my job to collect information about all kings, great and small, I have done a little research on King Suheldev. He is different. He spent several years waging a guerrilla campaign against the Turks. He is a true warrior. He fights to win.'

'Then we should help him,' said Rajadhiraja promptly. 'We should send the cursed Turks running back to their foul land with their tails tucked between their legs.'

Rajendra turned towards Kirtivarman. 'What do you say?'

Kirtivarman rubbed his jaw thoughtfully. 'I leave the political decisions to you, great emperor. What worries me are the logistics. Even if you were to give the order right now, it would take us time to mobilise the army. Then we would have to march them all the way up to Shravasti. We would almost certainly arrive too late to be of any use. For as Lord Kashinath said, Salar Maqsud has already entered India.'

There was silence for a while. The three men waited patiently for Rajendra to speak. From their long association with him, they knew the emperor had probably made up his mind right at the start of the meeting, but wanted to hear as many opinions as possible before announcing his decision.

They also knew what the decision would be. They knew what Rajendra Chola had done to Mahmud of Ghazni. They knew what he had done for the idol of the holy Somnath temple. They knew he would not allow the Turks back into India. Even if he had no clear personal benefit from stopping them.

Rajendra spoke finally. 'The Turks are a long-term threat to India. When we carried out the assassination of Mahmud, and triggered a civil war in Ghazni, I thought the problem had been taken care of for good. But it looks like we have to worry about the wolf's cubs too.' The great Chola leaned forward, and his men came close to him. He whispered, 'So, here's what we'll do.'

Chapter 25

Ajitpal bowed deeply as Maqsud dismounted. 'Lord Maqsud, it is an honour to welcome you to Kannauj.'

Maqsud nodded curtly and looked around. 'King Ajitpal. You needn't have ridden all the way to the border to greet me personally. You could have waited in the capital city.'

Maqsud deliberately used the term king to refer to Ajitpal, rather than emperor, which he knew was the preferred title of his Indian ally.

'Not at all, My Lord,' said Ajitpal obsequiously. 'It is my pleasure to personally escort you through my empire. Please come, the refreshments are ready.'

Ajitpal led Maqsud into a spacious tent and gestured at a large table heaped with dishes and carafes. 'The finest food and wine in all of North India awaits, My Lord.'

Maqsud wrinkled his nose at the spread. 'I am not in the mood for alcohol, King Ajitpal. As for food, I rather doubt that you would have the kind of meat I like.' He paused, then cocked his neck to one side and stared at Ajitpal. 'Or do you?'

Ajitpal gulped nervously and a trickle of sweat ran down his face. 'My Lord, there is chicken, lamb, peacock, partridge, camel … almost every kind of meat.'

'*Almost*,' emphasised Maqsud deliberately. He continued to stare at Ajitpal, gloating as he watched him squirm. Briefly, he debated whether to order Ajitpal to serve him some beef. Then, from the corner of his eye, he caught a slight frown on Kerim's face and an almost imperceptible shake of the head.

'Oh well, I will make do with water and sample some of these dishes,' said Maqsud finally.

Ajitpal almost slumped to the ground in relief. Maqsud concealed his amusement, then frowned as he saw Ajitpal's minister, Vrishabh, talking in a low voice to an attendant.

'Is something bothering you?' he demanded of the minister.

Vrishabh immediately bowed, hands folded. 'Forgive me if I have offended you in any way, My Lord. I was simply giving some last-minute instructions. We have a grand reception lined up for you at the nearest town.'

Maqsud grunted. 'I fear that by the time we finally get to the battlefield, my soldiers will be so fattened by all your hospitality that they will be in no shape to fight.'

'The army of Kannauj will fight side by side with yours, My Lord,' said Ajitpal. 'My house prides itself on always standing by its friends.'

'Yes, I'm well aware of the illustrious traditions of your dynasty, and how well you are following it,' said Maqsud dryly. To his surprise, Ajitpal actually preened at the barely disguised sarcasm.

Once again masking his amusement, Maqsud gestured to Ajitpal. 'Come great king, let us do justice to this feast your cooks have prepared. Please do me the honour of sharing a plate with me.' He picked up a plate, noting that it was made of silver, and began heaping various items on it. 'I insist that you take the first bite,' added Maqsud, personally offering a morsel to Ajitpal.

If there's any poison, the fat toad will be the one to die.

Ajitpal hesitated. 'My Lord, you do me too much honour.'

'Not at all,' said Maqsud smoothly. 'It is the least I can do for such a dear ally.'

Ajitpal looked at Vrishabh, who gave the slightest of nods. With a resigned look, Ajitpal ate from Maqsud's hand, as though he were a pet. From the corner of his eye, Maqsud scanned the reactions of Ajitpal's advisers. Shame and revulsion briefly crossed most of their faces before being quickly suppressed. Only Vrishabh remained completely nonchalant.

They're upset that their precious 'emperor' has been polluted by eating from my hands. The hands of a Mlechcha barbarian. Well, they'd better get used to it. He's not an emperor anymore. He's my stooge, to do with as I like.

─── ᕮ፱ ⵖ᠌ᘓꓵᢣᐃ ───

A few hours later, Maqsud and Ajitpal rode side by side through a richly decorated gateway into the town of Harsaran, the first major urban centre that one encountered after entering the kingdom of Kannauj.

There were flowers scattered all over the path on which they were riding. Residents of the town had been ordered to line up on both sides of the road and cheer as the two men rode by, preceded by a large number of infantrymen and followed by a sizeable cavalry contingent. As a precaution, and based on the demands of the Turks, Ajitpal had ordered that all the weapons of the Harsaran citizenry be confiscated. The weapons were to be returned to them when the Turks left a few weeks later.

'Welcome to Harsaran, My Lord,' said Ajitpal. 'As the name suggests, this town prides itself on offering shelter to everyone who comes here, regardless of caste, creed or nationality. It is a major trading centre and people of different faiths have lived here in peace for generations.'

Maqsud had barely opened his mouth to reply when a clump of mud flew close to Ajitpal. Startled, he hauled back on the reins of his horse. The animal reared up, almost throwing him off. Ajitpal struggled to regain control of the animal. By the time he succeeded, his guards had surrounded him. A few of them dashed into the crowd and pulled out the man who had thrown the mud. He was a bedraggled old man on crutches, with just one leg, long white hair that hung down his back and a crazed look in his eyes.

Ajitpal was livid. He yelled loudly, 'How dare you insult your emperor?'

'You are the one who is insulting the memory of your brave father, Ajitpal!' shouted the aged cripple. 'I was a soldier in the army of Kannauj. I lost a leg fighting for this empire. I never thought I would see the day when the emperor of Kannauj would lick the boots of a foreign invader!'

There was a stunned silence in the crowd. The old man was only vocalising what practically all the citizens of Harsaran felt about their ruler. But nobody expected such open defiance.

The old man turned to Salar Maqsud. 'Our ruler is a coward. But we common Kannaujias still have spines. We will never bow to a foreign plunderer!' The man hawked loudly and spat a gob at Maqsud, which landed on his leg.

There was an audible gasp from the crowd. People began to mutter loudly. This had gone too far. Even if they were angry with their emperor, many believed it was against *dharma* to insult a guest in such a manner. Some of the crowd started pulling the old man back. Telling him to calm down.

Maqsud, who had been observing Ajitpal's discomfiture

with a sly smile, flushed red at this insult. He had already reached for his sword when he felt a hand on his back.

It was Kerim. The whisper from the Turkic slave was soft. 'We need this city as a base ... Remember the main objective ... Let me handle this ...'

With great effort, Maqsud controlled himself.

In the meanwhile, the old man was still struggling against his fellow citizens. Showing surprising strength for his age. He was screaming constantly, about the bravery of the common citizens of Kannauj.

Kerim dismounted, walked up to the crippled old soldier and put a comforting hand on his shoulder. 'My friend, we were enemies before, but not now. Today, the great empire of Ghazni and the noble kingdom of Kannauj are—'

'Get away from me!' the veteran screamed agitatedly, interrupting Kerim. He pulled away from the Turk. While doing so, the old soldier also pushed hard against a Harsaran citizen holding him back. And he lost his footing. As he lurched forward suddenly with his crutch to balance himself, his head collided with Kerim's face. The blow was almost like a brutal head butt. Blood burst forth from the Turk's nose and mouth as he swayed briefly on his feet. Then he fell. Flat on his back, his head banging hard on the ground. Unconscious.

Maqsud erupted in fury. Roaring with rage, he drew his sword and slashed at the old man. Chopping his head off with one mighty blow. But Maqsud's anger was still not spent. He jumped off his horse, ran to the veteran's beheaded body, and hacked at it in a frenzy. Repeatedly. Blood burst forth in all directions.

The common people began to scream in terror. Some gathered the courage to start protesting against Maqsud's brutality. Soldiers of the armies of Ghazni and Kannauj immediately formed a protective wall around Maqsud and Ajitpal. Ordering the citizens of Harsaran to stand back.

But the crowd started shouting even more loudly. Screaming that the old veteran did not deserve to be killed.

'My Lord, this is going to turn into a riot,' Vrishabh told Ajitpal. 'Please calm Lord Maqsud down and let's get out of here.'

Ajitpal gulped nervously. But he remained paralysed. Unable to move.

Maqsud was still hacking away at the old soldier's body. Seeming to be in a mad frenzy.

By then, the entire crowd had become agitated. They began yelling slogans and pushing at the wall formed by the soldiers of Kannauj, who were reluctant to strike at their own citizens. They had not even drawn their weapons. The Ghazni soldiers, however, had already pulled out their swords. Clearly itching to kill. But held back by the absence of an order from their general.

A Turkic commander went up as close to Maqsud as he dared and said in an urgent voice, 'My Lord …'

Maqsud came out of his hysterical rage and looked around, assessing the situation. He closed his eyes for only an instant. But as soon as he opened them, he appeared calm. When he spoke, his voice was measured. 'This man attacked a commander of the Ghazni army. He should have been tortured and killed slowly over many days, but he got off lightly because I lost my temper. However, it seems the people of Harsaran have not learnt anything. I will teach them a lesson that no one in Kannauj will ever forget.' He turned to the officer accompanying him. 'Destroy the home of every *kafir* in this town. Not one brick should be left standing. Kill every male unbeliever—man, boy or infant. Enslave the women and girls, and sell them to brothels used by our soldiers. Spare only the believers. Report to me when it is done.'

Ajitpal was flabbergasted. 'What? Please, My Lord, no …'

Maqsud ignored the emperor as he lifted Kerim and laid him across his horse. Then he mounted behind Kerim's prone body, turned his horse around and galloped out of the town. Ajitpal hesitated, then followed. Behind them, screams began to ring out as Maqsud's soldiers began their grim task.

— ᴇᴊᴊ ꭗ� —

'The streets have turned red. The wells are choked with corpses of people who jumped in trying to escape the soldiers. The smoke from the burning homes is so thick that you can barely see your own hand. But even that could not prevent me from witnessing unspeakable horrors. I have seen soldiers raping pregnant women and leaving them to die bleeding. I have no fear of hell anymore. It cannot be worse than what I have already seen in Harsaran.'

In the Kannauj royal tent, housed within the Turkic army camp, Ajitpal was sitting on his travelling throne, listening to a thin man giving his report of what was happening in Harsaran. The thin man, named Subhash, was part of a network of spies painstakingly nurtured by Vrishabh over the years.

Vrishabh patted the man gently on the shoulder. 'Go and try to get some rest, Subhash.' As soon as Subhash had left, the prime minister turned to Ajitpal. 'My Lord, thousands of our countrymen have already died. Please, I beg you, at least now go and plead with Lord Maqsud to put an end to this slaughter. The town can be razed to the ground, but at least let us try to save some lives. A king's duty, first and foremost, is to protect his people. Please try to follow your *dharma* to some extent.'

Ajitpal put down the goblet of wine that he was holding. His hands shook, his eyes were bloodshot and his face was completely ashen. 'What kind of men are these? If they can do this with their friends ...'

Vrishabh shook his head sadly. 'They don't think of us as their friends, My Lord. We are simply their playthings, to be fondled or slaughtered as they please. You have made a deal with the devil. It is still not too late. You can regain your honour and dignity if we call off this alliance and—'

'Enough!' said Ajitpal sharply, holding up a hand. 'Be careful, Vrishabh. You are very close to uttering treasonous talk. I will go and speak to Maqsud and ask him to call off his men. But there is no question of going back on this alliance.'

—EJJ ꓘꙄꓵ꓾ꓔꗝ—

It was only a short while later that Ajitpal was waiting outside General Maqsud's tent. The Turkic guards had refused to let him enter. They had refused to even announce his arrival to Maqsud. Ajitpal was ordered to wait.

And Ajitpal, the emperor of Kannauj, descendant of men who until very recently had ruled large tracts of northern India, inheritor of a great dynasty about whom songs were still sung, swallowed his pride, and waited. Like a supplicant.

Inside the tent, Kerim was lying on a large bed placed in the centre. Bandages on his nose and head. Apparently, he had suffered a serious concussion as well. Strict bed rest had been advised. Maqsud was sitting on a chair placed next to the bed, concern and worry writ large on his face.

'Please … I beg you … stop the carnage …' Kerim whispered to Maqsud. 'They are common civilians … they are not soldiers … this is wrong …'

'You are too kind-hearted,' said Maqsud firmly, even as he gently caressed Kerim's hand. 'They have to be taught a lesson.'

Kerim began to shake his head, then winced as the movement sent a pang of pain shooting through his being. 'So many innocent lives … lost because of me … I can't bear it.'

'They are not innocent. They dared to hurt you.' Suddenly Maqsud looked towards the tent curtains and screamed loudly, 'Where the hell is the doctor?! He was told to do something about Kerim's pain!'

The chief guard spoke loudly from beyond the curtain, nervous. 'He is waiting outside, My Lord.'

The reply from Maqsud was immediate. 'Then send him in, you moron!'

The doctor drew aside the curtain and rushed in, being careful to push the curtain back in place.

The guard glanced at Ajitpal, then looked back towards the curtain and gulped nervously before he spoke, 'My Lord, Emperor Ajitpal is also waiting here for you.'

No response.

Ajitpal spoke up. 'Great general, if I may request a little bit of your time?'

Kerim held Maqsud's hand and squeezed gently. Maqsud sighed, and then ordered loudly, 'Come in.'

Ajitpal immediately drew the curtain aside and entered the tent.

He found Maqsud staring at him. A long, hard, cold stare. Ajitpal felt his guts turn to water.

Maqsud took a deep breath, like he was trying desperately to control himself. Then he smiled slightly, the disdain he felt towards Ajitpal clear on his face. He spoke with polite sarcasm, 'Great emperor, why are you standing there? Please come, have a seat. What can I do for you?'

Ajitpal shuffled uncomfortably to the seat indicated by Maqsud but did not sit down. He looked at Kerim and then back at Maqsud. 'General Maqsud ... I ... I hope the commander is well?'

Maqsud nodded, a cold expression back on his face. But before he could speak, there was a commotion outside the tent. Maqsud frowned irritably. 'What the hell is going on out there? I thought I had given a clear order for silence!'

A Turkic officer came rushing into the tent. 'My Lord, our troops have captured some fellow called Tarikh who is a resident of Harsaran. Though he is one of the faithful, he was sheltering some *kafir* neighbours in his home. When our men found out and tried to drag them out of his house, he fought our soldiers. He killed two and badly wounded three. Since you had said no believer should be harmed, he has not been killed. The men want to know what to do with him.'

'Son of a ...' growled Maqsud, standing up. 'These bloody Indian Muslims! Bring him in here!'

Tarikh was dragged in. A tall, broad-shouldered man, he struggled and cursed even though he had been badly battered and his hands were tightly tied together. His eyes were little more than puffy slits after the beating he had received. He found it difficult to see clearly. The first man he noticed was Ajitpal.

'Traitor!' roared Tarikh, his rage against the emperor of his land beyond breaking point.

Maqsud sniggered at Ajitpal's obvious discomfort.

Then Tarikh turned and noticed Maqsud. And his jaw dropped in shock.

The stunned Tarikh's whisper was barely audible. 'Aslan?'

The voice reached Kerim's ears clearly. The alarm on his face was obvious for an instant. He looked briefly at Ajitpal and Maqsud. Then he immediately controlled himself. Remaining silent.

But Maqsud looked at Tarikh nonchalantly. Giving the impression that he hadn't understood anything. 'Who the hell is Aslan?'

'You son of a dog!' bellowed Tarikh, with a sudden burst of furious energy.

Tarikh rushed towards Maqsud. But he was stopped in almost no time by the Turkic soldiers. Who began pummelling him once again. Brutally. Without respite.

— Ɛᴊ ᴎꜱᴧᴄᴧ —

The tent flap parted and an officer of the Ghazni army entered.

'Prime Minister Vrishabh,' said the officer, 'Lord Maqsud wishes to see you.'

Vrishabh smiled. 'And what if I don't wish to see him?'

'There are ten soldiers standing outside the tent, sir. I respect your age and position, so I would much rather not have to call them in. Please don't force me to.'

Vrishabh was genuinely surprised. 'You're very polite for an all-conquering Turk. What's your name, if I may ask?'

'Ozgur, sir,' said the man.

Vrishabh stepped up and looked at Ozgur keenly. 'Hmm … you don't look like a noble, if you'll pardon my saying so.

Neither are you a young man. But you're an officer, which can only mean that you were a soldier who has been promoted through the ranks. Is that correct?'

'With due respect, sir, I don't think this is the right time to be discussing my life.'

'Of course … So, what is your general calling me for?'

Ozgur's discomfort was obvious. But he was not the sort to disobey orders. 'I am not at liberty to say, sir.'

'A dutiful soldier indeed,' said Vrishabh. 'Right, Officer, lead the way.'

Even though Ozgur had not said anything, it was clear to Vrishabh what was going on. Subhash had come in just a little while ago and tipped him off. Tarikh, the former Kannauj army soldier whom Vrishabh had sent to fight with Suheldev's band in the forest, had returned to his family in Harsaran. He had gotten into a fight with Maqsud's men while protecting some fellow countrymen who were Hindus. Consequently, he had been dragged to the Turkic camp. Subhash had said that he was being questioned. Perhaps accompanied with torture. Tarikh was a strong man and they didn't expect him to break. But they had to be prepared for the possibility that he might do so. And if that happened, it would be only a matter of time before they found out about Vrishabh's role in the assistance given to the chief enemy of the Turks in North India: Suheldev.

Subhash had strongly advised Vrishabh to escape. But the prime minister had responded immediately and with no ambiguity. *Don't be silly. I am the prime minister. I cannot flee.*

But there was a practical reason for Vrishabh to stay as well. His disappearance would be noticed. And search parties would be sent out. But Subhash's disappearance would not be tracked, since he was not considered important enough. He had immediately ordered Subhash and two other men to ride to Shravasti using three different routes, and pass on every bit of the latest information on the Turks to Suheldev. Vrishabh had already prepared detailed documents, listing all that he had observed of the Turks. Their army strength, battle plans, tactics, weapons, etc.

That information would be priceless to Suheldev. It *had* to reach him.

It was Vrishabh's job now to misdirect the Turks. Or at least buy Subhash and the others as much time as he could.

Everyone has to die sometime. But only a few are blessed with a meaningful death. A death about which songs would be written.

—— EⅡ ℵℷⅉⅉℭⅉ ——

Vrishabh drew the curtain of Maqsud's tent aside and stepped in. And he immediately heard the voice of Ajitpal, his liege.

'You filthy traitor!'

Vrishabh turned towards the source of the voice. Only to see Ajitpal hurl a half-empty goblet at him. Vrishabh immediately ducked. But he wasn't fast enough. Leaving a trail of blood-coloured wine in its wake, the goblet crashed into Vrishabh's forehead. The prime minister of Kannauj staggered for a moment. And then collapsed on the ground, blood bursting forth from the deep wound. Ajitpal charged at him, and kicked him again and again. Screaming gutturally in rage. Vrishabh curled up on the ground defensively, in a foetal position, till Ajitpal got exhausted and stopped to catch his breath.

'When Lord Maqsud told me about you, I actually defended

you!' shouted Ajitpal, tears streaming down his face. 'I said there must be some mistake! Vrishabh is loyal to me!' He heaved a couple of deep breaths into his lungs, then spoke again. 'Why did you betray me? *Why*?' The last word came out as an almost stifled scream.

Vrishabh shook his head to clear it, then slowly rose to his feet. He was bleeding copiously. He winced as pain shot through his ribs every time he took a breath. With an effort, he forced himself to stand upright and looked Ajitpal in the eye. His voice was eerily calm, even if his words were laboured. 'I am loyal ... But not to you ... I am loyal to India ... I am loyal to Kannauj ...'

'I AM KANNAUJ!' screeched Ajitpal.

'No, you are not ... A land is not its king. A land is its people ... Kannauj lives in the people being massacred in Harsaran. The ones whom you cannot protect ... The ones for whom you will shed neither blood nor tears ...'

Ajitpal raised his hand to hit Vrishabh again, but the prime minister pushed the emperor back. Ajitpal gaped at him in shock, stunned at his minister's temerity.

Maqsud was sniggering now. Clearly enjoying the infighting among the Indians.

Vrishabh looked at Ajitpal with barely disguised disgust. 'You can raise your hand only on a defenceless old man ... You do not have the guts to fight the real enemies of your people ... You have betrayed our land ... You have betrayed your great ancestors ... You have betrayed your advisers and your brave soldiers ... You accepted humiliation to avoid war. Now you have both humiliation and war.'

'Be quiet, you insolent dog,' yelled Ajitpal, before turning to Maqsud. 'Execute him, My Lord. Kill this bastard. I will not protect him anymore.'

Maqsud was laughing openly now. 'Who are you to offer protection, you fool?' Then the Turkic general turned to Vrishabh. 'I respect the fact that you at least have the guts to fight. Tell me the names of the other traitors in your kingdom. Tell me the names of all the others supporting that bandit Suheldev. And you shall have a merciful, quick death. Otherwise ...'

'I am the only one. All the others are minor soldiers, and they have joined Suheldev already. I tried my best to join him too, but I wasn't of much use to him. Otherwise he would have accepted me in his kingdom.'

Maqsud stepped closer, as his voice dropped menacingly low. 'Do you think I am a fool? Do you think I don't know that there are nobles across Indian kingdoms giving Suheldev money, resources and, most crucially, information? I know much more about Suheldev than you think I do. But you ... I never knew about you ... Suheldev is one wily man. And I need to know more about him. You are going to talk ... Trust me, you don't want me to—'

Maqsud stopped talking. Stunned at Vrishabh's reaction.

The prime minister of Kannauj had yawned. Openly. Like he was bored of Maqsud's speech. He had even brought up his right hand to cover his mouth.

Maqsud had rarely been treated with such open disrespect. Not even by his mother. Not even by his father. Not even by the man he hated most.

'Who the hell do you think you are talking to?' roared Maqsud. 'Don't test me! You don't know the cruelty of my torturers! If they could make that foolish giant Tarikh break down, imagine what they will do to your frail body.'

Vrishabh laughed softly. He knew he was getting under Maqsud's skin. 'You bleat like a hyena ... You don't know anything about Suheldev ... He is a lion ... He is far better than you think ...'

Maqsud stepped closer. He laughed too. 'I will enjoy seeing you get tortured. I will make sure they keep you alive for weeks. You will know pain that you didn't even think was possible.'

Vrishabh chuckled.

'What do you think is so funny?' asked Ajitpal.

Vrishabh smiled at Ajitpal. 'I disappointed you earlier ...' Then he turned to Maqsud. 'And now, I am afraid ... I will disappoint him.'

As the prime minister said these words, a spasm went through his body. He clenched his fists. His eyes rolled back into his head as he collapsed to the ground. Froth began forming around his mouth. It all happened so quickly that the others had very little time to respond.

'What the hell!' shouted a startled Maqsud.

Ozgur suddenly rushed forward.

When he yawned ...

He grabbed Vrishabh's hand and turned it over. The gem on the ring on his middle finger was facing inwards. Ozgur sniffed at it and his nose wrinkled as he detected a strange odour.

'Get a physician quickly,' he barked. 'He has poisoned himself.'

As one of the soldiers scrambled out, Ozgur tried to shove a finger inside Vrishabh's throat to make him throw up. A second later, he screamed as Vrishabh bit down hard on his finger. He hastily pulled it out and clutched at it in agony.

Blood was trickling out of Vrishabh's mouth now. He rolled over, pressed the earth with trembling hands, and then touched his forehead. Almost like he was seeking blessings from the ground.

Farewell, mother ... This is all that this son could do for you ...

Then another spasm went through Vrishabh, and he lay still.

Chapter 26

It had been nearly three years since Suheldev had formed a confederacy under Shravasti's leadership. Those three years had been spent well. He had trained a strong army. And he had managed to get warriors from across the land to pledge loyalty to the anti-Turk alliance.

The time to test the preparations was finally here.

For Salar Maqsud and the army of Ghazni had returned.

Suheldev and his advisers were in consultation. News of the destruction of Harsaran just a few days ago had reached them. They knew it was just a matter of time before the Turks moved to their region. The battle that would decide the fate of their land would be fought soon.

Prayers were being conducted in the royal temple, which was not too far from the private office of Suheldev. Prayers for the souls of the victims of Harsaran. The Sanskrit chants wafted over into the sombre meeting.

The prayers, drawn from the *Garuda Purana*, pleaded for the safe journey of the souls to the abode of the ancestors. Souls that had met unhappy ends in their previous lives were believed to carry some of the negative energy with them. Prayers would help them overcome this. So that they could be prepared for their next life, here, once again, in this world of *maya*.

Suheldev had got special prayers conducted for Vrishabh.

Everyone in the Shravasti inner council was shocked to hear that the Kannauj prime minister had been an ally of Suheldev and had been secretly helping the king in his patriotic struggle. Kashinath had not been aware of it. Nor had Toshani, Abdul, or Govardhan, his closest aides.

Suheldev could really keep secrets buried deep in his heart. One of the qualities of a good leader.

'What now?' asked Govardhan.

'Should we wait here for them?' asked Kashinath.

Toshani was clear. 'I think we should move out. If we allow them to come close to Shravasti, we will be worried about what they will do to our citizens. They could use them as hostages against us.'

Abdul spoke up. 'But if we move out, we'll leave our towns and villages undefended. They could outflank our army and attack our people.'

'Perhaps we can continue our guerrilla tactics on them?' suggested Govardhan. 'They have always been effective.'

Suheldev leaned forward as he shook his head. 'No. They are here with a determined army now. From all the reports sent by Vrishabh*ji* before he died, it is clear that this army is better led than any Turkic force till now. Their camp defences are solid and conservative. It will not be so easy for our guerrilla assassins to break through. I have heard that their general Maqsud seems to understand our land and culture far better than any other Turkic commander before. He knows exactly what tactics to use against which kingdoms. It's almost like he knows India as well as us Indians. And from all the reports I have received, they have not come just to raid this time. They have come to conquer and stay.'

'Then we will have to take them on in one pitched battle,' said Toshani. 'And we will have to kill them all.'

'No Indian army has done that before,' pointed out Kashinath. 'Though the great Chandela king, Maharaj Vidhyadhara, fought Mahmud to a standstill once and later repulsed his siege of the fortress of Kalinjar.'

Suheldev sighed. 'Unfortunately, Maharaj Vidhyadhara can't help us. He's seriously ill, and I've heard he may not live much longer. And the crown prince, Vijayapala, has his hands full fighting the Kalachuris, who are trying to take advantage of the great king's illness.'

'The infighting amongst us Indians is what the foreigners take advantage of,' Kashinath said, shaking his head sadly. 'Anyway, I'd reached out to the prince and he promised to send a contingent of troops under Suryavir, one of his finest generals. But there can't be another Maharaj Vidhyadhara. If only we had him and the full Chandela army.'

'There's no end to wishful thinking,' said Toshani. 'We'll have to do the best we can with whatever we have.'

Suheldev glanced at Kashinath. He knew that they had to delay the battle for a few months. That's how much time they expected would elapse before Rajendra Chola's battalions could come in support of Shravasti. But nobody else, besides Kashinath and Suheldev, knew of the alliance with Rajendra Chola.

The chief guard suddenly made an announcement at the door. 'Your Majesty, your friend Aslan is here.'

Everyone turned towards the door. Suheldev immediately got up with a broad smile.

Perhaps Aslan will know something about Maqsud that can be useful. 'Let him in!'

A few moments later, Aslan entered the room, his arms already outstretched. Suheldev walked over to greet him. The two men hugged each other warmly.

The distrust on Abdul's face was obvious. Govardhan leaned over to him and whispered, 'It's alright, Abdul. King Suheldev trusts Aslan. We should trust him too.'

Abdul looked at Govardhan briefly and then back at Aslan and Suheldev. 'I don't trust that Turk. Something about his face … It troubles me … I hope that the king does not pay a heavy price for trusting someone from the enemy tribe …'

Govardhan patted Abdul's hand. 'Take it easy …'

In the meantime, Suheldev and Aslan had stepped back from their embrace, but still held each other's hands.

'My friend, it's so good to see you again!' Suheldev said. 'Where have you been?'

'I wandered around for a while, but I finally returned to settle by a lake where I'd had a mystical experience,' said Aslan. 'There, I set up a small hermitage where I began giving people whatever little medical treatment I could, in exchange for alms. Soon, some people started joining me during prayer sessions. Now, a little community has sprung up there. It has been a wonderful time for me. I have never felt so much at peace in my life.'

Suheldev smiled sadly. 'And that peace is under threat again. From the monsters of Ghazni.'

Aslan curled his lips in agreement. 'We Sufi Muslims have to realise that we cannot have peace as long as the radical Muslims remain. We have to fight them. For our own good. And for the good of the world at large.'

'They are not radical Muslims, Aslan. They are just radical monsters. But yes, all of us need to fight them. Together.'

'Without mercy.'

'Without mercy,' Suheldev agreed.

'And that's why I have come. You need me now.'

'Yes, I do. This general of the Turks, Maqsud … well, he has tactics that are …'

' … brilliant.' Aslan completed Suheldev's statement.

Suheldev nodded. 'Yes … And, apparently, his lover is his commander Kerim. Are there … any opportunities that can be exploited?'

There was a split second of intense emotion on Aslan's face. But he controlled himself quickly. He looked down, took a deep breath and whispered, 'I know you are better than this, my friend. Keep their love out of it. They are both warriors. We need to have tactics that will work against them.'

'Hmm … Your advice will be welcome.'

'I have come with more than advice,' replied Aslan. 'Over the past few months, a small group of young men, who insist on treating me as some sort of spiritual master, have gathered around me. Recently, they asked me whether one should fight for one's faith or one's country. I replied that India comes before everyone and everything. The motherland is greater than heaven.'

Suheldev smiled and held Aslan's shoulders. Remaining silent. Not stating the obvious.

Aslan's eyes softened. 'Wherever I may have been born, I was given a new birth right here, in India. This is where I was inducted into mysticism. Into the Sufi way. This is where I truly found Allah. This is the land of my mission. I think of India as my holy motherland. If she will adopt this barbarian Turk …'

'Our mother has adopted you already, Aslan,' said Suheldev. 'Mother India has a big heart. A foreigner who comes here and thinks of India as his own holy motherland, is a foreigner no more.'

Aslan smiled. 'My friends insisted on accompanying me

here. There are barely two hundred of them, but they are young, strong and enthusiastic. And I have given them some basic military training. They will follow you to hell and back, if need be. I suggest you keep them in your personal bodyguard corps.'

Suheldev nodded.

'Remember, Suheldev, we cannot allow you to die. If you die, the Indian army will scatter. The Turks know that. My people will protect you.'

'I welcome them into my bodyguard corps,' said Suheldev, visibly moved. 'Let's go meet them.'

As Suheldev and Aslan started walking out of the chambers, Abdul, who had heard everything, turned to Govardhan. He was visibly angry. 'How can the king do this?'

'Relax Abdul,' said Govardhan. 'You are still the commander of the bodyguard corps in peacetime. See it as you having two hundred more soldiers.'

'But those soldiers will be loyal to Aslan, not to King Suheldev!'

Chapter 27

The royal war council of Shravasti had congregated in Suheldev's private office chambers. Suheldev, Toshani, Kashinath, Govardhan and Abdul were gathered around a table, studying a comprehensive map of the region. The map was large, with details of the topography, cities, villages, rivers and even streams. Wise warriors have said that thorough knowledge of the terrain is half the battle won. Various earthen figures, depicting cavalry, archers, infantrymen and other military formations, were arranged on top of it. Aslan was by the other side of the table. All the confederacy kings were also present.

'We have the advantage of numbers,' said Aslan, 'but the Turks' cavalry gives them the edge. They are fast-moving, highly trained, and very skilled warriors.'

'We have our own cavalry too,' said Abdul, clearly upset at what seemed like a slight to Indian warriors. 'And we can battle them.'

'I have no doubt your cavalry is very good, brave Abdul,' said Aslan, his voice polite and calm. 'But they will not be able to defeat the Turkic cavalry. Trust me. They have three times the horses we have. And cavalry riders that have been repeatedly tested in war. If we can just hold them back during the battle, that itself will be an exceptional feat.'

Govardhan quietly held Abdul's hand below the table. And Abdul fell silent.

Aslan looked around the table. 'I believe that Maqsud will launch his cavalry from both wings and attack our flanks. The archers will be called in to assist them, raining arrows down on us. If his cavalry breaks through, which they have in every single battle till now, they will attack our infantry from both flanks. And that's when his infantry will charge in from the front. He will then have us neatly trapped in a pincer. And he will also call in his reserve troops then. After that, it will be pure slaughter.' While explaining Maqsud's tactics, Aslan had been moving the earthen pieces around on the map. To make the movements clearer. Now, he restored them to their original positions. He looked at Suheldev. 'Maqsud will not offer surrender. Not to you. He wants to kill every single person in your army. There will be no mercy.'

Suheldev smiled. 'Well, that's one thing we have in common. There will be no mercy from my side either. Because I intend to kill every single one of the Turks as well.'

'Har Har Mahadev!' said Toshani to that.

'Jai Shri Ram!' said King Karan, one of Suheldev's allies.

'Allahu Akbar!' said Abdul.

Aslan smiled broadly. 'More power to all of you. But the Gods will not be able to help you if you are not able to stop the Turkic cavalry. You need to have a plan for that. It is crucial. If we can somehow stop their cavalry, we can attack their vanguard with our infantry. And bring our superior numbers into play. Then, Allah may grant us victory.'

Suheldev narrowed his eyes. 'I have heard that, quite often, Maqsud's cavalry feigns a retreat as well?'

Aslan looked up. Surprised. And then smiled slightly. *This man is good. Really good.*

'Yes, you are right,' said Aslan. 'Sometimes the Turks pretend to be overwhelmed and start riding away. Luring the enemy cavalry to chase them. Pulling them further towards their side. Into a trap. They did this in Lahore. The entire enemy cavalry was crushed.'

Suheldev looked towards Govardhan and Abdul. 'No matter what, our cavalry must remain close to our army. Do not chase their cavalry if they retreat. Do not launch a charge. Just defend.'

Govardhan spoke up. 'If our cavalry is just going to defend, then how do you intend to win the battle?'

Suheldev looked down towards the map. 'If the horses can't win it for us, then we have to make the battlefield fight for us.'

Everyone looked at him, confused.

'We have to pick a battlefield where cavalry charges down the flanks will be difficult,' said Suheldev. 'Where are the Turks right now?'

'They're camping at Satrikh,' said Toshani. 'From what our scouts tell us, they're gathering supplies. Also, some of their divisions had gone off on raids to other kingdoms. Once they've reassembled, the Turks will head our way. It won't be very long. A few weeks at the most.'

Suheldev looked at Kashinath. An urgent message had been sent to Rajendra Chola. That help would be required much earlier than planned. But would Rajendra Chola's soldiers be able to reach in time?

Can't do anything about that now. Hope for the best. And fight.

Suheldev turned back to the map, ran his forefinger over the routes available to the Turkic army, then suddenly paused.

'Here,' he jabbed at the map. 'The Turks will have to come this way. There's a huge open plain, big enough to accommodate our entire army. There's a lake to the right and thick woods to the left. They form natural barriers. The Turks will not be able to ride around them to outflank us. They will have to charge at us head-on. If we can hold them on the naturally narrowed flanks, we can take the battle to them at the centre.'

Everyone leaned over and looked at the map again.

Toshani was the first to verbalise what everyone else was thinking. 'Yes, this can work.'

Suheldev looked up from the map, towards all his advisers. 'I think we should ride out right away and see if the field actually looks like this on the ground. If it does, then this is where we will make our stand.' His eyes settled on Aslan, who was looking troubled. 'What's the matter?'

Aslan sighed. 'The ground looks exactly like what is shown in the map. I should know. For the past few months, I was living there with my little group. It is a scenic, beautiful place and gave us immense peace. The water of the lake there is believed to have miraculous healing powers, and pilgrims often come there to bathe in the hope that it will cure their ailments. It breaks my heart to think of it as a site where blood will be shed and lives will be lost.'

Suheldev patted his friend's shoulder. 'We will build a beautiful place of worship there, open to all, after the battle is over. This place will not be defiled by blood. In fact, it will be sanctified by it. That is where we will offer up our blood, and that of our enemies, in defence of our motherland.'

Aslan remained silent. Keeping his thoughts to himself. *Let's see who all Allah favours with his blessings. There's Kerim. There is you. And there is me.*

Suheldev turned to the others assembled. 'Get the army

ready to move. We need to reach the spot well in time to prepare a fitting welcome for the Turks.'

The king of Shravasti smiled and thumped the backs of each one of them as they filed out of his tent. It was only when he was alone that he allowed his confident demeanour to slip. A look of anxiety settled on his face as he moved to the table once more and gazed at it.

This is where the future of India will be decided.

Help us, Lord Shiva.

Bless us with victory.

Take my life, if you must. But bless us with victory.

As Suheldev stared at the map, it seemed to fade away till only the spot that he'd pinpointed remained in focus. The name of the town nearest to the battlefield he had chosen stood out bold and clear, seeming to stare back at him.

Bahraich.

—— EʃJ ʜᢒ� ᢓᠶᠠ ——

Suheldev folded his hands and shut his eyes as Vijayalakshmi applied a *tilak* to his forehead. Only three days had elapsed since the strategy meeting in Suheldev's private office. And his army was ready to march. As tradition dictated, he had come to his mother's chambers to seek her blessings. And as tradition dictated, his mother had blessed him with victory. Only victory.

Vijayalakshmi's words were clear. 'Come back victorious or don't come back at all.'

Legends hold that proud family members have blessed the warriors in their clan with these words since the dawn of the Vedic age. In fact, many say that Lord Ram and Lady Sita also wished each other with this blessing before they fought battles. And that Lady Sati said this very line to Lord Shiva, many millennia ago, as he had ridden out to battle.

For true warriors never want to be wished with a long life. All they want is victory. Only victory.

A death in pursuit of victory is better than a life lived in compromise with defeat.

Suheldev bent to touch his mother's feet. The strong emotions of a mother slipped through Vijayalakshmi's proud, regal bearing for a short moment. She embraced her son. And almost immediately, released him.

'Go, my son. Bring victory to Mother India. Jai Maa Bhaarati.'

Suheldev repeated softly, 'Jai Maa Bhaarati.'

The king of Shravasti turned around and beckoned his attendant, who immediately proffered the royal helmet. Suheldev put it on and stood straighter, pushing back his shoulders as he walked out of his mother's private chambers. And then, out of the royal palace and into the square where his horse and personal guards were waiting.

The soldiers cheered as they saw their king approaching. Suheldev briefly raised his hand in acknowledgement.

Attendants led a horse up to Suheldev. The king held the saddle horn and smoothly mounted the horse, vaulting on with one effortless jump.

Suheldev looked back at his key lieutenants. Toshani, Abdul and Govardhan. And smiled.

Then he turned to his warriors. To Mother India's warriors.

'My soldiers! My friends! My fellow countrymen!'

The men and women of Suheldev's army fell silent. Listening to their king. Listening to their leader.

'We received a message from that barbarian Turk, Salar Maqsud of Ghazni.'

Shouts of anger and boos echoed from the soldiers. Hatred for that cursed name was at its peak. Suheldev raised his arm and they fell silent.

'He told us that, apparently, all land on earth belongs to his God. And since he is a representative of his God, he has come to claim ownership of his property. He ordered us to surrender!'

The rage against the Turks erupted once again. With soldiers screaming curses at Maqsud. They fell silent, once again, at a signal from Suheldev.

'I have just sent him a message, that in India, the earth itself is divine!'

The soldiers listened intently.

Suheldev raised his voice, his words ringing in every ear. 'How dare he claim to own Mother India?! Nobody owns Mother India! Mother India owns us!'

Roars erupted from the warriors. The warriors of Mother India.

'If he doesn't understand that, we will make him speak to Mother India! We will go to Bahraich! We will kill every single one of those Turks! We will behead that bastard Salar Maqsud! We will bury them all in the soil of Mother India! Then they can talk to Her!'

'Jai Maa Bhaarati!' bellowed Toshani, Abdul and Govardhan.

'Jai Maa Bhaarati!' thundered the army.

'Jai Maa Bhaarati!'

'Jai Maa Bhaarati!'

To the stirring roars dedicated to the motherland, the warriors began marching out.

To Bahraich.

To the call of destiny.

To the call of Mother India.

Chapter 28

It was just a week later that the Shravasti scouts had led Suheldev's army to a large open plain close to Bahraich. Being the first to reach, they had picked the advantageous side, and dug in well. The Turks had avoided coming close to the battlefield for a few days. They knew that the positions they would be forced to occupy was not the best for them. They did try to harry Suheldev's camp, trying to get their army to move. When that didn't work, the Turks had no choice but to march over to the battlefield chosen by Suheldev.

The Indian force outnumbered the Turks. The experienced Turkic commanders and spies had huddled together and come up with a figure of roughly seventy thousand Indian soldiers, which meant that they were outnumbered by at least ten thousand. But they were not too troubled by this. Their general, Salar Maqsud, seemed to possess intimate knowledge of the Indian army. He would disappear for weeks on end, secretly travelling throughout India, in disguise, gaining knowledge of the land that he wanted to conquer. Few among the Turks knew where all Salar Maqsud had travelled. But, clearly, the knowledge he had of India was a huge strategic advantage in battle. And since Salar Maqsud did know a lot about the Indians, he had prepared his commanders and soldiers to expect a larger enemy force. He had also convinced them that the numerical advantage of the Indians would not help them in battle. For they had greater numbers largely in infantry, and not in the far more important division of the cavalry.

But for all his knowledge of India and battle tactics, Salar Maqsud had been bested by Suheldev when it came to their position in this battlefield.

Their severe disadvantage at arriving late on the battlefield and being stuck with a far worse field position, was painfully obvious to the Turks.

They were lower down the course of the small river which flowed by the two army camps. Which meant that the refuse of Suheldev's camp would spoil the waters by the time it reached the Turks. This had already caused some diseases to break out in the Turkic camp. Furthermore, Turkic scouts had reported that the marching route from their camp to the battlefield was riddled with big ditches from an older, dried-up, water course. This prevented the Turkic soldiers from marching in ideal infantry and cavalry formations. The dense jungles on one side, and the lake on the other, hemming in the flanks of the chosen battlefield, also made it obviously difficult for the Turkic cavalry to bring their full force into the battle.

Suheldev had arrived early. And had taken good advantage of it.

The Turks knew that.

And they had been avoiding battle.

Until now.

It was late at night. The mounted Turkic raiding group moved stealthily through the dense woods. There were cloth coverings around their saddle stirrups to muffle their sounds. The swords and knives had cloth strips wrapped around them, which would automatically tear away when the blade was pulled out of the scabbard. The cloth strips stifled the sound of metal hitting against the insides of their scabbards. The horse shoes had been covered with leather, to mute the sounds of their cantering. Verbal commands had been strictly banned. Only bird calls, to be made by Turkic army heralds, were used to convey commands.

This was a daring and dangerous mission. But Salar Maqsud was not too perturbed. Much against Kerim's advice, he had decided to lead this raiding party himself.

He had been clear with Kerim. *Trust me, all we have to do is break in and kill Suheldev. The Indians will scatter after that. And then we will chase and massacre them all.*

Maqsud's plan was simple: break the traditional Indian rules of war, of not battling after sundown or killing unarmed and sleeping opponents. The Turks planned to attack the enemy camp at night, plunge it into confusion, and kill as many Indians and horses as they could, so as to incapacitate the enemy cavalry. But most importantly, a small troop of crack commandos intended to break all the way in to the royal tent and kill Suheldev. And then, the raiding party would send a signal for the rest of the Turkic army to launch a full-scale attack.

It will all be over by sunrise, thought Salar Maqsud, remembering the havoc the Turks had wreaked with a night attack on the Tomar army near Delhi.

But unlike the battle near Delhi, where the Turks had literally caught their foes napping, this time, the Indians were alert. The approach to the camp was reasonably well lit. Suheldev's sentries had been posted in pairs, each armed with a horn, to sound out warnings. The night guards were not allowed to sit around a fire, where the comforting heat might cause some to fall asleep. They had to communicate every two minutes, using specific light signals, with their neighbouring sentries stationed a hundred metres away. If any pair of night guards did not receive the standard signal from their neighbouring sentries by the appointed time, it was to be assumed that those guards had been killed and the warning horn was to be sounded.

The guard watch was disciplined, well-planned and alert.

The kafirs *are learning,* Salar Maqsud had thought grudgingly. *Suheldev is smart.*

The only path that was relatively less well-guarded was a part of the Indian camp flanking a dense jungle. Perhaps they had assumed that the Turks could not get a significant mounted force through there. This was the weakness that Salar Maqsud intended to leverage.

But little did he know that this was exactly what Suheldev expected the Turkic general to do.

Often, what appears as your enemy's weakness is actually a well-planned ploy.

As Salar Maqsud rode through the forest, there was one thing that he was sure of.

There are Muslims in his camp. Suheldev has naïvely accepted them. The believers will turn against their Hindu leader when they see a fellow faithful like me on the other side. Suheldev's inner camp and his bodyguards are the ones who will kill him.

I will win.

I will rule.

As the Turks continued riding silently, a loud bird call was heard. The tone and the length of the bird call was certainly not that of the Turks.

Everyone assumed the obvious. It must actually be a bird.

But something pricked inside Salar Maqsud. It didn't seem quite right.

However, the bird call was perfect. The tone. The pitch. The volume. The length of time. Everything was perfect.

Maqsud continued to ride. It was a short period of time before his raiding party would reach the Indian camp. And then victory would be his.

But his mind kept going back to that bird call. He shook his head. *It was perfect.*

And then Maqsud froze. As the instinctive warning he felt in his heart suddenly converted into a clear thought in his mind.

It was too perfect.

It's not a bird!

Maqsud immediately pulled his shield forward and bellowed at the top of his voice. 'Shields up!'

And almost immediately, the swoosh of an arrow flying in was heard. Which was followed almost instantly by a muffled cry of pain as it slammed into the throat of one of the Turkic raiders. He tumbled backwards, off his horse, and landed on the ground with a thud.

All the Turks had their shields up by now. But there were arrows flying in from all directions.

You can't protect yourself from a shower of missiles that you can't even see.

The raiders were halted in their tracks, frozen by the unexpected turn of events. Cowering behind their shields. Within seconds, several more saddles emptied as a torrent of arrows poured down upon the raiders.

The dense jungle ensured such darkness that the Turks couldn't even clearly see how many of their men were falling. But the sounds made it obvious that there were several.

And the clamour of Indians roaring loudly only added to the terror that had suddenly overtaken the Turks.

Maqsud had his shield held high. Staying close to the soldiers surrounding him. Using them as human shields. But he knew that the situation was hopeless.

They're picking us off like fish in a barrel.

A loud Indian order was heard. 'Lights!'

It was Abdul. He was leading the Indian archers in this ambush against the Turks.

Suddenly, light started appearing in the distance. The Indians had lit up some torches. Trying to spread some light to see the Turks. To make their arrows count for more.

The missiles continued to fly in, killing more and more Turks.

The Indians were all hidden high up in the trees. Protected well in *machans* there. They had planned this well. Maqsud had galloped right into a well-laid trap.

The desperate sounds of Turks screaming in pain scoured the night. Mixed with the insistent bellowing of the Indian battle cries.

'Har Har Mahadev!'

'Jai Shri Ram!'

But it was one battle cry that truly filled the hearts of the Turks with dread. It was a battle cry that normally infused them with power and strength. Now, it terrorised them. 'Allahu Akbar!'

A cry that resounded when the Turks attacked India, was now being heard as Indian Muslims defended Mother India.

'Allahu Akbar' linked seamlessly with 'Har Har Mahadev' and 'Jai Shri Ram', and then all these cries were mingled into the battle cry that truly mattered. The one cry to unite them all: 'Jai Maa Bhaarati!'

The Turks kept falling as Indian arrows tore into them.

A Turk to the left of Maqsud shouted loudly, 'This is a disaster, My Lord! Order the retreat! Order the retreat!'

The Turk's words were cut short as an arrow flew in, brutally ramming itself into the soldier's left eye. He fell from his horse, screaming in agony.

Kerim, on the other side of Maqsud, yelled, 'Order the retreat, Maqsud!'

Maqsud knew, even in this chaos, that retreat was impossible. Most of the arrows were coming in from behind them. He remembered the layout of this jungle well.

There was only one way out of this mess. No retreat. But a full charge ahead. The escape from this ambush was to burst through it. Out of range of the archers stationed high up in the trees.

And then flee through the woods to the right.

'Full speed ahead,' roared Maqsud. 'Charge forward!'

Maqsud kicked his horse into action. And the courageous Turks too started galloping behind their general. Screaming maniacally. Charging themselves into a frenzy.

It was a fight for their lives!

Suddenly, armed men, led by Ashvaghosh, rose from camouflaged positions in the ground or leapt off low tree branches to intercept the Turks. Shooting torrents of arrows repeatedly.

By now, the jungle had turned into a forest of light as the Indians lit more and more torches to be able to attack the Turks.

'Fight through!' roared Maqsud. 'Fight through!'

Ashvaghosh saw the Turk leading the raiding party hacking at the men who were trying to stop him. The gold-tipped helmet on the Turk and his high-quality armour made it obvious that this one was a senior officer in the Turkic army. Ashvaghosh knew that Suheldev would love for this commander to be taken prisoner. For the commander could be tortured for information.

'Get that Turkic commander!' bellowed Ashvaghosh, running towards the Turkic riders. 'Get him alive!'

Sanghamani, also a part of Ashvaghosh's ambush team, was right in the path of the riders. Maqsud picked up speed as he rode hard towards Sanghamani's platoon. The monk shot a couple of arrows, but they glanced off Maqsud's exceptionally sturdy armour. Sanghamani dropped his bow and drew out his sword.

'Jai Maa Bhaarati!' screamed the Indian platoon.

Meanwhile, Ashvaghosh, in the distance, began to race towards his friend.

Just before Maqsud reached Sanghamani, another of Suheldev's soldiers leapt at him. The rider chopped viciously, almost severing the sword arm of the Indian cleanly. The man spun around and fell to his knees. Maqsud rode past him and charged at Sanghamani, slashing hard at him with his sword. The monk rolled smoothly to the side, avoiding Maqsud's blow and slashing ferociously across the horse's legs. A standard tactic to bring an animal down. And with it, the mounted rider.

But Turkic horses were covered for such strikes. Leather armour ran down their legs, up to their knees. Making it difficult for blades to get through.

The horse didn't falter at all. As Sanghamani stared helplessly, Maqsud drew back his sword for the killing blow. Ashvaghosh arrived at that precise moment. The man whom Maqsud had wounded moments ago was still on his knees, clutching the gaping wound in his arm. Without breaking his stride, Ashvaghosh ran straight up to him, put one foot on his shoulder and used the leverage to launch himself through the air, crashing straight into Maqsud.

The two men tumbled off the horse together and landed on the ground in a tangled heap. Ashvaghosh rolled away, then put his hands behind his head on the earth and nimbly flipped himself back on to his feet. As the Turkic general staggered up unsteadily, Ashvaghosh delivered a roundhouse kick that snapped his head back and sent him sprawling to the ground again.

Meanwhile, Sanghamani was held back by another Turk who charged at him.

Kerim had been riding beside Maqsud through most of the encounter. But he had been blocked by two of Suheldev's men who were brandishing spears. He desperately tried to find a way around them to rescue his beloved general.

Even as Kerim continued to fight the soldiers in front of him ferociously, he screamed for the life of the man he loved. 'Maqsuuuuud!'

Ashvaghosh drew a dagger from his waistband and approached the disoriented Turkic general, who was scrambling on the ground for his sword.

Maqsud's helmet had fallen off. As Ashvaghosh drew back his dagger threateningly, he roared, 'Surrender!'

Maqsud turned, with one hand up, seemingly in surrender. His face, which had been in the shadows, was suddenly in the light.

Ashvaghosh froze. Stunned. 'Aslan?!'

He hesitated. The dagger suspended in mid-air.

And that hesitation proved fatal for the Buddhist monk.

Maqsud found his sword and immediately thrust it up

viciously. The blade ripped through the monk's abdomen, slicing through muscles and vital organs. Maqsud thrust harder, and the blade broke through the brave monk's back.

A gasping, agonised sound came out of Ashvaghosh's mouth. The dagger fell from his suddenly limp hand. His knees buckled and he clutched at the Turk's shoulder, fighting to stay on his feet.

Maqsud stood up, still holding his sword. He gripped Ashvaghosh by the neck, then slowly, almost tenderly, twisted in the sword even further before brutally yanking it out. Blood pumped out of the wound at a furious pace, turning the earth at his feet dark.

The monk swayed for a moment, then toppled to the ground.

Kerim had, meanwhile, broken through the two soldiers blocking his path. As he raced towards Maqsud, he held his hand out. 'Maqsuuud!'

The Turkic general grabbed Kerim's arm, and vaulted onto the horse.

The Turks kept riding.

Retreating from the failed attack.

Sanghamani had, by now, managed to kill the Turk he was fighting. He rushed towards his fatally injured friend. 'Ashvaghosh!'

Ashvaghosh knew he was going to die. The wound was too deep. Too many vital organs had been slashed.

But he was not afraid of his own death. He was afraid of something else. He held his friend tight and then pointed at the retreating Turks, whispering urgently. 'As … As …'

Sanghamani tried to pick Ashvaghosh up. To take him back to the camp. But Ashvaghosh struggled against his friend.

Pointing at the retreating Turks again, he found his last gasp of strength and whispered urgently, 'Aslan … That's … Aslan … Warn … Suheldev … Warn the … king …'

Sanghamani stared at the Turks riding away into the night and then back at his friend. Stunned. 'Aslan?!'

'Save … Suheldev …'

The enormity of the deception suddenly hit Sanghamani. *Suheldev … The bodyguards … Aslan's men …*

Oh, Lord Buddha!

Chapter 29

'Calm down, Abdul!' said Suheldev, restraining his friend.

It was late in the night. A clearly agitated Abdul was outside Suheldev's royal tent. Many more torches had been lit all across the camp now. And the area outside the royal tent was especially well lit. News of the devastation of the Turkic raiding party had electrified the rest of the Indians with positive energy, but Abdul was enraged. Enraged with Suheldev.

'I told you not to trust him!' screamed Abdul. 'I told you not to let him into our army! I told you!'

Suheldev kept his voice calm. 'Abdul … I don't think that …'

But Abdul was not listening. He turned to his soldiers. 'Arrest all of Aslan's men! Behead them right now! They are Turkic dogs!'

'Abdul!' Suheldev's voice was harsh. 'What has gotten into you? Calm down! We can't create divisions among our—'

'I told you! You trusted the wrong man! Aslan killed Ashvaghosh! That Aslan is a—'

Abdul stopped talking as the flap of Suheldev's tent lifted suddenly and Aslan walked out. Followed by Toshani and Govardhan. Abdul stared at Aslan. Stunned for a little while. Then, he uttered a cry of pure rage and lunged at him, wrapping both his hands around his throat.

'Abdul, stop!' cried Suheldev, grabbing Abdul and trying to pull him away. 'What are you doing?!'

Abdul was screaming in fury now. As Govardhan and Suheldev managed to drag him away, he kicked out, hitting Aslan straight on his chest.

Aslan slumped to his knees under the impact of the blow. Abdul managed to escape Govardhan's hold and kicked Aslan hard in the ribs once again, sending him sprawling to the ground.

'Abdul! Stop!' shouted Govardhan as he pulled Abdul back once again.

Aslan just lay there. He knew the truth was out. It had to come out some day. He was only surprised that the deception had lasted for so long.

Suheldev and Govardhan yanked and hauled Abdul away, even as he continued to scream abuses and kick ineffectually in the air. Toshani rushed up to Aslan, helping him up.

Suheldev held Abdul tight. Almost pleading with him. 'Abdul, please! Calm down ... He couldn't have killed Ashvaghosh ... There must be some confusion ... Aslan never left the camp. He was with me all along.'

'He was there!' bellowed Abdul. 'He killed Ashvaghosh! Sanghamani saw him!'

Aslan slowly straightened up, letting go of Toshani's supportive hand. All the colour had drained from his face. He looked tired. 'Sanghamani's eyes were not lying, brave Abdul ... But they weren't telling him the whole truth either.'

'Stop speaking in riddles, you snake,' snapped Abdul. He turned to his men. 'Kill Aslan! Kill all his men!'

'Wait!' ordered Suheldev, raising his hand.

And Abdul's men stopped in their tracks. Obeying their king.

Aslan looked down. Silent. Troubled.

The silence was broken by Suheldev. 'Aslan, speak!'

'Just kill him!' screamed Abdul.

Govardhan restrained a seething Abdul. Suheldev continued to stare at Aslan. There was fear in Aslan's eyes. And sadness. A profound sadness.

Suheldev spoke softly, but the menace in his voice was clear. 'Aslan, speak. What is going on? Speak, before I am forced to free Abdul's hands.'

Aslan looked up at Suheldev and drew a deep breath, as if steeling himself. When he finally spoke, it was as if every word was being prised out of him. 'I am not who I said I was.'

Abdul erupted in fury once again. 'I told you!'

Suheldev raised his hand for silence. And Abdul obeyed. The king of Shravasti held the hilt of his sword, ready to draw it quickly. Glaring at Aslan, he growled, 'Who are you?'

Aslan's eyes were downcast. *Allah have mercy on me.*

'Aslan, speak now!'

Aslan took a deep breath and spoke clearly. 'My name is Salar Masud. I am the nephew of the late Sultan Mahmud of Ghazni … And twin brother of the Turkic general, Salar Maqsud.'

— EJJ ⅍Ɜ∩ƈ∆ —

It had been almost half an hour.

Suheldev, Toshani, Govardhan, Abdul and Sanghamani had moved into the royal tent. Aslan was there. He had been disarmed. And there were ten guards within the tent. Ready to move in quickly at any sudden movements from Aslan. In the meanwhile, Aslan's soldiers were being kept under constant guard by Suheldev's soldiers.

Aslan had told Suheldev and the others the honest details of his life. His life as Salar Masud. That he was the younger son of Salar Sahu and Sitr-i-Mu'alla. While Sahu was a general in the Ghaznavid army, Sitr-i-Mu'alla was the sister of Sultan Mahmud himself.

Though he was born just a few minutes after his twin brother Salar Maqsud, their characters were as different as chalk and cheese.

He spoke of the fanaticism of his twin brother. And his own love for the knowledge and peace of the Sufi way. How their mother supported him. While their father loved his elder twin brother more. He spoke of how his brother was also the favourite of Sultan Mahmud of Ghazni. For Maqsud reflected much of the rigid fanaticism of the sultan himself.

And things had come to a head after an incident of particular cruelty carried out by Salar Maqsud. This was after yet another temple was destroyed by Mahmud's army. This time, that of a temple dedicated to Lord Ram in the largely Buddhist and Hindu city of Peshawar. The idol of Lord Ram Himself was also robbed from that temple. A few weeks after that, a contingent of Hindu Pashtuns had come to the royal court in Ghazni to beg for the return of the idol. In return, they were willing to pay a handsome ransom. Mahmud had wanted to raise some money for a war he intended to wage against the Mongols. And had hence agreed to the deal. Maqsud was appointed to work out the details.

Maqsud had negotiated hard for an astronomical price for the return of the idol. The Pashtuns had paid the money in advance, as they were told to. And when they came to the palace to receive the idol, Maqsud had greeted them with glasses of *sherbet*. It was only after they had drunk it that

Maqsud told them that the idol had technically been returned to them already. For the great idol of the God the Pashtuns worshipped had been ground to dust and mixed in the *sherbet* they had drunk. Maqsud had also taunted the idol-worshipping Pashtuns with a cruel interpretation of a deeply philosophical line. That since the Hindus believed that the divine was in everyone and everything, they had now been presented with the divine in their digestive tract as well. The enraged Pashtuns tried to battle Maqsud, but his guards had beaten them back and they were thrown out of the city. Every single one of those Pashtuns was distraught beyond all limits of endurance, at the sin they had committed by drinking the *sherbet*, even if unknowingly. Every single one of those Pashtuns had committed suicide outside the city gates. And with their dying breaths, they had cursed the city of Ghazni and its rulers. Maqsud had laughed at the sacrifice of the Pashtuns. But many of the Ghazni citizens had been shaken by what the Pashtuns had suffered. One of them was Aslan.

Aslan was enraged. He believed that this was against the tenets of Islam. He had confronted his brother Maqsud. And the confrontation had escalated into a pitched sword-fight between them. His mother had intervened to stop the battling brothers.

Disgusted by it all, Aslan had decided to leave Ghazni.

'Nobody stopped you?' asked Suheldev.

'Nobody cared,' answered Aslan. 'Except for my mother. And even she knew that my views were considered blasphemous among the Ghazni nobility. It would be a matter of time before even I would be called an apostate and killed. I fled the city with the help of a trusted soldier called Ozgur. A story was spread that I had fallen into the Jhikai river and drowned. I took on the name of Aslan, and made my way to India, where I found Sheikh Nuruddin and became a disciple. You all know that happened next.'

'Why didn't you tell us about your real identity earlier?' asked Govardhan.

Aslan made a helpless gesture. 'I wanted to, but I was trapped by the lie I had created. I had changed my name because I wanted to start a new life. When you met me, I was living as Aslan. If I had told you my story then and there, would you have trusted me, or would you have executed me as a spy? I hoped that I had put the life of Masud behind me and could simply live as Aslan without anyone being the wiser about it, but my past has finally caught up with me.'

Suheldev spoke up. 'Why are you helping us now?'

'I believe that what exists in India is precious. It's the only land, in this age of anger, where different religious groups live peacefully with each other. It's the only land where Shia and Sunni Muslims live in relative peace with each other. It's the only land where one can worship all truths, all Gods, and have nobody judge you. India needs to survive. Not just for the good of Islam or Hinduism, but for the good of humanity.' Aslan looked into Suheldev's eyes. 'And you, great king, are the only one in North India who is capable of leading a fight against the rampaging Turkic horde. That is why I must support you. For I had been searching for someone like you.'

Suheldev did not say anything.

'There are some in the Turk army who want peace as well.'

Toshani spoke up. 'Who?'

'You know of Kerim. Commander in their army and Maqsud's lover. He is an old friend of mine. Even he is not in favour of this war. He wants peace. So that he can take

Maqsud away and they can live happily in another land. He knows that as long as Maqsud keeps dreaming of conquering India, they will not know peace. They will waste their entire lives in endless war.'

Govardhan and Toshani looked like they believed Aslan's story. Suheldev's face remained impassive, non-committal.

But Abdul, clearly, did not believe a word. He turned to Suheldev. 'This is nonsense. Do you believe this fantastical story, My Lord?'

Suheldev remained silent. Staring into Aslan's eyes. Letting his instinct guide him.

'So, what do we do with him now?' asked Abdul, flexing his hands. He was clear about what he wanted to do.

Suheldev stood up and walked to the idol of Lord Shiva placed at one end of the tent. He didn't look back at the people sitting around the table. He kept on staring at the feet of the Lord. At the flowers and bilwa leaves that lay bunched there. At the ashes of the burning incense stick. At long last he turned and looked back at Aslan. 'You and your men will be right on the front line tomorrow. You will form a separate unit, backed up by my main infantry. You will have the honour of leading the charge into the Turkic centre.'

Aslan nodded and smiled. *Typically Suheldev. Kind. Yet pragmatic.*

Aslan knew that killing him and his soldiers would be the easiest thing for Suheldev to do. But, clearly, he didn't want to do that. Maybe because he believed that Aslan and his men were innocent. But he was not about to keep them prisoners either. He would have to post his own men to guard them; men who would be needed in the battle. And he didn't want to keep Aslan and his men in reserve. Just in case they did turn out to be traitors, they could cause severe damage to the Indian war effort from there. Much better to send Aslan and his men into the front line. In the centre where most of the fighting was done. It would be considered an honour. And in case they turned, there was very little damage they could do to the Indians from that position.

Kind. Yet pragmatic.

Aslan stood up and saluted smartly. 'My men and I will not let you down, My Lord.'

Chapter 30

The sun rose, bathing the sky in an angry red hue. Usually, most people would be barely stirring out of their beds at this early hour. But the two huge armies were already lining up on the vast field. It had been two days since the failed Turkic raid into the Indian camp. Suheldev had also got to know of a Turkic plan to have cows in front of their own army, so that the Hindus among the opposing Indian army would be wary of fighting, for fear of hurting the holy animals. He had sent a raiding party the previous night to the Turkic camp, under the leadership of Govardhan, to release all the cows from Turkish captivity. Govardhan and his band of warriors had succeeded. Subterfuge had failed. The time for open battle had come.

The soldiers had been up well before even the first pale light of dawn, greeting what many knew could be their last day on earth. They tried not to think about it as they hurriedly rushed through their ablutions. The older veterans wolfed down whatever food was available. From years of hard-earned experience, they knew that it would be a long, exhausting day, and they needed to store up as much energy as they could. Especially as the hours dragged on and the true fury of the baking hot Indian summer day would descend upon them. Many of the younger ones though were too excited, or too nervous—or both—to have much of an appetite. They nibbled distractedly at the rations offered to them.

Everybody prayed. There are no atheists on a battlefield. Some prayed for victory, some for honour and some to simply live through the day and see their loved ones again.

Then, orders were bellowed out and the troops swiftly fell into formation. Archers gently tugged at bowstrings to loosen stiff muscles. Others flexed their necks, backs and shoulders. A gentle breeze fluttered across the vast plain, caressing faces, and stiffening the flags. Alleviating the unbearable heat just a little bit.

Suheldev emerged from his royal tent. Suited in armour. Armed with weapons. Fired by courage. Ready for battle.

Toshani, Govardhan, Abdul and Sanghamani were waiting for him. Mounted on their horses. Suheldev smiled at them and nodded.

He turned as his horse was brought to him. He mounted quickly and rode out. And the rest followed closely behind.

All of them rode silently. To the front.

— ᨳ ᨠᨤᨶᨮ —

Aslan was already there on the frontlines. He was the first to see the king riding in. And he led the cheers.

The roar of the Indians on seeing their brave king grew louder and louder.

'Suheldev!'

'Suheldev!'

'Suheldev!'

Suheldev raised his hand. And the army fell silent.

'My friends!' bellowed Suheldev, as he rode up and down

the front line. He pointed at the Turks amassed on the other side of the huge battlefield. 'These monsters attacked the Somnath*ji* temple! They tore down that holiest of shrines to our Lord! They broke His great idol!'

The Indians clenched their fists in fury, anger coursing through them.

'How many of you are Shaivites?!'

A roar emanated from a third of the army, with loud shouts of 'Har Har Mahadev'.

'We will avenge our Lord today!' thundered Suheldev. 'These beasts also destroyed a temple to Lord Ram in Peshawar! They ground the idol to dust! How many of you are Vaishnavs?'

Loud roars of 'Jai Shri Ram' and 'Jai Shri Krishna' were heard from a third of the army.

'We will avenge Him today as well. They destroyed Buddhist monasteries! They burnt down Sufi shrines, calling our Indian Muslims apostates! They destroyed temples to Shakti Maa, calling Her worship sinful! How many of you follow these great paths of faith?'

Thunderous shouts of 'Jai Shri Buddha', 'Allahu Akbar' and 'Jai Maa Shakti' were heard.

'We will avenge them all today!' Suheldev now leaned over from his saddle, bending down and picking up some dust from the ground. He reared up on top of his saddle, raised his closed fist and bellowed, 'They have defiled this soil! They have insulted the earth of Mother India! How many of you are devotees of Mother India?'

The entire army roared in unison. 'Jai Maa Bhaarati!'

'Jai Maa Bhaarati!' boomed Suheldev.

Toshani, Govardhan, Abdul, Sanghamani and Aslan too repeated Suheldev's stirring cry. 'Jai Maa Bhaarati!'

'Jai Maa Bhaarati!'

'Jai Maa Bhaarati!'

Suheldev rode up and down the front line. His arm raised, his fist clenched tight. His loyal warriors kept repeating the cry.

'Jai Maa Bhaarati!'

'Jai Maa Bhaarati!'

Suheldev opened his hand and spread the holy earth across his forehead. Then he signalled for silence. His soldiers obeyed. 'A thousand years from now, poets will compose songs of this day ... A thousand years from now, the best bards in the land will write stories of this day ... A thousand years from now, Indians will stop what they are doing and listen in wonder to the brave legends that were formed today ... They will believe that mythic warriors arose from the bosom of Mother India to defend her from the most brutal killers in human history!'

The army was deathly silent.

'Those Indians of a thousand years from now, will stand in awe of their ancestors, who fought like Gods to defend freedom. They will stand in awe of you. They will stand in awe of the legendary warriors who fought and won the Battle of Bahraich.'

The soldiers stood tall, their backs straight, their shoulders back, their spirits strong.

Suheldev's voice dropped low. 'Now all we have to do is bring those legends to life!'

'To victory!' roared Toshani.

'To victory!' bellowed all the Indians.

'Jai Maa Bhaarati!'

'Jai Maa Bhaarati!'

'Jai Maa Bhaarati!'

Suheldev rode back to where his lieutenants waited. His order was simple: 'To positions.'

— EⅡ ꝋꝯꝺ —

As Aslan had predicted in their strategy meeting several days ago, the bulk of the Turkic cavalry was deployed on the two flanks. They appeared to have kept very few as reserves.

'Some good news from our spies ... The army of Kannauj will not be fighting against us today,' said Toshani. Abdul, Govardhan and she were mounted on horses and formed a loose semi-circle with Suheldev. Toshani continued. 'Apparently, revolts have broken out across Kannauj. The citizens are furious with the massacre at Harsaran and the death of Vrishabh*ji*. Ajitpal had to return to quell the revolts, otherwise Maqsud's supply lines could have been threatened.'

Suheldev nodded grimly. 'That's a reckoning for another day.'

'The army of Manohargarh is here, though,' said Toshani. 'King Jaichand is reported to be in the centre, along with Maqsud.'

'We fought and beat his soldiers often when we were bandits,' Govardhan said, chuckling at his distant relative. 'This is the first time he's dared to personally take the field against us.'

Suheldev looked at Abdul and Govardhan. 'You know what you have to do.'

Abdul reached across and embraced Suheldev. 'Allah be with us today, great king.' He then nodded towards Govardhan and Toshani. And galloped off.

Govardhan reached over and hugged Suheldev. 'May Lord Ram guide us to victory,' he said. Then he turned to Toshani and clasped her hand. 'Give them hell, brave lady!'

Toshani smiled and said, 'Make sure that you leave some Turks for me to kill as well.'

Govardhan smiled even more broadly, then spurred his horse and rode away.

Abdul was commanding the left flank while Govardhan was in charge of the right flank. Both reached their respective positions and quickly made sure their mounted troops were in full readiness.

On the Turkic side, Maqsud frowned as he surveyed the army lined up against him. The two Indian flanks were made up largely of infantrymen and archers, with just a few riders in support. The bulk of Suheldev's cavalry was concentrated in the centre.

'It's almost as if Suheldev is inviting me to crush his flanks,' he said. 'What the hell is he thinking?'

'The fool has no experience of major battles,' sneered Jaichand, the king of Manohargarh. 'He has only fought a few skirmishes in the forest and fancies himself to be a great general.'

Maqsud grunted irritably. Like any seasoned warrior, he preferred not to underestimate his foe, especially one who had repeatedly proven himself to be a wily tactician. But he was unable to make sense of Suheldev's plan.

'Well, only one way to find out,' he muttered to himself. He turned to his heralds. 'Signal a full charge by the cavalry on both flanks,' he ordered. 'Crush the *kafirs* and encircle them.'

Horns were blared, flags were waved and commands rang out. A few minutes later, the earth seemed to tremble as the Turkic cavalry thundered into action. As they charged headlong at their hopelessly mismatched foes, a massacre seemed inevitable.

Abdul allowed himself a flicker of a smile as he saw the Turkic cavalry bearing down at his men. 'Allahu Akbar,' he whispered to himself, shutting his eyes briefly. Then he reopened them and waited, counting down the seconds.

Suddenly, one of the charging Turkic horses neighed loudly—a sound of pure agony and anguish—and went crashing to the ground. Another shrieked in pain and abruptly broke off its charge, hobbling to a side—straight into the path of another charging horse. The two horses collided and the sound of the impact rang out clearly even over the noise made by galloping hooves and war cries. The two horses and their riders collapsed in a tangle of mutilated limbs and smashed bones. More and more horses were incapacitated in front of the stunned Turks.

Horrified, Maqsud turned to one of his officers. 'Get up there and find out what the hell is going on!'

The mystifying development was the result of work done on Suheldev's command the previous night. Soldiers had liberally scattered spikes across the ground on which the Turkic cavalry was expected to charge. The spikes, which looked like four-pointed stars, had been specially made by local Indian ironsmiths. Because of their design, one of the four sharp iron-spike points would always face upward from a stable base. Randomly strewn along the path of the advancing cavalry, they made for a simple but devastating trap, and the Turks had ridden right into it. The line of spikes was not very deep, but as the first few ranks of horses went down, they blocked the way for the cavalry coming up from behind, forcing the riders to pull up sharply. Some were unable to halt in time and their steeds went down too as they collided with the fallen horses, a few of which were struggling to get back on their feet, neighing painfully.

As the Turkic charge faltered on both flanks, Suheldev raised his right arm, then brought it down. Seconds later, a whirring sound became audible as hundreds of arrows were unleashed on the enemy cavalry. They were followed within a few heartbeats by another volley of arrows. Then another. And another. In a continuous flow.

The sharp arrows punched through the leather armour of the mounted Turkic soldiers. Only the senior officers had metal armour, capable of stopping these arrows. Terrified, agonised screams rang out from men and animals alike as death and destruction rained down upon them mercilessly.

Maqsud swore in frustration as he saw much of the cavalry that he had been heavily counting on torn to pieces in the first few minutes of the battle, before the two sides had even crossed swords. 'Call them back!' he roared, his voice thick with anger.

There was no response and he turned to find the officer next to him staring at the field, his jaw hanging open as he gazed in horror at the carnage taking place there. Maqsud lashed out angrily at the officer with his fist, breaking his jaw.

All eyes in Maqsud's vicinity instantly turned towards him. 'If I have to repeat an order again, I'll take the head of the person who fails to obey me instantly! Now, call them back.'

Horns blared out again and the Turkic cavalry disengaged and began to limp back. Abdul grinned and turned to his infantrymen. 'Follow them, but don't go beyond the line where the spikes end.'

On the other flank, Govardhan was giving the same orders to his men.

Maqsud looked around frantically as Suheldev's strategy finally became clear. 'Our flanks are in retreat, and he'll try to use his superior numbers at the centre to crush us,' he muttered to himself, wracking his brain for some way to save his army from the impending doom that loomed before it. Then his face suddenly brightened.

Govardhan was leading his men as they charged at the retreating Turks. 'Don't cross the line of spikes,' he yelled repeatedly as his men plunged into the shattered ranks of the fallen Turks, killing any survivors. He saw one soldier about to disobey him in his excitement, and slammed his mace down hard on his shield.

'I'll kill anyone who doesn't follow orders,' he shouted, waving his mace around in the air for emphasis. The men halted, some muttering discontentedly as they saw the Turks getting away.

There was a gentle cough. Govardhan turned and saw a young officer looking at him with a perplexed expression.

'What is it?' he snapped.

'I beg your pardon, sir,' said the officer diffidently. 'It's just that we have them on the run right now. Why don't we finish them off?'

Before Govardhan could answer, horns blared out again from the Turkic side. He looked towards them to see what was going on, then swore bitterly.

'That's why,' he said, pointing towards the left flank of Suheldev's army.

Like Govardhan, Abdul too had been ensuring that none of his men crossed the safe zone. Unfortunately, some of the Turkic archers had been providing covering fire to help their cavalry retreat. A stray arrow had hit Abdul in the left eye, sending him tumbling from his horse. With Abdul no longer in charge, his excited men ignored their instructions and poured after the retreating Turks, stepping on the fallen bodies of Turkic men and horses to avoid trampling on the spikes that still littered the ground.

As Maqsud observed this, his flagging spirits lifted. Fate had offered him a slim chance and he gratefully seized it.

'Turn around,' he bellowed in excitement. 'You're on safe ground now. Form up again. Charge at the *kafirs* and wipe them out. They won't be able to stand against a cavalry charge on plain ground!'

Orders were relayed. And the Turks obeyed.

The hunted suddenly turned into hunters as the Turkic riders swiftly yanked their horses around and charged at the Indian soldiers who were still pursuing them. Seething from the mauling they had received just a few moments ago, they struck furiously at their opponents.

With the spikes no longer impeding the cavalry charge, and Suheldev's archers unable to shoot as they feared hitting their own troops, it was a hopelessly one-sided affair. Within a few moments, Suheldev's left flank was shredded. As his men tried to retreat, many were hacked to pieces.

Suheldev cursed as he saw the dramatic turnaround. 'We need to shore up that flank before it collapses completely!'

Toshani's regiment was closest to the flank. She signalled to her troops and rode off at a fast gallop. More regiments followed as fresh Indian soldiers raced to reinforce the left flank.

Standing up in his stirrups to get a better look, Maqsud surveyed the battlefield. 'Things are a lot better now than they were a short while ago. Too bad we couldn't damage their right flank like we did the left.'

'That lake is protecting them,' observed Kerim. 'Otherwise we could have outflanked them.'

Maqsud swallowed, suddenly aware that he was painfully thirsty. He had not drunk water for what seemed like hours and he felt like he had sweated buckets, the damp clothes under his armour clinging to him like a second skin.

'Give me some water,' he ordered. A waterskin bag was hastily passed to him and he took a deep, grateful gulp. 'Damn the heat in this blighted country,' he cursed, mopping at his brow. Then, suddenly, he paused.

It's peak summer. The water level in the lake must be lower than usual.

Maqsud turned to Kerim. 'Get somebody to ride a horse into the lake and see just how deep it is.'

Kerim knew that this would call for the equivalent of a sacrificial goat. Some poor soldier would drown in case the lake was too deep. But in case it wasn't so, a new flank could be opened against the Indians.

Kerim knew better than to argue with Maqsud during a battle.

Orders were issued. And a Turkic soldier rushed to obey. Stripping off his armour hastily, he rode towards the lake and urged his horse into it.

The animal hesitated, reluctant to enter the water. The officer spurred it on, and a couple of men prodded it from behind. Finally, it gingerly stepped into the lake. Within the first few steps, water had reached its knees, then its shoulders.

It's not going to work, thought Maqsud bitterly.

Then he noticed that the water was not rising any further even as the horse continued to wade across the lake. Soon, it had crossed the halfway point. As it moved further, the water receded and fell to its chest, then to its knees.

Maqsud's orders were issued immediately. 'Ford the lake

and come out on the other side. Then ride towards the rear of the enemy and cross the lake one more time to take him from there.'

The Turks on the flank hastened to comply.

Govardhan frowned, puzzled as he saw the manoeuvre being carried out. Then in a flash, he understood what Maqsud was trying to do.

'Pull back!' Govardhan yelled to his men urgently. 'When they cross the lake again, make sure we're facing them. Don't let them get behind us.'

The Indians scrambled to take their new positions, the archers making sure that they would be ideally situated to greet the Turkic soldiers with a deadly shower of arrows the moment they came into range.

Suheldev grunted in satisfaction as he saw Govardhan's move. The burly general had done exactly what Suheldev himself would have in his place. Then he turned his attention back towards what lay in front of him.

In the process of trying to outflank Suheldev by ordering his left cavalry to cross the lake, Maqsud had opened up a huge gap between his centre and left flank. Trying to fill the gap would mean thinning his ranks considerably.

So far, Suheldev had avoided committing the bulk of his cavalry to the battle. Now, the vacant area seemed to gape invitingly at him.

I can charge into that area and then smash straight through Maqsud's centre.

He looked around and saw Aslan and his men in the front line, waiting patiently. Aslan felt Suheldev's gaze on him and looked at him questioningly. Suheldev beckoned to him to approach.

'Do you see what I see?' Suheldev asked when Aslan got within earshot.

Aslan nodded but said nothing.

'It's time,' Suheldev told Aslan. 'Lead the charge on the enemy centre.'

Aslan bowed his head and touched his chest with his hand. 'It will be an honour.'

Then he rode back swiftly to his small contingent. A roar of excitement went up from them as they heard the orders. Almost immediately, the charge began. Aslan's band raced towards the enemy. The rest of Suheldev's central cavalry followed a short distance behind.

'Here they come,' said Kerim as the opposing cavalry swept towards them.

Maqsud nodded grimly, his face drawn. He was fully aware that the next few minutes could seal the fate of the battle one way or the other. 'Hold the centre at all costs,' he yelled at the top of his voice. 'No retreat, no surrender, no prisoners!'

The order was shouted up and down the ranks as the Turks waited for the Indian centre to converge upon them.

Chapter 31

Toshani slashed viciously with her sword, hacking the neck of a Ghazni soldier as he was about to strike an Indian who had been knocked down to the ground.

The soldier's headless corpse collapsed onto the prone man. With a shudder, he pushed it away and scrambled to his feet, smiling in gratitude.

The man's face was covered with blood and gore, but his features seemed vaguely familiar. Toshani squinted hard, and with a start realised that it was Sanghamani.

'What happened here?' she asked. 'Where's Abdul?'

Sanghamani shook his head. 'I saw him get hit by a stray arrow. Bloody bad luck. I don't know what happened to him.'

Shit, it's a complete mess, thought Toshani. *But maybe I can still retrieve the situation.*

She quickly looked around, assessing the scene, then raised her voice. 'Fall back and regroup! Fall back!'

Her heralds rushed to call out the orders.

Just then a grating voice was heard. 'What's the hurry, sweetheart?' It was a Turkic officer who had ridden up along with several other cavalrymen. Toshani had initially been accompanied by many bodyguards but most of them had either fallen, or been left behind, in her daring charge to reinforce the collapsing flank.

Toshani looked around. She was heavily outnumbered.
Lady Kali be merciful.

She didn't allow her despair to show on her face. She pointed her sword at the officer who had addressed her. 'My only hurry is to send you to the gates of hell, you dog.'

With a roar of anger, the Turk charged at Toshani. The sound of clashing blades rang out as Toshani blocked his blow, feeling the shock of the impact jar her wrist and shoulder.

As the man prepared to swing again, Sanghamani jabbed at him with a spear. The man warded off the attack but was momentarily distracted. Toshani immediately plunged her sword into his throat. Blood sprayed from the wound, drenching Toshani's face and stinging her eyes. She blinked and wiped away the blood, trying to clear her vision.

There was a sudden blur of motion to her right. Toshani instinctively brought up her sword. She managed to deflect the blow but the heavy enemy mace clashed with her helmet.

A white light flashed before Toshani's eyes as the helmet was dislodged. Her ears began to ring. Dazed by the blow to her head, barely registering what was happening, she fought on, drawing upon muscle memory, defending herself purely by instinct. Just then, another rider charged up from behind and slashed at her. Toshani felt a blinding pain shoot through the right side of her face, then her body went numb and the world went black.

—— EJJ ꝴꝋᏨᎴ ——

The Turkic lancer lunged towards Suheldev, his weapon aimed straight at the king's chest. Suheldev turned the tip away with his sword, forcing the lance wide. As the lancer rode onwards,

Suheldev struck with his sword, cutting off the man's head. It rolled on the ground but the horse galloped on, the headless body listing slightly to the left and jetting blood in all directions.

Suheldev's men had descended upon the Turks like a hammer blow. The Turkic centre had held under the charge, but only just.

It's a matter of time before they buckle and break.

The Mahadev will grant us victory today.

Another rider loomed up. Suheldev swung his sword. It bit through the Turk's leather armour, but got lodged in his shoulder.

As the man screamed, his horse moved away. Suheldev was almost yanked off his saddle and felt a burst of agony in his shoulder. He let go of his sword, which was still trapped in his opponent's body, and grabbed at the reins.

Aslan, fighting nearby, saw that Suheldev had been disarmed. And he still hadn't reached for the reserve sword in his saddle. Aslan began to ride towards him and then his eyes widened as he saw Kerim charging at Suheldev, his lance at the ready. Aslan shouted a warning to Suheldev, which was drowned out in the din.

Suheldev became aware of the danger in the nick of time. As Kerim thrust at him with his lance, Suheldev managed to block the blow with his shield at the last possible second. The impact of the blow shattered the lance. Suheldev, already off balance, felt the shockwave go through his entire body. He flew through the air before crashing to the ground.

Kerim threw away his useless lance and drew a sword. Suheldev looked around desperately and saw a spear lying next to the body of a dead soldier. He scooped it up and lunged upwards just as Kerim drew back his sword for the killing blow. As he saw the spear being thrust at him, Kerim tried to jerk his head away, but it was too late. The spear went through his right eye and emerged from the back of his head, killing him instantly.

Kerim's horse, still running, cannoned into Suheldev, knocking him to the ground. He hit his head hard and passed out instantly. Seeing him lying senseless, a Turkic officer prepared to finish him off.

'Ozgur, no!' cried out Aslan. He arrived just as Ozgur was about to strike and blocked his blade with his own.

Ozgur looked first at the prone Suheldev and then at Aslan. He was a loyal soldier of Ghazni, but had enormous affection and respect for Aslan—whom he still addressed by his old name, Salar Masud. The conflict was written large on his face.

'He's our enemy, My Lord!' pleaded Ozgur.

'He's my friend!' roared Aslan. 'You'll have to kill me first.'

Ozgur hesitated for a split second. It was long enough for several of Aslan's disciples to rush to his aid. Ozgur disengaged from Aslan and retreated.

Aslan sighed with relief. He had been prepared to battle with Ozgur if need be, but was much happier not having to fight him. Quickly dismounting, he lifted Suheldev and slung him over his saddle. He turned to one of his disciples. 'Get the king to the hospital tent. Take as many of our men as you need. Keep him safe at all costs.'

—— EJ ж𝟹ꓵↄ⊿ ——

'The king has fallen!'

Aslan whipped around as he heard the cry from one of Suheldev's soldiers.

'The king will be back! Fight on!' he yelled, but he could see the rumour spreading rapidly through the ranks, unnerving the men. The charge was in danger of failing.

'Come on, my brave warriors!' thundered Aslan. 'This battle is not over while we live! Allahu Akbar!'

His disciples cheered and rallied around him with roars of 'Allahu Akbar!'

'Death to the Ghaznavids!'

Seeing their fellow men charge at the Turks, Suheldev's soldiers rallied as well. And launched another charge with cries of 'Har Har Mahadev!'.

News of the ferocity of the charge of the Indians in this part of the battle reached Maqsud quickly through some heralds. He also knew that Kerim was in charge of that wing of the army. He was surprised that Kerim was not able to hold the Indians back. The heralds had, wisely, not told Maqsud that Kerim was dead. They knew that this would break the Turkic general.

Maqsud gathered his forces and rushed towards where Aslan and his forces were causing havoc.

While riding, he called out to a herald and said, 'Get Kerim to meet me! I'll tell him what to do.'

The herald kept riding. Remaining silent. Eyes downcast.

It was only moments later that Maqsud realised that there had been no reply from the herald. He looked at the man. And from his eyes, the answer was clear.

That Kerim was dead.

'Where is he? Take me to him.'

'My Lord, please don't,' begged the herald.

'Take me to him!' screamed Maqsud, on the verge of hysteria.

The herald bowed his head and rode towards where Kerim had fallen. A platoon of Turkic soldiers was fighting to keep their commander's body from falling into the enemy's hands. Kerim's body had been hastily covered with a flag of Ghazni that had fallen along with the flag-bearer.

Maqsud fought his way through, dismounted, and reached for the flag.

The Turkic herald pleaded, 'My Lord, please don't! I beg you ...'

Maqsud ignored him and pulled away the flag, uncovering Kerim. He howled in agony when he saw Kerim's beautiful face, horribly ruined by the death blow. He clutched at his chest and sank to his knees, tears streaming down his face.

Rage and misery ravaged Maqsud's soul. He hugged Kerim's body and tenderly kissed what remained of his lover's forehead.

I will see you in Paradise, my beloved.

Then he placed Kerim's mutilated head back on the ground. He turned around and mounted his horse, his face like thunder.

'Kill the *kafirs*!' roared Maqsud to his men. 'Kill them all! Don't leave a single one alive!'

Maqsud spurred his horse and rode towards a spot on the battlefield where the fighting was particularly intense. As he drew closer, he saw his younger twin brother. Maqsud had found out just the previous day that his twin was still alive. And that he had allied with the Indians.

'Masuuuuud!' screamed Maqsud, all his grief and rage channelled at his brother. 'Fight me, you treacherous cur!'

The cry rang out across the field. Aslan looked up and saw Maqsud riding full tilt at him, a furious expression on his face.

Suddenly, an Indian arrow hit Maqsud's horse. Right through the rear flexor leg muscles. The incapacitated horse crumpled to the ground, throwing Maqsud clear. Showing remarkable agility for a man of his bulk, he rolled away and scrambled to his feet, snatching up a sword and shield that lay beside a fallen soldier.

Aslan hesitated, then reined in his horse. He dismounted and stood in front of his brother. There was regret on his face, but there was a look of resolution as well.

'If we're going to fight, let's do it fair and square,' he said.

Maqsud's face was streaked with tears and his eyes were bloodshot. 'You killed Kerim!' roared Maqsud, his voice that of a man who had nothing left to live for.

For all his differences with his brother, Aslan felt a pang of empathy for his pain. 'I did not … And I am sorry for what happened to him.' He meant it. He had always been fond of Kerim, whom he saw as a moderating influence on his brother. Kerim had been a friend of his too.

A look of pure hatred flashed on Maqsud's face. 'I will not leave a single person in this idol-worshipping, infidel hell-hole alive! Beginning with you!'

Aslan rolled his shoulders and flexed his neck, trying to work the tension out of his joints. Then settled into battle position, balancing himself lightly on the balls of his feet, his sword held up.

Deep down, he had always known that one day he would end up in a battle to the death with his brother over the soul of a religion.

'Allahu Akbar!' thundered Aslan. And then added, 'Har Har Mahadev!'

For a few seconds, the two brothers circled each other warily. Then Maqsud let out a roar and attacked.

Maqsud began with a swing towards Aslan's head, which

he blocked with his shield. Aslan's counter-strike, in turn, was thwarted by Maqsud's shield. Maqsud swung again, and Aslan ducked under the blow. As Maqsud's sword completed its swing, he was momentarily off balance. Aslan barrelled into him with his shield, knocking him off his feet. Maqsud scrambled away hastily and came to his feet again, still holding on to his sword, but without his shield.

Maqsud took a deep breath, composing himself. Then he rained a series of blows on Aslan, who used his shield to ward them off. Abruptly, Maqsud kicked out at his twin's knee. As Aslan stumbled, his brother grabbed the rim of his shield and yanked it forward, following up with a blow of his sword's pommel to Aslan's mouth.

Momentarily stunned, Aslan let his sword slip from his hand. Maqsud let out a triumphant roar, wrenched away Aslan's shield and hurled it to the ground. He raised his sword for the decisive blow but Aslan grabbed his wrist and clung on grimly.

Maqsud grabbed his brother by the throat and tried to choke him even as the two wrestled for the sword. Aslan clawed desperately at his brother's grip, but it was too strong. With only a few seconds of consciousness left, he jabbed his fingers at Maqsud's eyes.

Maqsud howled in pain and jerked his head back, loosening his grip on Aslan's throat. Aslan pushed Maqsud's hand away and hastily backed off, snatching up his fallen sword.

Maqsud charged and swung his blade wildly at Aslan's head. Aslan parried the blow and then punched Maqsud hard on the mouth, rocking him back on his heels.

Maqsud retreated a couple of steps and shook his head to clear it. He spat out blood, wiped his mouth and roared in anger. Then he brought up his sword in the classic defensive position and glared at his brother, taking deep breaths to compose himself.

Aslan moved unhurriedly towards Maqsud, then suddenly snapped into motion and thrust his blade at him with lightning speed, hoping to catch him by surprise. But Maqsud was ready and waiting. He responded by deflecting Aslan's blade upwards, then cut at his brother's stomach. Aslan leapt back in the nick of time.

'We had the same teacher, brother,' smirked Maqsud. 'Remember?'

'Yes. And I was the better student.'

'So you think!'

'Save your breath for the fight,' said Aslan, launching a series of rapid thrusts and cuts. Maqsud countered them, but was steadily forced back by the fury of his twin's onslaught.

Unable to see where he was going, Maqsud stumbled upon a corpse lying on the ground and fell. As he quickly got up on one knee, Aslan slashed at him hard. Maqsud blocked him with his sword, but his grip was loose and the force of Aslan's blow knocked the weapon out of his hand.

With an animal cry of rage and desperation, Maqsud pulled out a dagger from his waistband and lunged at Aslan, even as his twin tried to strike him with his sword. Maqsud took a vice-like grip on Aslan's right hand, preventing him from bringing down his sword. Aslan did the same with Maqsud's right hand, preventing him from thrusting up with his dagger. The veins stood out on the foreheads of both brothers as they strained against each other, each exerting his formidable strength to the utmost. Gradually, though, Maqsud was able to push Aslan back. First one step, then another, and then another.

Aslan abruptly changed tack. Instead of trying to overpower

Maqsud, he stepped forward, hooked a leg behind Maqsud's, and pushed. The startled Maqsud went sprawling to the ground. Aslan kicked hard at his wrist, sending the dagger spinning out of his hand.

Yet again, Maqsud showed remarkable athleticism for his bulk. He came off the ground like an uncoiled spring, wrapping his arms around his brother's waist and knocked him off his feet. As Aslan tried to rise, Maqsud grabbed his neck with one hand and an arm with the other hand, lifted him up and hurled him through the air.

Aslan landed hard on the ground, the breath knocked out of him. He struggled to his knees, searching for his sword. Maqsud came storming up and kicked him hard in the ribs.

Aslan groaned in agony and doubled up. Maqsud wound up for another kick but, as he launched it, Aslan grabbed his foot and tugged hard, throwing him off balance. As Maqsud crashed to the ground, Aslan hurled himself upon him. The two brothers rolled over and over, grappling as they once used to playfully do in a far more innocent time, when they were still children. But now, they were hell-bent on tearing each other apart.

The two finally wound up with Maqsud on his back and Aslan straddling him. Their helmets had long since fallen off and their faces were bloody and torn wherever they had clawed at each other with their nails. They pummelled each other with their bare hands, years of pent-up anger and animosity finally finding release.

Aslan backhanded his brother hard across the face. The back of Maqsud's head slammed against the ground. With a roar, he raised his torso and punched Aslan hard on the cheek. Aslan rocked back and Maqsud pushed him off his stomach. Aslan fell to the ground and rolled away.

His breath coming in ragged gasps, Maqsud staggered to his feet. Blearily, he saw Aslan lying on the ground. He strode towards him, intent on bashing in his head with a kick.

Aslan slowly rolled onto his stomach. Through eyes that had been reduced to little more than slits, he saw his brother advancing purposefully towards him. Exhausted, he placed both hands on the ground to push himself up. His right hand touched something. He peered at it and realised that it was the handle of a sword.

As Maqsud drew up, Aslan pushed himself upwards with his left hand and swung hard with the sword. The blade sliced through Maqsud's thigh, opening a deep, bloody gash. Maqsud cried out in pain and shock as his leg gave way. As he collapsed, Aslan pushed him onto his back and loomed over him, sword in hand.

'Please, brother!' Maqsud levered himself onto his elbows and raised a beseeching hand. 'Mercy! Mercy!'

Aslan paused, then his expression hardened. But before he could do anything, Maqsud spoke again, in a wheedling tone. 'Think of our parents, I beg you! You have already abandoned them. Will you leave them without any sons?'

Aslan stopped as if he had been struck. The bloodlust fading from his eyes, replaced by a look of uncertainty.

'Please!' Maqsud pleaded again. 'Spare me! I promise I will leave India and never come back.'

Aslan stared at his elder twin brother. *I had promised Kerim that I would not kill Maqsud.*

Kerim had once saved Aslan's life, when he was still Salar Masud. Aslan always felt that he owed Kerim for this. And the death of Kerim was a blow to him as well.

The tension in Aslan's posture eased. 'Do you surrender to me, brother?'

'Yes, yes, I do!' said Maqsud eagerly. 'Please, just let me go. I will spend the rest of my days in Mecca. I will spend the rest of my days in prayer. Let me grieve for Kerim in peace. Please.'

Aslan lowered his sword. 'I accept your surrender. Order your army to stand down.'

'Yes, of course,' replied Maqsud, raising his hand. 'Help me up, my brother.'

Aslan reached down and extended his hand to his twin. Maqsud smiled and grasped his brother's hand. Aslan pulled him up. As Maqsud came to his feet, his smile widened. Then he suddenly grabbed Aslan by the hair and viciously head-butted him.

Aslan blanked out for a few seconds. When he came to his senses, he was flat on the ground. The sun beating into his face. And then a shadow fell over him. He looked up and saw Maqsud standing by the side, a sword in his hand.

Aslan gave Maqsud a look filled with contempt, but said nothing. Maqsud waited for Aslan to do something. Anything. Perhaps he would beg for mercy, shout at him in anger, or even just avert his gaze in fear. Aslan did none of that. He just stared at Maqsud in an unnerving manner.

It was Maqsud who finally broke the silence. 'Rot in hell, my brother,' he said, his voice bursting with hatred.

Then he swung his blade at Aslan's neck. Decapitating him in one mighty blow. Aslan's severed head rolled to the side. As it came to a halt, it was positioned such that his eyes were staring up at Maqsud. At his brother.

There was pure disgust in those eyes. Disgust at Salar Maqsud.

Chapter 32

Toshani cried out in pain as the medic applied an antiseptic-soaked cloth to her wound. Her body convulsed briefly and then became still again.

'Suhel … Suhel …' she muttered.

'I'm here,' said Suheldev, tightly gripping her hand.

'She's delirious, great king,' said the medic gently. 'I don't think she's hearing you.'

Suheldev had been brought unconscious to the field hospital, but a quick inspection had revealed nothing more serious than a concussion and a shoulder strain. The doctor had told him that he needed to rest. Suheldev had curtly responded that with the battle still raging, that was simply not an option.

He had been about to leave when he heard that Toshani was lying wounded in another hospital tent, and rushed to check on her. Now, he gently stroked her arm, trying to comfort her.

Just then, a senior officer burst into the large tent. 'My Lord, Aslan is dead. He had his brother at his mercy but spared his life. In return, his treacherous brother deceitfully killed him.'

Suheldev came to his feet. Enraged.

'My Lord, the men are panicking,' continued the officer. 'They are on the verge of breaking. Perhaps we should consider retreating and fighting another day?'

Suheldev shook his head. 'If we run now, we'll spend the rest of our lives running. How many fresh men left in the reserves?'

The officer shrugged. 'A couple of regiments at best. If we deploy them, then we have no reserves left to cover a retreat.'

Warfare in these set-piece battles was hugely dependent on when and where the reserve troops were brought in to play.

'Get them ready to charge. It's all or nothing now.'

Saying this, Suheldev strode out of the tent.

A fresh horse was brought for Suheldev. Like all the steeds meant for the king, it was a tall, magnificent animal and had been specially trained for combat. Suheldev stroked its face gently. 'I'm counting on you, Pawan. Take me to victory today and I'll give you a wonderful retirement, with all the juicy grass and pretty mares that you could desire.'

Then he swung onto the saddle.

A boy who looked like he had barely entered his teens was holding the flag of Shravasti.

'Hold that flag up high, boy. Let all our soldiers see it,' ordered Suheldev. Then he signalled to the men. 'Let's go.'

As Suheldev led the men towards the carnage, he encountered a group of Indian soldiers who were retreating, panic writ large on their faces. The men halted when they saw their king.

'Deserters,' growled an officer. 'Shall we execute them, My Lord?'

'Wait,' said Suheldev. He addressed one of the men, a grizzled veteran. 'I remember seeing you this morning, taking an oath along with me to protect our motherland till our last breath. Were those mere words? Do you have no sense of pride? Or honour? Then why did you become a soldier?'

'Forgive us, great king,' said the shame-faced soldier, unable to look Suheldev in the eye. 'We thought you had left the battle.'

Suheldev rose and stood up tall in his saddle. 'Go back to the battle, all of you! Shout it out loud for everyone to hear. I am here! I never have and I never will abandon any of you!'

'The king is here!' shouted the veteran loudly.

The cry was taken up by the other men, and it rippled through the battleground, infusing fresh hope into Suheldev's troops.

'The king is here!'

'King Suheldev is here!'

Suheldev turned to the troops following him and spread his arms wide as if to embrace all of them. 'My brothers, I will need all your strength and courage today. Will you ride with me?'

All the men spoke in unison. 'Yes, My Lord!'

'Will you ride with me to victory?'

'Yes, My Lord!'

Suheldev raised his sword high and brandished it. 'Fight for our land. For our people. For Mother India. Har Har Mahadev!'

The roar was taken up through the ranks. 'Har Har Mahadev!'

Some of the survivors from Aslan's troops shouted, 'Allahu Akbar!'

Suheldev looked at them and roared, 'Avenge Aslan! Allahu Akbar!'

A loud cry went up from the brave warriors.

'Charge!' bellowed Suheldev, urging his horse into a flat-out gallop. The men followed, the hooves of their horses making a thundering sound.

Suheldev's fresh attack smashed through the ranks of the Ghazni army, slicing through its core like a knife going through butter. As the Turks scattered, the soldiers of Shravasti who had been fighting through the day poured in after Suheldev, finding a fresh burst of energy in their exhausted limbs.

The first significant resistance Suheldev encountered was from a group of soldiers dressed in Indian-style armour. As he watched them in action, he couldn't help but grudgingly acknowledge their skill and courage.

It's a shame they're fighting on the other side.

A rider suddenly loomed up from the right and struck at Suheldev with a sword. Suheldev parried the blow and rode past. Just then, Suheldev felt a sharp pain on his left. While he had been distracted by the sword attack, a lancer had attacked from the other side. Only Suheldev's armour had saved him from being run through. Even so, the lance had inflicted a wound that hurt like hell.

The lancer thrust again. With only a split second to react, Suheldev dropped the reins that he was holding in his left hand, grasped the lance from just under the tip and pushed it away from him. The lancer let out a frustrated cry, but before he could do anything else, Suheldev used pressure from his knees to guide his horse, Pawan, straight onto a collision course with the other man's mount.

The two horses rammed into each other with a sickening thud. For a brief moment, both animals staggered and teetered. Pawan managed to regain its footing but the other horse toppled over, falling on its rider.

'Good boy,' said Suheldev, patting Pawan.

Then he saw the first rider charging back into the fight. Again, Suheldev blocked his blow. Before the rider could strike again, one of Suheldev's men buried an axe into the back of his head.

Suheldev nodded to his soldier and turned again to his left. The lancer seemed to have fractured a leg but was determinedly hobbling towards Suheldev. He tried to grab Suheldev and pull him down from the saddle. The king took his foot out of the stirrup and kicked the man in the face, sending him sprawling to the ground. As he tried to rise again, Pawan reared up and smashed the man's skull with his hooves.

Suheldev felt his heart hammering in his chest and took a couple of deep breaths, trying to steady himself. Pawan was equally agitated and Suheldev stroked him gently, soothing him. He looked around the battlefield, trying to take stock of the situation. Then he paused, unconsciously sucking in his breath as he saw a thickset, heavily-bearded man with a curled moustache and a hawk nose scowling at him. His armour was metallic but had a golden sheen, and the emblem of a rising sun was emblazoned on the chest.

These men are his guards.

'Jaichand!' bellowed Suheldev.

The king of Manohargarh growled. 'Suheldev!'

'Your men fight well!' shouted Suheldev. 'They deserve better than a king like you!'

Jaichand snarled in anger and rode towards Suheldev, his sword held high. Suheldev pulled his shield forward. As he came close, Jaichand hacked at the king of Shravasti with his sword, in a standard top-to-down kill strike. Suheldev blocked the blow easily with his shield, then countered with his own sword.

Jaichand moaned in agony as Suheldev's blade hammered down on his gauntlet. The protective covering absorbed some of the blow's impact, but it was still hard enough to leave Jaichand in acute pain. Before he could recover from the first blow, Suheldev hit him on the same spot again. Jaichand's hand went numb. The sword slipped out of his paralysed fingers.

Jaichand's faltering resolve broke completely. He tried to turn his horse around and flee. Then his eyes bulged in shock as Suheldev drove his sword through the side of his neck.

Jaichand stared incredulously at the tip of Suheldev's sword as it emerged from his throat. He tried to speak but only gurgling sounds came out. He coughed once and a mouthful of blood poured out. Then he slumped forward in the saddle. Dead.

Chapter 33

Jaichand's corpse had fallen off his horse. His guards had surrendered already. Suheldev ordered them to fight on his side. With the Indians.

Just then a tense voice was heard. 'My Lord! My Lord!' It was Suryavir, the general who had been sent with a division of Chandela troops to fight alongside the confederacy led by Suheldev.

Suheldev turned towards Suryavir. 'What happened?'

'Our left flank has broken! We need to fall back to avoid being encircled!'

Suheldev cursed. 'Send a messenger to Govardhan. Tell him to send some troops to shore up the flank.'

Suryavir shook his head. 'Govardhan has already sent as many men as he can. If he sends more, his own position in the right flank will be weakened and he will be overrun.'

Before Suheldev could reply, he heard the sound of horns blaring from behind the Indian positions. From the left flank.

What the hell?

He edged up on his horse and peered into the distance. Deep behind his own left lines. There were about five thousand fresh horsemen galloping into the fight.

Lord Shiva have mercy!

Suryavir was stunned. 'Reinforcement cavalry for Maqsud?! Where the hell did they come from?!'

Suheldev said nothing. There was nothing left to say. He had gambled everything he had on one last throw of the dice. He had no reserve troops left. And fate had sprung a surprise on him. A cruel surprise.

Suryavir continued staring at Suheldev. He didn't say anything either. But the silent message from his eyes was obvious. *It's over. It's over for us.*

Suheldev straightened his back and clenched his sword hilt tighter. 'We may die today, General Suryavir. But we will give them hell before we do so.'

Suryavir smiled. 'It has been an honour, My Lord.'

Suheldev smiled too. 'I will be honoured to die with you, my friend.'

Suryavir held his sword high. 'Until death!'

'Until death!'

The cavalry riding towards the Indians started slowing down to a canter.

What's going on?

Suheldev pushed his feet deeper into the stirrups and stood up in his saddle. To look further behind his left flank. The new horsemen riding into battle had their spears raised. They weren't in attacking position, where the spears would be pointing forward.

And then he heard the war cries of this cavalry.

'Veera …'

'Vetri …'

Suryavir turned towards Suheldev, confused. 'What are they chanting? Who are these people?'

A bolt of electricity ran up Suheldev's spine as he finally understood what was going on. As he heard the war cries clearly for the first time.

'Veeravel! Vetrivel!'

Vel was the spear that was used by Lord Karthik, the fierce warrior son of the Mahadev, Lord Shiva. A lance that was considered invincible. His followers honoured him with this battle cry, celebrating the greatest warrior that ever walked the holy land of India.

Courageous vel! Victorious vel!

'Veeravel!'

'Vetrivel!'

'Veeravel!'

'Vetrivel!'

Suryavir turned to Suheldev. 'Who are they?'

'They are ours!' said Suheldev, his voice cracking with excitement. 'They are our countrymen! The Cholas!' Suheldev turned to his troops. 'Part! Part!'

This was a manoeuvre that Suheldev had trained his people for. To move back, part positions, and offer space for reserves to ride through into battle.

The army of Shravasti immediately obeyed their king. Moving back to offer an opening to the Cholas at the left flank. The Cholas riding in understood immediately what was going on. They goaded their horses and picked up pace.

'Veeravel! Vetrivel!'

The Cholas were now close enough that their faces were distinguishable. Suheldev saw a massive man at the head, riding his horse hard. Tall, well over six feet in height. Fair-skinned. Chiselled muscular physique. Handle-bar moustache. Very obviously the commander. Suheldev looked at him and nodded. The commander nodded back.

And then the Chola commander goaded his horse into a quicker gallop as he lowered his spear threateningly forward. And roared loudly, 'Brave Cholas! Kill them all!'

The Chola troops followed their commander. Lowering their spears. And charging headlong into the startled Turks.

Suryavir couldn't contain his excitement as he saw the Cholas crash into the Turks. Killing all in their path mercilessly.

Suheldev turned to his troops and raised his voice. 'Men, we have the enemy on their knees now. Finish this battle once and for all. No prisoners! No mercy! Kill them all!'

'Jai Maa Bhaarati!'

The battle cry echoed through the field as Suheldev's soldiers dug deep within their emotional and physical reserves, and unleashed one more attack. Trapped between Suheldev's army in the centre and right flank, and the freshly charging in Cholas in the left, and exhausted from fighting all day, the Ghazni army collapsed.

Suheldev hacked, stabbed and slashed in a frenzy, losing count of the number of Turks he killed. His soldiers followed suit, exultant, as a gritty stalemate turned rapidly into a triumph. The field became slushy with blood and corpses piled up as the battle became a one-sided carnage. Many soldiers of Ghazni threw down their weapons and pleaded for mercy. But none was given.

The army of Ghazni broke, the myth of Turkic invincibility shattered loudly. A few soldiers turned and ran, then more followed. It began as a trickle, and turned into a flood, as the Turks fled for their lives. They were relentlessly followed and ruthlessly struck down.

Every last Turk was chased. Every last Turk was killed.

Save one.

One was kept alive.

For the justice of Suheldev.

—— EJI H3JCΔ ——

It was late in the night. After the massacre of the Turks earlier in the day, the Indians had gathered in their camp. To celebrate. To recuperate. To sleep.

Doctors had worked steadily to save many Indian soldiers. Though the Indians had lost only around fifteen thousand soldiers, the entire Turkic army of sixty thousand had been wiped out.

This had been one of the most one-sided encounters in recent history. More of a massacre than a battle.

Suryavir and all the other commanders of the confederacy were searching through the entire area for Salar Maqsud, who had escaped. The orders to the soldiers were clear. Search for a Turk who looks like Aslan. And bring him back alive.

Suheldev was sitting in the royal tent, his wounds having been dressed. He was tired beyond measure. But sheer excitement and the remnants of adrenaline pumping in his body did not allow him to fall asleep. Toshani had recovered enough to be conscious, but she had spent the afternoon and evening in a fitful sleep. She reclined in a comfortable chair. Not far from where Suheldev was sitting. Awake, but a little groggy.

Abdul had been found. Fortunately, the wound wasn't very serious. He had lost his left eye, but the arrow had not penetrated the eye socket. He too was sitting on a chair, a short distance from Suheldev, a patch over his eye, bandages all over his body. Weak, but conscious and alert. And deliriously happy at the Indian victory.

Govardhan had just entered the tent and was sitting in a chair closer to the tent curtain. His left arm in a sling and some bandages on his body, but relatively unscathed.

'You didn't suffer much,' Suheldev said with a smile.

Govardhan laughed softly. 'Apparently, I've got a few

broken bones. But my fighting arm is intact. By the grace of Lord Ram.'

'By the grace of Lord Ram.'

Then Suheldev turned to the tall, fair-skinned stranger with a handlebar moustache and trimmed beard, who had entered with Govardhan. He didn't bear any serious injuries at all. He had been offered a seat next to Govardhan and was sitting there.

Suheldev folded his hands into a namaste and spoke in Sanskrit, the language that the educated classes across India knew. 'I can guess who you are, noble Arya. My love, respect and honour to the great emperor Rajendra Chola. Your help arrived just in time.'

The man smiled and folded his hands into a namaste. 'My emperor, the great Rajendra Chola, sees you too as an Arya, noble Suheldev. You have fought for our land, for our Gods. It was our duty to help you.'

After Kashinath's meeting with Rajendra Chola, the emperor had decided to help Suheldev's war effort. But he knew that his entire army would never be able to get to Bahraich in time. So he had ordered his general to rush to the northernmost outposts of the Chola empire, in Bengal, and gather as much light cavalry as he could, and then race to Suheldev's support, through the riverine route. It meant that they could get to Bahraich quickly. But it also meant that they could come with only a relatively small force of five thousand cavalry.

Fortunately, that cavalry had been enough. It had been more than enough.

'What is your name, great general?' asked Suheldev.

'My name is Narasimhan.'

Suheldev rose from his chair with great difficulty, refusing help from the attendants close by. Then he walked over to Narasimhan, who too had risen from his chair.

Suheldev reached over and embraced Narasimhan warmly. 'Lord Shiva bless you, noble Narasimhan.'

Narasimhan was genuinely surprised with the warm personal gesture from one who was a king. So he took a few seconds to respond. But respond he did. Warmly. He put his arms around Suheldev, careful not to make his grip so tight that it hurt the injured king. And he said, 'May Lord Shiva continue to bless you too, noble king. As long as time keeps running, the world will remember you as one of the greatest devotees of Lord Shiva, and one of the finest sons of Mother India.'

Suddenly, Suryavir entered the tent, parting the curtains rapidly. He was obviously excited.

Suheldev stepped back from Narasimhan and looked at Suryavir, his eyebrows raised in question.

'My Lord,' said Suryavir, 'we have found him. He was hiding in a ditch like the coward that he is. But we found the bastard. He is outside.'

Suheldev held his breath.

Salar Maqsud.

He looked back at Toshani. Steel in his eyes. She looked at him and nodded.

— ᴇⅉ ꜱꙅ∩ċ∆ —

A short while later, the main leaders of Suheldev's army were gathered in the open area outside the royal tent. Suheldev, Toshani, Govardhan and Abdul were sitting on chairs. The Chola general Narasimhan too was sitting by them. So were the

Chandela general Suryavir and all other allies from Suheldev's confederacy. The badly injured Sanghamani had also been brought out. He was on a reclining chair, his head raised, so that he could see justice being done.

Numerous torches had been lit all across the open ground. Spreading light far and wide.

Indian soldiers stood at the back, kept at a distance. They were jeering and hooting at the hated Turk, who was on his knees, in the open ground between them and the royal tent.

Hands and legs tied together. Bleeding. Head covered in cloth.

Salar Maqsud.

'Remove the head cover!' ordered Suheldev. 'Let us see this dog of Ghazni.'

Two soldiers standing close to Maqsud held him tight and quickly removed the cloth.

Shock rippled through the Indians present.

Maqsud barely looked human. One terribly swollen eye was completely shut. The other was bright red, the blood capillaries inside having burst open. His hair and face were caked with blood, gore and dust. The left ear had been partially cut and was barely hanging on to the rest of the head by a slender thread of skin and sinew.

But it wasn't the sight of his injuries that had shocked the Indians. They felt no sympathy for a man who had only recently massacred an entire city of innocent, unarmed civilians.

What shocked them was Maqsud's face. It was an almost exact replica of Aslan's. Or Salar Masud, as they had come to know. The same hazel eyes. The same Central-Asian features. Skin colour. Everything. It was unnerving to see a face that they loved and trusted on another man who they saw as a monster.

How could the same face be shared between one who was so Good and another who was pure Evil?

Suheldev flicked his hand, gesturing his order to his soldiers. *Pull him up.*

Two men seized Maqsud and roughly hauled him to his feet. He stood briefly, then groaned and slumped to his knees, his wounded leg unable to bear his weight.

His armour had been pierced at several places, and while much blood had clotted, some still trickled out of his numerous wounds. The massive injury on his thigh, inflicted by Aslan, was especially severe. Maqsud had managed to staunch the blood flow there by sealing it with a scalding knife and tying a piece of cloth tight around it. Quick battlefield first aid.

'Mercy,' he pleaded in a hoarse voice, licking his dry lips. 'Mercy ... That is what ... your *dharma* ... dictates.'

Suheldev looked at Maqsud incredulously. 'Mercy? *Dharma*? Don't defile those precious words with your cursed tongue.'

'I deserve ... a fair trial. I ... know your *dharma* ... I deserve—'

Suheldev interrupted Maqsud. 'You deserve nothing. Except a public execution.'

Maqsud looked at Suheldev with barely disguised disgust. 'Go to hell ... *kafir!*'

Suheldev got up from his seat. His injuries forgotten. The rage flowing through his veins had gripped his soul and steeled his body.

He walked over to Maqsud. Slowly.

Maqsud spat towards Suheldev. Globs of viscous spit landing on Suheldev's shoes.

'Kill me, *kafir* ...'

Suheldev remained silent. Letting his angry eyes speak.

Maqsud suddenly took a deep breath and found the strength to raise his voice. So that all could hear. 'Kill me, all you *kafirs*! In any case ... I will go to heaven ... Allah will take care of me ... You idolaters will all go to hell ...' Then Maqsud looked around. 'And I know ... that there are Muslims among you ... You sided with the heathens ... Allah will punish you ... You will all go to hell ... You will never see heaven ... Prepare for hellfire!'

Suheldev looked back at Abdul.

Abdul stood up slowly. 'I am a Muslim ... Allah will praise us for fighting for our country ... And as for heaven? I am already living in it ...'

Cries of 'Allahu Akbar' rang out among the crowds. From the tongues of both the Muslim, and the Hindu Indians.

Maqsud looked at Abdul and spat again. Then he turned to Suheldev. 'Kill me ... And be done with it ...'

Suheldev spoke up. 'I am worried about you, Maqsud. Because if you have to go to heaven, isn't your body supposed to be properly buried?'

For the first time, a look of pure terror descended on Maqsud's face. 'You ... you can't ...'

'Yes ... I was thinking of beheading you ... And then burning your body ...'

Maqsud actually believed in what he preached. He was not scared of dying. But he was scared of dying in a way in which reaching heaven was impossible, at least according to his own beliefs. He looked towards Abdul. 'You are a Muslim ... you cannot allow this to happen to another Muslim ... I must have proper funeral ceremonies ...'

Abdul said loudly, his voice ringing with emotion, 'You are not a Muslim, Maqsud. A man who kills innocent, unarmed civilians cannot be a Muslim. I don't give a shit what happens to your body.'

A petrified Maqsud turned to Suheldev. 'You cannot do this … You have to honour your *dharma* … You have to treat your enemy with respect … You have to give me proper funeral ceremonies …'

Suheldev drew his sword slowly. The eerie sound of the blade, as it edged out of the scabbard, reflected the rage of a civilised country, fighting back against barbarians, in the only language they understood.

Maqsud kept pleading. 'I deserve a proper funeral … You have to follow your *dharma* …'

Suheldev's lips curled up in a cruel smile, and he whispered, 'Your body will burn.'

The king of Shravasti swung his sword in a mighty arc, decapitating Salar Maqsud with one brutal stroke.

Maqsud's headless body fell back to the ground, a dark red pool rapidly forming as murky blood pumped out of his gaping neck in torrents. His head rolled to the side. His vacant dead eyes resting on the soil that he had dared to defile.

Suheldev dropped his sword to the ground. And he slowly pulled out a pendant that he wore around his neck. It was the miniature Shiva Linga that had been gifted to him years ago by his elder brother.

He spoke to his brother. He spoke to his motherland. He spoke to his God.

'You have been avenged.'

Chapter 34

It had been just half an hour since the execution of Salar
Maqsud. His decapitated body lay where it was. A platoon of
Govardhan's soldiers guarding it.

Suheldev was back in his royal tent, sitting at his desk,
signing orders. Toshani was lying on the bed, recovering. Two
physicians were in constant attendance. Suheldev had put her
in his own tent so that he could personally look after any of
her needs. Govardhan and Abdul had just been announced in.

'What is it?' asked Suheldev, surprised at the intrusion,
laying the feather-tipped pen down.

Govardhan and Abdul remained silent. Govardhan seemed
nervous. And Abdul looked angry.

'What is it, my friends?' asked Suheldev, his tone softer.

Abdul stared at Govardhan. Clearly unhappy. Suheldev
too turned towards Govardhan and raised his eyebrows
questioningly.

'Umm … my king,' said Govardhan. 'You are not actually
going to … Are you?'

'Going to do what?'

'With Salar Maqsud, I mean.'

'What about Maqsud?'

'Are you actually going to burn his body?'

Suheldev sighed and leaned back in his chair.

Abdul spoke up. 'My Lord Suheldev, I have made my stand clear already. I spoke with many maulanas after the massacre ordered by Maqsud at Harsaran. They were all unanimous. Maqsud is not a Muslim anymore if he committed a heinous crime like that. We do not accept him as one of us. We refuse to take his corpse. You can do what you want with it.'

'It is not about what the maulanas say, Abdul,' said Govardhan.

'It *is* about what they say, Govardhan,' said Abdul. 'You were telling me just a little while back that he should receive Islamic funeral ceremonies. I can tell you that no Indian Muslim burial ground will accept his body. We will *not* do his funeral ceremony. He is not one of us. And you are insulting us Indian Muslims by trying to treat him as one of us.'

'I am not trying to do that, Abdul,' said Govardhan, his tone placatory. 'I am not saying that Indian Muslims have to carry out any ceremonies for Maqsud's body. I am saying that my men and I could do it. We can bury him ourselves. With respect. It's not about Salar Maqsud. It's about us. It's about how we should behave.'

'And how should we behave, Govardhan?' asked Suheldev.

'My king, I agree with you that we had to be ruthless when we fought them. But there is a difference between the Turks and us. We are not monsters. We are the descendants of Gods. Of Lord Shiva and Lord Ram. Of Lady Sati and Lady Sita. History will look at us. *Dharma* will look at us. By showing respect to their dead, we will honour our own way. We should not give in to anger.'

'Do you really think it's about anger?' asked Suheldev. 'You think I want to do this because I'm angry?'

Govardhan remained silent.

Suheldev turned towards Toshani. She nodded. And he turned back to his friends.

'Let me tell you why I want to do this,' said Suheldev. 'The Turks are not afraid of death. If they were, they wouldn't have conquered so much of the world. The fact that we have massacred their entire invading army will not stop them. In fact, it may spur them to mount even more attacks on us. Martyrs are the fuel of their fanaticism. But if they think that we can be as monstrous as them, that we will burn their dead bodies, then they may pause to consider.'

Govardhan seemed unconvinced. 'But …'

'Why do you think they attack our temples and destroy our idols?' asked Suheldev. 'Wouldn't it be more logical and rational of them to treat the idols as hostages and force us to give them money? They don't do that because they are using our beliefs and faith to destroy our morale. To destroy our spirit. Because they think that conquering a demoralised populace is much easier. We have to pay them back in their own coin. We have to use their beliefs and faith against them. They want heaven in the afterlife. And they believe that they cannot get heaven if we burn their bodies. I don't know if their belief is true or not. But I do know this, if we use their belief against them, then they will not dare to come back to India. If they know that we will not just kill them, but burn their bodies, they will not try to invade us.'

'But why do we have to do that? Even if they come back, we will defeat them again. We will kill them all.'

'And how many of our own soldiers will die in another war?'

'I understand what you are saying,' said Govardhan. 'But—'

Suheldev interrupted Govardhan. 'Don't think that I am disrespecting your Kshatriya way. I know that true Kshatriyas have always been willing to die for the country. I have always respected your courage.'

'No. No. I didn't say that. I know you will never think like that. You respect all the different Indian ways. However, doesn't *dharma* say that we must win wars, but we must win the right way?'

'*Dharma* … A simple word … But so many complicated philosophies behind it …' Suheldev got up from his chair and hobbled closer to Govardhan and Abdul, refusing the help offered by them. And then sat down close to the both of them. 'What is *dharma*? Our ancestors agonised over this question for millennia. Let us agonise over it as well. What is a warrior's *dharma*?'

Govardhan's answer was immediate. 'To fight and win. But without taking a sin on …'

' … his soul,' said Suheldev, completing Govardhan's words.

'Yes. Without taking a sin on his soul. Defeating the enemy, but with honour. Winning the war, while following the laws of true warriorhood.'

Suheldev smiled. 'That would be ideal, wouldn't it? If a warrior could win a battle without breaking the laws of warriorhood, without committing any sin. But what if life does not give you that choice?'

Govardhan remained silent.

'Consider this, Govardhan,' said Suheldev. 'What if life has brought a warrior to a fork on the road where he has *only* two choices. On one road, he can keep his honour and protect his soul from committing a sin. And he also, thereby, allows the enemy to come back. Something that will lead to the deaths of thousands of innocent civilians who were looking to that warrior for protection. However, on the other road, the warrior takes a sin on his own soul. Even though he knows that, according to the laws of *karma*, he will be punished for that sin. In this life or the next. But by committing that sin, the warrior ensures that the enemy never returns and his people do not die. What does *dharma* say? What should the warrior do?'

Govardhan remained silent.

'Do you remember what Lord Parshu Ram had said?'

Govardhan nodded. He knew. All warriors knew.

'Lord Parshu Ram had said that a true warrior loves his country more than he loves his own soul. And if, by taking a sin on his soul, by sacrificing his own chance at *moksha*, he can protect the people who depend on him, then he should do it. Without hesitation.'

Govardhan, Abdul and Toshani remained silent.

Suheldev paused, and then said clearly, 'Maqsud's body will burn.'

— ЕЛ НЗЛĊΔ —

It was early in the morning when Suheldev rose from his bed, stepped out of the tent and walked towards the stable. His bodyguards quietly fell into step behind him, no words exchanged.

It had been four days since the execution of Salar Maqsud. As Suheldev had ordered, Maqsud's body had been burnt. But his head had been treated with special chemicals to maintain it. Suheldev still had a message to deliver to Ghazni.

As the king of Shravasti reached the army camp stables, the stable boy scrambled to his feet, rubbing away the sleep from his eyes. Without saying anything, Suheldev helped him saddle his horse. Then, the king mounted the animal and rode out, his guards following close behind.

The camp had been shifted a fair distance from the battlefield, but Suheldev didn't mind the ride. At that hour, the breeze was pleasant and there was a restful peace that he rarely encountered as the day got busier.

As he got where he wanted to, he pulled the reins and slowed his horse down. Dismounting, he handed the reins over to one of his bodyguards.

Then he walked a short distance. To the grave of his friend. The final resting place of Aslan. Of Salar Masud.

When he was alive, Aslan had loved a spot by the lake and had hoped to eventually return there to set up a Sufi hermitage. Suheldev had remembered that. And had ordered that Aslan's corpse be found in the battlefield, and that the body be buried, with all proper Islamic funeral rituals, at his favourite spot by the lake.

He had also started coming to the grave for a few moments early every morning and talking to Aslan as though he were still there.

'I'll be leaving tomorrow, my friend,' said Suheldev to Aslan's grave in a soft voice. 'Thank you for all that you did for me. For my motherland. For our motherland.' The breeze briefly picked up, seeming to sigh. Suheldev reached out and gently touched the grave. 'Rest well, my friend. You have earned it. None of us will ever forget you. May Allah and Lord Shiva continue to bless you.'

He looked towards the lake. To a view that he knew Aslan loved. Then he noticed that the guards seemed to be pushing back a group of women who were holding flowers.

'What's going on?' asked Suheldev.

'We've come to pray at Aslan Baba's grave,' said one of the women. She was wearing the traditional Hindu *bindi* on her forehead. Another woman next to her had the *abaya* of a Muslim. 'Prayers at such a holy site will surely be answered.'

Baba was the native word used for a saint. The locals of the area had heard of the role that Aslan, or Salar Masud, had played in defending India. They had come to honour him. Even worship him. For what are great people, but those who discovered the divine within themselves.

'What superstitious nonsense,' began one of the guards. He stopped abruptly and muttered a hasty apology as Suheldev glared at him.

'By all means … If it gives you peace, please go ahead and pray,' said Suheldev, as he looked back at Salar Masud's grave. 'For this site has been blessed by both Lord Shiva and Allah.'

He beckoned to the guards to follow him, mounted his horse and rode away.

—— ᴇᴊᴜ �∩ᵭ△ ——

A year had elapsed since the Battle of Bahraich.

Reconstruction in many of the lands devastated by the Turks had begun. One of the places being rebuilt was the holy Somnath temple on the coast of Gujarat.

Suheldev and his band, responsible for ending the Turkic menace, had been invited as guests of honour as the temple was rededicated to the Mahadev, the God of Gods, Lord Shiva.

The majestic Shiva Linga gleamed, reflecting the rays of the sun that fell upon it. It had been installed in a makeshift temple and consecrated while the Somnath temple was being rebuilt. But today, it would take its rightful place in the main temple.

Suheldev bowed before the idol. 'It's a truly wonderful gift from Emperor Rajendra Chola,' he said to Narasimhan. 'A worthy replacement indeed for the original Shiva Linga.'

Narasimhan smiled enigmatically. 'Yes ... But you should also know that a part of the original returns today as well.'

Suheldev gaped at him, stunned. 'You mean ... But I thought that Mahmud ...'

Narasimhan continued to smile, enjoying Suheldev's astonishment. 'It is a long story, My Lord. But Mahmud didn't die naturally. And we got our vengeance there too.'

'But how?'

'I will tell you ... And perhaps, one day, some author may write this tale as well. In another book. But for now, let's complete the ceremonies.'

Suheldev continued to stare at Narasimhan, overcome by curiosity. 'My friend, immediately after the ceremony, you will have to tell me the entire story.'

Narasimhan bowed his head. 'As you command, great Arya.'

Suheldev grinned and held Narasimhan's arm in a friendly gesture. Then he turned towards the large crowd that had gathered there.

Right in front were Toshani and his comrades, Govardhan, Abdul and Sanghamani. His mother too was present. As were many members of the Shravasti alliance, the Chandela general Suryavir, King Karan, and the many others who had fought the Turks bravely. And Indians from across the land.

They knew a speech was coming. It was due. And the audience started chanting the name of the hero they all saw.

'Suheldev!'

'Suheldev!'

'Suheldev!'

'The rebuilding of this temple,' said Suheldev, raising his hand for silence, 'is not just the rebuilding of a structure.'

The audience listened to him in hushed silence.

'It is not just the Lord Mahadev returning to this seat. How can the Mahadev return when he had never left?'

The crowd seemed confused.

Suheldev clarified. 'Every pore of the universe has Lord Shiva in it. Not just you and me, but every drop of the rivers and the oceans, every atom in all bodies and things, the very stardust in the skies, they all have Lord Shiva in it. Even the destroyed temple here still had Lord Shiva in it.'

The Indians listened quietly. There was one stray shout of 'Har Har Mahadev'. All of us are Mahadevs. The Mahadev is in everything.

And almost instinctively, everyone present repeated: 'Har Har Mahadev!'

'Then what was the point of rebuilding this temple?' asked Suheldev.

The king of Shravasti looked around. There was no answer. For they all waited for Suheldev to give them the answer.

Suheldev's voice rose as he said, 'The rebuilding of the Somnath*ji* temple is a statement! A statement to the world! Many of our fellow ancient cultures have died out. Nobody in Rome believes in the Roman Gods anymore. Nobody in Greece worships in the Greek temples anymore. The ancient Egyptian culture has been forsaken by the Egyptians themselves. All the Schools of Mystery around the Mediterranean Sea have been abandoned. Across the world, many who began their road to civilisation with us have ended their journeys. They have died out!' Pointing to the temple behind him, Suheldev roared, 'But as Lord Shiva is our witness, our Indian civilisation will not die!'

The crowd roared in unison. A cry from the depths of their soul. A cry of pride.

'Those civilisations did not die just because foreigners

invaded them. For is there ever a time when the civilised are not attacked by the barbarians? They died out because the civilised stopped caring about their own civilisations. But as Lord Shiva is our witness, we Indians will not stop caring!'

The crowd began to cheer and call out Suheldev's name. They started hailing Mother India. Suheldev held up a hand to silence them.

'A land does not die because there are some who hate it. For has there ever been a time when hatred has not existed in the world? A motherland dies when her own children stop loving it! A nation is not built by those who hate it, it is built on the shoulders of those who love it!' Suheldev raised his balled fist in the air. 'And as Lord Shiva is our witness, we Indians will never stop loving our land!'

All the people around raised their hands, the fists held tight, the bodies exultant with pride, their souls filled with purpose.

And there was only one thing left to be said.

'Jai Maa Bhaarati!'

Glory to Mother India.

'Jai Maa Bhaarati!'

'Jai Maa Bhaarati!'

'Jai Maa Bhaarati!'

Suheldev raised his hand for silence. And everyone obeyed.

'Everyone will have the honour of touching the Lord. Of taking the Mahadev back to His rightful place within the temple. Of carrying His idol. Everyone here. Everyone.'

This was unorthodox. But nobody dared to question the great Suheldev.

'Let's begin!'

At Suheldev's gesture, Toshani stepped forward. So did Govardhan. Abdul, wearing a patch over one eye, stepped forward too. Followed by Sanghamani. Narasimhan, the Chola general, Suryavir, the Chandela general, and King Karan stepped up as well. One by one, Suheldev's numerous allies and senior officers came forward. They bent together, gripped the platform on which the Shiva Linga was mounted, and tensed.

'Har Har Mahadev!' called out Suheldev.

'Har Har Mahadev!' was the answer from everyone.

They all straightened, heaving the platform onto their shoulders.

As they carried the Shiva Linga a short distance towards the temple, the crowd continued to roar.

'Har Har Mahadev!'

'Jai Maa Bhaarati!'

The cry resounded around the temple, echoed by the thundering of the sea. One by one, everyone got a chance to carry the platform. To carry the Lord Mahadev back to His rebuilt home. To be restored in the sanctum sanctorum of the reconstructed Somnath temple.

Suheldev felt goose bumps rise as the cries rang out again and again, getting louder and louder. Till the roars reached a crescendo that drowned out the sounds of the waves crashing against the shore.

Far at the back, close to the gate of the temple, an old man, who had seen the carnage carried out at the Somnath temple a few years earlier by the hated Mahmud of Ghazni, looked at his young grandchild. 'No invader will ever dare look at our country as long as it has children like the king of Shravasti. Learn from Suheldev, my child. Learn from him.'

The Ghaznavid Turks had certainly learnt their lesson. For their entire army in India had been massacred. To the last man. It was a loss they would find difficult to recover from for decades. Salar Maqsud's body, along with the bodies of every single Turkic soldier, had been burnt. And the ashes of Maqsud's body had been gathered in an urn, which had been sent to Ghazni. It had been accompanied with a message. A message carved on the forehead of the decapitated head of Salar Maqsud.

The message was simple.

Come to India as devotees, and our motherland will open her heart for you. Dare to come as invaders, and we will burn every single one of you.

The Turks learnt the lesson well. There was no attempt to invade India for the next one hundred and fifty years.

'Learn from Suheldev, my child. Learn from him. Jai Suheldev!'

Glory to Suheldev.

The little child looked up at her grandfather. And then towards Suheldev. She knew what she wanted to be when she grew up. She wanted to be a warrior. A warrior for India.

She folded her hands together with respect, and bowed her head towards the king of Shravasti in the distance, repeating her grandfather's cry. 'Jai Suheldev!'

Om Namah Shivāya.
The universe bows to Lord Shiva. I bow to Lord Shiva.

Other Titles by Amish

The Shiva Trilogy

The fastest-selling book series in the history of Indian publishing

THE IMMORTALS OF MELUHA
(Book 1 of the Trilogy)

1900 BC. What modern Indians mistakenly call the Indus Valley Civilisation, the inhabitants of that period knew as the land of Meluha – a near perfect empire created many centuries earlier by Lord Ram. Now their primary river Saraswati is drying, and they face terrorist attacks from their enemies from the east. Will their prophesied hero, the Neelkanth, emerge to destroy evil?

THE SECRET OF THE NAGAS
(Book 2 of the Trilogy)

The sinister Naga warrior has killed his friend Brahaspati and now stalks his wife Sati. Shiva, who is the prophesied destroyer of evil, will not rest till he finds his demonic adversary. His thirst for revenge will lead him to the door of the Nagas, the serpent people. Fierce battles will be fought and unbelievable secrets revealed in the second part of the Shiva trilogy.

THE OATH OF THE VAYUPUTRAS
(Book 3 of the Trilogy)

Shiva reaches the Naga capital, Panchavati, and prepares for a holy war against his true enemy. The Neelkanth must not fail, no matter what the cost. In his desperation, he reaches out to the Vayuputras. Will he succeed? And what will be the real cost of battling Evil? Read the concluding part of this bestselling series to find out.

The Ram Chandra Series

The second fastest-selling book series in the history of Indian publishing

RAM – SCION OF IKSHVAKU
(Book 1 of the Series)

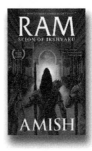

He loves his country and he stands alone for the law. His band of brothers, his wife, Sita and the fight against the darkness of chaos. He is Prince Ram. Will he rise above the taint that others heap on him? Will his love for Sita sustain him through his struggle? Will he defeat the demon Raavan who destroyed his childhood? Will he fulfil the destiny of the Vishnu? Begin an epic journey with Amish's latest: the Ram Chandra Series.

SITA – WARRIOR OF MITHILA
(Book 2 of the Series)

An abandoned baby is found in a field. She is adopted by the ruler of Mithila, a powerless kingdom, ignored by all. Nobody believes this child will amount to much. But they are wrong. For she is no ordinary girl. She is Sita. Through an innovative multi-linear narrative, Amish takes you deeper into the epic world of the Ram Chandra Series.

RAAVAN – ENEMY OF ARYAVARTA
(Book 3 of the Series)

Raavan is determined to be a giant among men, to conquer, plunder, and seize the greatness that he thinks is his right. He is a man of contrasts, of brutal violence and scholarly knowledge. A man who will love without reward and kill without remorse. In this, the third book in the Ram Chandra series, Amish sheds light on Raavan, the king of Lanka. Is he the greatest villain in history or just a man in a dark place, all the time?

Non-fiction

IMMORTAL INDIA

Explore India with the country's storyteller, Amish, who helps you understand it like never before, through a series of sharp articles, nuanced speeches and intelligent debates. In *Immortal India*, Amish lays out the vast landscape of an ancient culture with a fascinatingly modern outlook.